"I MISS YOU."

Closing her eyes, she whispered, "Don't."

His lips brushed across the side of her brow. "Don't what? Tell you that I miss you? Miss us?"

"Us?" She laughed hollowly as she turned to face him. "There *is* no us, remember? You said that. There's *me* . . . and there's *you* . . . and sometimes we're together, but there's no *us*."

His gaze held hers. "I never wanted it to be that way. And maybe there was more of an *us* than I realized. Seeing you . . ." He paused, took a deep breath. "Seeing you just drives that home."

. Those intense, hypnotic eyes held hers. Her heart kicked up a few beats, stealing her breath away. As he started to dip his head, Shay stood there, frozen. *Shit. What now . . .*

His mouth, so warm, brushed against hers. She gasped and then almost wished she hadn't as he used that opportunity to tease the inside of her lips with his tongue, moving deeper and deeper. His hands came around her waist, tugging her closer.

This is a bad idea . . .

BY SHILOH WALKER

Stolen
If You Know Her
If You Hear Her
If You See Her

STOLEN

SHILOH WALKER

BALLANTINE BOOKS
NEW YORK

A Ballantine Books Mass Market Original

Copyright © 2012 by Shiloh Walker

Published in the United States by Ballantine Books, an imprint of The Random House Publishing Group, a division of Random House, Inc., New York.

BALLANTINE and colophon are trademarks of Random House, Inc.

ISBN 978-0-345-53190-2
eBook ISBN 978-0-345-53191-9

Printed in the United States of America

www.ballantinebooks.com

9 8 7 6 5 4 3 2 1

Ballantine mass market edition: November 2012

For my family, always. I love you all so much.

For Irene, my agent. Thank God I've got you around
to keep me sane and focused.

For all of my readers. You all are wonderful.

STOLEN

CHAPTER
ONE

MyDiary.net/slayingmydragons

I had another dream.

I'm in the closet. Again, hiding like always. I hear a baby.

And *he* is here. I can hear him shouting. Yelling. Swearing. He's angry . . . but he's always angry.

I hear somebody giggling this time—this is new . . . I don't remember this. She's giggling, and I hear her talking about a princess.

I'm hungry.

I'm cold.

I wait until it's quiet, because I need to get some food. I think the baby is hungry, too.

Then there are sirens. And I think there's blood. I hear the baby again, but these screams are different. . . .

LEANING BACK AWAY FROM THE COMPUTER, SHAY Morgan closed her eyes and sighed. The dream was already fading away, the threads of it escaping her grasp even as she tried to hold on.

Even as she tried to put the terror into words. The pain.

Moments passed and the dream lost some of that vivid, powerful punch. But still, she was shaken. Sickness gripped her and in the back of her mind, she could hear a pitiful, broken scream.

Shifting her attention to the screen, she started to read back over what she'd written.

"You're going to hold down the fort, right?"

The man bent over the desk didn't look up at first.

Lorna Winter sighed and leaned her shoulder against the doorjamb.

"Elliot!"

Her brother looked up, eyes a little clouded. Lack of sleep, lack of caffeine, or just general crankiness could account for the dark scowl he sent her way. He hadn't exactly been a ray of sunshine the past few months.

"What?" he asked, reaching for the cup of coffee sitting in front of him.

It must have been empty because he gave it a look of such disgust, one might think it had kicked him in the face.

"You're going to take care of things here, right?"

He frowned. "I am? Why?"

"Because . . . I told you yesterday I needed the day off," she reminded him.

His frown deepened, then abruptly, his face went as smooth as glass. "Right. The hospital." He bent back over the computer as though it had him hypnotized. If she didn't know better, she'd think that catalog for Baker and Taylor held the secrets to the entire universe, the way he stared at the screen.

"You know, if you want, you can go pick Shay up," she offered.

Elliot just grunted.

"Is that a yes or a no?"

For a long moment, he didn't move. Neither did she. She knew her brother. She knew his moods, she knew his quirks . . . and she knew when he was hurting. Right now, he was hurting, even if he never admitted it. Finally, he slid her a look from under his lashes. "Shay doesn't need me to pick her up, Lorna. We broke up months ago, remember?"

She just watched him and waited.

He stared back at her. "It's over, sis. Deal with it. I have."

Then he focused his attention back on the monitor and started making notes. Knowing she wasn't going to get anything else out of him, she sighed and turned around.

Dealt with it, my ass, she thought darkly.

The man hadn't dated since he'd broken things off with Shay and she'd *seen* the look on his face when they heard about Shay's accident. She'd been completely shocked that he hadn't gone tearing down to Anchorage to be with her.

Hell, every damn time the phone rang, he'd practically attacked it. Yeah. He had dealt with it just fine.

But she couldn't make him see reality until he was ready to see it, she knew.

Of course, it might *help* if Shay would open her eyes and see what she was missing. The two of them were giving her a headache, damn it.

CHAPTER
TWO

AREN'T YOU HAPPY, PRINCESS—

A mad little giggle brought Shay gasping into wakefulness and pain splintered through her abused body as she rolled up to a sitting position.

Three days after her discharge from the hospital and she still felt like she'd been run over by a freight train, although she'd take the pain over the nightmares any day.

Sick at heart, her belly twisting with nausea, she sat on the edge of the bed and tried to banish the echo of that maniacal laughter, the rasping, ragged breaths of a brutal monster.

Dragon's breath.

Some people had inner demons.

Shay had always called hers an inner dragon.

A diary had been her first way of slaying it, and the dreams it brought.

She'd actually managed to go a few days without the dreams—this had been the first one since her release from the hospital. This had been a bad one, though. The price she had to pay for a few quiet nights, she guessed.

Her hands were still shaking as she clambered off the bed and her knees felt like wet spaghetti. It was a minor miracle that she didn't collapse as she made her way down the hall.

She hit the light in her office and stumbled over to the desk she hadn't used much since her return home from the hospital a few days earlier. There was so much work she needed to catch up on, such as emails to answer and a book to be written, but she couldn't even think about that.

Right now, she had a dragon to slay.

MyDiary.net/slayingmydragons

It was a bad one this time . . . an ugly monster, although it shouldn't seem all that bad. I just felt more scared than normal. I don't know why. I didn't really see anything different, and I don't remember much more. A little, but not a lot.

I'm just more scared. More shaken. I almost feel sick, I'm so scared.

I closed my eyes to sleep, and I wake up in the closet. I'm covered in blood and something isn't right. I've got blood on me and I know that closet. I dream of it all the time.

None of this seems right. I've dreamt of it so many times, but this was . . . different.

I can't hear the baby.

I can't hear the yelling.

I just hear . . . breathing.

Almost like somebody is watching me.

I reached up to touch my face and it was my face. As it is now, and I realized it's the me from now. It was so weird. I could think so clearly. I could feel my scars and I could think that this wasn't normal.

And then I heard that laughter. A kid laughing. It's not him. It's somebody else. I've heard her before, but it's never been quite this intense.

I heard her laugh and then everything changed.

I wasn't me anymore. I was the little girl, and I was trapped and I heard the baby screaming . . . and that giggling. Why was she giggling?

Sometimes I think the pain medicine they have me on has screwed up my head until I can't think straight. Then I think maybe the car wreck knocked something loose—not that car wrecks can really do that, but ever since then, it's like I'm trying to remember more.

But I don't want to. I don't want to remember anything about then.

Shit, I'm such a baby.

Better go. I'm supposed to have lunch with a friend. I need to try to get my life back to something resembling normal so I can focus again. After lunch, I see the doctor. Yay.

Not.

Staring up at the bookstore, Shay closed her eyes.

Next to her, one of her few friends stood with a bright smile on her face. "Come on. I'll buy you a couple of books." Lorna Winter went to open the door.

Shay sighed. She wasn't up to this; she was still so damn tired. Yeah, she had to go into town for the follow-up visit with her doctor, but hitting the bookstore?

This bookstore? Although this one was the only one around, unless she wanted to drive another thirty minutes.

Coward. It's not the exhaustion *that has you down. You just don't want to see Elliot.*

That wasn't it at all, she insisted. She would *love* to see Elliot. The problem was Elliot didn't want to see *her.* He'd dumped her. Months ago. Seeing him now . . . *that* was what she wasn't up to. Seeing him, thinking about what she didn't, couldn't, wouldn't have . . .

"Shay? Sweetie?"

Grimacing, she eased her way out of the car and met Lorna on the sidewalk.

"Are you not up for this? I mean . . . well." She looked down, plucking at a loose thread on her shirt. "Never mind. This was a stupid idea. I promised you lunch before your checkup, not a shopping spree."

The guilt in Lorna's voice pricked at Shay's conscience.

"It's okay," she said tiredly. "I'm fine. It's been a few

days since I left the hospital, you know. I'm not a complete invalid. I even get myself dressed now."

"I know. You just . . ." Lorna blew out a breath. "I shouldn't have dumped this on you. You look worn out. Come on, we'll go eat."

"No." Shay made herself smile. And damn her heart . . . she realized she *did* want to see Elliot, even if it would hurt. "You promised me books. You can't back out now."

Lorna meant well, Shay knew. Meant all sorts of well. It wasn't her fault Shay avoided the bookstore like a plague, just as she had for the past six months. Ever since the problems with Elliot . . .

Don't think about that right now. Turning her head, she stared at the brightly lit windows of Winter's End. Earth's End was a small town; the town's sole bookstore was a popular place. People came to grab a hot drink from the little coffee shop in the back of the store. They'd sit for a while, enjoy their drink and chat . . . read. Several different book clubs met here once a month.

And up until six months ago, this had been one of the few places in her life she actually *loved*. Outside of her house.

Was she really going to let a bad breakup get to her like that?

Was she actually going to spend the rest of her life avoiding this place just because she was too afraid to see Elliot?

Why not? a sly voice in her head whispered. *You're afraid of everything else.*

Damn it. She hated that it was true.

"Shay's here."

Looking up from his desk, Elliot met his sister's gaze. The look on her face held something of an impatient demand on it, but he didn't pay much attention to demands anymore. Demands were too similar to commands, and he'd left those behind when he'd walked away from the army nine years earlier.

He didn't do demands. Didn't do commands. If anybody didn't like it, screw it and screw them.

Actually, that was kind of his outlook on most things in life anyway these days. He was who he was and if people didn't like it? Screw them.

With the exception of his sister, Lorna. She was the one exception . . . the one person he still stopped to think of, for the most part.

Liar . . .

There was one other. Shay. The woman he loved. The woman who couldn't trust him. The woman he still needed—the pain was a punch to the gut as he once more made himself accept the fact that she might be the woman he needed, but she was the woman he wouldn't ever have.

Damn it. It had been six fucking months. He ought to be used to this by now. Six months without her. Why wasn't he over it? Over her? They'd only been together a year, and he'd spent more than half that time just trying to get it to where she wouldn't bolt if he so much as came within two feet of her.

And yet, here he was, in knots, because he'd heard her name.

Shay . . .

Closing his eyes, he leaned back in the chair. "Why in the hell are you telling me this?" He opened his eyes to meet her gaze. "You can . . . wait. You're not working today."

"Nope." She smiled at him serenely. "I told you I needed the day off to help out a friend . . . Shay."

"Yeah? Then what are you doing in here?" He tried to focus on the paperwork in front of him, but he couldn't.

Lorna kept staring at him and he knew she'd wait him out. Leaning back, he crossed his arms over his chest and studied her face. "What do you want, Lorna?"

"I want you to go out there. Talk to her."

He scrubbed a hand over his face. "It's done, Lorna. Over. Done."

"Liar." Her golden eyes, so like his own, focused on his face. "You can't hide in here forever."

Wanna bet? he thought sourly. No point in chasing after what he couldn't have, he figured. He'd spent so much time doing just that. It had taken him a year just to get her to relax around him, months to get her to go out with him, and they'd had one year together . . . and now? Nothing. There was just nothing. He wasn't getting his heart thrown back at him again.

"I'm not *hiding*—I'm *working*," he pointed out, gesturing to the mess of orders, invoices, and bills that littered his desk. "Becca can check her out. That's why she's here—to work with customers."

"Stubborn bastard," Lorna muttered, staring at him through narrowed eyes. It reminded him, disturbingly, of the same look their mother had given them once upon a time. "You do realize she just got out of the hospital, right? That wreck of hers was worse than I thought. I talked to Mike. He tracked down one of the county boys who worked the accident. She could have died."

A cold chill settled low in his gut and he looked away from the pile of work to stare at his sister. *She could have died . . .*

Yeah. He knew about the wreck, all right. Of course, nobody here in Earth's End had learned about the wreck until several days *after* it had happened. Shay hadn't called anybody. Hadn't told anybody. Hadn't told *him*. Yet even after he'd heard about it, he'd waited by the phone, for hours, for *days*, hoping she'd call him. But she never did. It served as just one more reminder how little she wanted or needed him in her life.

But . . .

Swallowing, he glanced up at his sister. "It was really that bad?" he asked gruffly. If it had been that bad, how could she have called him? Maybe she had needed him and she just couldn't call—aw, hell.

"Yeah." Lorna stared at him, her gaze intense. "I managed to get a little bit of information out of her on the drive into town today. She wouldn't tell me anything when I went to see her in the hospital, but . . . yeah. It was bad. She spent days in a coma. Then she was laid up in ICU. Alone, because she didn't have anybody down as next of kin and she didn't call me until nearly two weeks later."

Alone . . .

It hit him like a punch straight to his chest, and he groaned.

Images flashed through his mind. Shay, alone and frightened in a hospital. Shay, hurt and alone.

But that wasn't enough torture . . . no, his brain just *had* to keep going. Shay's lovely dark eyes, a shade between blue and purple, lifeless. Her face still. Shay . . . gone forever. *Fuck.* Just thinking about that was enough to turn his stomach to ice. He scrubbed his hands over his face. "Why are you doing this? What do you want me to do, Lorna? We broke up, remember?"

"Yeah. I remember. And you've been a moody, mean bastard ever since." She crossed her arms over her chest, watching him with flat eyes. "You still have feelings for her and you can't honestly tell me you don't."

"It's not about whether or not I have *feelings* for her." Hell, yes, he had feelings for her. But Shay had so many secrets—she kept herself so closed off. It had been killing him inside, bit by bit. He loved her, but she wouldn't open up. Wouldn't give him anything.

She was alone . . .

Fuck.

"Then what is it about? What in the hell is so awful that it's keeping you locked in here even though I know you want to go out there and see her?"

Lorna had disappeared into the office.

The second she did, Shay promptly moved to the very back of the store, far away from the long wooden counter that held the computer, the cash register, and everything else. Far away from the door where she'd last seen Lorna.

She was in there talking to Elliot. Shay knew it. Her friend still hadn't come to grips with the fact that the two of them were over.

There was an ache in her chest—a dull one that had nothing to do with her still recovering body. Yeah, she knew Lorna hadn't come to grips with the fact that her friend and her brother weren't together anymore.

Shay still hadn't come to grips with it.

She still thought about him all the time.

He'd been the first person she wanted to see when she woke up in the hospital. And she had almost called him, too. But he had told her he was done.

So she hadn't called. Maybe he was done, but she wasn't. She missed him, thought about him all the time.

She still dreamed about him.

She still wished she'd be working and hear the phone ring and just know it was him.

Not that many other people ever really called her.

There'd been a number of business-related calls, but those didn't really count. Lorna. Shay's assistant, Darcy, but that was about it. Hell, the only phone calls she really looked forward to anymore were Lorna's. Guilt tugged at her, because there had been a time when she'd loved talking to Darcy, but lately . . .

Hell, you ought to be thankful you've got Darcy to talk to. Darcy and Lorna, both? You should dance. That's two friends.

Yet neither of them did anything to ease the loneliness that had been a part of her life for as long as she could remember. Only Elliot had done that. But she hadn't been able to keep him . . .

You won't share any damn thing with me, Shay . . . how long are we supposed to keep this up?

He'd asked her that, and she hadn't been able to answer.

Are you ever going to let me in?

That, she could have answered. The answer had been no. But she hadn't wanted to hurt him, so she kept the answer trapped behind her teeth. He'd seen it anyway, in her eyes, in the way she watched him.

I guess that's it, then.

They were over . . . just like that.

He hadn't been unkind and he hadn't tried to force anything out of her. But it was over just the same and her heart had been an aching, empty mess ever since. She missed him so much. There were times when she wanted to talk to him, wanted to see him so bad . . .

A shiver danced along her spine and she looked up, turned her head. Even before she saw him standing at the end of the aisle, staring at her, she knew.

He wasn't too tall, his height brushing in just under five-ten, but there was a caged strength to his body that might have frightened her if it had been anybody but Elliot. Hell, at first, he *had* made her nervous. But he'd been patient, as though he knew if he moved too fast . . .

Golden eyes stared at her over the distance that separated them and even now, they managed to make her shiver.

Swallowing, she swiped her hands down her skirt and tried to get herself to calm down—to settle down, but her heart was racing away inside her chest and he hadn't said a damn thing. He was staring at her, his gaze roaming over her body, as though searching for any sign of injury that lingered from the wreck.

Well, he was about to see one.

As if her face wasn't already screwed up enough.

Bracing herself, she turned fully toward him.

But he didn't do the double take just about everybody else had done upon seeing the bruises that still lingered. The swelling was finally going down and thank God, her nose had healed fairly well.

Most of the other injuries were hidden by clothing, but even Shay had been a bit dismayed by how awful she'd looked.

"You look like you should still be in bed," he said bluntly.

Yes, I look awful. You look amazing. Hell, he always looked amazing. Long and lean, strong without being too bulky, nice shoulders. Man, she'd always loved his shoulders. Right now, they were covered by a denim shirt that lay open over a Bob Marley T-shirt. It stretched over a lean belly and was left untucked over a pair of beat-up jeans.

Here at Winter's End, the owners went for the casual look. Very casual, in Elliot's case.

The look suited him.

But then again, if you were Elliot Winter, just about any look would suit you. She'd seen pictures of him from his army days and he'd worn his uniform with as much ease as he wore those jeans of his.

A powerful body, a face that was almost too pretty. Thick hair, a shade between rich auburn and brown that blazed with just a little more red during the summer. His eyes also blazed with color—burnished gold.

Like whiskey, they made her drunk, but without that pesky hangover.

He wasn't hers anymore, though, and it hurt. It hurt like a bitch. He wasn't hers anymore because she couldn't be what he needed. Acknowledging that had broken her heart.

Because just looking at him made the ache worse, she looked away. "I spent almost three weeks flat on my back. I'd rather not spend any more time in bed unless I have to." Peering around him, she looked for Lorna—she had to kick that woman's ass. "Did Lorna send you out here?"

"Not exactly. I wanted to see you." Dark russet hair fell into his eyes and he brushed it back absently as he closed the distance between them. "I heard the other driver walked away with barely a scratch."

Scowling, she shrugged and turned back to the books. She'd been in such a reading slump lately—it wasn't just the car wreck, either. It had been going on since . . . well. The breakup. She hadn't been able to read or focus on much of anything all that well since he'd walked away from her.

"Is that right? He just walked away?"

"No." She gave him a dark look and stroked one of her few remaining bruises. "The jerk *stumbled* away. The bastard was nearly twice the legal limit. And he didn't stumble far—the police had him locked up before I even made it to the hospital, I think. It's his third DUI in eighteen months, too."

"You're shitting me."

"No." A title caught her eye and she reached for the book. Skimming the blurb, she pursed her lips. It actually sounded almost intriguing. She dropped the book into the basket by her feet, but when she went to grab the handle, Elliot already had it.

"I can carry a few books," she pointed out.

"So can I. And I didn't just get out of the hospital."
The resolute look on his face made it clear that arguing
with him wasn't going to do much good.

It never really had.

Still, she had to at least try. "I didn't *just* get out. I left
the hospital a few days ago."

"Yes. And you spent nearly a week in a coma, several
days in ICU, and another week recovering. I'm carrying
the damn basket," he said. He paused and then added,
"You know . . . I would have come down to be with
you . . . Hell. If I'd known it was that bad, they wouldn't
have been able to keep me away. I figured you'd call if
you wanted me around. If you'd called, I would have
been there."

Shay swallowed. "I know you would have. But we're
not together anymore, right?"

"Does that mean you can't need a friend with you?"
He touched her shoulder.

That light touch sent her heart skittering around in
her chest, a mad little dance that made her breathless.
Breathing was already difficult. Being near him made it
so much worse.

"We're not friends, though, are we, Elliot?" she said
quietly.

"So not dating means we can't be friends?"

"You didn't want to be friends." She hugged herself
tightly and closed her eyes so he wouldn't see the truth
in them. She couldn't handle being friends with him
anyway. It would hurt too much. "You just wanted us
to be over, remember? You said we were done. So we're
done. Besides, I managed okay."

"Always gotta be so tough, huh, Shay?"

No. Miserable, she gave him her back and circled
around the back edge of the store. She wasn't tough at
all. She was miserable and lonely and she wished like

hell she could be what he needed, give him what he wanted. She just didn't know *how*.

At the back of the store, she headed for the fantasy section, bypassing the romance. Once upon a time, it had been her first stop in the store.

"A couple of your favorite writers had books out last week. Don't you want those?"

"I'm not much into romance these days." Depressing as hell, reading about a happily-ever-after when it was painfully clear she wasn't very likely to find one. She'd have to settle for a humdrum-ever-after. Besides, as grim and moody as she was these days, she found herself connecting to action or gore or violence better.

Stopping in front of the shelves featuring the newest releases, she studied them, all too aware of Elliot standing at her back. "You've probably got business to do, paperwork and all that crap. You can go back to it."

"Thanks for your permission," he murmured.

A warm hand settled low on her back. As he bent his head, Shay shivered at the feel of him. *Damn it*. Coming in here had been a BFM. Big fucking mistake. She should have just waited in the car . . .

"I miss you."

Closing her eyes, she whispered, "Don't."

His lips brushed across the side of her brow. "Don't what? Tell you that I miss you? Miss us?"

"Us?" She laughed hollowly as she turned to face him. "There *is* no us, remember? You said that. There's *me* . . . and there's *you* . . . and sometimes we're together, but there's no *us*."

His gaze held hers. "I never wanted it to be that way. And maybe there was more of an *us* than I realized. Seeing you . . ." He paused, took a deep breath. "Seeing you just drives that home."

Those intense, hypnotic eyes held hers. Her heart kicked up a few beats, stealing her breath away. As he started to dip his head, Shay stood there, frozen. *Shit. What now . . .*

His mouth, so warm, brushed against hers. She gasped and then almost wished she hadn't as he used that opportunity to tease the inside of her lips with his tongue, moving deeper and deeper. His hands came around her waist, tugging her closer.

This is a bad idea . . .

The warning was already screaming in her head. She couldn't give him what he needed. And he couldn't accept what she had to give. They would just hurt each other again—

Tearing her mouth away, Shay ducked to the side. "We . . . we can't do this." She pressed a hand to her buzzing lips. "I'm just getting to the point where I'm used to going through the days without you calling. I'm just getting to where I can pass a few nights without dreaming about you." *Liar.*

Well, she *did* manage to go a few nights, she told herself. Usually, on *those* nights, she had nightmares, but so what? She wasn't dreaming of Elliot, and that was all that counted, right?

"Shay . . ." He reached up and touched her shoulder.

But she didn't want to hear what he had to say. She wasn't going through this again. She wasn't whole inside and she had to accept that and stop pretending otherwise, and it fucking *hurt*.

Stooping down, she grabbed the basket of books from where he'd placed them on the floor. Without looking back at him, she headed for the front of the store.

She had to get out of here. She could pay for her damn books and meet Lorna at the Italian place. It was two doors down—she could walk two fucking doors.

Maybe not *well*. She was already weaving a little, lethargy and weakness still pervading her body, but she damn well wasn't going to linger—

She stumbled, her feet all but giving out under her. Crashing into a book dump just next to her, she flung out a hand, but there was nothing to grab. Books from the display went flying and just before she would have crashed to the floor, a pair of strong, steady hands gripped her waist. "I've got you," Elliot murmured.

I've got you . . .

The room stopped spinning around her, even though her legs still felt like spaghetti noodles. Her heart slowed back down to its normal speed for a few seconds before embarrassment settled in. Swallowing, she closed her eyes and reached for some level of control.

Stumbling all over the place.

Running away from Elliot.

She needed to get herself together.

Sucking in a desperate draught of air, she blew it back out. Carefully, she eased away from Elliot, checking her legs. Okay, she could walk. This was good.

Grimacing at the book dump she'd knocked over, she opened her mouth to apologize. The display had been holding a *lot* of books, she thought inanely. Foil lettering on one of them caught her eyes.

Familiar lettering the shade of blood.

Familiar . . .

Her stomach dropped to her knees, and the waning strength in her abused body disappeared. Sinking to the floor, she reached out to touch one of the books.

"Shay, I'll pick it up," Elliot said.

His voice seemed to come to her from a tunnel. Her blood roared in her ears and black dots danced in front of her eyes for a long, ugly second. *Stop it, Shay—breathe!*

No more panic attacks. She didn't do panic attacks anymore.

She looked down at the book in her hands—a book

with a gold foil sticker on the top right corner that read, *Signed by the author!*

Touching that sticker, she swallowed.

No.

This . . . this wasn't happening.

There was no way the author signed books here.

Ever.

He'd never seen Shay look *that* pale before.

Considering she had a milk-pale complexion, that was saying quite a bit, too.

He hunkered down next to her and reached out, touching his fingers to her cheek. There were still bruises there. The sight of them flooded him with fury and pain, and the need to touch her, *really* touch her, was almost overwhelming. Touch her to assure himself that she really was okay. Touch her . . . and try to convince her that she could trust him. Come back to him.

But it wouldn't happen. He should know that by now.

"Shay . . . it's okay," he said tiredly, watching the way her hands trembled as she scooped up one of the books. "I'll take care of it."

She jerked her gaze to his, but he had the weirdest feeling she wasn't seeing him. There was a glassy, disconnected look in her eyes, one that had him worried. Hell, should she even be out of the hospital?

"Can you stand?" he asked quietly.

Two seconds later, she was lurching to her feet, clutching one of the Shane Neil books she'd picked up from the floor. "I need to go home."

She barely made it halfway upright before she wobbled again. Scowling, he rose to his feet and steadied her. "I think you should sit down. Eat. Have a drink or something."

"I'm not hungry." Her head swung to the left, then the right.

Searching for Lorna, he knew. "You're never hungry. Maybe that's why you're feeling so awful."

"No." And to his surprise, she started to laugh.

It was a harsh, ugly sound . . . one that hurt him just to hear it.

"I need to go *home*," she said again.

She still clutched the book. He stared at it and then shifted his gaze up to her face.

"Are you okay?" he asked quietly.

Something's off. Those dark eyes of hers, a color caught between the dusky purple of a twilight sky and the darkening navy of the coming night, stared into his, and he could see her trying to hide it.

She was afraid.

He could see it as clearly as he could see the bruises on her face, and the faint scars along her left cheek.

"Tell me what's wrong," he said softly. *Please, damn it . . . for once, will you talk to me?*

Her lips parted. Something flitted across her face.

His heart skipped a beat as she took a deep breath and looked down at the books all over the floor.

Then the bell over the door rang and the moment shattered.

"Nothing's wrong," she said hoarsely. "I just need to go."

It was a lie. He knew it. And she knew he knew.

But still, she turned on her heel and slowly, carefully, made her way to the counter.

Once more, she'd pulled away.

It was why they'd broken up.

It was why he never should have kissed her.

Setting his jaw, he crouched down to gather up the books. It wasn't until he heard the bell over the door again that he looked back to the front of the store. She was gone.

He righted the book dump and put all the books back

in place, positioning Neil's latest release at the top, the gold foil of the autograph sticker displayed.

"Hey, where's Shay?"

Looking up, he saw Lorna heading his way. He jerked his head toward the door. "Outside. Upset. She won't tell me why. Maybe she'll tell you."

Although he wasn't counting on it. She didn't open up for his sister any easier than she opened up for him.

Lorna's face fell and he sighed. "Lorna . . . it's no good. We tried, but it just isn't going to work."

As she walked off, he tried to convince himself of the same thing. He'd seen her. Seen for himself that she'd come through the wreck okay. And he'd seen for himself that, without a doubt, Shay wasn't any closer to changing *now* than she'd been a few months back.

That was why they'd ended.

That was why they had to *stay* ended.

He started to go back to his office but stopped when the toe of his battered hiking boot kicked something. Looking down, he saw the basket with all of the books Shay had picked out.

She'd left without her books.

But she'd been at the cash register . . .

Frowning, he called out, "Hey, Becca . . . did Shay buy anything?"

"Yep. A book by the thriller guy you like—Shane Neil's newest."

Shane Neil.

Shay didn't read him. Hooking his hand over the back of his neck, he continued to stare at her books. He'd tried before to get her to read the Neil books—they had similar tastes—but Shay had told him, more than once, she wasn't interested in reading any of them.

But she'd just bought one . . . ?

CHAPTER THREE

Shay had barely stepped foot inside her house when the phone started to ring.

She ignored it.

"You want me to get that for you?" Lorna offered from behind her.

Glancing over her shoulder, Shay shook her head. "No, the machine can get it. And see? I'm fine. I made it up the steps and everything."

Sure, she'd shuffled and shambled along like a zombie, but so what? People really didn't give zombies enough credit.

"It was too soon for us to try and do lunch," Lorna said quietly. "I'm sorry. You should have been resting. What did the doctor say? You're acting awfully weird. Are you sure everything is okay?"

Okay? A hysterical laugh bubbled in her throat, but she fought it back down. *No, nothing is okay right now, but I'll deal. I'll fix it. I just need to be alone for a while.*

Instead of saying that, she made her way into the kitchen. She wanted to sit, but if she sat down, she'd have to fight herself to get back on her feet and she had things to do once she got Lorna out of here.

So instead of a chair, she settled for leaning against the kitchen island, letting it take some of her weight.

"Lorna, I could have said 'no' just fine if I thought I shouldn't be going out to get a bite. It's not like we were going out to party or anything. I had to go into town anyway."

"Yeah, but I dragged you into the store." A guilty flush pinkened Lorna's cheeks and she shifted her gaze away. "I just . . . I thought maybe you and Elliot would see each other and maybe . . ."

Shay smiled sadly. "It's not going to happen, Lorna. Your brother needs something I can't give him. It's just not in me." *Trust. The ability to believe in somebody or something*—hell, she didn't even believe in *herself*. The ability to open up, to confide in someone . . . The secrets of her past were hers, and hers alone, and she couldn't share that darkness with him.

She couldn't share *herself* with him.

Hard to do when she was practically living a lie, every day of her life.

Can you tell us what happened . . . the ghostly voice danced through her mind. She pressed the heel of her hand against her temple as one of those early memories slipped out to taunt her. It had been happening more and more since she'd woken up from the coma and it was driving her nuts.

"Do you want me to hang around?" Lorna offered. "We never did eat. I could make something . . . ?"

Shay laughed. "Not if we want something edible. Look, I'm just tired," she hedged. "I'll grab a granola bar or something and go take a nap."

For a long moment, Lorna watched her, and Shay had to fight to not look away from those golden eyes—eyes too much like Elliot's. Intense and soul-searching, the Winter siblings had a way of looking at you and stripping you bare.

"Okay. If you're sure."

It took another five minutes to get Lorna out of there.

It took Shay another three minutes to shuffle her way to her office.

Once there, she reached into her purse and pulled out the book she'd bought from the store.

Not that she really *needed* a copy of this book.

Shay had *written* the damn thing.

She had forty author copies waiting in neat rows on one of her work desks. She'd been planning to send some of them to soldiers stationed overseas. Then she'd gotten into the car accident and it fell to the wayside.

There was a problem with this book, though—that problem of the autographed sticker. And the autograph inside might read *Shane Neil*, but it sure as hell wasn't *her* autograph.

Touching it with the tip of her finger, she whispered, "Who in the hell did this?"

The phone started to ring again.

Glancing over, she saw a familiar name.

Her assistant, Darcy Montgomery. Shay groaned. Talking to Darcy was the *last* thing she wanted to do. There had been a time when she'd loved calls from Darcy; she was one of her few connections to the outside world, but lately . . . hell. It was a chore.

Not that she'd ever admit that. Darcy was something very rare in Shay's world . . . a real friend. They'd met in college, but Darcy sure as hell hadn't had a bulldog level of persistence back then. Well, she *had*, but it had been different. Back then, Darcy had been all about dragging Shay into the land of the living.

She'd dragged her shopping. She'd been the one to convince Shay to stop hiding in baggy jeans, and even baggier shirts. She'd been the one to talk her into taking some self-defense courses, and *that* had led to her discovering that she actually almost enjoyed it. There was nothing quite like sparring with somebody to get rid of pent-up aggression and fear. From there, she'd gone on to earn her black belt in tae kwon do and for a while, both she and Darcy had even gone to class together.

So many of the *good* memories in her life were tied to Darcy, but lately, the woman just seemed to drag everything down.

Sighing, she reached for the phone. The calls wouldn't stop until Shay talked to her. And knowing Darcy, the woman was freaking out over the fact that she hadn't answered.

Deal with *that* problem first, she decided. Plus, she could multitask.

Grabbing the phone, she answered with a curt, "Yeah?"

"Hey, you!" Darcy's voice, like always, was all bright and happy. Sometimes talking to her made Shay feel like she was trapped in a cheerleading training session—all pep and bounce and optimism. "What took you so long? You aren't up and moving around, are you?"

"No." Shay had her ass firmly planted in her office chair. She just didn't want to fricking *talk* to anybody.

"You should be in your bed, with the phone on one side, books on your lap, and coffee on the other side."

"If I had coffee in bed, I'd spill it, and then I would have to sleep on the couch and my back would hurt even more than it already does," Shay said, sighing. She pinched the bridge of her nose. "Darcy, I need to get some work stuff done. I don't really have time to chat for a while."

Chatting was something that would have to wait until she'd figured out just what in the hell was going on. Not that she really felt like shooting the breeze anyway. Guilt nagged her, but she pushed it away. Even if she didn't have a majorly weird problem going on, she had a book to finish, others to write, and she was going to fall behind, thanks to the damn wreck.

"Oh, I know you're busy. I just wanted to check on you . . . and . . ."

Her voice faltered.

"And what?" Shay asked. *Shit*. This wasn't going to be a quick conversation, was it?

"Well, I just . . . I dunno. I can't believe you did all of that without telling me." Darcy sounded a little despondent. If it had been Shay using that tone of voice, it wouldn't mean much. For Darcy to sound that down, somebody must have been kicking a puppy or something in front of her. Darcy just didn't *do* down. It was kind of like Shay doing *up*. They were total opposites.

"Did what, Darcy?" She scowled, still staring at the book. She shouldn't have gone to the bookstore. If she hadn't, her head wouldn't be pounding, her gut wouldn't be a twisted, tight snarl, and she wouldn't be sitting there, holding a copy of her latest release with some fake's signature on it.

Granted, the book would still be at the store, but Shay could have found out about it at a time when she was a little more equipped to deal with it.

"Well, the Facebook thing. You know. You always said you hated that stuff, so why did you go and start up the page without telling me?"

Facebook. That snarl in Shay's gut jerked itself into a sudden, tight knot, one that was almost viscerally painful.

"What did you say?"

Darcy repeated herself—yes, Shay had just heard what she thought she'd heard.

"Darcy, what Facebook page?"

"Well, *your* Facebook page, silly." She laughed, but it was strained. "I mean, I'm glad you're doing it and all, but you could have told me. Could have let me help.

And how were you even able to keep up with it while you were in such bad shape at the hospital?"

Shay's heart skipped a beat or ten as she tossed the book down.

Just *what* in the world was Darcy talking about?

Spinning around in her chair, she bumped the mouse and watched as her desktop came to life. She opened up her browser and went to the search bar, typing in *Shay Morgan Facebook*.

There were a few entries, but none of them were her.

Her gut was a raw mess as she typed in another name. Several hits came up . . . but again, not her. Sucking in a desperate breath, she silently said, *Thank God*. He wouldn't be able to find her that way. *Nobody* would—

"Shay, are you going to explain this or what?" Darcy asked, her voice edging into that plaintive, whiny zone.

"Just give me a minute," she muttered, wedging the phone more securely against her shoulder. Staring at the screen, she tapped *Shane Neil Facebook*.

And there it was.

"What in the fuck is this?" she muttered.

"Huh?"

"The damn Facebook page," she replied as the page loaded on her computer.

The cover of her latest book seemed to glare at her mockingly from the screen. It was the same book that had a fake's signature on it, too. *What the hell?*

"This Facebook page—it's actually an author-owned page, right? Not one of the fan communities?" Shay said, her voice tight and rough.

"Of course, it's an author page . . . it's yours. That's why I called."

"Darcy. That page isn't mine."

There was a pause and she thought she heard Darcy muttering on the other end of the line, but she couldn't quite make out the words.

"You mean you didn't set up the Facebook page?"

Am I speaking in code? Shoving back from her desk, Shay snapped, "No. I did *not* set up the Facebook page." She went to stand up, but the twinge in her ribs had her remaining in her seat.

She needed to be conscious to handle this, after all.

"Darcy, what do you know about that damn page?"

"Well. Not much. I just found out about it. But I thought you'd done it."

Shay heard her swallow over the line and then Darcy laughed, a strained sound. "I mean, it's *way* popular. Has like ten thousand fans already and it looks like it just went live a few weeks ago. There's a blog and stuff, too. Readers are so excited to see you out more. Can't you tell? It's amazing, isn't it?"

"Amazing. Sure. It's amazing." Shay could feel a muscle starting to pulse behind her eye. A headache would come next and it wouldn't be long before she wanted to claw her brain out, just to relieve the pain. "There's just one problem. I *didn't start a fucking Facebook page!*"

On the other end of the line, Darcy was silent.

The silence stretched out between them and guilt dropped down on her hard. This wasn't Darcy's fault. It was the fault of whoever had set up that page. And Shay now wanted to *strangle* that person. "Sorry for snapping. But, Darcy . . . you know me better than that," she said, trying again. "Why would I have started a Facebook page? I don't do that social media crap. And shit, I was in the hospital for more than two weeks. For a solid week, I couldn't even *sit,* much less type on a computer and update it. I wasn't even conscious."

"Oh. Um. I guess . . . I don't know. Shay, this is weird."

Gee, ya think? "Yes, it's damn weird. That page isn't mine. I don't do these things. You know that." She couldn't. Not even under the guise of her pen name.

Most of the world thought Shane was a guy—which was exactly *why* she'd picked that name. It was just one more way to help her stay hidden. Damn near everything she did was done with the purpose of either *staying* hidden or making it harder to *find* her. Making it harder for *him* to find her . . .

It's your fault . . . that ugly voice jeered at her from the back of her mind, loud and angry and awful.

Your fault. And you won't forget—

She flinched as the screams echoed in her head.

Swearing, she pinched the bridge of her nose. *Not now. No falling apart now.* As the memories tried to push in, she pushed them out. It didn't matter that they were so much worse lately than they used to be. The memories were from *then,* and they didn't affect the crazy shit that seemed to happening right now.

Deal with that; *then* she could have her freak-out.

Freak out, then purge herself of the poison, just her and her diary.

"Darcy, think. Why would I have set up a Facebook page when the last thing I want to do is draw attention to myself?"

Another silence fell. It was so complete, Shay could hear Darcy's ragged intake of breath. "You're right. I never even thought of that. I was just so surprised to see your name . . ." She laughed nervously. "Surprised. Excited. All of that. I know why you keep to yourself and all, and I understand, but I guess I just thought enough time had gone by."

No, Darcy . . . you don't know why. Swallowing, Shay said, "There's no such thing as *enough time.*" She knew people wouldn't understand that. They probably couldn't. But they didn't need to understand it. It wasn't any of their business.

Absently, she reached up and touched the scars along the left side of her face; then, as panic tried to claw into her, she touched one of the ridged lines under her shirt. Those scars were hidden, under her bra and T-shirt, but she saw them every day. Lived with them every day.

They reminded her. She'd lived through hell. She'd gotten out of hell. Nothing could be as bad as that.

Still, there was no such thing as *enough* time.

Crazy bastards didn't care about the passage of time or much of anything else. Crazy bastards didn't care about who they hurt, or how much damage they caused, as long as they got what they wanted.

One more reason why she kept to herself . . . fewer people to get hurt in any potential crossfire.

Looking away from the computer, Shay stared out the window. Her house was the only one around for miles. She'd chosen the isolated area because she felt safer here, away from anybody and everybody, but sometimes the isolation got to her, and now was one of those times.

The snowy, barren landscape seemed to be closing in around her and although it was only three in the afternoon, it was getting dark outside. One of the weird things about living in Alaska—the sun set damn early in the winter. This time of year, they had only a few hours of daylight before darkness enveloped the land again.

It had taken her a couple of years to adjust to it, and sometimes it still took her off guard. Damn it, sore body or not, weak legs or not, she had to move. Cradling the phone on her shoulder, she used the desk for balance as she climbed to her feet.

The room didn't start spinning—that was good.

Okay, a few steps . . . still no spinning. Even better. Slowly, she moved to the window, resting her brow on the icy glass.

"Are you okay?"

Shay laughed, but there wasn't any humor in it.

"Okay? Yeah. Sure. Why not?" Sighing, she lifted her head away from the glass and turned back to her desk. The computer sat there, the screen glaringly white. Okay, so somebody had set up a Facebook page for her. She could deal with that mess—she'd just get it shut down. It wasn't her page, she didn't want it there, end of story. Since she hadn't set it up, that made it a fraud and there had to be rules on Facebook's site against that, right?

Shay always dealt better with things when she had a solution in sight.

There was still the problem of the book—of *all* of those books back at Elliot's store—and she'd deal with that one, too.

First, she had to get off the phone, though. "Darcy, look, I need to figure out what's going on. So we'll talk later."

"But—"

She hung up. Darcy would keep her on the phone for the next two hours and although Shay loved her dearly, she just didn't have time for it.

The woman she remembered from school was just . . . different. Oh, Darcy still loved to talk, but the funny, free-spirited chatter had been replaced and more often than not, Shay was stuck listening to chatter about TV shows, or hot guys that Shay had never heard of, or why wasn't Shay getting better placement at some bookstore in Boise, Idaho.

A pang of longing hit her. She missed her friend. But she just didn't have time to deal with the chattering or nonsense right now.

Surrounded by the peaceful silence of her home, Shay pushed Darcy out of her mind. She bent over the desk and set to work. She didn't use Facebook, although she'd set up a dummy account for a book she'd written a year ago where the killer had stalked his victims through the social media site and she'd needed to understand how the platform worked.

Using that persona, she logged in and started poking around.

"This isn't good," she muttered as she did the *LIKE* thing. More than ten thousand fans. Shit. Shit. *Shit.*

Six weeks ago . . .

All of the info on the page was crap that could be found on Shane's admittedly minuscule website. She kept it short and sweet for a reason—it was all about the books, what had been written and what was coming. Next to no info on her—or him, as the world thought Shane was a guy.

There weren't any author photos on the Facebook page. The images were all of her book covers and that sort of thing. She was both grateful and a little frustrated. While it would have been terrifying if somebody had pictures of *her* and freaky if somebody had been posting pictures masquerading as her "other" self, having a picture of somebody might have clued her in to what was going on. Maybe.

What was really disturbing, though, was how this person related to the world. Although there was no *way* Shay would be doing this, it sure as hell sounded like her. A lot. She recognized phrases she used, her general attitude . . . everything.

The worst thing of all was that the imposter "Shane" sounded like a woman.

It was pretty damn clear by the interaction on Facebook that many of the readers there didn't seem to buy the *guy* bit anymore. The commentary on the page from the *Shane* wannabe had a decidedly female voice to it and about two weeks ago, the imposter had up and stated:

Yes, I'm female . . . I admit it . . . lol!

"Lucky guess? Or did you know?" Shay murmured, stroking one of her scars and steaming. The more she read, the angrier she got. Hardly *anybody* knew. A few might suspect, but the people who *knew*? She could probably count them on her hands and still have fingers left over.

She'd kept as much of her real identity—name, gender, where she lived, everything—as hidden as she could, and this freak went and blasted something in the open. Even if it was just her gender, it was too much.

"Who are you?" Shay stared at the monitor, but it didn't yield any answers. Not that she was expecting any.

Absently, she touched the ridges along the right side of her face, ridges left by burns.

I'll find you . . .

She swallowed, shoving that voice out of her head. She'd escaped. He'd been put in prison. She'd left and hadn't been found.

That was what mattered. Not those terrifying, ugly memories. Even if what had happened to her had destroyed any carefree nature she might have had. Everything she'd hoped to be, everything she'd been—it had all withered and faded and ultimately it died, one ugly, awful night.

But she'd remade herself.

Frowning, she clicked on the link on the *Shane* page, skimming over the "likes." It was a sucker punch when she saw a name she recognized.

Winter's End. Shit.

That was *Elliot's* store.

Winter's End . . .

She had an imposter masquerading as her online, and there was somebody who'd gone and signed her books, at least *once*, at that store. Just miles away. Coincidence?

Shay was too paranoid to believe in coincidence.

With a pounding head, and a heavy heart, she started to dig further. She'd seen other links when the search results had come up, and sure enough, there was plenty to find.

A blog.

A Twitter account.

The longer she read, the more disturbed she got.

"Son of a bitch," she muttered.

Swallowing, she reached for the phone. She needed to contact whoever on Facebook could handle this mess, but she also needed to let her agent know something very strange was going on.

She felt a little bit better as she dialed the number. It would be late in New York, but Anna would have an idea where to go from here. It was also Friday, but Anna would answer, and if she couldn't, she'd call back. Then they could get this mess straightened out.

Anna *always* knew how to handle things. Although they had never met in person, Anna was definitely somebody Shay could count on and when it came to all things writing, she was like a port in the storm.

Anna would know what to do.

Anna was Shay's port in the storm.

But Shay's port in the storm, it seemed, was closed.

Scowling, she lowered the phone after the message finished playing. "That sure as hell is the right number." She punched it again and waited, listening as she was told the number was no longer in service.

"Okay, it hasn't been *that* long since I called her, has it?" Bringing up her email, she did a quick search and found the phone number on Anna's last message.

Yep. It was right.

So what the heck was this?

Sighing, she shot Anna an email.

Hey, I've got something really freaking weird going on. I tried to call, but I keep getting told the number is disconnected.

She cut the link to the Facebook page from the browser bar and added it to the email.

My assistant told me about this—only she thought I'd started this thing up. It's not my page. You *know* how I am about this shit. Look at how many fans are on the page, too. What in the hell do we do about this? I'm going to file a complaint or whatever I need to do with Facebook after I send you this, but I wanted to give you a heads up. I've only just started poking around—there's a Twitter mess, a blog mess, and other messes, too. I'm hoping this will be easy to fix. *Hoping.* But I'm probably not that lucky.

She sent off the email and switched back to the Facebook page, scrolling down until she found the *help* option. Which *wasn't* particularly helpful.

By the time she'd finished with that, her head was throbbing, her shoulders were tight, and she was so pissed she couldn't see straight. She kept shooting her phone hopeful glances, thinking Anna would call. Any minute now.

As soon as she got the email, Anna *would* call. Instead of wasting time worrying about that, she went back to her Googling. Her brain almost exploded at what she saw next.

Yeah, she'd seen the blog. The Twitter account.

But that wasn't all.

LinkedIn, Goodreads, an Amazon author account— pretty much every damn social media thing an author could do. Pretty much everything she'd avoided.

It was all there now.

And she hadn't done any of them.

Son of a *bitch*—

* * *

Nearly six hours after she'd left, Elliot sat at his desk, still brooding over Shay.

Fuck, he missed her.

Just seeing her made him ache.

Even when she pulled away.

Not too many things had left a hole in him. Losing his parents. Yeah, that had done it—their abrupt death in a freak accident years earlier had left both him and Lorna reeling.

He'd reeled himself right into the military, but it had been a good fit. He'd belonged there. It had left another hole in him when he finally realized that something could happen to change that—ugly accusations, nasty lies, a disaster that had ruined his career. Eight years he'd given them . . . and it had ended in a nightmare that had sent his life spinning right out of control, again.

But he'd put it back on track. He came back home to Alaska, opened the bookstore with Lorna. Good choices, both of which had worked for him, and he hadn't had to worry so much about what others thought. His life had been his own and he was ready to live it just as he saw fit.

Then he met Shay. Once more, his life was jerked off course, but in the best way imaginable. For a while. Until he realized she'd never let him in. But shit, he missed her. Maybe—

"No." He shook the thought off, reminding himself of just how miserable he'd been those last days before he'd finally acknowledged the truth. He wasn't going through that with her again. Not with her, not with anybody. He'd either be able to trust her, and have her trust, or it just wouldn't happen.

Determined to distract himself, he logged into his email. That was a chore that would keep him glued to the desk for another two hours and by the time he was done, he'd be stupid-tired—too tired to think.

Excellent.

Thirty minutes into the job, he came across a request that made his eyebrows go up.

A friend request.

From Shane Neil.

Running his tongue along his teeth, he read it again, studying the book's cover image that served as her picture.

He'd been surprised as hell to find out that Shane Neil wasn't a man, but a woman. Very much a woman, with dark hair, curves out to there, and a wide, flirtatious smile. She'd done a little heavy-handed flirting, including inviting him out to dinner, but he had about as much interest in that as he would have had in an IRS audit. Maybe even less. He liked the woman's writing, sure. Outright loved it. But she'd left him cold . . . in so many ways. Something in her eyes just hadn't been right.

She'd brought bookmarks. An advance reader's copy of her next book—one not due out for four months yet. The new book he had in the store now was the paperback issue of the hardback that had come out earlier in the year. He'd read it in one sitting. He'd done the same with the ARC she'd brought in.

Yeah, he'd been surprised when she'd come strolling into his store a couple of weeks ago, but this caught him a little more off guard. What was a big-name author doing friending him on his personal page?

He almost deleted the request but figured it wasn't a big deal. Hell, she had only a couple hundred personal friends and he even knew a few of them—booksellers, industry people that he'd met here and there. What was the problem?

* * *

MyDiary.net/slayingmydragons

Normally it's nightmares that have me writing here . . . I come here to slay my dragons, after all. But I've got a new one . . .

Shay stared at the online diary she kept. She'd started doing it after a therapist had suggested writing things down. The nightmares had started coming more frequently after college, and although nothing had been clear, they didn't need to be clear for her to relate feelings, thoughts, or even the vaguest bit of memory.

Writing things out by hand in journals hadn't seemed to work for her. The online diary, though, *that* worked. She could think things through, and something about putting those thoughts out there, sending them out into the world . . . it made it easier. She felt less isolated. It was totally anonymous and she had no clue if anybody read the entries; she didn't *want* to know. But he hadn't silenced her. This was proof of that.

This had always been a diary for the nightmares, for the trauma . . . not for real-life shit.

Yet now she had some heavy, heavy shit going on. And it was choking her, just thinking about it.

This is a different kind of dragon—a different nightmare. Somebody is trying to take me over and I hate it. Somebody is trying to claim the one thing I take pride in . . . and I don't know how to stop it.

Well, that's not entirely true, I guess. It's just not moving fast enough. I've contacted the right people, but they haven't gotten back to me yet. It's only been a few hours, but it feels like a lifetime.

I've worked too hard to get where I am . . . I'm not letting this happen.

By the time she finished the entry, there was a headache brewing at the base of her skull and her eyelids were heavy.

But no rest for the weary. Not yet.

Shay let herself break long enough for some coffee and half a sandwich. Her gut didn't even want that much, but she knew better than to totally skip eating. While she munched on her sandwich, she checked her email.

Nothing from Anna. A couple of automated replies from some of the sites she'd sent complaints to, and a whole shitload of emails in her inbox.

Three hundred of them.

Three hundred emails in the span of a day. Shit. And most of them were recent. Shay checked email every day, but it was usually after Darcy had winnowed it down. There were messages Darcy couldn't answer and Shay handled all of those, but she didn't usually log in until the evening when Darcy had cleared out a lot of the extraneous stuff.

Was this *normal*?

Of course, she hadn't been doing much of *anything* in the way of email since her accident. Nothing much in the way of email, work, eating, sleeping . . . no. Scratch that—she'd slept. But beyond that? She hadn't accomplished much of anything.

Plus, things had been a little crazy in those weeks before the wreck. She'd been finishing a book, trying to put together a proposal . . . maybe she hadn't been as good about paying attention for a few days.

But still. This just didn't seem right.

With her gut churning, Shay stared at the emails, scrolling through them. The subjects ranged from things like *Viagra . . . make your lady friend happy* to *I loved your latest book!* to *Blog party invite . . .*

It was those last ones that really had her gut clenching in dread. Blog parties.

Interacting.

With people.

That was Shay's biggest fear. Hell, she'd barely been able to interact with Elliot. And she'd fallen hard for him. But if she couldn't interact with *him*, interacting with total strangers would never work.

She'd managed to get through college, although it had been hard. Once she'd graduated, she'd worked for a while at a bank—a nice, safe, secure job. It had sucked. She'd been around too many people and it drove her crazy. So she'd tried a library. Books had been her refuge, and she'd been working on selling hers, so why not a library?

Because, again, libraries had people.

Selling her books had been her salvation. Virna had left her enough money that as long as she was careful, she'd be okay for a while, but the book sales had been her godsend. It wasn't *huge* money, but she'd be able to work at home indefinitely.

Away from *people*. No interaction. Unless she wanted it. Years passed, she'd moved to Earth's End, and as time ticked by, it got to the point that her only interaction with people was via email, the occasional phone call, or the rare trip into town.

Interacting with people *terrified* her, especially if it was on their terms. Working a job outside the house, it had always been on somebody else's terms and it had almost driven her mad. Why she'd been able to get through college but hadn't been able to cope well working with others, she didn't know. Maybe it was because she hadn't *had* to do the college thing. That had been in her control. Sooner or later, though, she'd known she would have to get a job. Virna's gift to her wouldn't last forever.

She could handle email. She could handle her diary posts—she was in control there. She could handle her trips to town—again, she was in control.

As long as she was in control, she was okay. But this situation had spiraled out of control some time ago and she'd been too busy being all comatose and shit to realize it.

Come guest blog with us!
Interested in setting up a signing . . .
Facebook party . . .

"Hell." The longer she read, the more tangled her gut became.

It seemed as though she could vaguely recall seeing some of these emails during those last few weeks before the wreck, but those memories were hazy. The doctors had told her it wasn't unusual. They also told her they didn't know whether her memory would get any better with time.

Not that it mattered right now.

All that mattered was fixing this mess.

A massive wave of self-pity tried to rise inside her but she pushed it away. She could feel sorry for herself later.

Grimly, she started to tackle the problem. She wouldn't get any damn work done, considering how upset she was, so she might as well start tackling some of the emails and letting people know, upfront, she didn't *do* blog parties, chats, and all that stuff.

At least *then*, she'd be in control.

"He's going to find you . . ."

A girl's voice. But it didn't stay that way long. Morphing from the young, childish voice of a girl to the deeper, husky voice of a woman.

"He'll find you!"

"No!"

On the bed, Shay muttered into her pillow. But her sleeping form didn't move. It was a lesson learned early, and a lesson learned well. She hid like a rabbit, cowering still and silent for fear the predators would see or hear her if she moved. Even now, she couldn't break that conditioning.

And as the dream changed, going from terrifying to merely heartbreaking, silent tears slid from under her lids as she dreamt of a little girl in a room surrounded by people who watched her with sad, serious eyes.

One woman had been called Virna, and she'd often visited the little girl back at the house where she'd lived. Sometimes, she'd even sneak her doughnuts.

Shay woke to silence.

Sweet, blissful silence . . . and the sad, wistful memories of Virna lingering in her mind. Shay was pretty certain the social worker hadn't planned on taking in a kid when she'd come in to work that day. But in the end, Shay had gone home with Virna Lassiter.

And in the end, Virna had been the one to adopt Shay.

Of course, she hadn't been called Shay, then.

But Shay was who she'd become.

And Virna had made the girl she'd been a promise. Several promises, actually. She'd be safe, she'd always have a home with Virna. And she'd always have chocolate doughnuts.

It wasn't Virna's fault that she'd died and that the safe home had disappeared. But Virna had kept her promise . . . in a way. She'd left Shay with the means to provide her *own* home. Her own chocolate doughnuts. Her own means of safety.

Virna hadn't been safe, though.

All because of *him*. Shay's bastard of a stepfather and his twisted, warped view of the world.

Him . . .

Bile roiled through her belly, rushing up her gut, and she swallowed, forcing it back down.

This was why she had such a hard time putting on weight—waking up with the nightmares made her less likely to eat and the more stressed she was, the less she wanted to eat. It was a nasty, ugly cycle, one that wore her out, but she didn't know how to break it.

Weary already, she sat up, braced for the pain it would cause, but to her disappointment, it wasn't so bad this time. Pain would be a welcome distraction on a morning like this. Covering her eyes with her hands, she took a deep breath, then another.

"He's gone," she whispered. "Gone."

Not completely gone, of course. Not like Virna. But out-of-her-life gone—because he didn't know where she was. Or even *who* she was. She'd seen to that. She'd been almost eighteen by the time the trial had ended, and the first thing she'd done once she had turned eighteen was have her name legally changed. Since there was very clear proof that her safety was at risk, it had been a closed proceeding and her new name had been kept hidden. It would take a court order to have the new identity revealed.

And there wasn't a big likelihood of that happening.

With a new name and the money Virna had left her, Shay had disappeared.

Disappeared . . . and moved to Alaska. Connecting Shay Morgan to the young woman who'd testified against Jethro Abernathy, who'd helped lock him away, wouldn't be as easy as doing a name search online, or trying to follow the social security numbers.

She was safe here. Safe, as long as she didn't draw attention to herself. She was as far away from the deserts of Phoenix as she could get.

And she tried to forget. Why *shouldn't* she forget? She'd forgotten so much of her life. The early years of her life, right up until the night she'd met Virna, were nothing but a black void. Virna was the first clear memory she had. If she could forget whatever had happened before then, why not forget about *him*?

Working her way through college, writing her nightmares down on paper, she'd tried to forget. Forgetting wasn't happening . . . but she'd managed to purge the nightmares enough so that she could sleep. Most days, the diary was enough, and she'd found escape, relief, and an odd form of therapy through her fiction writing.

As long as she was able to get those dragons out, put them down on paper or on the computer, she didn't lie awake at night, choking on screams.

It was a fucking weird twist of fate that she actually had people paying her to write those books—the therapy she needed to stay sane. Those books, many of them at least, stemmed from her nightmares, created by her inner dragons, and she used them to haunt the dreams of others.

It was a bizarre trade-off, she figured.

Lowering her hands, Shay stared out the window into the darkness of the early morning. It was almost seven, but the blackness of the sky made it look like midnight.

Lost in the silence of the room, she thought back to the way she'd spent the past day. Somebody was trying to steal her life. All of the hard work. All of the anguish. Her dragons.

A faint sneer curled her lip.

If somebody wanted to take that past, maybe it wouldn't bother her so much. But if whoever was doing this realized just what it had cost Shay to create those stories, maybe that person wouldn't be so eager to try and claim credit.

"It doesn't matter." Her voice was a harsh slap in the quiet of the room.

Her heart started to thud against her rib cage in slow, heavy beats as she realized the truth of those words. It *didn't* matter. Her past, brutal as it was, ugly as it was, had made her. *She* had survived it. Another child might not have and if that was the sacrifice it required . . . so fucking be it.

She'd earned this life—this uneasy peace that really wasn't so very peaceful. But it was what she had, and it was hers, damn it. Shane Neil was hers, this place was hers, this *life* was hers, and whoever was trying to masquerade as her was in for a rude fucking awakening if he or she thought Shay would just *take* it.

Mentally bracing herself, she eased herself out of bed.

First things first—get the dream in her diary. Then she'd see if any progress had been made getting that Facebook page down.

And if not, she was going to bring down unholy hell.

After that . . . she was going back to Earth's End, and back to Winter's End. She'd talk to Elliot and find out what in the world was going on with those damn books.

Grimacing, she realized she was going to do what he'd wanted her to do from the very beginning. She was going to open up to him. Because there was no other way he'd understand just why it was so important for her to know everything he could possibly tell her about the person who'd claimed to be the author of *her* damn books.

MyDiary.net/slayingmydragons

The dreams keep getting weirder. More real. More complete. And I'm not forgetting them the way I used to. They are staying with me, clear and solid in my head. I hate it.

I dreamt about the closet. There was a baby crying . . . again. The girl, whispering.

And then it changed and it was the day I met Virna. I remember her talking to me, and offering me doughnuts. I wanted a powdered sugar one, but she talked me into trying chocolate ones . . .

One hour, one chocolate doughnut, and two cups of coffee later, the phone rang.

"Hello?"

"Hey, it's me!" Darcy's bright, cheerful voice was almost like a nail in her ear. Two cups of coffee still wasn't enough to face a perky person.

Hell, *ten* cups couldn't make perky manageable.

Still, this was Darcy. Forcing herself to smile, she said, "Hey, it's you."

"So what are you up to today?"

"Right now, I'm topping off my coffee." Shay studied the bottom of her cup and rose to her feet.

"You've probably had more than you need already." Darcy sighed. "Think you'll get any work done today? You've been having trouble with your book since the wreck."

Shay rolled her eyes as she shuffled into the kitchen. Yes, she was aware that she hadn't written much in a while. Shit, she hadn't been out of the hospital *that* long. "I dunno. I'm having these issues . . ." Sighing, she poured her coffee.

It would be good to talk about it, she supposed. If anybody would understand, it would be Darcy. That was what friends were for, right?

After adding cream and sugar, she headed back to her office. She might as well tackle email while she talked to Darcy. They needed to discuss how to handle things until the impersonator problem was cleared up but until they had that worked out, Shay would much rather be the one declining any and all invitations.

A few minutes later, she finished summing things up and sat there, staring at her computer and waiting for a response.

Silence greeted her.

"Darcy?"

"I'm here," Darcy said quietly. "This . . . well, this is weird. You're serious about all of this?"

"Yes." Shay pinched the bridge of her nose and said, "Somebody is pretending to be *me*."

"What do you mean, somebody is pretending to have written your books?"

Sighing, Shay skimmed another email—*hello, we would like to link our blog to yours . . . delete*. "Darcy, I mean just what I said. Somebody went into the bookstore in Earth's End and signed the damn books. Pretended to be me. Acted like they had a fucking *right* to sign *my* books." Damn it, the more she thought about it, the angrier she got—and she still needed to get into town and talk to Elliot.

She shot a look at the clock; it was ticking close to noon.

But here she was, on the phone with Darcy. Fighting with email, Facebook, WordPress, Twitter.

Clicking on another email, she barely made it through two lines before her head wanted to explode.

Dear Mr. Morgan
We're contacting you to see if you would like to come to our store for a signing. We're located in Portland . . .

It wasn't the *Mr.* that set her off, either. Portland. Bookstore. Come in for a signing. *Shit.* Another one. People actually wanted her to come in for actual signings.

That so couldn't happen. Shay would freak out before she even made it out the damn door.

She groaned and dropped down to thump her head on the desk. Hard. Several times.

"Shay? What's that noise?"

"I'm hitting my head on the desk."

"Ah . . . you just got out of the hospital after you hit your head in a car crash. Should you be banging your head?" Darcy asked worriedly. "I mean, you were in a coma."

"I came out of the coma, too, thanks." A headache

started to bloom, but she was pretty sure it was stress related.

"Well, still, that's not a good thing to do. You know, you're worrying about this too much," Darcy said. "I mean, you deal with weird shit all the time. Just get to work on the book and this will work out. I'll handle the email and everything, and maybe I can figure out what's going on for you. You'd feel better if you weren't messing with it anyway."

"No." Shay scowled. "I'd feel better if none of this was happening."

But *that* wasn't possible, so the next best alternative was to find answers—do something.

So far, all she'd done was send out complaints, and she hadn't gotten one *damn* answer. That was stopping. *Today.*

There was one person who had some sort of answer. Elliot Winter.

He would have met the Shane imposter.

He was a nut for those books. It had always given Shay a dull rush of pride, even as it made her nervous and uncomfortable. He liked her books. *Elliot* liked *her* books, damn it.

He'd know something about the person who'd signed them—so why in the hell was she sitting here *chatting* instead of getting on the road?

"I need to go, Darcy."

"Hey, wait!"

"I can't." Shutting down her desktop, Shay eased back from the computer and turned around. "I need to go to Earth's End. So far, I'm not having any luck shutting things down on this end and I'm going to go crazy if I don't find some sort of answers. Anna must be out of town or something and *she* isn't answering me—nobody will be at the publisher's until Monday. I've got to talk to somebody. So Elliot is it."

"Elliot?" Darcy asked warily.

Grimly, Shay smiled. "Yeah. That guy I used to date. This faker signed books at his store. He'll know something, or have remembered something about the imposter. That's just Elliot for you. He remembers things. I'm going into town to pick his brain."

"You're driving down there?"

"Too cold to walk," Shay pointed out, glancing outside. The sun was up. It would be up until around three or so and then it would set—the days were short and cold, very cold. She didn't have to go outside to know that. It was January, for crying out loud. "Plus, it's thirty minutes away."

"I wasn't suggesting you walk, silly," Darcy said, laughing. "But you shouldn't go *now*. You need to be resting and taking it easy."

"I've done enough of that." If she stayed here, she was just going to brood, and steam, and brood some more. At least if she went to Elliot's, she'd feel like she was *doing* something. "I'll talk to you later, Darcy."

"But—"

Dropping the phone into the cradle, Shay stared outside at her truck.

She hadn't driven since the accident.

She'd been in her car—a beautiful Dodge Charger. Or it had been beautiful. It now resembled a tin can. Swallowing, she rubbed a hand over her chest, vaguely recalling the way it had felt right before she'd passed out. Pain. Lots of it.

For a minute, the fear almost kept her trapped.

But then she threw it off. "What are you going to do . . . never drive again?" she muttered.

Like *that* was an option.

Some days the nightmares were so bad, she had to leave the house just to escape them. She couldn't run fast enough to get away from herself. She could barely drive fast enough.

Besides, if the nightmares from what had been done to her all of those years ago weren't enough to paralyze her in terror, then she sure as hell wasn't going to let a fucking *car wreck* do it.

CHAPTER
FOUR

"WHAT IN THE *HELL* DO YOU THINK YOU'RE DOING?"

At the sound of his sister's irate voice, Elliot closed his eyes and just remained where he was, sprawled on the floor, straightening out the mess the Danver kids had left when their parents had finally vacated the store.

Considering how pissed off she sounded, he knew he wasn't in any mood to tangle with her.

They'd already tangled over the Danver kids. She'd wanted to tear into the mom and dad the second they'd stepped foot in the store. The last time the kids had been there, they'd left bubble gum inside books and one had thrown a board book down a toilet.

Elliot had decided to give them the benefit of the doubt.

He'd been in the wrong—as evidenced by the thirty or forty dollars' worth of destroyed merchandise surrounding him.

Bunch of hooligans. He honestly didn't mind if parents wanted to bring their kids in to just *browse*—very often *browsing* led to *buying*. And a bookstore couldn't exactly stay in business if people didn't *buy*. But who in the hell was going to buy the books that those kids had trashed?

After he'd pointed that out to the parents, they'd gotten rather insulted and informed him, "We'll just take our business elsewhere."

He'd then felt the need to mention, "You don't exactly do any business here anyway, so that's just fine."

They hadn't approved.

Lorna had barely managed to keep the *I told you so* quiet until they'd taken their five kids out of the store. Once the bell jangled shut behind them, though, she'd whirled around and laid into him as if the kids had destroyed bricks of solid gold.

Elliot was a wise man. He knew when to advance . . . and when to retreat.

He'd retreated into the aisles to clean up the mess; he was perfectly happy to stay right there until she cooled off.

Tuning out the low murmur of voices coming from the front, he picked up a scrap of paper and stared at it glumly. Hell, didn't those idiots bother to teach their kids that books were for *reading*? *Not* for tearing up? He could have understood if any of the kids had been under five or so, but the youngest Danver kid was about seven or eight.

Hearing a soft footstep behind him, he said, "Give me a second to clear the mess up—sorry."

"It's okay."

Need punched through him a second before the recognition hit. His body, his heart . . . those parts of him remembered Shay just a little better than his mind did. He looked up in time to see her easing her way down to the floor, a wary look on her face.

The bruises were still there—those faint shadows of color lingering on her pale, soft skin. He'd seen them yesterday and it had been like a kick to the gut. She didn't look much better today—tired, strained, and in pain.

Yet she still looked amazingly beautiful.

And she smelled so damn good. Like the first snow, springtime, and citrus, all wrapped up together. Sitting as close as she was, he had that scent flooding his head now, making it hard to think. For weeks after he'd broken up with her, he'd caught the faintest ghost of her scent on his jackets. Now he was surrounded by it again and it was torture.

"What are you doing here?" he asked, tearing his gaze away from her and forcing his attention back to the mangled remains of children's books.

"I wanted to talk to you about something," she said softly. She reached out and touched one of the books, her fingers brushing against the cracked spine. "Man, somebody had fun back here."

"The Danver family was in."

"Ahhhh. That would explain it." She gathered up the books around her.

"I can get them." Hearing the terse sound of his own voice, he sighed and rubbed a hand down his face. "Sorry. I'm in a bitch of a mood. But I'll take care of the mess. You should be back home, taking it easy, anyway."

"Handing you three or four books isn't going to slow my recovery any, I promise you, Elliot." She smiled at him.

The dimple in her cheek winked and his heart stuttered in his chest. That dimple had always gotten to him. Damn it, how could she still get to him like this? Hadn't he decided he was better off without the complication of Shay Morgan?

Shit. Clearing his throat, he focused his attention back on the books in front of him, stacking the books that he wouldn't have to trash in one pile and the rest in another. "So how is that recovery going? You going to need physical therapy or anything?"

"No. I was lucky. If it hadn't been for the coma and

the head injuries, I probably would have been able to go home within a few days, but those complicated things. I ended up with pneumonia in ICU, but that's not as bad as the other stuff." From the corner of his eye, he saw her shrug. "It could have been a lot worse."

"It sounds like it was bad enough." He held up a hand and ticked the problems off on his fingers. "Coma. Head injuries. Pneumonia. Any of those could have been bad, just on their own. But all three? You should be taking it easy. So why aren't you resting?"

She wrinkled her nose. "I've rested. Two weeks, flat on my back." Her fingers toyed with the folds of her long denim skirt, twisting them, smoothing them out. Twist, smooth, twist, smooth . . . over and over . . . He wanted to reach over and catch her hands in his, hold them and get her to tell him what was wrong.

That wasn't going to happen. So he focused on the obvious.

She was nervous about something. Very nervous. She wasn't looking at him and she was fidgeting.

Elliot had learned to read people pretty damn well. It had come in handy during his years in the army and in the years since he'd bought the bookstore.

Reading Shay wasn't always easy because she was about as open as a closed book, but right now, she was nervous as hell.

Shifting around, he faced her and waited her out.

She shot a quick look at him, her eyes bouncing around to land somewhere in the vicinity of his chin before moving to linger on his right shoulder as she said, "Besides, I need to ask you a question."

"I'm all ears."

She paused in her endless twisting and folding of her skirt to reach for a book by her side. Seeing the copy of the book she held, his curiosity stirred. He'd almost forgotten about it. "I heard you'd picked one up. What made you change your mind about trying these?" he asked, reaching for the copy of *Death Sigh*. It was one of the store's copies. He recognized his store's autographed copy sticker.

Her fingers uncurled from the book slowly as he tugged it out of her grasp, but it struck him that she was reluctant to let it go. From under his lashes, he watched her.

"I didn't exactly change my mind," she said quietly. Her tongue stroked across her lower lip.

For a moment, he was distracted. He wanted to lean in and trace the path her tongue had taken with his own. *Focus, Winter.* Flipping the book open, he looked at the flowing, flowery script on the title page, giving himself a minute before he looked back at Shay. "So what's up?"

"I want to know about the person who signed it."

Elliot cocked a brow at her. "Okay . . . although I'm curious why the sudden interest. I'd tried to get you to read these for years. Why the change of mind now?"

Shay closed her eyes.

Elliot had always been good at realizing when things were about to go to hell—five seconds before it happened. It was a weird feeling. A tension of sorts, something that lingered in the air and all but choked the oxygen out of it in some bizarre way.

This was one of those moments—everything was about to go straight to hell and he knew it. Adrenaline slammed into him and his heart raced along at about two hundred beats a minute, or at least it seemed that way. He had to work to keep his breathing level as he watched Shay, as he waited.

And then she opened her eyes and said quietly, "I need to know about whoever signed this book, Elliot. Because whoever did it is a fucking *liar*. Whoever did it isn't Shane Neil. *I* am."

* * *

I am—

Shay had thought it would be hard to say that.

She'd thought she would have to force herself to admit something she'd kept such a closely guarded secret.

Oh, yeah, sure. A few people knew, but only two of them knew her in real life, knew the *real* Shay. Darcy knew and Shay's adopted sister Angie knew.

That was just about it.

The rest of them, none of them really *knew* her—not in person. Her agent, her editor—neither of them had met her in real life. All of their contact had been online, through email. Shay had never met any of them out in the real world—no conventions, no signings, no business lunches. Not a one of them knew what she really looked like.

None of them really knew *her*.

But Elliot did.

He knew her better than Darcy did. Better than anybody, probably even better than her sister . . . she hadn't seen Angie in years and while Angie knew the girl she'd *been*, Elliot knew who she was now.

And nobody had ever made the impact on her life that he had; what he thought about this *mattered* in a way she couldn't describe. Swallowing, she dared a quick look at him but saw that he wasn't looking at her. He was staring at the book he held.

A lock of hair fell into his eyes, shielding his gaze from her. Seconds ticked away into minutes, and finally, she said softly, "Elliot?"

A harsh sigh escaped him and he stood up.

"Yeah?"

She managed not to flinch at the abrupt sound of his voice, but just barely. It was enough to make her heart bleed, though. He didn't believe her. She could tell, just by the way he sounded, just by the tension in his voice and the rigid set of his shoulders.

Tears burned her eyes, but she blinked them away, refusing to let them fall.

You can do this.

And there was no doubt that she could. She'd gotten through hell. She could get through this without letting him see how he'd hurt her.

Swallowing, she shifted around until she had her legs beneath her before she started to get up. She still had to grab hold of things to stand—her strength was coming back, but it was slow.

A hand came around her arm, gently. A blush stung her cheeks and she would have pulled away if she could have figured out a graceful way to do it. "I'm fine," she mumbled.

"You're not." He dropped a kiss onto her head and stroked a hand down her back. "It's okay to need a hand every now and then, Shay."

She shrugged and turned away the second he let go of her arm. Coming here had been a waste of time, she realized.

Okay to need somebody? She resisted the urge to laugh. She'd come here because she *did* need somebody. She'd needed him. But he hadn't even realized it.

Hunching her shoulders, she turned away, staring at the brightly decorated kids' area of the store, trying to figure out what to say, what to ask—

"What's the deal here, Shay?"

"I told you. I'm Shane Neil."

She heard another heavy sigh come from him. "And I'm just supposed to believe that?"

"Hell, why would I *lie* about it?" With a harsh laugh, she nodded at the book he still held. It hung from one long-fingered hand and she could see, faintly, how the light glinted off the red foil of the title font. She'd been so excited when she'd heard about what they were doing with the cover of that book—it was the kind of cover that authors hoped for, prayed for, and it was *hers*. And damn it, somebody else was trying to claim it. Trying to take it over. "You just believed it from somebody else easily enough, didn't you?"

"Shit, she came in here with an advance reader's copy and bookmarks. Those don't exactly fall off of trees, Shay."

Something stilled inside her. Bookmarks . . . and an ARC—that was something. "It's not that hard to get your hands on bookmarks, Elliot," she said softly. "I can show you ten different sites where you order them and have them shipped right to the doorstep. All they need is the artwork—they don't care if it's the author or not. They just need the art, and the money."

She came in here with an advance reader's copy . . .
She . . .

Narrowing her eyes, she studied him closely. "She? It was a woman who came in?"

"Yes." With a pointed stare, he said, "But then again, so are you."

Ignoring that, she said, "And you weren't surprised by her showing up out of the blue?"

"Actually, I was pretty damn surprised. But she had the ARC. She had the bookmarks. What was I going to do, tell her to leave and come back with some sort of written proof? She wanted to sign the damn books!" He looked down at the book he held and then swore, tossing it down by the pile on the floor before turning away to pace.

"The problem with that is that they aren't her damn books." She wrapped her arms around her midsection, eyeing the book on the floor. *Mine*, she thought. *They are my damn books.*

"And how in the hell was I supposed to know that?" he growled.

Shay swallowed. "You weren't, I guess."

Silence stretched out between them, hanging there like a heavy, musty curtain. Shay shivered, but it had nothing to do with cold. The silence grew so weighted, she jumped when Elliot shattered it with his next words.

"Look, I'm sorry. I don't know what to think about any of this. It's just too . . . it's too bizarre."

"Tell me about it," she said. Closing her eyes, she tried to level out, reaching for some sense of calm, of peace. It had always eluded her. Always. But she could fake it. She'd been faking elusiveness, distance, for years, right? Once she thought she could look at him without his seeing that he'd hurt her, she opened her eyes and turned to face him. "You kept saying that you just wanted me to open up . . . to trust you. You just said it's okay to need a hand. That's why I'm here, Elliot . . . I need help. I'm trying to trust you. But you—"

"Elliot?"

Lorna appeared at the end of the aisle. Shay stiffened. The look on her face was angry. So very angry.

"Not now," Elliot said, his gaze locked on Shay's face, eyes burning, intensely hot.

"Yes, damn it. *Now*. Shay, I'm sorry, but things just went to hell. Elliot, come on."

"I said not *now*," he bit off.

"Elliot, damn it!"

As he continued to stare at her, Shay asked softly, "Just tell me one thing, Elliot. Do you believe me?"

His eyes clouded. "Shit, Shay. Hell, I don't know . . . this is just . . ."

"Yeah. It's just." Nodding, she edged around him, taking great care to keep as much distance between them as she could. "You think about it, then. Take all the time you need and think about it."

Not that it would really make a difference. She'd done what she could. She'd reached out. She'd tried. And failed. She could always come back, bring her contracts and shit to convince him, but she didn't see the point. He trusted a total stranger so easily. But not her.

He caught her arm, tugging her to a stop, but when he tried to ease her closer, Shay leaned away. "Damn it, Shay . . ."

"Go on," she said, staring up at him. "You've got a business to run and I've got things to do."

"We'll talk about this later."

No. We won't. She'd be damned if she'd try to convince him.

As he disappeared down the aisle with his sister, Shay lowered her gaze to stare at the book on the floor—her book. The one she'd written—the one she hadn't signed. Gingerly, she bent over to pick it up. To her satisfaction, her head didn't start spinning around like a Tilt-A-Whirl—each day was getting a little bit better. Curling her hand around it, she started for the front of the store. The longer she stared at the *autographed copy* sticker, the more furious she got.

She'd always had a bit of a thrill seeing her books in a store. Yeah, she'd wondered what it might be like seeing signed copies of her books, but she wasn't about to leave any sort of sign as to *where* people might find her. Even changing her name wasn't enough.

Nothing was enough.

Plus, there was the little fact that she completely and utterly *freaked out* at the thought of putting herself out in public that way. Not just leaving a trail for him to find her, but putting *herself out there*—having to interact with people. It froze her with fear. Shay didn't know if she had some warped sort of social anxiety disorder or what, but just the *thought* of having to face people and claim credit for work she was extremely proud of . . . talk about a mess of contradictions.

But she wasn't letting somebody masquerade as her, either. On her way out of the door, she stopped by the book dump and collected the rest of the books, using a handbasket to carry them all to the register.

Becca, the part-time employee, stood at the register and smiled in Shay's direction, but her smile wobbled a little as Shay dumped the books out onto the counter.

"Ah . . . you want all of them?" Becca asked.

"Yes."

Becca blinked. "But . . ."

"Hey, the books are there to buy, right?" Shay offered what she hoped was a charming smile. She suspected it fell short, but it was the best she could do. "What can I say—you don't get signed books in here every day, right?"

"No." Becca smiled. "That's for sure. We're such an out-of-the-way little place, we hardly ever have authors who come in just to sign stock."

While Becca finished ringing her up, Shay stood there, shifting from one foot to the other, the pain in her head blooming like an ugly, poisonous rose. She needed to get home and lie down.

"Hey, are you all right?"

Absently, she looked up and realized she'd been rubbing her temple and swaying on her feet. Forcing a smile, she nodded. "Yeah, I've just got a headache." She glanced at the total and reached into her purse, pulling out her wallet. Extricating her credit card, she gave it to Becca. As the girl swiped it, Shay looked away, searching for the clock. She'd left her phone in the car and without it, she had no way of telling time. She had a habit of losing watches.

But instead of finding the clock, she found herself staring at a strangely familiar book.

The ARC the Shane imposter must have given Elliot. Her next book.

Blood roared in her ears.

"Here you go, Shay. Just sign my copy."

Blindly, she took the receipt and scrawled her signature on it, barely able to drag her eyes away from the book lying just a few feet away. "Here," she whispered, her voice reed thin.

"Thanks. Shay, are you sure you're okay? Do you need some water?"

Man, had things gone to hell or what?

Staring at the computer was like being punched in the face.

Elliot had dealt with some rough-ass shit in his life. He had only been nineteen, Lorna just a year older, when they'd lost both of their parents. It had been a harsh blow—Paul Winter was their stepfather, but in all the ways that counted, he'd been their real father. Their *only* father. He'd married their mother when Elliot and Lorna were kids, and the car accident that had killed them had been a devastating blow.

Finding the woman he thought was *right* for him, only to have her remain as distant as the moon—that was the sucker punch that just kept on giving.

That fucking disaster in the army—the one that had been the beginning of the end for him—this reminded him of that. Another crazy-ass bitch trying to ruin his life.

I barely got away . . . That was what she'd written in the Facebook note. And it was eerily similar to what somebody else had once tried to say about him.

"What in the hell is she talking about, Elliot?" Lorna asked quietly.

Shit, it was almost verbatim, too, he thought. *I barely*

got away—he was just too strong. Crazy, and he wanted to hurt me. I could see it—

Swearing, he ground his fist against his brow and shoved the memory of that awful time out of his head. *Charges were dropped, man. The people who matter know she lied.* Granted, there weren't a lot of them. A lot of the guys he'd thought were his friends had believed—*fuck, Winter, you need to focus*, he told himself.

He had another nightmare on his hands. *Another* one. How in the *hell* had he ended up with another crazy bitch out to try and destroy his life? He'd met this woman *one* time and he hadn't touched her for longer than it had taken to shake her hand.

"Elliot, damn it, would you concentrate?" Lorna snapped. "What the fuck is she trying to pull?"

Glancing over his shoulder, he met his sister's furious gaze and shook his head. "I don't know, Lorna."

There was a knock at the door. "Not now," he called out.

The knock came again thirty seconds later.

Swearing, he shoved back from the computer and stormed over to the door. With a savage twist of his wrist, he jerked it open and glared at Becca. She shrank away from him. "I'm sorry," she blurted out before he even managed to open his mouth. "I'm sorry, Elliot, I just . . . I didn't know what to do. It's . . . the book is missing."

"If somebody stole a damn book, we can deal with it in a few minutes. I've got a bigger problem on my hands," he snarled.

"It was Shay," she said, as though she hadn't even heard him.

He stilled. "Shay?"

She started twisting one of the numerous rings she wore on her hand. "She was at the register and she did the weirdest damn thing. She bought every last one of the signed Shane Neil books—I mean, *all of them*. It was like over a hundred dollars' worth and a lot of them were copies, ya know? Duplicates of the same book. But every signed book. She bought them all. Then, she was looking all white and pale, like she was going to pass out. I heard about her wreck and all and I was worried, so I asked her if she wanted some water. I went to get her some from the break room and I brought it out here. She was leaning against the counter, acting fine. Still pale and everything, but she drank it. Said thank you. Then she left. I swear, Elliot, the book was *there*, on the counter behind the register, when I went to get the water. I was reading it before I checked her out, I know it was there. But now it's gone."

The words came spilling out of her in a rush and it took a few seconds for him to process them all. He was still confused. "What book?"

"That one from Shane Neil . . . the advance reader's copy you got from the author. I'm sorry . . . I know you two used to have a thing going, but I think . . . I think Shay stole it."

CHAPTER
FIVE

"IT'S NOT REALLY STEALING," SHE MUTTERED, SHOOT-ing a look at the ARC on top of the books. It was her damn book. Whoever had it couldn't have a legit right to it. That was her line of thinking. So whoever had it, when she'd given it to Elliot, had done it under false pretenses and besides, the bitch had fucking *signed* it. It had a false signature on it—that made it a lie.

If Elliot wanted a signed book, she'd give him one.

But he wasn't keeping *that* one. Wasn't selling the other ones in his store, either.

Nearly an hour had passed since she'd rushed from the store as fast as she could. It wasn't very fast. She was finally back up over half speed. She figured she was at 70 percent now. Snow had moved in and it had taken her nearly fifty minutes to get home instead of the nor-mal thirty. But now she was settled in front of the fire-place. It was already set with wood. She had matches. And she had the books.

It was time to watch them burn. The damn things weren't going to exist in a few minutes and that was exactly how she wanted it.

The only thing she wasn't going to burn—yet—were the autographed pages. She wanted to scrutinize those title pages, see if she could recognize the handwriting.

So far, nothing clicked, but one could never tell.

Striking one of the long matches she'd bought for the fireplace, she leaned in close and touched it to the kindling at the bottom. She watched as the flame flared, then steadily grew brighter. Once it was crackling away, she added a book. Then another. And another. She hadn't quite managed to add the fourth when the phone rang.

Sighing, she picked it up.

She wasn't surprised to see Elliot's store on the caller ID. She'd known Becca would figure it out. She'd also known Becca would rat her out. What surprised her was that he hadn't called before now.

"Hello?"

"Did you take that fucking book out of my store?" Elliot snapped.

"You own a bookstore," she pointed out. "I imagine you have many people taking books out of your store." She reached for the ARC, lifting it to study the cover. It was the first time she'd gotten the nicer ARCs, too. This imposter was putting a pall on her success—tarnishing it.

"You know what book I'm talking about, damn it. You had no fucking right to take my damn book," he growled.

"Hmmm." She carefully ripped out the signed title page before tossing the ARC into the fire. As the flames greedily ate it up, she watched. "Well, we never did get to finish talking. If you want your book back, you come up to my place—we can finish talking, and you can have your book." *Well, a replacement. One with a* real *autograph.*

Signed by *her*, damn it. Not some fake.

And maybe if he saw all of *her* copies, he'd believe her. She had first editions, foreign editions, large-print editions, all of them—things that he wasn't likely to see just *anywhere*. And the ARCs. She had ARCs, too, damn it.

"I've got a fucking mess on my hands. I can't."

Her heart sank inside her chest—a heavy stone weight.

He had a mess? She was battered from that wreck. Somebody was trying to screw with her life. And somebody was trying to lie about her books. But *he* had a mess?

So much for that friendship you talked about, she thought miserably. Self-pity started to rise inside her, but she shoved it down. Feeling sorry for herself wasn't going to get her through this. She might be half-broken inside and she might jump at her own shadow and she sure as hell was fucked-up beyond fixing. But self-pity wasn't going to help. There was little room for it in her life.

"You've got a mess, huh?" she asked quietly.

"A big one, damn it, and I need that book."

The impatient, demanding tone in his voice had her frowning, but she didn't care *why* he wanted the book so much. If he wanted an ARC, he could have one of hers. Reaching for the poker at her side, she nudged the ashy remains of one of the books farther back inside the hearth. It fell apart under the pressure. Distantly, she felt as if she just might do that—fall apart under even the lightest touch, into nothing but bits and pieces.

"I'm sorry to hear about your mess, Elliot, but I've got one of my own. You take care of yours and I'll muddle through mine and sooner or later, I'll get your book to you."

"If you hadn't fucking stolen it, you wouldn't have to worry about going out of your way to bring it back to me, now would you?" he snapped. "I need that damn book back."

"Well, I'm a little busy with my own mess . . . and

stolen is such a harsh word. Perhaps we should say *bor-rowed*."

"Borrowed. That implies I actually gave you permission, that you didn't just take off without getting my okay, Lorna's okay, that you didn't sneak behind my counter and take it, that you didn't sneak off without letting anybody know." His voice was as sharp as broken glass, cold as the arctic ice. "Bring me my fucking book, Shay. Whatever your problems are, they aren't my problems, and trust me, mine are pretty fucking bad."

She watched as the inner pages curled and turned black, catching fire one by one. "Doesn't life just suck, Elliot?" Bitterness crept into her voice and she couldn't hold it back. "It's ironic, you know. You kept talking to me about trust. You said it was okay to reach out, to need somebody. I did it. I tried to trust you. I needed to talk to you and you wouldn't spare me five minutes. You go deal with your problems . . . and have a nice day. I'll get your book to you when I can."

Without wasting any more time, she disconnected and dropped the phone onto the floor. One by one, she fed the books to the fire until they were all gone, saving nothing but the signed title pages.

By the time it was done, she had more than twenty sheets of paper at her side.

And the phone had rung six times.

An empty ache settled in the middle of his chest. *I tried to trust you—*

Shit. This was just *insane.* He didn't need to be trying to think through the complication of an ended relationship when he had a woman out to ruin his life. That was what he tried to tell himself. Yet the ache in his chest wasn't going away.

"Is she bringing the book back?" Lorna asked.

"No." He dialed her number again, but he wasn't surprised when she didn't answer. *Damn it, Shay.* The words burned on his tongue, but he wasn't frustrated over the damned book. He just . . . hell. *Pick up the phone.*

It rang four times and rolled over to voice mail. She was pissed off and ignoring him now. *Damn it. I tried . . .*

How many times had he hoped she'd reached out to him? But *fuck*, this was insane. If she was Shane Neil, then why the hell hadn't she said—

A hand smacked him across the side of his head. Shooting Lorna a dark look, he hung up the phone. "Watch it," he warned her. He just wasn't in the mood for any of this bullshit now.

"Stop drifting off into la-la land." Hands fisted on her hips, she glared at him. "Exactly *why* won't she bring the book back?"

"Because she's pissed off at me," he growled, shoving out from behind the desk. He started to pace.

"That doesn't sound like Shay."

No. It didn't. He'd seen her sad. He'd seen those solemn smiles on her face and after a few months, he'd slowly worked around to where he'd brought her to a slow, surprised arousal. But she rarely got angry.

Damn it, none of this made sense. It was as if he were trying to jam a giant, uneven square peg into a neat little round hole.

Why would Shay lie about this?

That was the first thing that didn't make sense.

There was just no *reason* for her to lie. If she really was Shane Neil, though, why hadn't she said anything about it *way* before now? Why drop this bomb on him now?

Because until now, there was no reason for her to.

*Except for the fact that we were seeing each other . . .
and it would have been kind of cool to know . . .*

Stopping in midpace, he turned around and eyed
Lorna, debating about sharing that little kicker with
her.

*You know your friend? That one I was so fucking
crazy about? The one that I thought was* the *one . . .
well, she's claiming to be a writer—one of my favor-
ites, no less.*

Yeah, that all sounded like bullshit.

Especially the bit about how he'd *thought* she was the
one.

She *was* the one for him. It just didn't seem as though
he was the one for her.

And none of this was solving the current problem,
that ugly, weighty one that was getting heavier all the
time.

The phone rang and he jumped on it, hoping it was
Shay.

"Hey there, man."

Recognizing Mike's voice, he sighed. Mike, Lorna's
boyfriend, was not the person he wanted to talk to.
"Hey, Mike. Hold on a minute. Lorna's right here."

"No. I'm calling to talk to you. I . . . ah. Well, I had a
call from Deloris Golden about something she saw online. She just thought . . ." Mike paused, and Elliot
could hear him blowing out a breath on the line. "Shit.
I'm just going to lay this out. She wants me to know
there's a sexual deviant living in our midst."

Curling one hand into a fist, Elliot closed his eyes as
the world started to go red.

"I asked her what in the world had gotten into her
and she told me. Elliot, have you ever met some writer
by the name of Shane Neil?"

Elliot closed his eyes. "Yes. Yes, I have."

They finished up the conversation in short, terse

terms, and then he hung up before looking at the computer. He was tempted to smash the damn thing to smithereens.

Instead, he moved back over to the chair and sat, staring at the Facebook page that had exploded and turned into an ugly, fire-breathing monster on him.

"I still think you need to call a lawyer. What she's doing is slander," Lorna said.

I barely got away. Elliot Winter tried to rape me. Ladies, please be careful around him . . . I think he's done this before . . .

"Shit." Every time he thought about what that bitch had written, he wanted to punch something. He couldn't believe he was going to have to live through this . . . *again*. But Mike's call had just proven to be one hell of a wake-up call.

"Elliot, are you *listening* to me? We need to call a damn lawyer. See if we can sue her for slander or something. This is *bullshit*. You've never hurt a woman in your life."

No. No, he hadn't. Reaching up, he rubbed at the back of his neck. "Actually, I think it would be libel," he said absently, still staring at the computer and that godforsaken Facebook page. "Remember your Spider-Man . . . slander is spoken."

"This isn't funny!" Lorna shouted. "That crazy bitch is saying you tried to rape her! Right here, in our store. She's calling you some kind of fucking *monster* and you're sitting there joking about it. This is serious, and you're copping off about the difference between slander and libel. Grow *up*."

Lowering his hand, he spun around in the chair and faced his sister. "Lorna . . . I know how serious this is," he said quietly. "Trust me. Nobody knows this any better than I do. Remember why I left the fucking army, for crying out loud?"

"Shit." Lorna's face crumpled and she sighed, turning away.

"Eight years," he murmured, staring off into nothing. He'd given them eight fucking years and had been prepared to give them even more. Then some crazy bitch had come along and decided to screw it up for him.

And now somebody else was doing it.

I fought him, but I just couldn't get away . . . he's so strong . . . That was something *Tracy* had said. Reading it again, *now*, here . . . in his home? It was like a sucker punch, right to the gut.

Blood roared in Elliot's ears as he stared at the computer, reading the screen for the hundredth time while memories of that time played back in his head.

I barely got away . . . he's so strong. Those words, there in black and white on the screen, seemed to mock him, a twisted version of the event that had sent his life shooting down a completely different road.

"It's happening again," Lorna muttered.

"No." Elliot slanted a look at her over his shoulder, shaking his head. "It's not. This isn't the same." He wasn't just going to ride it out, just take it in the hope that it would get better. He wasn't going to assume that the people who mattered would believe in him.

Shane Neil was screwing with his life—with his sister's too, because what affected him affected her. She ran this bookstore with him; there were women's groups in here all the time, a teen reading group, a couple of church groups, and a victim's support group that chose to meet here rather than at people's homes.

If people started believing he was a rapist . . .

Bile churned in his gut.

"I guess I do need to call a lawyer," he said quietly.

"Yes. You do. And then you need to turn that lawyer loose on that Shane chick."

He blew out a breath, but instead of answering that,

he found himself thinking about Shay. What she'd said. How she'd taken the ARC. How she'd bought all of the books.

And he wanted to know more about the woman who'd been in his store.

Yeah, he could call a lawyer . . . but if that woman wasn't really Shane Neil, what good would it do?

None at all.

And going after Shay wasn't going to happen.

Hell. He really did need to know what was going on.

He needed to know, for sure, just who Shane Neil was.

Get the facts; then, after he had them, he'd draw his line in the sand.

Nobody was going to ruin his life again.

* * *

Dear God, don't let him kill me.
  Dear God, don't let him kill Virna.
  Dear God . . . I'm not ready to die . . .

Shay came awake on a gasping sigh, that prayer still echoing through her mind. Tears stung her eyes and she swiped them away. She'd prayed, all right. She probably should have been more specific.

She'd prayed that he wouldn't kill Virna. Virna hadn't died until a few days later, but her heart had given out—she'd died as an *indirect* result of his beating. Shay hadn't even realized he'd beaten the shit out of her foster mother until later.

She'd prayed that he wouldn't kill her—and Jethro hadn't killed Shay, because he'd wanted his stepdaughter to suffer.

And she still didn't completely understand why. Oh, she knew he hated her. She just didn't understand *why* and nobody else could explain it to her, either. Virna, perhaps, had the answers, but she'd chosen to take them to her grave.

The only answers Shay had were from what she'd learned during the course of the trial. All she remembered were those fragmented dreams from her childhood. She didn't even remember her own name. Virna had given her a new name, a new home . . . things she'd lost when Jethro Abernathy had found her.

All she had from those early years were those vague bits of memory.

Screams. Angry shouts. Ugly whispers. Soft words. A baby crying.

And a closet.

She hated closets.

Jethro had been locked away after he was found guilty of abusing her, neglecting her—apparently, he'd spent those years developing a serious animosity toward her. When he'd gotten out, he'd spent his time tracking her down. Even though Virna had legally changed her name when she adopted her, it hadn't been enough. He'd tracked down Virna . . . and lo and behold . . . there was his stepdaughter.

He'd hunted her for weeks, and neither Shay nor Virna had realized it. He'd hunted *both* of them, learned their habits, where they went, who they saw. And then he struck. After he'd beaten Virna senseless, he'd gone for Shay, kidnapping her and holding her captive for more than forty-eight hours.

A fist gripped her throat and she swallowed the spit pooling in her mouth, fighting the urge to puke. He hadn't won—

You thought I wouldn't find you, you little cunt . . . ?

"You didn't win, you son of a bitch," she whispered in the quiet, predawn stillness of the room.

Rising from the bed, she grabbed her robe and pulled it on. She'd gotten away from him. He'd gotten shit-faced drunk and passed out and once he did that, she'd managed to loosen the ropes, then she'd stumbled out of the building where he'd held her prisoner. The neighborhood was a slum, but even in a slum if somebody saw a bloodied, bruised girl, most would offer to help. And Shay had found one decent person . . .

Jethro had lost . . . and when the case went to trial, Shay had faced him. She'd been too young the last time but this time, she'd faced him down and she'd been the one to help send his ass back to jail.

Her diary beckoned. After a quick stop in the bathroom, she headed for her computer and logged on, not even hitting the coffeepot first.

* * *

MyDiary.net/slayingmydragons

It was bad tonight. I dreamed about the time when he kidnapped me. When he killed Virna. I dreamed about how he cut me, how he laughed. All of it. I heard him screaming at me—

Then he told me how it was my fault. I feel like I can hear the baby screaming, even now.

I wish I knew more about the baby.

Who was he?

And why did that bastard hate me so much? What was supposed to be my fault?

It was a draining, exhausting hour, those minutes she spent in front of her online diary. But when she finally hit *post,* the weight on her shoulders lessened a little.

Lessened enough that she could move, that she could breathe. That she might even be able to handle coffee.

Shuffling into the bathroom, she hit the light and stared at her reflection. Out of habit, she angled her face to the side, staring at the first collection of scars he'd given her. He'd been disappointed. Shay had forgotten about the stepfather she'd lived with for the first four years of her life, even if she hadn't forgotten the nightmares.

Virna had given her a happy home, a place where she felt safe, felt loved. And she forgot the horror that had been her life before Virna came along. Jethro had sought to undo all of that, and more. He wanted to give her brutal, visible reminders so that she'd never forget. Not again.

Blowing out a sigh, she shrugged out of the robe and hung it up, then reached for the hem of her shirt. She turned away before she saw the next set of scars. She didn't need to see them—they were emblazoned forever on her mind.

The third set of scars wasn't quite so easy to see, but like the other scars, they were embedded in her memory. No mirrors were necessary. Although she'd do just about anything to forget.

Shay wasn't even halfway through her shower when the phone started ringing. What time was it . . . eight o'clock? Eight-thirty?

It was probably Darcy. Not too many others would call her this early on Sunday . . .

Unless it was Anna?

That decided it. She rushed through the rest of the shower, wrapped her short black hair in a towel, and grabbed her robe instead of getting dressed. As a result, she was freezing as she went to check the phone. That was okay. She could be cold, as long as she got to talk to her agent.

Except Anna's number didn't come up on the caller ID. Just Darcy's.

Depressed, she skimmed through the numbers, but Anna's number didn't pop up once, not *once* in more than three months of calls. Hell, had it really been that long since they'd talked? Granted, they didn't talk on the phone much and sometimes, Anna called her on her cell . . .

"This is kind of depressing." Twenty calls. In three months. Back before Elliot had broken up with her, at least *he* had called her at home from time to time, but since then?

Almost every single call was from Darcy. A few were from Lorna.

"I need to get a life," she whispered, scrolling through the numbers. Darcy, Darcy . . . a couple of charities looking for donations. Darcy. Lorna. But not a single call from Anna. None from Elliot, either—not until she'd swiped the ARC yesterday.

Of course, he had no reason to call. Why would he call? Unless he'd suddenly changed his mind . . . *Hey, I've decided I'm okay with you holding me at arm's length. And yeah, maybe I can buy that crazy story. You want to start going out again? Maybe we can spend another year going out every week while you work up the courage to let me do more than kiss you . . .*

She made a face. That wasn't fair. Elliot had never been less than patient with her. It wasn't his fault that the lightest touch from *anybody* was sometimes enough to send her into a panic attack.

Yeah, no reason for him to be calling. And another day had passed without a call from Anna.

What in the hell was going on?

Shit, this is ridiculous. She *knew* her agent. Anna was always checking for important stuff, and this was important. So why wasn't she getting back to her?

Somehow, she had to get at least one thing accomplished today. She had to stop thinking about the hopeless situation with Elliot. She had to get through to Anna or get hold of somebody at the websites—something,

anything. Or she was just going to lose her ever-loving
mind . . . and that wasn't a very big leap for her.

With lunchtime came progress . . . *some* progress.

An email hit Shay's inbox and to her somewhat vicious delight, it was from WordPress. They were very
sorry for this trouble and they had shut the blog down.

She immediately went to the blog, and lo and behold . . .

She got a little message saying the blog didn't exist.
There was also a little note at the bottom about possible
terms-of-service violations. A smile curled her lips as
she leaned back. Crossing her arms over her chest, she
muttered, "Stick *that* in your pipe and suck it, bitch."

Of course, that warm, fuzzy glow of satisfaction
lasted only a few minutes. It took only one look at the
Facebook page she had just opened for that glow to
fade, fizzle, then die an abrupt death.

There was a note—an ugly one. And somebody was
tagged in it. Somebody Shay knew all too well.

What the hell . . .

Her gut clenched on her. Her heart raced and blood
roared in her ears. Her palms were sweaty and she
couldn't fucking breathe.

It had been years since she'd had a full-blown panic
attack, but she hadn't ever forgotten what one felt like.
Can't breathe—

The panic was like a beast, trying to rip her apart inside.

Can't breathe—

Endless moments passed. The weight of the terror
rode her down, blackening out everything around.

Can't breathe . . .

But a name, a face . . . they beckoned to her. She'd just
seen him on the screen—*Elliot. Gotta focus. Think.*

I can breathe . . . and I can do this.

"I can breathe," she whispered, her voice a thready whisper. She sucked in a desperate gulp of air just to prove it. "You can breathe. This is just in your head. You *can* breathe."

Squeezing her eyes shut, she waited for the spiraling sensation in her mind to ease a little. She needed to be able to think, and she couldn't. She needed to focus, and she couldn't. For now, she had to be content with being able to breathe. The rest of it would come. Eventually, the panic eased back. After another minute, the vicious grip of terror that had wrapped around her throat had lessened and she made herself open her eyes, look back toward the monitor.

What she *wanted* to do was shut the damn thing down.

Run away.

Hide. Because she knew just *seeing* that note was going to trigger her panic again. It had been years since her rape . . . *years*. She should be stronger than this, better than this. At least that was what she *thought*, but she wasn't. Just hearing about things like this, seeing them on TV . . . online. That was all it took to trigger her. And she couldn't walk away from this. Couldn't run or hide no matter how hard she tried. She had to face it.

She had to face that awful, ugly Facebook note and read how the so-called *Shane Neil* had tagged Elliot Winter.

It was titled . . . *This man tried to rape me*.

The second attack hit almost as hard, almost as fast. And once more, she had to bring herself through it. Sweat soaked through her shirt; her heart was pounding so hard she thought it just might explode through her rib cage and through the wall of her chest to land on the desk in front of her.

But it passed.

It happened a third time, but that time, she'd actually managed to read the first few lines of the note.

By the fourth time, she was over it.

Over it, because she accidentally hit the mouse when she bent over the desk and when she did, it minimized the browser window. She found herself staring at a picture . . . of her and Elliot. They didn't have too many of them. Lorna had taken this one. It had been taken out at Earthquake Park last summer, not long before they'd broken up. Right before Shay had realized things were about to go straight to hell. Back when she'd still been enjoying one of those *happy* periods of her life.

Since then, everything had kind of sucked.

Absently, she lifted a hand to the image of Elliot's face.

He'd been smiling down at her, his fingers brushing over the curve of her cheek.

And there was a look in his eye. One that made her heart ache even now.

Shay kept her wallpaper set to rotate and she hadn't seen this picture in a while. That it would come up now, in just this moment . . .

Closing her eyes, she lowered her head. The raw, battered lump of her heart bumped against her ribs as she took a deep, calming breath. Then she squared her shoulders and lifted her head, reaching for the mouse.

When she looked back at the note on that fucking Facebook page, she did it without flinching. Yes, this imposter was talking about being raped . . . but it was a total sham.

Because Elliot wouldn't have raped anybody.

As many of you have guessed, I am, in fact, a woman. I have an urgent message that I need to share with my sisters . . . and if you are a woman, you are my sister.

This man, Elliot Winter, is a monster. He tried to rape me—

"You bitch," Shay whispered. "You evil, awful bitch."

Reading that note infuriated her. For so many reasons. This was *Elliot*, and it would do awful things to him, but it went so much deeper than that. She'd lived through rape, had suffered through the humiliation, the degradation, the pain . . . even now the nightmares haunted her. And this bitch was lying about it . . . *why?* When women did this, it made it that much harder for the real victims to be heard.

This time, she made it through the entire note dry-eyed and stone-faced, and when she finished, she reached for the phone. She needed to talk to him.

But when the phone at the store was answered, it was Becca on the other end of the line.

And Becca's voice was tight and cold.

"I'll let him know you called."

Then the call was disconnected, without another word. Shay didn't wait another second before punching in Elliot's home number. When that rolled to voice mail, she left a message, and then she dialed his cell. She left another message.

"I need to talk to you. Immediately. Call me. Elliot . . . it's urgent."

After that, she dialed his sister. But Lorna wasn't answering either.

CHAPTER
SIX

"WELL, FOR CERTAIN, I CAN TELL YOU THAT THIS IS A mess."

Elliot leaned back in the padded booth and waited for his lawyer to finish talking. They'd met at a restaurant in Anchorage; it was the only way they'd get any privacy while they talked, without everybody in town knowing they'd arranged to meet up.

Elliot had no doubt that Johnson S. Jones, Jr., out of Louisiana, would have quite a lot to say. He was a transplanted Southern gentleman who'd moved to Alaska with his wife some three decades earlier . . . and he *always* had something more to say.

"And you do know, for a fact, that the woman who wrote this on Facebook is not the author?"

"No. I don't know that for a fact. But there's a possibility it isn't her." He hedged about those details, shrugging and shifting his gaze to stare outside. He hadn't said anything to Lorna about his discussion with Shay the previous day, although he *had* made it clear they were dealing with somebody off their rocker. Of course, which one was the lunatic . . . the woman who'd come to his store? Shay? Elliot, for wanting to *believe* Shay? And he did, he realized.

The more he thought about it, the more he did believe

her. Or the more he wanted to. Was that the same thing as believing? Hell. He didn't know. Right then, he didn't feel like he knew *anything.*

"What makes you think that?" Johnson asked, his eyes shrewd, watchful.

Insightful old goat, Elliot thought sourly.

"Just a feeling," he muttered. "Look, I don't *know* much of anything about this woman. What I do know, for a fact, is that I haven't raped anybody. Ever. So what does it matter if she's the author or not?"

"Damn it, Elliot, the woman has a frigging Facebook page up. What other proof do you *need*?" Lorna stared at him.

He shrugged again. Too many things weren't adding up lately and until he had more concrete evidence, he wasn't going to buy into any particular story.

Lorna grumbled while Johnson stared at him with practiced eyes.

"Look, Mr. Jones, my brother has some crazy woman posting to thousands of people that he's a rapist. We're getting calls at the store about it, for God's sake. What in the hell can we do?" Lorna, her gaze full of fire, leaned forward and glared at the attorney.

"For now, the best thing you can do, Miss Winter, is let me talk to your brother so I can get the facts straight." He smiled as he said it, but the look in his eyes was clear. "I can't help if I don't have all the information I need."

Elliot's phone started ringing. He frowned, recognizing the ring tone. *Spooky.*

Love is kind of crazy with a spooky little girl like you . . . Immediately those lyrics went through his head, even though he'd already silenced the phone. Shay. It was the ring tone he'd programmed for Shay.

From the corner of his eye, he could see Lorna watching him. He ignored her. Staring at Johnson, he said,

"I've given you about as much information about this woman as I can—I don't know anything about her but what she told me. She claims she's Shane Neil, but I don't know if she is."

"Why wouldn't she be?" Lorna asked, her voice overriding the lawyer's.

"Lorna . . . please." Elliot gave her a narrow look.

She groaned and slumped against the seat.

Shifting his attention to the lawyer, he waited.

"Hmmm." Johnson tapped his pen against his lip. "Maybe you start by telling me why you think maybe she isn't . . . ?"

Lorna's phone started to ring.

Pretending to be distracted by that, he glanced over, trying to decide if he should just lay this out on the table here and now or wait until he had some time alone with Johnson. It wasn't that he didn't want Lorna to know what was going on with Shay . . . especially if Shay wasn't being honest. But if she was . . . if she was Shane Neil, he had to assume she had reasons for keeping that to herself all this time.

Especially considering that she knew how big a fan he was of her books.

As that line of thinking unfolded in his mind, he closed his eyes and muttered, "Shit."

He realized something. He didn't know if it made him the world's biggest idiot or not, but he believed her. If she was shooting straight with him, he had messed up in the worst fucking way imaginable. *I'm trying . . .*

Elliot, you fucking fool.

Lorna frowned. "That was Shay."

He blinked, his attention caught by the very mention of her name. "What? Where is she?"

"On the phone, weirdo. Damn, this shit really has your head screwed up, doesn't it?" Lorna held up her phone, showing the missed call and Shay's phone number on the display. "She tried to call me when you didn't answer—unless you have that ring tone for somebody else besides her. I wonder if something's wrong . . . should I call her? I know you're pissed off at her."

He started to say no. After all, he planned on heading up to talk to her. But then he glimpsed Johnson's very intent gaze out of the corner of his eye and he changed his mind. Screw it. "Yeah, maybe you should. Why don't you go to the ladies' room or something, though? I need a few minutes to talk things out with Johnson and I'm distracted as hell. I need to focus and I can't do it if I'm thinking about Shay."

Good cover-up . . . he thought.

But not good enough. He saw that measuring gaze in his sister's eyes and knew he hadn't covered up the truth well enough.

Too bad. He couldn't talk this out with his sister until he knew for sure what was going on. If Shay was being straight up with him, then she'd kept that secret for a long time for a good reason and it wasn't his to share. If she was jerking him around, he'd find that out soon enough and he'd let Lorna know because all this shit was going to affect her, too. But somehow, he suspected that talk wasn't one he'd be having with her anytime soon. He suspected he wouldn't be having it at all.

He slid out of the booth to let Lorna leave and watched her disappear into the depths of the restaurant before he turned and met his lawyer's eyes.

"So."

Johnson linked his hands loosely in front of him and smiled. "So."

When the phone rang, the last person Shay expected it to be was Lorna, despite the fact that she'd requested her friend call back ASAP. Well, maybe the last person she expected to hear from was Elliot. Or Anna. The way things were going, she never expected to actually be able to talk to the people she needed to reach.

Scrambling for her cell phone, she managed to answer before the first ring even finished. "Hello!"

"Ah, hi. Everything okay?"

Hearing that overly anxious snap in her own voice, she cleared her throat. "Um, sorry about that, Lorna. I . . . Hell. Crazy few days."

"Tell me about it," Lorna muttered.

Taut moments stretched out between them until Shay shattered the silence like glass when she finally spoke. "I saw something really fucked up about Elliot online."

"If you tell me that you actually believe that crazy-ass bitch, I'm going to drive up to your place and punch your lights out. I don't care how many fucking black belts you own and I don't care that you just got out of the hospital."

The venom in Lorna's voice made Shay smile. "Oh, trust me, lady. I don't believe a word of it. Besides, I only have the one black belt and it's possible that if I ever had to use it, I'd panic and forget everything I learned."

"Good. Well, not that you'd panic, but good that you don't believe her." A heavy sigh gusted out of Lorna. "So . . . since when were you on Facebook? Or has it stretched out past that site now, too?"

"Nah. I saw it on Facebook." She swallowed, wondering if Elliot had told his sister anything about what she had told him. She danced around the edge of it carefully, uncertain how to proceed. "Has Elliot mentioned anything about this author to you?"

"No." Lorna snorted, and the derision she felt came through loud and clear. "We don't even know her. She came in the store one time. And we were both there. Exactly how was he supposed to try and rape her when I was there in the fucking store? What was I supposed to do, just sit around and watch while he did it? Is it a spectator sport or something?"

Both relief and nerves bloomed inside Shay's mind and she managed to battle back the panic that tried to creep in. It helped that she was staring at his picture on her monitor the entire time. Whoever would have thought that the trick to guiding her through panic attacks was seeing his picture?

"You were there," Shay said quietly.

"Yep. The entire time."

Lorna had been there. Elliot had a witness. He had proof he hadn't done anything.

Shay's mind ran wild at the thought that Lorna had also seen this woman. Lorna had information, too. Should she ask? It wasn't as if Elliot was talking to her. Would Lorna? Moving to the window, she stared out at the watery, wintry sunlight streaming through the clouds. Resting her head on the pane of glass, she closed her eyes.

No. First, she needed to talk this over with Elliot. Elliot was now personally invested in this . . . and she was still personally invested in him, whether he wanted to be with her or not. She had to fix things, because this crazy woman, whoever she was, was fucking things up for Elliot in the worst way.

Swallowing the knot in her throat, she asked quietly, "Is Elliot with you? I kind of need to talk to him."

"He's around. But he's got his hands full right now. He's . . ." Lorna's voice trailed off. Over the line, Shay heard the gurgle of conversation ebbing and flowing. Once it quieted, Lorna spoke again. "He's talking to our lawyer, Shay. Now, he's just our family lawyer and he can't do much to help with this other than advise us which way to go next, but what that woman is doing is slander. I mean, she could fucking *ruin* us."

"Libel," Shay said faintly, horror blooming inside her

as she realized what Lorna was getting at. She hadn't understood just how bad this could get for Elliot. *Oh, hell.*

She had to fix this.

"It's libel," she said again. "She's not speaking it— she's putting it down in print, and it's on the fucking Internet, so it's *forever* unless it gets retracted."

Or proven wrong . . . Shit, why didn't I think of that?

Turning back to stare at her computer, she said quietly, "I have to go, Lorna. Tell Elliot I need to speak with him as soon as he has time. It's important, but I know he has a mess going on, so when he's got a few minutes."

Without waiting another second, Shay disconnected and moved back to the computer.

Once more, she pulled up the complaint page for Facebook. She had to shut this bitch down.

She started another complaint about the fake page, and she also included the fact that the impersonator was now making false allegations against an innocent man and provided links to the statements.

Of course, they were very likely to claim it was just her word against the impersonator's. As a cynical smirk curled her lips, she muttered, "I ought to just put a fucking statement on my website . . ."

Then, as that idea hit her full in the gut, she whispered, "My website."

Shay swore. She was a fucking *idiot*.

Why hadn't she thought of this before?

Her website had a *news* section. It was basically a blog.

Shay didn't use it as one, but that's what it was.

Her hands were sweating as she stared at the computer and told herself she needed to do this.

"Are you there?"

She nodded, forgetting that Angie couldn't see her. Of

her three sisters, Angie was her favorite and the one closest to her in age. She was the only one who knew *who* Shay was now, where Shay was now, and what Shay did. She'd been close to all of her sisters before . . . well. Before. But now it was just Angie. Angie was also the only one who knew about Shane.

After the attack, Shay had been determined to cut all ties and while the others hadn't completely understood, they'd respected her decision. Shay had been terrified Jethro would come after her again someday and she didn't want to endanger any of her adopted siblings, even though they had all been out of the house by that time, and most of them were married.

While she'd been able to cut ties with most of them, though, she'd missed Angie too much. One year after she'd run away from Arizona, she'd hunted Angie down.

And they'd kept in touch, through phone calls and then through email; their contact was infrequent, but it was enough.

Angie lived in North Carolina, and she was the one person who knew all of Shay's deepest, darkest secrets.

Angie handled everything that had to do with Shay's website, including the graphics and updates. And she'd hold her hand through this. Nobody but Angie could possibly understand how hard this was.

"This bitch is fucking whacked," Angie said, her voice flat and angry.

"You must be checking out my so-called Facebook page," Shay muttered, still staring at the computer. She was kind of hoping it would just disappear. Or that she could will the website into doing what she wanted without actually having to *do* anything. It wasn't working so far.

"Yep. I went and checked out the page of the bookstore guy, too. He's hot."

Yes. Hot . . . that described Elliot to a *T*. Shay took a

brief mental break to ponder that. Some of the tension tightening her shoulders faded and she was able to take a deep breath. *Hold it . . . relax. Again . . .* As some of the panic receded, she laid her hands on the keyboard and asked quietly, "This isn't a totally stupid thing to do, right?"

"Right." Angie's voice was solid and steady, just like the woman herself. "Sweetie, it's the only *smart* thing to do. That bitch is pretending to be you, and you have to stop it. But first you have to have proof she *isn't* you. This is proof. So do it. And give that hottie up there in Earth's End a break. Maybe he'll decide to come cuddle with you in your igloo as a way of saying thank you."

Shay snorted. "I've lived here for years and I've yet to see an igloo."

"That's a shame. I think an igloo would be really cool—literally and figuratively. Hey, I know . . . he could help you build one and then cuddle with you."

"You're rotten." Shay suspected Angie was trying to distract her. Swallowing, she flexed her hands, then reached up and adjusted the headset she wore so she could talk to Angie and still type. She could do this— she *had* to do this.

The looming, bright white of the screen seemed to glare at her, mocking her.

"Oh, shit. Angie, I don't know if I can do this." Shay closed her eyes, blocking out the image of that terrifying white screen. A few years ago, she'd written a short story about an agoraphobic who'd had to leave her house to escape a killer. This was kind of like that for her. She wasn't terrified of the outside world, but she was terrified of exposing herself. And even this little bit was too much.

But what else could she do? *Nothing?* She'd done that, and look what had happened.

"Are you there, kid?"

Kid. It made her smile, despite the fear fluttering inside her. Angie was seven years older than she. In some ways, Shay felt years older . . . and at the same time decades younger than her big sister.

"Yeah." She made herself open her eyes and face that white screen.

"You have to do this. You know what she's doing is wrong—it's so fucked up, it's not even funny, and you can start to set things to right. If you don't do it . . ." Angie didn't finish the sentence, but she didn't have to.

Virna had drilled a certain set of values into her kids, including the one she'd adopted . . . Shay.

If you allowed an evil to continue and you did nothing to stop it, and there was something you *could* have done, you were just as bad as the evil-doers. How many children could have been saved from abusers if the people who knew about the abuse spoke up? How many victims of assault?

Ignoring evil perpetuated it.

And what this woman was trying to do to Elliot was evil . . . it could destroy him. Then there was the matter of the wrongful rape accusation—shit like that made it so much harder for real rape victims.

Shay had the power to step in and make things right.

She might be a terrified coward, but she couldn't let that fear stop her. Elliot had talked about how she always had to be tough, yet she *wasn't*. She was a damn wreck—she just knew how to fake it. So she'd fake it now. Fake it until she made it and she'd get through this.

Clearing her throat, she squared her shoulders. "Okay, Angie. I'm doing it."

"Good girl."

Silence hummed between them, but it wasn't a heavy, awkward silence, wasn't flooded with that awful need to fill it. Shay wrote. On the other end of the line, Angie waited.

Moments later, Shay said, "Okay, so I want to read this through before I post it. How do I do that?" The setup was different from her online diary and the words had to be just right.

"You can save a draft."

Shay fiddled around until she saw the option. *Okay*—

A *preview post* link came up.

Her hands were sweating as she clicked on it.

REGARDING RECENT ISSUES—FACEBOOK, TWITTER, BLOG, ETC.

"Shay?"

She whispered, "Yeah?"

"Are you okay? You're starting to breathe kind of funny again."

"I'm fine." Damn it, this shouldn't be so hard. It wasn't as if she were taking out a public notice: *I'm in hiding in Alaska—come find me*.

"Yes, you're fine," Angie said, her voice soothing. "Nobody knows *who* you are. Remember that. Also, keep in mind, this is the best way to spread the word. Anybody can set up a Facebook page, after all. Not everybody can access your website and make these changes. Do it." Angie's voice was firm but gentle.

"I know, I know . . ."

I've recently been made aware of a number of issues online.

A Twitter account, a Facebook page, and a blog have been set up by somebody claiming to be Shane Neil.

I was attempting to settle this matter quietly, but I haven't had much luck so I need to discuss these matters with my readers.

The Facebook page, the Twitter account, and the blog formerly located at shaneneil.wordpress.com do not belong to me.

The blog has been shut down and I would like to thank wordpress.com for being so prompt in their response. I'm hoping other sites will also soon take action.

There are also a number of other social media accounts that appear to be connected to my name, but I did not set these up or authorize them.

I wasn't made aware of these issues until just a few days ago.

My publishers have been made aware of the matter and please know that we are looking into it and trying to resolve this issue.

Additionally, and more troubling, the woman who has set up the Facebook page is making allegations against a bookstore owner in Earth's End, Alaska. She is claiming that this man, Elliot Winter, attempted to rape her.

While I cannot speak about what happened when she went to his store, as I wasn't there, I can say that this woman is not me. As she has lied about who *she* is, I would question the truth of anything she says.

I would like to apologize to everybody who has been deceived by this person and I'd like to extend a special apology to Elliot Winter, the owner of WINTER'S END BOOKSTORE, for the trouble she has caused him.

Again, please accept my apologies and know that I'm trying to resolve this matter.

Sincerely,

Shane

She saved it. Chewing on her lip, she asked Angie, "Can you go in and read it?"

"Yeah, sweetie, I can."

A few seconds of silence stretched out between them, and then finally Angie came back and said, "Sounds good to me. You did just fine. Now . . . *publish the damn thing.*"

A smile cracked her lips. "Okay."

She hit *publish*, and that's when the shaking *really* started. "Oh, shit. I . . . um, I think I need a drink."

"So get one."

Her knees shook as she stood up to do just that. It didn't matter that it wasn't even noon yet. What did the song say again . . . *it's five o'clock somewhere* . . . that meant it was okay for the rum and Coke, right?

Over the line, she heard a few taps and clicks. "What are you doing?"

"A few widgets and things I need to update on the site. I'm also going to make sure I've got things as secure as I can get them. No site is one hundred percent hacker-proof, but we'll do what we can."

Shoving a hand through her hair, Shay said, "Hell, you think a hacker is doing this?"

"I don't know. But we're going to do every damn thing we can to make it secure. Have you changed your email passwords and everything?"

"No. Hell." Squeezing her eyes shut, she tried to think past the headache that was threatening to eat her alive. "I guess I need to get that done, huh?"

There was a pause, and then Angie muttered, "Help me. Please. Just give me patience." Then she sighed. "Yes, sweetie, you need to get that done. Immediately. Look . . . somebody is pretending to be *you*. She had one of your books. She had your fucking bookmarks. What else does she have access to? Maybe nothing . . . but just in case . . ."

Something uneasy settled in Shay's gut. "Yeah. Damn it. You're right. I'm a moron."

"No. No," Angie snapped, her voice hard. "You're not a moron. You were in the hospital less than a week ago. Then you come home to this mess and you're doing the best you can to deal with it. Just start changing the passwords and shit, okay?"

After Angie hung up, Shay fixed her drink and then returned to her office, settling behind her desk. She stared at her website. The front page had an area that highlighted any updates to the *News* page and now there was a notice about the shit happening in her little place in the world, how somebody was trying to steal it from her.

For a long, quiet moment she stared at it, even though she knew she needed to change her passwords.

First, she finished up that complaint to Facebook, including a link to the updated news on her website. "There. That ought to be proof enough for them," she muttered.

She sent another complaint to Twitter—that was another experiment in fun. But this time she had proof, hard proof, right there on her website, and nobody could change it.

Now . . . about those damn passwords . . .

Her phone started ringing. Sighing, she reached for it. "Hey, you!"

"Hi, Darcy," she said. She reached for a piece of paper and a pen, scratching out a note about the passwords. She'd never remember if she didn't write it down, not now that Darcy had her on the phone.

"So how are things going?"

Shay scowled and lowered the phone. Darcy's overly cheerful voice just seemed . . . wrong. How in the world could she be *that* happy right now?

Okay, so maybe it wasn't *Darcy's* world that was coming crashing down around her, but still. "Well, frankly, things suck," Shay said, staring at the computer, clicking back to her website and rereading the note that had made her all but sweat blood just to post it.

"Aw, hon, I'm sorry . . . the recovery going rough? You know, I could come up and stay with you for a while."

Shay frowned. "Recovery?" Shaking her head, she said, "No, Darcy, it's not the recovery. I'm moving around slower than normal, but that's not the problem. The problem is that damn Facebook page, that damned imposter, and the fucking *lies* she's telling."

Silence crackled between, heavy as the stillness before a summer thunderstorm.

Darcy broke it with a forced laugh. "Oh . . . that. I'd forgotten about it. I mean, since it wasn't your page and all . . ."

"Yes. That." A nerve ticked in Shay's forehead and she reached up, pushing on it. "*I* haven't forgotten about it. It's getting worse, Darcy. Hell, it's getting *much* worse."

"Oh, honey." Darcy made a soothing noise, humming under her breath a little.

Shay felt some of her tension ease up and she sighed, rolling her shoulders, trying to brush off the anger rising inside her. Maybe what she needed to do was just talk this out. She hadn't really talked with Angie all that long. They'd been focused on the note, but if she talked about it, she'd feel better. Darcy would listen. She could offer some advice and Shay could decide if she liked it not, but somebody would *listen*, and she'd feel better.

Right?

"Internet scandals always get hot, but they fade away pretty fast," Darcy said softly. "How bad do you think it can get?"

"She's trying to take my life over. She's telling lies about a man I care about." She stared at the computer, at the note. She remembered what Angie had said . . . *what else do they have access to?*

Shit, that was a scary thought.

"I'm afraid it could get pretty bad." Spinning around in her chair, she stared toward her books. There was one on the shelf that had been a favorite of hers for years—it was out of print, but she'd always loved it. She found herself staring at it now, though, and a chill raced down her spine. *She's trying to take my life over . . .* Rising from the chair, she moved toward her shelves and pulled it down, staring at the bright red cover. It was worn, faded, and well-read. Dog-eared, the spine cracked. She'd lost count of how many times she'd read that book.

"I've got this book," she murmured. "It was written back in the nineties. The hero was a writer . . . and some guy tries to take over his life. All of his contracts, all the proof that he was who he says he was, it all burned up in a fire. And nobody believes him. Except the heroine. She doesn't believe him at first—he actually kidnapped her. But she comes to believe him. But nobody believed he was who he said he was. Not even his agent."

Shay swallowed, thinking about how Anna hadn't returned her call. Fear threatened to swallow her but she shoved it back. She'd lived through a screaming hell the likes that others couldn't imagine. This wasn't going to defeat her. And she was just being paranoid now. She'd get hold of Anna tomorrow and everything would be fine.

"Wow. That's freaky. I want to read it. Can you send me the book?"

Shay put it back on the shelf. "Maybe later." Turning away from the books, she moved to the window. Lately, she found herself at this spot more and more, as though she'd find the answers written in the pristine white of the snow.

Darkness had fallen and the moon was high, falling across the icy expanse in silvery swaths.

"You sound so depressed," Darcy said, her voice soft. "Maybe you should stop worrying about all of this for a while. Do something that makes you feel better."

Scowling, she shook her head. "Hell, I *can't* stop worrying about this."

"You need to." Darcy's voice took on a no-nonsense quality and she pointed out, "It's not like worrying non-stop is *accomplishing* anything, right? Is worrying about this making you feel any better?"

Caught off guard, she stopped in midstep. *How is it*

making me feel better? "Darcy, what am I supposed to do? Ignore it? She's trying to take away everything I worked for."

"But worrying isn't helping. I mean, what have you accomplished?"

"I got her fucking blog down," Shay snapped. "And I went to the store where the books were and I bought them, brought them back, and burned every last one. And let me tell you . . . *that* made me feel better."

Silence crackled between them, so heavy and thick, the hairs on Shay's arms stood on end. Her gut clenched and crawled and the moment stretched out, endless and tight, before Darcy whispered, "You did *what?*"

Her voice was low and ugly, just a few steps above a growl. Just a few steps above angry.

That awkward, horrible silence lingered and Shay turned away, staring at her bookshelves, concentrating on them. Easier to do that than think about how uneasy she suddenly felt.

"I went down there." Frowning, Shay turned away from the window. The peace she'd been trying to find staring out into the moonlight had shattered. Returning to her desk, she sat down and maximized the browser that had her email. She needed to get to work on those passwords.

"But what good did it do to go and burn a bunch of books? Or even go down there to begin with? I mean, you can't help that somebody is pretending to be you."

"No, I can't *help* it, but for one, I know the guy. We used to date and she's fucking with him now, too. And for another, seeing somebody else's signature on *my* books makes me sick to my stomach." Shay clenched a fist, angry all over again, but this time, it wasn't *just* at her imposter.

Why did it feel like *she* was suddenly in the wrong? She hadn't done a damn thing wrong, had she? She wanted her life to stay *her life*. What was so wrong with that?

"It's just a signature," Darcy pointed out. "The people who buy it don't know if it's hers or yours!"

"*I* know." Pain flared in her hand and she made herself relax her fist. Opening her hand, she realized she'd been squeezing so tight, her nails had bitten into her palm. "Don't you get that? *I* know . . . and it's a lie. Whoever she is, when she signs her name to my books, it's a damn lie. Seeing those books in *his* store, with her signature . . . it's a lie. And what's more, what she's doing to him? That's another fucking lie . . . and it's *wrong*."

"How do you know?"

Shay tensed at the low, flat tone of Darcy's voice.

"I mean, you weren't there, right?" Darcy continued. "That's what your website says. You weren't there, so how do you really *know* what happened? Maybe he *is* a rapist. Do you really think you can trust him? Are you sure you can take such a chance? I mean, seriously, it's not like you've ever been all that good at relationships. Maybe you just trusted the wrong guy."

Curling her hand around the edge of the desk, Shay shook her head, even though nobody was there to see it but her. *Maybe you trusted the wrong guy . . .*

No. Hell, *no*. Her voice was a thready, bare whisper of a sound as she said softly, "Elliot isn't a rapist."

"You don't know that . . . you never really know about people, do you, Shay?" Darcy paused and then asked softly, "Do you even know *me*?"

You never really know . . .

Those words tried to settle in her heart, tried to take root. There was fertile soil there, and the seeds of distrust were already planted deep—it was second nature for her to fear, for her to doubt.

But not Elliot.

"Shit. Enough of this, Darcy. Yes, I do know you. We've been friends for years."

They had been *best* friends. For the longest time, Darcy had been her only connection to the world, aside from Angie. She loved her, trusted her, needed her.

"We've known each other for more than ten years, Darcy," she said quietly. "I know you. And I *know* Elliot. He's not a damned rapist." She let go of the desk and reached for the mouse, clicking to the folder on her computer that held her pictures. She searched for the one of them together at Earthquake Park and once she found it, she made it the desktop background.

Just seeing him grounded her. The aching in her chest eased and she could breathe, could think, could focus. Reaching up, she touched the image of his face. Heavy with five o'clock shadow, laugh lines fanning out from his eyes, a smile on his face as he stared down at her. She didn't have to doubt him. Whether they were together or not, she could trust him.

"You don't know him. I do, Darcy. And I'm not going to listen to this . . . as a matter of fact, you don't seem to understand my problems with this anyway, so I'd rather just not discuss any of it with you, period. I'll talk to you later."

Darcy was in the middle of saying something. But Shay didn't know what, nor did she much care. She'd already disconnected the call.

For another minute, she let herself stare at Elliot's picture.

Then she brought up her email; she wasn't going to hide in the sand over this anymore. Come tomorrow, if Facebook and Twitter hadn't taken any action, she was contacting a damn lawyer.

First . . . the passwords.

Yeah, yeah, she knew it was a bad idea to store passwords in her email account, but she was always forgetting them. Plus, some of them were passwords Darcy needed, too, so it only made sense to keep that information all in one place. It wasn't the smartest solution, she knew, but she didn't keep any financial information stored and that was what would cause the biggest problem, she knew.

Out of habit, she did a quick skim through the inbox, looking to make sure neither Anna nor the evil overlords of Twitter or Facebook had emailed in the last five minutes since she'd checked—*nada*.

Shit. Why in the hell hadn't she heard from Anna . . . ?

That niggling worm of paranoia, the one that had arisen when she'd thought about that book—another author with a stolen identity—rose to taunt her, and all thoughts of changing passwords slipped from her mind.

Anna had yet to email. Yeah, it had only been two days and it was the weekend. But Anna would realize this was important—unless she was either sick or out of town, she would have *called*. And if she couldn't call, she would have emailed.

Hunching over the keyboard, Shay clicked on the folder that held the correspondence between her and her agent. Except . . . there was nothing there.

Empty—

"Now, that's not right," Shay whispered. And that niggling worm of paranoia grew, shifting into a massive, bloated monster in the blink of an eye. That folder should be fucking *full*.

"Shit." Her gut twisted and an odd, sick sensation slithered through her.

She loved Gmail. It had all those nice little folders where she could keep things organized, and it even had little bolded numbers to indicate emails she hadn't read—useful when she was keeping track of receipts, or just keeping email responses in case she needed to go back and check on things later.

As she was staring at the screen, one of those folders went from having a bolded *5* to nothing. The one below it did the same thing. A bolded *8* to nothing.

Hissing out a breath, she scrolled down and stared at the bottom.

Gmail also had a nifty little feature—it let her see when her account had been accessed last . . . and from what IP. The IP at the bottom wasn't hers. Swearing, she copied it and then clicked on the link that would let her sign out of all other sessions. Somebody had hacked into her email.

"Crap. Angie, I shouldn't have waited," she muttered.

Quickly, she changed her password and then, since she wasn't sure if her backup email was secure or not, she changed that password, too. This time, she didn't let herself get distracted, and she kept at it until she'd changed every single password that she could think of.

Her desk was littered with notes by the time she was done, but she didn't trust those little pieces of paper. Just staring at them made that ugly paranoia monster in her gut roll and thrash around, so she did a search online and found an app that would store the passwords on her iPhone, with the ability to back it up to her desktop. It also randomly generated passwords and she'd have to copy and paste the damn things, because there was no way she could remember *those*.

She secured *that* app with another password and it was one that nobody but she . . . and maybe Elliot . . . would think of.

It took almost an hour, and by the time she was done it was nearly eight o'clock. Nearly eight, and she hadn't eaten since breakfast. Hunger was a gaping hole in her belly and she took a few minutes to make herself a sandwich before returning to her computer.

How much is missing? she wondered.

Logging back in with the new password—one so

complicated she'd *never* remember it—she stared at the folders listed along the left. The bite of sandwich in her mouth turned to sawdust, but she kept chewing. She wasn't going to do herself a damn bit of good if she kept forgetting to eat.

"Years' worth of shit, gone," she muttered. Not everything was lost—that was a relief. That monster of paranoia currently tormenting her wasn't always a bad thing. Important stuff, she'd always copied—paranoia was sometimes a blessing. But still, her idea of important was probably skewed.

She was skimming the emails she'd backed up when a message popped up on her computer.

I'm sorry I made you mad.

Darcy . . .
Shay ignored it. Maybe she just didn't understand friendship that well, but shouldn't Darcy be . . . well . . . supportive? She sure as hell *used* to be supportive.

Another message popped up almost immediately.

I was going to log into your email and take care of things there, but I can't. The password isn't being accepted and I know that's the right one. Was it hacked?

Shay frowned. And that paranoia monster started to growl and lumber about. Once more, her mind started to spin. Started to churn. It couldn't . . . *Nah.* No. It just wasn't possible.

Still . . . nibbling on her lip, she did a quick search on the IP she'd copied from Gmail. Darcy lived in Michigan. When the IP address turned out to be located somewhere in Texas, she felt a little better. A little. But not much. What was going on?

Shay didn't know. But it was too damn weird.

And Darcy kept firing off messages—the more she sent, the worse Shay felt. She read each one. She didn't respond to any.

So we need to decide what to do contest-wise for the next book.

Shay leaned back in her seat, arms folded across her chest, nails tapping out a rapid beat.

You going to send me books again to mail out to the winners?

A brief pause, followed by another message.

Of course you are . . . silly me. You'd never want anybody knowing you live in Alaska, right?

"Riiigggghhhhtt. . . ." Shay snagged the rest of her sandwich and took a bite, washing it down with a drink of Monster.

Okay, I just checked the website's email and I can't get into there, either. This is really weird . . . I'm getting worried. Let me know if it was hacked or not—I'll try the backup email real quick, just to be sure. But if it wasn't hacked . . . never mind.

Shay lifted a brow. *If it wasn't . . . what?*
Seconds ticked by while that paranoia monster shrieked and danced through her skull, having a fine old time as it smashed down the secure walls she thought she'd built around her life.
You never really know anybody . . . That was what Darcy had told her.
"Is it you?" she asked quietly, staring at the screen, at the now silent IM box. "Are you the one, Darcy?"
Although the very idea turned her stomach, it wasn't an idea she could brush off. Not just yet.

But, shit. It couldn't be Darcy. She was one of Shay's *real* friends. Somebody she'd known for years—and they really *knew* each other. They'd gone to college together, for crying out loud. Darcy was somebody Shay loved dearly, somebody she had trusted for years. Her inescapable humor and enthusiasm had pulled Shay through so many dark years.

God, please don't let it be her . . .

CHAPTER
SEVEN

"THIS IS . . . WEIRD."

Glancing over at his sister as he pushed the car into park, Elliot smirked. "You're just figuring that out? And 'weird' isn't what I'd use to describe it. 'Weird' doesn't touch it."

Lorna glanced at him, a frown darkening her face. "That's not what I meant." She turned her phone around. It held a mobile website. "Read this."

He glanced down, and the name at the top of it immediately caught his attention. "What the . . ."

"I think it's a trick."

He took the phone from her and started to read.

Lorna continued to talk. "I mean, the woman is whacked out. And here's just another sign of it. She comes into our store, signs the damn books, she accuses you of rape, and now she's denying any of that ever happened—trying to act like somebody *else* did all of it. Maybe she figured out she could get her ass in major trouble with libel or something—hey, I got it right, by the way. Maybe she realized how much trouble she could get in and she's backtracking. Hell, is she going to come up with a one-armed man scenario next?"

"Lorna . . ." He waited for her to pause. Then he said,

"Be quiet for five seconds, please? And I'm pretty sure there's no one-armed man in the future."

She made a face at him but relaxed against the seat, staring outside as he read the post on Shane Neil's website.

REGARDING RECENT ISSUES—FACEBOOK, TWITTER, BLOG, ETC.
I've recently been made aware of a number of issues online . . .

Eyes narrowed, Elliot read it through a second, then a third time before he gave Lorna her phone back. "When did that show up, do you know?" he asked softly.

"Today." She tapped something on the phone. "It's time-stamped, see? A friend of mine on Facebook saw it and she tagged me about it. I just got it a few minutes ago and I had to read it about five times before I figured out it wasn't a gag thing. But it has to be bullshit."

You kept saying that you just wanted me to open up . . . to trust you. You just said it's okay to need a hand. That's why I'm here, Elliot . . . I need help. I'm trying to trust you. But you—

How long had it been since she'd stood in front of him, saying those very words? A day? Why did it seem like it had been longer? It was the moment he'd hoped for, waited for . . . and when it had come, he hadn't even seen it. He'd been too caught off guard by what she'd been saying. He was a total fuck-up.

Lorna was oblivious. "I mean, it's got to be bullshit. Right?"

"Wrong. It's not," he said grimly, shaking his head. *I need help . . . I'm trying to trust you.* She'd reached out to him. And he'd just stood there, like a fool. *Fuck.* Nodding toward the store, he said, "Head on inside, would you? I gotta go. I've got to do something."

"What do you mean it's not bullshit?" she demanded, twisting around in the seat to glare at him. "That's gotta be the biggest bunch of crap ever. Who in the hell could believe that?"

Cocking his head, he met her eyes. "I do."

Lorna gaped at him. "How? How can you believe this?"

"I just do. Now . . . do you mind? I need to go. I have somewhere to be." *I need to go see if I can fix the mess I made. And it's kind of important, so can you just let me do it?*

"Look, El, I know you have this weird obsession with Shane Neil and this was like a sucker punch, but come on. How in the hell can you believe that just because you saw it posted on the Internet? I wouldn't believe it unless I saw hard proof. With my eyes." She swung her hand, gesturing to the dark, quiet town. "The real Shane Neil would have to be here with a written affidavit or whatever they are, proving to me that the woman who was here a few weeks ago wasn't the real deal."

"I don't know if they give out written affidavits to authors like candy," he murmured, staring out at the store. He had to admit, if it had come from anyone other than Shay, he wouldn't have believed it. Shit, it had taken seeing that note on the website to make him fully *believe* her, and he owed her one major apology for that. He should have believed her. Before anybody, and anything else, he should have believed *her*.

He hadn't, and now on top of everything else, he had to fix this. And *this* was more important than everything else, too. Maybe that wasn't how anybody else would see it, but Shay was . . . shit. Even after all of this, she was too important to him and he had to fix what he had done.

Damn it, this was a mess.

There was more going on than just this crazy bitch who'd come into his store, more than her telling bullshit stories about him, more than her trying to take over bits and pieces of Shay's life. There had to be. His gut was screaming, and he always listened to his gut.

"Are you even listening to me?" Lorna asked quietly.

Slanting a look at her, he sighed. "Not much more than you're listening to me. Lorna . . . I have to go, I told you that. I have to go talk to somebody. It's urgent."

"And this . . . this lunatic isn't important? She's trying to ruin your life."

No. Elliot was starting to realize he was just collateral damage. The fear he'd seen in Shay's eyes, the anger . . . this was personal. He guessed any writer would be pissed if somebody was trying to steal their work from them, but somehow, he knew it went deeper than that for Shay.

And that's what this was.

It was *all* about Shay.

Whoever this woman was, she was trying to get to Shay. That was why she'd come after him. It had nothing to do with him . . . and everything to do with Shay.

Elliot couldn't help but wonder just how far she'd go to get what she wanted.

"Lorna, look, I've got answers to some of your questions, but it's not my place to tell you . . . not yet. I will tell you what I can . . . when I can. But you have to trust me for now. Okay?"

For a long, quiet moment, she watched him. "Son of a bitch," she finally muttered, reaching up to cover her eyes with her hands. "Is *this* why you kept rambling on to Johnson about that Neil chick maybe not being the real deal? Is it?"

"Lorna . . ." He stared at her.

She glared at him. "Damn it, this bitch is screwing with both of us. You get that, right?"

"Yes. And I'm going to do what I can to fix it. But *we* aren't the only ones involved, either. So can I go? I need to talk to somebody."

The fury continued to glint in her eyes. "You're a bastard sometimes, El." She jerked open the door and climbed out. "I hope you know what you're doing."

"I do."

A few minutes later, as his sister disappeared into the store, he muttered. "I hope I know what I'm doing, too." Then he put the car into reverse and pulled away from the store.

He was going to Shay's place. This time, he was going to listen to what she had to say, and nothing was going to interrupt them.

Michigan.

Michigan.

Michigan.

Shay went through letter after letter she'd gotten from Darcy. All were postmarked from Michigan—the address had been the same for two years now. Shay was something of a pack rat; she kept everything. She hit her email next. Not all of the messages had been erased by whoever had gotten into her account—the person had gone through the folders alphabetically. It was just a nasty little bitch that things like AGENT, BIZ, and EDITS happened to come before PROMO and PERSONAL. But that meant she still had plenty of emails from Darcy. Including all the messages where Darcy had sent her phone number changes. For the first few years of their correspondence, Darcy had seemed to change her phone number about as often as Shay had changed her hairstyle . . . and that had been pretty damn often for a while.

The earlier emails had been more tentative—Darcy had been content to just follow Shay's lead. She'd been excited . . . so thrilled for Shay, and so happy to be helping her do this. Reading them made Shay smile a little.

It had been cool, finding a way to keep that connection with the one real friend she'd made in college. To have somebody else she could trust to share that news. Darcy had never let her down and she'd made things so much easier for Shay—she was her go-between, somebody who could handle some of the interaction that was so hard on Shay.

And Shay could *trust* Darcy.

At least, she'd always thought she could.

Darcy helped Shay keep details straight, helped her remember things like contests and deadlines. She handled keeping stuff together for the website updates so Shay didn't miss getting the info to Angie, sent out all the material for the various group promo sites, everything. Shay couldn't even keep track of all the stuff Darcy handled for her now.

But the longer she read, the more Shay wondered if Darcy hadn't been managing her. It wasn't there . . . at first. But later on? Things had just changed.

She couldn't quite pinpoint what it was, but there were little things. Sites that Shay used to use . . . had liked, even. She'd never had any problems with them, but then a few years after Darcy had come on board, things had started going wrong—Darcy would claim *this* had gone wrong, or they weren't getting the promo they'd been promised, or *that* had been changed.

Little things, but still. She'd let Darcy switch things, shift things, because that was what she paid her to handle.

But had she *really* been managing Darcy? Or had it been Darcy managing her?

Sighing, Shay started making notes about everything. She had to go back and check things. Maybe some of this shit was legit, maybe it wasn't, but she couldn't ignore the crawling in her gut.

"Stop it," she muttered the first time that thought circled through her mind. "Just stop."

But when she got to the emails from last January, that warning in her brain really started to scream at her—hard, harsh, and strident—so urgent and piercing, Shay wouldn't have been surprised if the glass in the windows had started to rattle.

It was a conversation between Shay and Anna—contract negotiations that had fallen apart. Shay had wanted to try something new, and things just hadn't happened the way they'd hoped. The project hadn't caught the interest of any publishers and they'd decided to table it for a while.

Darcy wasn't supposed to read the emails from Anna. They weren't part of her job, but she'd read that one. Then . . .

"Shit."

Resting her head in her hands, Shay remembered that phone call.

Who does that high-and-mighty bitch think she is? She says table it and you just do it? She's your fucking agent—you decide what to do, not her.

It doesn't work that way, Darcy, Shay had told her. She'd been tired and depressed, and while it had felt good to have somebody upset on her behalf, Shay had known Darcy really just didn't understand. The publishing business was a lot more complex than people thought, and Shay couldn't just wave a magic wand and make things happen. It didn't work like that.

But Darcy hadn't been convinced.

And for weeks after, Darcy had nagged Shay to fire Anna.

Weeks.

"This is insane," Shay muttered. Darcy couldn't have managed to interfere with her agent, not all that time ago. Not without Shay realizing before now. Shit, that had been almost a *year* ago and Shay knew she'd talked to Anna since then. She knew it.

Just fire that high-and-mighty bitch . . .

Shay closed her eyes and groaned. "Shit. I'm going insane."

Ghostly echoes of Darcy's voice danced through Shay's mind and she shoved back from the desk to pace around her office.

Hell, it didn't even *sound* like Darcy. Not really. Except it was. Shay knew her friend. Knew how she acted, how she talked . . . except, well, Darcy didn't exactly seem to be herself now. Darcy hadn't acted like herself in a long while, but it was way worse now. More than Shay wanted to deal with. Guilt and the little fact that Darcy was one of her few friends . . .

Sighing, she rubbed her temple and muttered, "You can't let that shit get in the way, damn it. *Think*."

Her feet sank into the plush, dark red of the carpet, her footsteps muffled as she padded back and forth. Now that the idea was there, she couldn't stop thinking about it.

Had Darcy somehow managed to get in between her and Anna? *How?*

"Shit," Shay muttered, pressing a fisted hand to her forehead.

It wasn't as if Anna wouldn't check with her, right?

A knock at the door kept her from pursuing that line of thought any further. She needed to think it through, first. And she needed to talk to Anna. Now more than ever. She was desperate. Tomorrow, she'd call the office and she'd damn well not get off the phone until she talked to her.

The knock came again and she muttered, "All right, all right."

She paused at a window on the way to the front door, even though the third knock was even more impatient than the last. The sight of that familiar SUV sitting in her driveway had her breath catching in her throat. Elliot . . .

"What's he doing here?" Nerves and need knotted deep inside her, a twisty little mess that had her even more unsettled.

Swallowing, she smoothed a hand down the front of her shirt, then through her hair, only to stop and swear. *Shit.* She was wearing yoga pants and a T-shirt that was five years old, stretched out of shape and all but colorless from being washed so many times. Her hair was limp, she was paler than death, and she'd lost too much damn weight—between the hospital stay and her lack of appetite, she just wasn't up to eating. Not to mention that she wasn't sleeping. The nightmares were bad and getting worse all the time.

So why was she wasting her time primping when it wasn't going to do a damn thing to make her look presentable? Not without about two hours in the bathroom, with a brush, a blow dryer, and some serious "me" time.

Grimacing, she made herself walk past the hallway bathroom, straight to the door. She opened it right as Elliot was getting ready to knock a fourth time. "Sorry . . . I was in the middle of something," she hedged.

Trying to figure out if a friend is fucking with my life. Having a minor mental meltdown over my personal appearance . . . you know, girl stuff, she thought.

"I need to talk to you," he said quietly.

Shay arched an eyebrow. "Really. And here I was thinking you drove up from Earth's End at eight o'clock just because you had nothing better to do."

A faint grin slanted his mouth. "You really are a smart-ass," he murmured.

"One of my finer qualities," she responded, stepping aside to let him enter. She shut the door behind him, shivering as a wicked burst of cold air came slicing through. Wrapping her arms around herself, she turned to face him.

He was slipping out of his parka and she felt her mouth go dry as she watched his sweater stretch over his shoulders. Man, she loved those shoulders . . . she'd always loved those shoulders. For some reason, looking at him managed to stir the hormones she was able to ignore at any other time.

Why was it she'd managed to go most of her adult life without feeling these pangs of lust and need, but whenever he was around, they were about *all* she felt? It made it even harder to think.

As he turned back around to face her, she forced herself to look away, staring at her feet so he wouldn't see all those things she didn't want him seeing—he'd always seen too much. That had been one of the problems.

He saw the things she hid, saw the secrets nobody else had ever guessed. Saw the pain and the fear she'd always managed to keep hidden behind her mask . . . and he'd always wanted to help take it away. But she couldn't share that pain with him without sharing the source. And Shay wasn't about to do that.

She'd actually tried to share some small piece of herself yesterday and it had been a disaster. If he couldn't accept the simplest, easiest truth in her life, the cleanest truth she had to offer, he'd never be able to accept the uglier, darker secrets that were just as much a part of her.

You're not being fair, a voice inside her whispered. *You dumped something on him and didn't give him much of a chance to think it through. Maybe that's why he's here.*

Maybe it was.

But if it was . . . did that change anything? Did that mean she was really ready to open up to him?

Shit. She wasn't certain she could. And if she did . . .
he might not want her anymore. That part of her was
really fucked up. It was one thing to not care about the
scars he could see; it was another thing to know he'd
have to handle all the scars neither of them could see.
And if he wanted to be with her, he'd have to handle
them. Hell, Shay *had* to live with those scars and she
could barely handle them.

Now you're really getting ahead of things, she thought
morosely. He probably didn't even care about that anymore.

"You got any coffee or anything?" he asked.

"Coffee?" She cocked her head. "What, you don't
just want to demand I give you your book and storm out
of here?"

He sighed. "Hell, Shay. I'm here to talk. Demanding
a book and storming out doesn't sound like *talking,*
does it?"

"Guess not." She edged around him, avoiding any direct contact with him even though that long, lean body
of his managed to take up a hell of a lot of space. She
excelled at avoiding contact—it was one of her skills. For
years, she'd avoided contact with anybody and everybody. It had been second nature. It wasn't until Elliot
had come into her life that she'd actually wanted contact, that she wanted to have somebody else inside her
isolated little bubble.

She just hadn't been able to open up enough to keep
him.

He followed along behind her, and Shay was painfully aware of his gaze resting on the back of her head.
When they went past her office, she grimaced, thinking
of the door she hadn't closed. It had always been shut
when he'd been over before—she'd kept that part of her
life closed from him. She hadn't thought to come back
here and close it before she let him in. But it wasn't as

though she could just tell him to wait here while she went and closed that door down the hallway, right?

Rude, much?

So instead, she just went to the kitchen and made some coffee. Caffeine was the last thing she needed a few hours before she went to bed, but maybe she could use the extra time awake to get some work done. She hadn't made any decent progress toward her deadline in weeks—not since before the accident—and if she didn't get something done soon, she was going to have to ask for an extension.

Of course, she was going to have to do that anyway. There was no way she was going to get her head cleared enough to work until this was settled. She just knew it.

Once the coffeepot was making its nice little hiss and bubbling sound, Shay turned around to face Elliot. He was leaning against the island, watching her. Those whiskey-colored eyes rested on her face, intent and somber. Just that look was enough to make her heart flip over in her chest. Her breath hitched a little and she reached back, gripping the counter to steady herself. *Breathe* . . . she just had to remember to breathe, after all.

"So," he murmured, still watching her face, his stare unblinking. As if he was waiting for any sign of a reaction. "Have you been online much today?"

Online . . . ? Ah. Ah, yes. That. So he was here about that. "Hmmm. Saw it already, did you? You're fast."

"Why didn't you make a statement about this sooner? You knew the Facebook thing was going on before today, right?"

Shay shrugged, turning around to pull a couple of mugs down from the cabinet. "Well, there are a number of answers to that. For one, I just found out what was going on the day before yesterday—when Lorna brought me to the store. I couldn't do anything when I didn't know this was going on. For another, I just didn't think to."

She slid him a look over her shoulder, staring at him through her lashes. "You've made the comment before . . . Shane Neil has next to no online life—and you're right. I email. I make sure my website stays updated, and that's about it. There are the group sites my publisher has been hooked up to and a few contests run through those or my newsletter, but that's it. I'm not wired into the online world the way some are. I don't normally do the updates on my site. I hardly ever do anything on the site, to be honest. I knew how I wanted it to look, knew what features I wanted it to have, so I was mostly involved in the design, but I rarely log into it. It just . . ." She closed her eyes and sighed.

Resting her hands on the counter, she shook her head. Quietly, she said, "Honestly, it just never occurred to me."

"I guess I can see that," he said softly, nodding. "I . . . shit. Shay, look, I'm sorry. I should have listened a little better. I wasn't—screw it. I didn't give you the benefit of the doubt and I should have."

Head cocked, she studied him. An apology. Huh. She hadn't expected that. Coming for the book, coming to ask more questions . . . but the apology? No. That wasn't anything she'd expected at all.

Golden eyes bored into hers. Once more she felt as though he was trying to see clear through her. It was almost painful; all those other secrets felt closer to the surface. She'd managed to hold everything in, keep it all together for so long, and now it was ready to come spilling out. But *she* wasn't ready.

Tearing her gaze from his, she shrugged. "No problem. Anyway, it's done. Took me awhile to think about posting it to my site, but I did and it should help. It's not much, but at least it's something."

A hand touched the back of her neck. She tensed, then groaned as he curved his palm around it and curled his fingers into the tight muscles. "Not much?" he asked. "There are comments like crazy going on. Haven't you looked online since you posted it?"

"Not so much. Been a little busy," she murmured. *Trying to fix the mess that is my life . . . you know, little details like that . . .*

"Hmmm. So. Where is your computer?"

Even under those talented fingers, Shay could feel her muscles tensing. "My computer?"

"Yeah. You should see what's going on, after all."

She narrowed her eyes, trying to decide if that was a challenge she heard in his voice. Then she decided it didn't matter. Seriously, if somebody had just dumped a surprise like this right in *her* lap after months of no communication, as distrustful as she was . . . would she believe the person? With absolutely no proof?

And besides, he'd just apologized. She couldn't let herself get hung up on this. She had plenty of other things to get tripped up on, anyway.

With a sigh, she eased away from his hands and poured herself a cup of coffee, lacing it liberally with cream and sugar. Then she poured him a cup, black. He took it and stood there, staring at her.

"Come on," she said, wearily. Damn it, she was tired. The wreck, coming home to this hell, having Elliot thrust back into her life, and now Darcy's possible involvement . . . all of it left her exhausted. And the nightmares . . . mustn't forget how much worse the nightmares had gotten.

But life wasn't going to get any easier, not anytime soon, because she was still trying to untangle all of the snarls and until she did that, nothing was going to change.

Elliot followed along silently in her wake.

She didn't bother turning on any lights. The office was her refuge and she'd made this walk in the dark countless times. When the nightmares sent her gasping for air as she came hurtling out of sleep, the office was where she went. She'd pour the nightmare out in her diary, and then she'd take refuge in her books—at least *there* she could kill the people who caused such pain.

Once inside her office, she hit the light. Absently, she was aware that Elliot had stopped in the doorway, but she didn't turn to look at him. She wasn't in the mood to give a tour.

The office had wall-to-wall bookshelves on three walls. The western wall was dominated by a huge window. It had a built-in window seat, although she didn't use it much in the winter.

It got chilly in there sometimes with that window, so there was a freestanding electric fireplace, the kind that looked like one of those old-fashioned stoves. It was off right now and she was cold, so she grabbed the remote to the fireplace from her desk and turned it on. It came on with a cheery glow, emitting a faint crackling sound. She'd thought about having a real fireplace built in here, but with all the books, and with her decidedly scattered brain, the electric one was safer.

The desk was massive and cluttered with paperwork that had been neglected during her stay at the hospital. It was piling up with alarming frequency and sooner or later, she was going to have to devote a few days to catching up on things. A problem for another day, she figured. From the corner of her eye, she saw Elliot studying her bookshelves. Particularly the one that held her author copies. The muscles along her shoulders started to tighten and she winced as a warning spasm went screaming up her spine.

She forced herself to relax and then sat down at her desk, tapping the mouse until the screen came to life.

The browser was still active from her last session. She hit the link to view the website so she wasn't in under the administration area and found herself staring at the notice she'd posted.

"Why did you do it?" Elliot asked from just behind her.

"A better question would be the one you asked . . . why didn't I think to do it sooner." Shay shrugged. Then she groaned and reached up, cupping a hand over her neck. The muscles felt tighter than bowstrings and her head was pounding, throbbing . . . she thought she just might puke if this kept up. "I'm sorry she's doing this to you."

Elliot brushed his fingers down her neck, almost as if asking permission.

Slowly, she eased her hand away and let him curve his against her nape, as he had in the kitchen. This time, he just let it rest there for a moment, the heat of his hand seeping into her skin, easing some of the tension with just that one touch. "Something occurred to me earlier. I came out here to tell you what it was, and to try and think this through with you. Well, that, and to apologize. I've apologized. Now I think we need to talk about the other shit. I think I'm just collateral damage, Shay. She doesn't give a flying fuck about me. It's you she's going after."

She closed her eyes.

He pressed the heel of his hand against the knotted muscles, lightly, then eased up. He did it a second, then a third time, waiting until the muscles relaxed before doing anything else. "Am I right?"

"How in the hell am I supposed to know?" she asked quietly. Even though the words sent a bolt of fear darting through her.

"Well, you have to have a better clue than I do . . . it's your life she's jerking around with, isn't it?"

Shay snorted. "I'm not the one she accused of rape."

"But she expected you to have a reaction to that. Didn't she?" He shifted his attention to another spot, repeating the process he'd used. "I mean, I could be off here, I know that. I could be way off. Maybe this is some crazy chick who's got a hate-on for me, and it's just coincidental that it's all playing out at the same time you're dealing with this crazy shit. But . . ."

"It sure doesn't seem likely," Shay finished. Her head slumped forward. The muscles felt looser already, and she wished like hell he would just stop talking and keep touching her. Forcing herself to focus on his words took more effort than she could possibly imagine; of course, that could be because she didn't *want* to think.

All she wanted to do was let him touch her. And keep touching her. Then she wanted to turn around and touch him, keep touching him. Maybe this time she could do it without those demons slipping in. She'd never been able to do it before, but then again, she'd never been that determined to try. Elliot had never pushed. He'd known there were issues . . . had known she had secrets. And maybe that was why she'd kept him locked out. Shay had understood, deep inside, that sooner or later she'd have to let him in, and she just hadn't been prepared for that.

Am I now?

The very thought filled her with terror, but one thing was certain . . . if she had a chance to have him back in her life, she was going to grab it. Grab it and hold on tight.

Except none of that could happen while somebody was out there screwing around with their lives.

Forcing all the need and frustrated longing in her body aside, she took a deep breath and opened her eyes, staring at the computer, at the message she'd written. Then she opened another browser window and went to

Facebook, using the fake persona to go to the "Shane" page.

She skimmed it over, but didn't see much to get excited over.

Except the *LIKE* count was down. By maybe a thousand . . . ?

Shrugging, she glanced over her shoulder at Elliot. "I don't see anything to get excited over," she said.

"She's been deleting shit, then." He nodded toward the computer. "May I?"

She eased over to the side, starting to rise, but all he did was lean over her. For a moment, just the nearness of him, the warmth of him, surrounded her and she felt goose bumps break out even as heat flooded her and her heart jumped up into her throat. Fear and desperate desire tangled inside her and she had to clench her hands into fists to keep from reaching for him. *Months* . . . it had been *months* and he still got to her like this. Having him so close left her heart racing and her skin felt tight.

She missed him. She needed him—

"Yeah," he murmured, his voice just a breath away from her ear. "There."

She swallowed and stared at the screen. It was a little different now.

"She's been deleting the comments," Elliot said. "But she can't keep up with it . . . look again."

Forcing her brain to focus on the matter at hand, not on the fire burning in her belly, Shay leaned forward. Then she tensed as the outer curve of her breast brushed against his arm. A gasp lodged in her throat and the slow crawl of blood up her neck warned her that she wouldn't be able to hide her blush from him. Keeping her gaze focused on the screen, she told herself, *Fake it until you make it.* She reacted to him . . . she always had. And yes, she wanted to try this with him again, if he was willing.

But she needed to get this straightened out first.

One fucking disaster at a time—that was all she could handle.

She would start by focusing on the messages on the page in front of her.

One of them read:

What the fuck, Shane? Somebody sent me a link to your website and I saw that message. Are you screwing with us? Are you for real or not?

Another comment—

Oh, shit. UR so fake. I can't believe I've been buying into this shit ur selling us. Crazy bitch.

The next one was a little more sympathetic, but still, the disbelief was there.

I realize you must have some strange things taking place, but whether you are Shane Neil or not, you clearly have a lot of issues going on. I think it's time you got help. It might be best if you shut this page down until you have your life straightened out.

There were more of them . . . dozens, at least.

"Huh." She clicked to refresh the page, and immediately wished she hadn't. Because all of those comments were gone. "What the hell?"

"Told you. She's deleting them. She'll just keep it up, too. Have you contacted Facebook about this?"

Shay sighed, resting her chin in her palm and staring at the glaring white screen. "Yeah, as soon as I realized what was going on. And it did zero good." The headache pounding behind her eyes seemed to gain in strength and she rubbed the line between her eyebrows, but it didn't do anything to ease the pain.

"It probably takes a few days, and I doubt they do

much over the weekend. Give it time." He brushed his fingers down her cheek, a light, questioning touch.

Shay turned her head to look at him. He was so close . . . so close. She could smell the coffee on his breath, the scent of the soap he used. The gold of his eyes seemed to darken and she could recall how his gaze would do that right before he'd kiss her.

Was he thinking about that now?

Her heart skipped a beat and she thought about leaning in, pressing her lips to his. What would he do if she did that? Her heart didn't just skip a beat this time. It all but jumped into her throat and she couldn't help but think about what *she* would do . . .

The blaring ring of the phone shattered the silence of the night. Shay jolted and then swore, swinging around in her seat to stare at the phone.

Not now, she thought glumly as disappointment crashed into her. She already knew who it was.

Not that many people would be calling her, especially after eight-thirty. She could always hope that Anna had finally gotten around to checking her email, but that wasn't likely. Her gut told her something really screwed up was going on with her agent.

It wasn't Anna, and as much as she could hope it might be Angie, she knew it wasn't her either. It was Darcy.

Taking a deep breath, she reached for the phone.

And prepared herself to discover something very unpleasant about one of her only friends.

CHAPTER
EIGHT

"HEY, IT'S ME!" DARCY STARED AT THE COMPUTER AS she waited for Shay to respond.

The message on the screen was so plainly, simply stated. Even though she'd had a few hours to steam about it, she still couldn't believe this had happened, and Shay hadn't given her any of the damn passwords, so she couldn't get in and change the damn thing, either.

She'd never seen this coming.

Darcy didn't know why exactly, except for the fact that Shay just didn't interact with the outside world. Not unless she absolutely had to—and this wasn't an absolute necessity, not as far as Darcy was concerned. If Shay had found it necessary, why hadn't she allowed Darcy to do it?

Of course, that would have been interesting, Darcy thought, muffling a laugh. Interesting. To say the least.

"Hello, Darcy," Shay said quietly, her voice strangely reserved.

"I saw the message on your site. That's . . . well, unexpected. You know, I could have handled that." She paused, and then added, "Except you haven't gotten me my new passwords. Did you ever find out what happened to my access?"

"I'm working on it." Shay was quiet; then, off in the background, Darcy heard a low voice. Too low . . . deep, rougher.

A man's voice.

Darcy narrowed her eyes. What the *hell* was this? What was going on?

She made herself smile. It was easier to pretend to be happy if she was smiling. "Shay! You tramp. Do you have somebody over there?" It was like spitting out glass, making herself sound excited.

What was that little bitch thinking? Didn't she remember how badly things went the last time she tried to actually have a fucking relationship? They just didn't *work* for her.

"Yes. I do."

Again, her voice was cool. Almost closed off. Turning away from the computer, Darcy started to pace, moving to stare out the window. The moon gleamed in the sky, shining down on the snow like silver.

"Sooo . . . should I call back?" she teased. *You better not tell me no.*

"Actually, no. This is a good time to talk."

Oh, excellent . . . this is excellent. Shay knew she wasn't ready to get involved with anybody. She wasn't ever going to be ready. The only person she really needed was Darcy. "If you want, I can wait while you tell him good-bye . . . ?"

"Nah, Elliot doesn't mind waiting for me."

The satisfaction Darcy had been feeling abruptly started to fade. A muscle twitched in her brow. "Elliot." Rage gripped her, twisted her. "So you're still talking to that asshole who dumped you. Isn't he the one who raped . . . well, I dunno who she is, but I saw something on Facebook. If he's dangerous, should you be alone with him?"

Shay snorted. "Well, if she's lying about being *me*, it stands to reason she'd lie about that, too, doesn't it?"

Darcy reached up and grabbed a fistful of her hair, jerking at it. The sharp pain flared, but it wasn't enough to keep her focused on the conversation. Her voice came out razor sharp as she said, "But how are you so fucking *sure* she's lying, huh? Men do assaholic things all the time, don't they? And come *on*, you know hardly anything about him—there was some kind of mess when he was in the military. Did he ever tell you that?"

"What in the world are you talking about?"

That bite of anger in Darcy's voice wasn't exactly an unfamiliar one. No, Shay had heard it before, dealt with it before—it was the rage Darcy seemed to show when things weren't exactly going *her* way. Sort of like the fight they'd had when Darcy had been adamant that Shay fire her agent.

She hadn't always been that way, but it seemed that Shay saw it more and more lately.

When Darcy didn't answer right away, Shay rose from her chair and moved to stare out the window. She was vaguely aware that Elliot was watching her, but her attention was focused on Darcy now. "Just what do you know that you aren't telling me, Darcy?" she asked softly. "You've never even met him."

As she talked, she wound the cord around her fingers, keeping her gaze on the dark of the night. If she turned and looked at Elliot, she was going to lose her focus and she couldn't do that right now . . .

"He got in trouble like this before, Shay. Really, don't you ever pay attention to things?" Then she laughed softly. "Wait, that's why I'm here, right?" On the other end of the line, Darcy sighed, her voice heavy with that put-upon tone—*poor me, I'm so unappreciated* . . .

Normally, Shay would start feeling guilty right

about . . . *now.* Except for the first time, she heard the calculation lurking below Darcy's voice. The almost sly taunting. It was more than that needling little whine—a lot more. The needling whine hid that clever manipulation, Shay realized.

"Just how have you been paying so much attention to a man you've never met, Darcy?" Shay asked.

"That's what the Internet is for."

"I don't pay you to spy on the people in my life, Darcy." Shay gripped the phone tighter and tighter. She was tempted to throw it. Tempted to smash it against the floor until the plastic was nothing but broken, busted bits.

"It's my job to take care of you, Shay," she said quietly.

"Your *job*?" Shay was pretty certain her jaw just about hit the floor.

"Yes. You pay me to take care of you."

Take care of me? Now she was certain of it—her jaw was all but dragging on the floor. She literally could feel it hanging open and it took a few seconds of letting it do that before she could manage to snap it shut with an audible click. "I pay you to help me keep business shit in order. I don't pay you to *take care* of me. I had a mother for that, thanks."

There was a pause, followed by a low, malicious chuckle. "And she did such a wonderful fucking job taking care of you . . . didn't she . . . *Michelline* . . . ?"

Then the phone went dead.

But Shay never noticed. At the sound of that name, she went flying back.

"Michelline, do you remember what happened to you?"

"No." She was sleepy. And tired of sitting here in this room with that grim-faced, sad-eyed man. Even though

he wasn't mean or anything, even though he hadn't yelled. And the woman next to her wasn't much better. She'd promised she was there to take care of her, but Michelline knew better.

Nobody took care of her. And she didn't want anybody taking care of her . . .

The door opened.

Another woman stood there. The other two stood up and moved to talk to the woman. They all spoke in low tones and then finally, the others left, leaving Michelline alone with this other woman.

Michelline thought she looked familiar.

"Hello, sweetie. Do you remember me?" The woman lingered in the doorway, holding something. A plate, Michelline thought.

It was a plate.

And on it were doughnuts . . .

Her belly rumbled.

She remembered the doughnuts better than the woman.

Slowly, she nodded. The lady had come out to the house a few times. And Michelline was always supposed to lie. She didn't like doing it, but she had to. The lady was nice, though. And she always managed to sneak in doughnuts or bananas . . .

"Can I sit down, Michelline? I'd like to talk . . . if that's okay."

Michelline had talked to enough people. But this woman had doughnuts. Maybe she'd let her have one . . .

Slowly, Michelline nodded.

"Michelline . . ."

That name. Shit, that name—

She wanted to puke, just thinking about it.

Shay sat there on the floor without even realizing how

she'd gotten there. Shit, she hadn't had a panic attack *that* bad in years. Maybe ever. She hardly remembered *anything* and now she was on the floor, with Elliot crouching in front of her. He had his hands on her face and the look in his eyes was just this side of terror.

But when she spoke, he hauled her against him and muttered, "Thank God. Damn it, you gave me a heart attack."

"She called me Michelline," Shay whispered, curling her fingers into the bulky weave of his sweater and cuddling against him. His warmth seeped into her chilled bones and if she could have, she would have stayed there, just there, for the rest of her life.

His hand curved over the back of her neck. "Who, baby?"

"My assistant . . . my friend." She swallowed and eased away, staring up at him while the knot in her throat threatened to choke her. "Elliot, I think she is the one doing this. All of it."

She'd suspected Darcy was involved, but damn it . . . it could be worse than she'd feared. So much worse. *Michelline—*

"Okay." He pushed her hair back from her face, his thumb tracing one of the scars by her cheek. "But I'm not tracking the deal with the name . . ."

Shay closed her eyes and let her head sink back against his chest.

"I . . ." She took a deep breath, tried to brace herself. "I think it was *my* name."

"What?"

Curling her hand into his sweater, she said quietly, "I don't remember the first few years of my life, Elliot. They're just a blank. But I think I was Michelline."

CHAPTER
NINE

ELLIOT STARED AT THE SCRAPBOOK IN FRONT OF HIM, battling so much anger and sickness, he couldn't think straight.

He'd wanted Shay to open up to him.

There was no denying that. Although, shit, it would have been easier if she were just a reclusive author, dealing with agoraphobia or something.

They'd broken up because he couldn't be with a woman who would share only half of herself with him. He couldn't live his life in a vacuum and he'd wanted her too much, cared too much to watch as she suffered alone. She wouldn't let him in, wouldn't share her burdens with him, and he'd been dying inside. All he'd wanted was for her to let him in.

Now she had. And oddly enough, he still felt like he was dying inside—he hadn't been prepared for this.

But how did any sane, decent person prepare for this kind of horror, he wondered.

Daughter testifies against stepfather for kidnapping, rape, and torture.

Phoenix man found guilty.

Local social worker dies.

He went through the scrapbook, stopped to read each article. There were many—articles about the trial, follow-up pieces, and letters from the Arizona Department of Corrections. The final letter was about the man's release.

"They let him out," he said quietly. Rage bit into him, tearing out chunks of him, and he wanted to scream, wanted to break something. Instead, he just focused on the scrapbook.

Behind him, Shay said softly, "He's served his time."

"His time," Elliot muttered. *Fuck that.* He closed his hand into a fist to keep from hurling that scrapbook and its vile contents across the room. Then he turned around and stared at the woman in front of him.

In the article, the girl hadn't been named.

But he knew, without asking. She was sitting before him now, curled up in the window seat and staring outside at the snow, a lost look on her face, grief in her pretty eyes, dealing with more pain than he'd ever thought a woman could carry.

She'd been under eighteen and that name would be kept quiet, since she'd been a minor.

The social worker's name had been Virna Lassiter.

"Is your real name Shay Morgan? Or is it Michelline Lassiter?"

She drew her knees to her chest and shivered. "Shay is my name *now*. But that's not my birth name . . . I don't know what my real name used to be," she whispered softly, her voice breaking.

The broken, awful pain in her voice all but killed him.

But he didn't go to her . . . not yet. Somehow, he didn't think she'd want it. Not until she had this out.

Yet he wanted so badly to go to her. To hold her.

To stroke away the naked fear, the pain he'd always glimpsed in her eyes.

To do something to ease the burden of the secrets she carried inside.

Secrets . . .

He needed to understand those secrets. Desperately.

Taking a deep breath, he blew it out and then focused. One small step at a time. If he could get her to talk to him about one secret at a time, he could begin to understand.

"You don't remember your real name?" he asked.

"No. Not the name I was born with, at least." She shook her head, staring outside for another moment before turning her gaze to his. Those eyes, with all their misery and secrets, stared into his.

"The man in the article was my stepfather—Jethro Abernathy. I doubt I shared his last name, so I don't think I was Michelline Abernathy. And I'll be honest, I don't *remember* the name Michelline. Up until I changed my name after the trial, I went by the name Michelle . . . I didn't realize I'd had another one. I don't know much about Abernathy, except for what I was able to piece together. Virna, the woman who adopted me, would have known some of his history, but she died before she could tell me much and all of those records are sealed." She shrugged and said, "I *might* be able to get my adoption records, but the records from her investigation of my family and all of that? Hell, I've thought about trying, but I don't know if I want to dig up those skeletons just so I can find out what I already know."

"And what is that?" Elliot asked.

She shrugged. "That I was taken away from him when I was young. I don't remember why. I don't remember him. I don't remember my mother. I have some vague memory of being told she abandoned me, but I don't know. I don't remember much of anything before Virna."

Just darkness, Shay thought. *Darkness, fear, hunger.*

And a baby crying—and the angry, awful shouts that always followed.

Somebody shut that baby up—

Swallowing, she closed her hands into fists until her nails dug into her palms. As the pain grounded her, focused her, she sucked in a desperate breath. Once she could think, she said, "Virna was the part of my life that mattered. She was my mom. In every way that counted. I had her from the time I was four, until I was sixteen."

"What happened when you were sixteen?"

At the low, angry throb of his voice, Shay looked back at Elliot. His whiskey eyes glinted with rage, but oddly, it didn't scare her. She found herself comforted. Eased by it. He wouldn't hurt her. He'd move heaven and hell to keep that from happening, she realized.

And he wouldn't reject her, either. That was a realization that shook her to her core. Closing her eyes, she rested her head on her knees, waiting for the trembling in her limbs to stop. He wouldn't reject her. He wasn't going to see all the scars she had and turn away.

She just knew it in her bones.

Tell him, something inside whispered. *Just tell him.*

Before the sudden burst of courage faded, she slid off the window seat and grabbed the hem of her shirt, pulling it off. She heard the surprised intake of his breath. And then she heard nothing but the roaring in her ears as the blood started to pound. As her heart raced and black dots danced in front of her eyes.

The room started to spin around her, and then it steadied as Elliot closed his hands around her elbows.

"He did that," he rasped, staring down at her chest.

Her scarred chest.

"Yes." Forcing herself to look up at him, she said it again, "Yes."

It was ugly, the scars stark against the paleness of her skin. Even after all this time, the initials were visible.

She wasn't wearing a bra—she rarely did unless she was leaving the house. It wasn't as if there was ever really anybody who'd come by, right? But now she was standing there, bare-chested, in front of Elliot, with nothing between him and her scars.

The letters *J. A.*

"Why?"

"I forgot . . ." She whispered, staring past him. "That's what he said. I don't know *what* I forgot, but that's what he kept shouting. I forgot and I'd never forget again. He'd make sure of it. This was his way of doing that. He . . ." She stopped and swallowed. "He marked me so I'd never forget again."

"Forget *what*?"

"I don't know."

"Your father tortured you and you don't know why?"

She started to shake, and as the cold got to her, some of the shock in her head receded. Trying to find something of herself left in the pain and the grief, she said, "Stepfather. As to why? Well, he's a crazy-ass bastard . . . we can always use that as a reason. But . . . no. No, I don't really know why."

A hard shiver racked her body and she wrapped her arms around her middle, trembling. Lost, she looked down, searching for her shirt.

"Here."

Elliot grabbed a blanket from the window seat and wrapped it around her shoulders. She gripped it, a ragged sigh escaping her, but it hurt to even breathe around the knot in her throat. Each breath was almost a sob.

"Are you okay?" Elliot asked, his voice quiet. Then he swore, taking a step back. "Okay . . . fuck. How in the hell can you be okay?"

He turned away and started to pace.

Staring at him, Shay gripped the edges of the blanket.

"Do you need anything?" he asked.

"Yes."

He stopped and turned, facing her, his hands hanging loose at his sides. "What?"

"Stop moving around so much . . . and . . ." She licked her lips, closed her eyes. Then, taking a deep breath, she asked, "Would you maybe just sit with me for a while? I mean . . . I know you and I aren't together anymore, and maybe you don't have anything left in you for me, but I'm feeling kind of . . ."

"Shay."

She opened her eyes.

He came toward her and stopped just a breath away. One hand came up and cupped her chin. And as those whiskey-gold eyes met hers, all the pain and chaos and misery inside her fell away and once more, she was lost. But it was okay, because she was lost inside him, and that was where she wanted to be, where she needed to be.

"You think I don't have anything in me for you?" he murmured, lowering his head so that the words were whispered against her lips. "Baby . . . *everything* I have in me *is* for you. You're my *everything*. You are it for me. I knew that months ago. And it was killing me that you wouldn't let me in."

A harsh breath escaped her. Tears burned her eyes and despite her best intentions, one of them broke free, rolling down her cheek. He brushed it away. Then, he caught her up in his arms.

"Come here," he said quietly, lifting her.

"Hey!" Startled, she shoved against his chest as he carried her over to the window seat. But almost as soon as he had picked her up, they were sitting down, and she was cradled in his lap, up against his chest. The warmth of his body seeped into hers and some of that awful cold began to ease.

He urged her head to his shoulder. "Close your eyes for a few minutes, Shay," he whispered. "You look so damn tired."

"I am." Giving in to the urge, she rested her head and did just as he'd suggested. Closed her eyes. Breathing in the warm scent of him, she let herself relax. He smelled just like he always did . . . of wood and smoke from the fires he liked to burn in the store, of books and after-shave and man. He smelled perfect. And he felt safe. He *was* safe. She knew, as well as she knew the shape of her hands, that she was safe, right here with him.

Although she couldn't quite believe he *was* here, holding her again. After he'd walked away. He was here with her. He still cared. And he'd seen her scars, but they didn't matter. Elliot had looked at those awful, ugly scars without flinching.

If he could look at them . . .

"He kidnapped me," she blurted out. "He stalked me and Virna. For months. After he got out of jail, he acted like the good citizen, like he'd paid his debt to society. He went to church, went to work, did everything he was supposed to do. And all the while, he was looking for us. They found the evidence after he'd kidnapped me, during the investigation. He learned our routines, learned what we did, where we were . . . when I was alone, when I wasn't. Then one day, he broke into the house. He beat Virna." Her voice broke. "He hurt her so bad, she ended up dying from it. Her heart was already in bad shape. She died a few days later. And he took me. I don't re-member all of it, but I was tied up . . ."

Her breath started to hitch, and she could feel the blackness weighing in on her. She shook, and no matter how tightly he held her, she was still so cold. So damn cold.

"Shay, you don't have to do this," Elliot whispered against her temple.

"Yes, I do." Swallowing, she whispered again, "Yes, I do. He tied me up—kept me that way for a couple of days. He cut me because I forgot about the time when I still lived with him. He'd yell at me about how everything was my fault. This crazy shit, because I had to be the princess and I wasn't a fucking princess and it was all my fault—I had no right to forget and he'd make sure I never forgot again. He cut me, and he beat me, and he raped me . . ." Her voice broke and she sobbed against his chest. "He raped me. Over and over . . ."

Elliot closed his eyes. Inside his throat, there was a howl of denial, of fury.

Be careful what you ask for . . .

He'd wanted her to let him in. Now he was. He wanted to rage, to scream, to hurt the bastard who'd done this to her.

But Shay clung to him, trembling.

And all he could do was hold her and stroke her back, and listen as she cried. His heart shattered.

"He hurt me," she whispered. "And he loved it. I don't even know why . . ."

When she buried her face against his neck, he opened his eyes and stared off into the night. *God, baby. I'm so sorry . . .*

Time passed. It could have been minutes. It could have been hours. He didn't know, didn't care, because finally, those awful, awful sobs eased and she breathed easily against his chest.

He thought she might have slept, but then she spoke again, her voice soft and steady. "I'm tired. I'm so damn tired. I have nightmares," she murmured. "I've always had them. But they get bad sometimes, and lately, I've been having them all the time. It's like something flipped a switch in my head and they are there all the time . . . I hear echoes even when I'm awake, and I can hardly sleep anymore."

"Try to get some sleep now." He pressed his lips to her brow. "I'll be here if the nightmares start."

She started to ask what good that would do, but she stopped. She felt safer with him. Even her mind felt calmer.

Talking about it should have made it worse, she thought. Should have made it more vivid in her mind. But it hadn't. Her mind was easier, calmer. She always dreaded closing her eyes, but she didn't now. Maybe she could rest a little.

"Go to sleep, Shay," he whispered again.

"That's not even my real name . . ."

"Yes, it is. That's who you've made yourself. Now . . . sleep."

She was out in the next minute. Elliot sat there holding her, but he didn't dare look at her. Not yet. He had to get himself under control. The fury and the grief was a monster inside him that threatened to rip him apart.

Every time he closed his eyes, even if it was just to blink, he saw the scars. He saw what had been done to her. If he thought the narrow lines on the left side of her face were bad, what was hidden under her clothes was so much worse.

He laughed silently, bitterly. *Shit.* He'd thought he'd been prepared . . . no matter what she told him, if she ever opened up, he had thought he'd be prepared for it. All those months ago, he'd waited. He thought he was ready to hear what she had to say.

But he'd been so fucking wrong. Even if he'd been a little right.

He'd known it would be bad.

The way she'd flinched around him at first . . . how nervous she was.

It had taken her almost a damn year just to stop being so nervous around him. Another four months of him badgering her before she'd agree to a date. And they'd dated a good two months before he'd suspected she wouldn't bolt in fear if he did much more than give her a friendly peck on the lips.

Yeah, he'd known it would be bad. He'd suspected she'd been assaulted, and that was why he'd moved so slowly. Why he'd waited, and hoped, and prayed she'd talk to him. Open up to him. But days turned to weeks, then months. Almost a year after they'd started dating she still wouldn't open up to him, even after he'd started trying to press her just a little at a time.

The more he pressed, the more she'd shut down, too.

But by then, he'd been so fucking gone over her, he felt that he was damned if he did, damned if he didn't. Things couldn't stay as they were, but they weren't moving forward, either.

He hadn't handled it well.

Looking back, he could admit that, although he didn't know how else he should have handled it, what else he should have done, or not done.

Hindsight wasn't always twenty-twenty, it seemed.

Finally, when he thought he might have things under control, he let himself look down and study her face. She was so damn pretty. Looking at her was a punch to his gut, to his heart, to his soul. Even now. But it was even more heartbreaking because he knew some of the secrets beneath those scars.

The scars.

Swallowing the bile rising in his throat, he slowly reached up with his right hand. All Shay did was turn her face into his chest and cuddle closer. It exposed the scars along the left side of her upper cheek and jawline. They rode along the edge of her face, up to her temple, before disappearing into her hair. They looked practiced—he had thought that the first time he saw her, and he'd been right. Her stepfather.

Rage—ugly, vivid, and rabid—twisted inside him. Closing his eyes, he accepted it, breathed it in. He couldn't block it out, couldn't pretend that he didn't feel it. There was no way anybody with any sort of decency inside could think about what had been done to her and *not* feel some kind of disgust, some kind of anger. But this wasn't just *somebody* to him. This was Shay . . . and as he'd told her, she was his everything, and knowing that somebody had taken the child she'd been and tortured her, tried to break her . . .

He had to take the rage, had to accept it and find some way to live with it.

His fingers were trembling as he traced them down one thin line, then the next, and the next. By the time he'd traced each one of them, he was almost blinded by his own fury. And Shay was sleeping. Completely unaware. Gently, he shifted her on his lap until he could brush the blanket aside.

Her skin was pale against the vivid weave of the bright red blanket. Pale, soft . . . and although he knew she wasn't fragile, her skin certainly seemed that way. Fragile, silken. How in the hell . . .

Put it away, he told himself. A muscle pulsed in his cheek; he could feel the damn thing ticking away as he mentally braced himself to look again. Would it be as bad—

It was.

Each scar stood out in stark relief against her skin, rather neat in its perfection. She would have fought, if she could have. It was the human way. If she'd fought and moved around much, those marks wouldn't be so neat. So she'd been restrained. That monster had re-strained her, and then carved those letters into her flesh.

He stared, until he knew he could see it again without it coming as such a brutal shock.

Because he'd damn well see her again. He'd see *all* of her again, unless Shay got it in her head to run away. Elliot wasn't going to let her go this time. He couldn't.

He never should have given up so easily last time.

Shay shivered in his arms and he eased the blanket back up over her. Lowering his head, he pressed his lips to her brow. "Sleep, baby," he murmured. "I'll be here."

CHAPTER
TEN

"THAT'S LONG ENOUGH," DARCY MUSED, REACHING for the phone.

She'd heard that startled, shocked gasp right before she'd hung up. Two hours had passed . . . enough time for Shay to wonder, to worry, to remember. Darcy knew the nightmares sometimes came on fast. Maybe she was even having one now . . .

Or maybe she was just wondering where the name had come from. Maybe she hadn't remembered that far back yet. Maybe she was just too clueless. But sooner or later, that name would slip out from her subconscious along with more memories.

She needed to remember. Really, she did. This waiting . . . it was so tedious. Nobody liked to be forgotten, after all.

And Shay had forgotten almost everything—all the important things.

That much was clear just by what she wrote in her little *diary.* She thought that thing was so damn secret, that nobody knew who was writing those words.

Shay didn't *have* secrets. Not from her.

She only thought she did. Seriously, Shay didn't know shit. After all, she was letting that son of a bitch in her house . . .

"Hello?"

It was a guy's voice.

Darcy blinked, caught off guard. Not *once* had she called Shay's number and anybody *but* Shay answered. Not *one fucking time*. "Who the hell is this?"

A dumb question, she realized a split second later. It was Elliot Winter, of course.

"Not exactly your place to ask," he replied. "Who is this?"

Eyes narrowed, fury biting at her, she still managed to put on her oh-so-cheerful and friendly persona. "I'm sorry about that . . . I was just a little surprised to hear a guy answering. I need to talk to Shay."

"Sorry. She's sleeping."

And then he hung up. Just like that. Snarling, Darcy went to punch the number back in but then she stopped. Okay, so the bastard didn't offer to take her name. Or her number. Granted, Shay had caller ID and it wasn't necessary, but still—it was common fucking courtesy, right? Points against him, as far as Darcy was concerned, and if he thought she wouldn't mention how much of a bastard he'd been, he was in for a rude awakening.

Shay thought the sun fucking rose and *set* on Darcy.

Stupid bastard.

Setting the phone down, she reached up and smoothed her hair back from her face. No problem.

This was infuriating as hell, but it wasn't a problem. She'd just call again tomorrow and talk to Shay. There were other things she needed to do anyway.

Shay was forgetting how much she needed Darcy, and she needed to be reminded of that.

Shay awoke to darkness and silence.

Silence in her mind, silence all around her.

And warmth. There was an arm around her waist and a long, lean form pressed against her back.

Stiffening, she jerked upright and whipped around.

Light filtered in from the bathroom—she hadn't left that light on. Well, she didn't *think* she had, but she never left that light on. But if that light hadn't been on, she wouldn't have been able to see Elliot's face. *Elliot's face*. Which meant Elliot was there.

In her bed.

Elliot was in her bed.

Shay gulped.

"Morning," he murmured, his voice a low, sexy rumble.

She gulped a second time and managed to squeak out, "Morning." Then, as terror and nerves gripped her, she scrambled out of the bed and took off for the bathroom.

Halfway there, she realized she wasn't wearing a shirt. But she was wearing her jeans. *What the . . .*

Forget about it. She'd figure it out in the bathroom.

She slammed the door behind her and sagged against it, covering her face with her hands. She stood there trembling for a minute and then she stormed across the bathroom floor and turned on the water, washed her face. As she was brushing her teeth, she tried to think; she needed to think. The entire night was nothing but one black pit. She didn't remember much of anything . . .

Not much of anything . . . Slowly, Shay lowered her hands. She didn't remember the nightmares. That was almost always the first thing on her mind when she woke and they weren't there.

Wait . . .

She spit out a mouthful of toothpaste and rinsed her mouth out, staring into the black bowl of the sink. "No nightmares," she whispered.

And Elliot's words from the past night came back to her . . . *I'll be here if the nightmares start . . .*

She put the toothbrush down and then rested her hands on the black marble. It felt cool and solid under her hands, and without it, she might have sagged to the floor.

Slowly, she made herself straighten, made herself stare at her reflection in the mirror. She rarely looked at it for more than a minute or two while she brushed her teeth and combed her hair. But now she stared at herself, saw the scars on her still bared chest.

Scars she could now remember showing Elliot.

And he hadn't flinched.

She'd asked him to hold her, even though she didn't dare hope he still had those kinds of feelings for her—he'd walked away from her, after all.

Now, those words from last night came back to her, a warm whisper that echoed around and around inside her head.

You think I don't have anything in me for you? Baby . . . everything I have in me is for you. You're my everything.

And then she'd told him what had happened, and he'd stayed. Had held her through the night.

Tears burned her eyes and she reached up, pressing her fingertips to them. "God," she murmured. "Did that really happen?"

There wasn't an answer, though.

Everything after the phone call with Darcy was a dazed rush of adrenaline, fear, and nerves. She couldn't remember it clearly, but she was pretty certain he'd said that.

Pretty certain wasn't good enough.

Before she could lose her nerve, she grabbed a towel, clutching it to her bare chest before opening the door. The room was empty. *Shit—*

Modesty forgotten, she dropped the towel and took off running.

Only to stop halfway down the hallway as she smelled coffee. Swallowing, she took a deep breath and glanced back. Okay, she needed to get a grip. Turning around, she went to her room and grabbed the first shirt she could find—it was one of her workout tanks—and she tugged it on and left the room. Already, her courage was fading and she needed to do this. Needed to ask, before she chickened out and spent the next week wondering and worrying and—

"Hey."

She came to an abrupt halt as she saw Elliot in the middle of the living room.

He had a hesitant smile on his face. As if he wasn't sure exactly what to do or say.

"Are you okay?" he asked softly. He glanced past her toward her room, then back at her. "I thought I heard you running . . ."

"Ah. Um." She shoved her hair back and shuffled her feet. "I thought you might have left." Then she shrugged and gestured toward the kitchen. "Then I smelled the coffee, and . . ."

Hell. She *sucked* at this. Turning away, she stared at the floor, curling her toes into the carpet and eyeing the badly chipped polish on her toenails. She hadn't given herself a pedicure since her accident—she liked painting her nails. Odd little thought, that. *You're procrastinating*, she chided. *Stop it*.

Spinning around, she stared at him. "Did you hold me last night?"

"Yes," he said cautiously. His gaze was guarded.

She swallowed and looked down at her chest, at the scars hidden by the thin, ribbed tank—horrified, she realized it was *too* thin. She could see the outline of her nipples, stabbing into the cloth. Blood rushed to her cheeks and she crossed her arms over her chest, embarrassed. Turning away, she stared at the cold, dark fire-place.

"You . . ." She stopped, her mouth painfully, achingly dry. *Shit*. Turning back to him, she gestured to her chest. "I showed you, didn't I? And you . . ."

"Shay." He came to her then.

The words she was reaching for died and she looked at him, lost.

As he cupped her face in his hands, he dipped his head and pressed his lips to her mouth. "Yes, you showed me. And the only thing about it that bothers me is how much you suffered . . . and how much I want to hurt the bastard who did it to you."

She sagged against him. Out of reflex, she reached up and grabbed at his waist, her fingers curling into the belt loops of his jeans. "So that means . . . the other stuff I thought you said . . ."

He smiled against her mouth. "Yeah. I said that, too."

"Oh." She pulled her head back and stared at him. "Oh . . ." Blowing out a breath, she smiled at him.

"Oh?" He grinned at her. "Is that all you've got to say? I lay my heart out for you and you say . . . *oh*?"

To her surprise, she giggled. Dropping her head against his chest, she sighed. "I thought maybe I'd . . . I dunno . . . thought I'd dreamt it."

"No nightmares?" He skimmed a hand up her back, then down, resting it low on her spine, just above her butt.

"Not that I can remember." Closing her eyes, she murmured, "You don't know how rare that is. The only time I usually sleep without nightmares is when I work myself into exhaustion or go a few days without sleep."

"Well, don't take this wrong, but I don't think you were that far off." He nuzzled her temple. "How long has it been since you really slept, Shay?"

"Beats me." She didn't care, either. She felt halfway decent just then. Rested.

"Somebody's been calling. Your caller ID said it was Darcy Montgomery."

Shay grimaced and pulled back. His arms fell away and she almost wished she hadn't moved, but the easy, relaxed moment had disappeared the second he'd mentioned Darcy's name. Jamming her hands into her back pockets, she started to pace. "Darcy."

"That's who you were talking to last night."

She slid him a look over her shoulder. "Yes."

"The one who called you that name."

Shay stopped. "Michelline," she whispered, staring down into the cold fireplace. Abruptly, she grabbed the matches from the mantel and knelt down. She needed to occupy her hands and her mind, even if it was with something mundane—

Can you tell us what happened, Michelline?

"Stop it," she whispered.

"Shay?"

She shook her head. "Not you. I . . ." She struck a match and touched it to the kindling. She always tried to keep a fire ready to go. She loved having a fire going in here. It was soothing. Calming. Once the flames were crackling away, she remained there, watching the flames as they danced. "I think I'm remembering something. Or trying to."

"Remembering what?" Elliot asked.

She glanced back at him as he moved closer and sat down beside her.

"From when they took me away from him—when I was little," she said softly. "I don't remember much of *anything*. Not until Virna. Before that, everything else is blank. As far as I'm concerned, my life started when Virna . . . Mom took me home."

She laughed sadly, the ache in her heart twisting. It

had been so many years and that ache was still there. By the time she'd escaped her stepfather, Virna had already died. No good-byes, no chance to say she was sorry. Nothing.

"It took me *years* to call her Mom, even though that's who she was to me. And I still think of her as Virna. Up here." She tapped her forehead. "But to me, *Virna* meant mother. I remember the cops asking me about my mom. Maybe that's why part of me doesn't like the word *mom*. It doesn't have pleasant connotations for me or something."

She licked her lips and looked down, staring at her hands.

"Sometimes I dream of blood. I dream of it, and I wake up thinking I'll be covered in it."

Elliot reached over, twining his fingers with hers. "You were hurt damn bad by him. Whether it was then, or when you were older, blood and pain often go hand in hand. Maybe it's just from that."

"Yeah." She shrugged and shifted around, settling on her bottom next to him. "And maybe it's because a very big part of me blames myself for Virna dying. He never would have gone after her if she hadn't adopted me. Part of me still feels like her blood is on my hands—that could explain it right there."

"But you don't think so."

Shay didn't answer. No, she didn't think so. Sometimes, she had a fleeting image in her head. As if she'd seen herself as they led her out of her house one last time . . . seen a mirror or something.

And there had been blood on her. A small, thin child . . . splattered with blood.

Shay closed her eyes.

Can you tell us what happened, Michelline?

The phone started to ring.

Her eyes flew open and she swore. Shooting to her

feet, she moved across the living room. Behind her, Elliot said, "You know, if you don't want to talk to anybody, just ignore it."

She glanced at him. "Can't. I keep hoping it's my agent."

It wasn't.

Shay stared at the display. Darcy's number. And once the ringing stopped, her cell phone showed that she'd already missed a call this morning. Sighing, she hit a button and checked. Darcy.

There was also a text from Lorna. Shay frowned as she read it.

Tell my brother he needs to check his car. Immediately. He's not answering me, but maybe you will. He can thank me later if it's necessary. Tell him it's a present from the just-in-case fairy.

She checked her home number. No calls from New York. Right now, that was the only number that mattered. Well, that or North Carolina.

Turning around, she said, "Darcy called last night?"

"Yeah." He half-turned to face her, long legs stretched out. "Her exact words . . . 'Who the hell is this?'" Elliot shrugged. "I told her that wasn't any of her business. Then she puts on this nice act and asks to speak to you. I told her you were asleep and hung up."

Shay laughed. "Oh, she's going to love that."

"Like I give a fuck." Then he winced. "Sorry. She's a friend of yours, so . . ."

Then he stopped. "What?"

Shay looked away. "I . . . hell. I don't know. She used to really *be* nice, you know. It wasn't an act. Lately, though, I've been feeling like she's working me. I'm being manipulated somehow. And that makes me even more suspicious that she's behind this."

Elliot's eyes sharpened and he got up off the floor. As

he crossed toward her, she found herself staring at him, at the way his worn jeans clung to his thighs, the way his sweater stretched over his chest. She licked her lips, remembering the feel of his hands . . . the way it felt to touch him.

"Behind this . . . you mean behind the mess with your books?" Elliot asked.

She blinked and jerked her gaze upward. "What?"

"You think your friend might be the one impersonating you?"

"Well, if she's impersonating me, she's not exactly the friend I thought she was," Shay said softly. "But . . . yeah. And it doesn't make sense. She's one of the few friends I've got. Lorna, my . . . ah. My sister. And Darcy. I *know* Darcy. I love her. She wouldn't *do* this. But it's the only thing that's adding up, so I don't get it." She didn't *want* to get it, she thought. It hurt too much.

"People can do crazy shit," Elliot said sourly. "Stuff you never would have thought they'd do. Maybe something just pushed her over."

"Maybe." She didn't want to think about it anymore. Easing closer, she reached out and curled her hands in the front of his sweater. Under it, she felt the warmth of his chest, the strength of him. It went straight to her head.

Elliot went still. It was amazing, she thought. He'd been all but vibrating with intensity—she had *seen* the anger burning in him, as if it had been coming off him in invisible waves. That was Elliot . . . *life* came off him like that. It was something about him that had attracted her from the beginning. He was life . . . and she was emptiness.

But now, it was as though he'd cut himself off and he was so still. All the intensity that was Elliot was silent and still.

She shifted her hand just a little to the side until she

could feel the rapid *bump-bump* of his heart against her hand. "I don't really want to talk about Darcy right now," she said quietly, still staring at her hand on his chest.

The sweater was that weird, not-quite-white color. Off-white. She looked awful in that color. Like a washed-out corpse. Not Elliot. But Elliot looked amazing in anything.

For the first time, she thought she really, really might be ready to see what he looked like in *nothing*. Not in fantasy, but in reality. She'd fantasized about it plenty. But she didn't want to fantasize. She didn't want to think.

She wanted to live. She wanted to feel.

Elliot's hand came up, curled around her wrist. "Shay . . ."

She shifted her gaze up, staring at him through her lashes.

Dull flags of color rode high on his cheeks and the gold of his eyes glittered hot and bright. *There*, she thought distantly. There was all that intensity. Her head started to spin a little and she swayed closer to him, bracing her other hand against his chest.

Elliot's lids drooped low and she felt his chest rise and fall.

"Damn it, Shay."

She rose on her toes and pressed her mouth to his.

Elliot groaned as she used the tip of her tongue to trace the line of his lips . . . he liked to do that when he was kissing her. And she'd always liked how it felt. So it would work for him, too, right? When he opened his mouth, she thought . . . *yeah, that works*. She smiled inwardly as she took the kiss deeper. Heat flashed through her, pulsating bursts that seemed to work in time with her heart, spreading through her body in a rhythmic pattern. It centered low in her body and unconsciously, she rocked her hips with it.

A harsh sound came from Elliot and Shay stilled, lifting her head to stare at him.

He caught her hips in his hands, watching her through slitted eyes. "Shay, what are you doing?"

Blushing, she asked, "Isn't that kind of obvious?"

"Fuck." He closed his eyes and then dropped his head down, resting it on her shoulder. "Damn it, this . . . give me a minute."

"I . . ." She scowled. Then, as the heat faded enough for embarrassment to settle in, she twisted away from him. "Never mind. Take all the minutes you need. Don't you need to get to the store anyway?"

She made it two steps before he snagged the back of her jeans, tugging her to a stop. "Wait just a damn minute," he said, his voice just above a growl.

"I've got work to do."

"Thirty seconds ago, the only thing you seemed interested in doing was me," he pointed out, circling around until he stood in front of her.

Jerking her chin up, she glared at him. "Well, you needed a minute and I changed my fucking mind," she snapped.

"I needed a minute because you go from fragile to hot-damn in five seconds flat and I can't seem to keep up." Frustrated, he shoved a hand through his hair, temper glinting in his eyes. "Damn it, you don't seem to get how much you matter to me, and I don't want to screw this up."

"You're doing a damn good job of showing that," she said, her voice thick with sarcasm. Crossing her arms over her chest, she glared at him. The ache in her chest expanded and she hurt—she actually *hurt* inside because she'd felt lost for want of him and now . . .

"Shay, I don't even know everything that happened to you."

She stared at him.

And the pain shifted and went from hot to cold. Ice took the place of the pain and she spun away, covering her face with her hands. "Go away," she whispered. "Just get the fuck out."

"No." He covered her shoulders with his hands.

She struck backward, driving her elbow hard into his gut. He grunted and muttered, "Good hit."

"I said, *go away*." When he didn't move this time, she brought up her foot to smash the ball of her heel down on the top of his foot. He saw it coming and managed to shift at the last second, but she still caught him with a glancing blow.

"Damn it, Shay—"

His arms came around her, pulling her against him.

She tried to twist away from him. "You son of a bitch, let me go. I thought what happened didn't *matter*," she snarled.

"It doesn't." He slid one arm around her, bracing his hand against her belly. "Not the way you're thinking. But how in the hell am I supposed to touch you without scaring you? And how can I live with myself if I do scare you?"

His lips brushed over her shoulder, left bare by her tank. "I don't want to scare you . . . I don't want to hurt you . . . but I want you more than I want to breathe and you're killing me," he whispered against her skin. "I don't know how to handle this and you're moving at the speed of light here."

As he skimmed a hand up her arm, she shivered. Some of the ice gripping her heart melted, though, as he used the hand on her belly to ease her body closer to his. "Do you really want me to leave, Shay?"

Closing her eyes, she tried to think around the roaring in her ears. Did she want him to leave? She didn't know—did she? And why in the hell was she suddenly expected to think?

Hedging, she asked, "Shouldn't you be at the store?"

"I called Lorna last night and asked her if she'd be okay covering today if I didn't make it in until later." The words were spoken against the curve between her neck and shoulder, and the feel of his lips moving against the skin there was a minor torment.

She groaned and tipped her head to the side.

He kissed her. But that was all he did. That one, soft kiss. Then he murmured against her ear, "You didn't answer me. Do you want me to leave? You can get some work done. I can come back later. Tonight, or in a few days. We can go out to dinner. Talk."

He was leaving this completely up to her, damn it.

Why was this so much harder now?

But she already knew the answer.

She'd slowed down enough to think.

And it was always harder once her brain took control from her body.

Swallowing, she turned around and stared at him.

"You don't want to scare me," she said quietly. "Is that the reason you want to stop?"

CHAPTER
ELEVEN

MyDiary.net/slayingmydragons

DARCY STARED AT THE PAGE, HIT THE REFRESH BUT-ton.

Nothing.

She did it again.

Cleared the cache.

Nothing.

It was after nine in Alaska. Shay rarely slept past seven. She should have done her online journaling by now. It was the one thing that kept her sane, and while she didn't do it every day, she did it on the days when the dreams had been bad.

Last night should have been very, very bad.

Those dragons of hers should have all but eaten her alive.

So what the hell was going on?

And she did such a wonderful fucking job taking care of you . . . didn't she . . . Michelline . . . ?

That was a little surprise she'd been clutching close to her chest for a long, long time. Darcy had damn well expected some kind of response. Her throat ached as she reached up to touch the screen. Although they talked on the phone all the time and emailed, *this* was her strongest connection to Shay.

The online journal.

When Shay was scared, this was how Darcy knew what to say.

When she was pissed, this was how Darcy knew what had upset her.

Although the way Shay was upset lately . . . really, Darcy didn't get that—maybe she needed to think it through a little more. Shay cared about selling books so she could sell *more*, right? Darcy was trying to help her do just that—sell more books by promoting her. Obviously, she'd miscalculated and she needed to fix things, but how could she do that when Shay wasn't reaching *out*?

Touching the monitor, she stared at it, as though that alone would *make* the damn post appear.

She needed to know what happened to Shay last night. Had she dreamed?

Had she made him leave?

Or . . . worse?

"Please, no . . ." Darcy covered her eyes. She didn't even want to think about that. It just wasn't right.

Elliot stared down at her heart-shaped face and wondered if she had any idea how fucking hard it was for him to *not* touch her.

"I don't want to stop," he murmured, shaking his head. He brushed the back of his knuckles down her cheek. "I want you naked and if I have my way, I'll have you naked sometime very, very soon. But I want to know I can do it without scaring you. I want to know I won't hurt you."

She gave him a faint smile, the dimple in her cheek flashing. "Elliot, I don't think you have it in you to hurt a woman. I'm not worried about that." Then she sighed and reached up to rest her hands on his chest. "But I can't promise you I'm not going to get scared. I just can't. Hell, I've never been able to have a sexual relationship, casual or otherwise. Period."

She paused, biting her lip as she worked up her nerve. "You know I'm . . . jumpy," she settled on, glancing at him. She didn't have to explain that. He'd already figured it out and she knew that without asking, because she'd seen it in the way he'd treated her over the years. "But you haven't seen anything. Once, I . . ." She stopped and blew out a breath.

Elliot just waited.

"When I was in college, there was a guy. It was my junior year and we'd been flirting . . . or I'd been trying to flirt and he flirted back." She looked away, staring off into nothing. "I just wanted to feel normal. And he was a nice guy. I liked him. A lot. He was . . . sweet. Patient. He was going to medical school, and I think he knew what had happened with me. He was . . . well, like I said . . . patient. We tried. One time." She grimaced and shot him a look. "I broke his nose. I freaked out the one time we tried to sleep together and I broke his nose."

Elliot cupped his hand over the back of her head and pressed his brow to hers. "My nose has been broken before. I can handle it."

She laughed, the sound caught between tears and relief and other emotions she couldn't define. "Elliot, he told me the same thing. But *I* couldn't handle it. There was this wonderful guy and he couldn't touch me the way we both wanted without me losing it. How do I know I'm not going to do the same thing when *we* try?"

Jealousy burned in him for a brief moment, but he brushed it off. *Doesn't matter—he was important to her and she needed that.* Hell, Shay needed a hell of a lot more than what she'd gotten in life. Taking a deep breath, he stared into her eyes and asked softly, "Do you trust me?"

"If I didn't, I never would have opened my door." She touched his cheek.

"Okay. Then I'm going to do something and if you feel the need to punch me, just let me know. Or . . . well, you could punch me, but you'd probably be sorry for that later. But here's the deal: if you do hit me, you're not allowed to run." He paused and watched as she pulled her head back, still watching him. "Deal?"

"What are you going to do?" she asked warily.

"Not telling you. Just remember . . . you trust me. Deal or not?"

She grimaced. "This is more entertaining when Howie is offering a suitcase full of money."

"Oh, you'll be entertained, I think." Either that, or he'd be dealing with a busted nose. "So . . . deal?"

"Deal." She watched him warily and when he rested a hand on her side, she glared at him, her mouth turning down in a scowl.

"That's it?"

"No." He leaned in and slanted his mouth over hers, stroking his tongue along her lower lip until she opened for him on a shuddering sigh. As she did, he slid his hand up and cupped one round, small breast in his hand.

Shay gasped as he stroked his thumb over the hard, pebbled crest of her nipple. Lifting his head slightly, he whispered, "This is."

Staring into her eyes, he circled her nipple with his thumb. "I've been going out of my mind ever since you came out of your room wearing this damn shirt . . . why did you even bother?"

Shay just shuddered and her gaze darkened to near black. As a weak moan escaped her, he asked, "Are you thinking about punching me?"

"No . . ."

"Good." He continued to toy with her nipple, watching her face, her eyes, for any sign of fear, any sign of nerves. Her slim, strong body was tense and trembling . . . but her fingers dug into his arms and then moved to his waist, gripping him closer.

And every now and then, she moved, slow, hesitant shifts of her hips that had her brushing against the aching ridge of his cock. This was going to be an experiment in control . . . and in sweet, sweet torment, Elliot realized.

Stroking his hand down her side, he rested it under the hem of the tank. "Can I . . . ?"

Shay stared at him, her eyes glassy. "Can you what?"

He eased the shirt higher.

"Oh . . ." She blushed and then nodded, reaching down to tug it up.

"Let me," he whispered, nudging her hands down.

She stood there and let him strip it away and he watched as she started to cover herself—watched as she stopped and lowered her hands, standing there with her head bowed, the dark, choppy strands of her hair falling into her face.

Then he watched as she squared her shoulders before she lifted her head to look him in the eye. As if she was prepared for him to flinch, for him to look away. Reaching up, he cupped her face in his hands and took her mouth. In his mind's eye, he could see the scars, and in another moment he'd see them again, but when he looked at her, all he really saw was her . . .

Her tension had returned when he stripped off her shirt, but as he kissed her, he could feel it creeping away. As she sighed into his mouth, as she swayed against him, he rested his hands on her waist. He stroked them upward until he could cup her breasts. He could feel the faint ridge of a scar here and there, but more, he felt the silken, sweet flesh of her breasts, the hard crests of her nipples . . . and her. Shay. He felt Shay.

But it wasn't enough. Lifting his head, he stared at her. "Do you trust me?" he asked again.

Shay swallowed. Then slowly, she nodded.

As he dipped his head, he loosened his grip on her waist. From the corner of his eye, he saw her hand move. As he closed his mouth around one nipple, she reached for him.

With a cry, she buried one hand in his hair. Her body sagged against his and he braced her weight with his arm around her waist. It was awkward—she was small, almost delicate. Groaning, he boosted her up, balancing her weight in his hands and lifting her breasts so they were level with his mouth.

"Elliot," she yelped, startled.

He slid her a look, staring at her over the curves of her breasts, the taste of her still lingering on his tongue. Squeezing the taut curve of her ass, he said gruffly, "Should I stop?"

Shay stared at him. And then she whispered, "No." She tightened the hand she had in his hair, urging his head back to her breasts. He licked, teased, and softly bit until she was groaning and arching against him, her hips rocking back and forth slowly. The friction was driving him nuts and he doubted she was in much better shape.

Kissing his way up over her collarbone, along the line of her neck to her mouth, he fisted his hand in her hair and covered her mouth with his. She caught him off guard when she cupped his face in her hands and plundered his mouth, her tongue sliding out to tangle with his, a sleek, hot little dart that rubbed over his and toyed and tangled.

It wasn't until they were both starving for air that they broke apart, gasping.

He slid his hand down her back, just inside the waist of her pants, and toyed with the lace he felt along her panties. "I think now sounds like a good time to talk about getting you naked," he whispered against her shoulder.

"We don't really need to talk about it."

Lifting his head, he stared at her flushed face. "You sure?"

She laughed nervously, her eyes glinting with hunger . . . and resolve. He could see that certainty and it burned him straight through to his gut. "Yes," she whispered, wrapping her arms around his neck and pressing her naked breasts to his chest. Shay lowered her head and started to nibble at the flesh along his shoulder. "I'm sure."

The blood drained out of his head and for a moment, he thought he was going to drop her—his knees were feeling . . . No. He was good. His cock pulsed hard, like a bad tooth, and he had to . . . fuck, he had to get her naked, and now sounded really good. Naked, so he could get inside . . .

"*Shit*," he bit off as something occurred to him.

Shay lifted her head from his shoulder. "What?"

"I don't have anything with me, damn it." He groaned. This wasn't happening. Damn it, this wasn't happening.

"What do you mean, you don't have anything?" she asked, some of the heat clearing from her eyes.

"Protection." He unlocked her ankles from behind his back and eased her to the floor. "I wasn't . . . hell, Shay. I came up here to talk to you about the trouble going on, not for this. *Damn* it. Hell of a time for the just-in-case fairy to not be around."

Shay blinked at him. "Did you say 'the just-in-case fairy'?"

"Uh . . ." Elliot felt the slow rush of blood creeping up

his neck. *Shit*. Had he just said that? "Ah, that's a Lorna thing. She used to tease me about making sure I'd have that kind of thing on hand . . . since I wouldn't have a just-in-case fairy . . ."

"Ah, Lorna said you did have one . . . said to check your car." She circled around him and grabbed her phone from the counter, shoving it into his hands. "I didn't know what she was rambling about, but . . ." She finished with a shrug as he read the text.

Elliot blinked at the phone. Then he reached out and hooked his hand over the back of Shay's neck, hauling her against him. Startled, she barely even had time to breathe before his mouth came down on hers with sudden, shocking intensity. And then he was gone, moving out of the kitchen at a pace that was almost a run.

"Elliot?"

She reached up to touch her buzzing lips, but he didn't pause.

"What the . . ."

With a scowl, she grabbed her shirt and tugged it on, then trailed along after him. A blast of cold air came through the door just as she reached the front hall and she saw his back right before he shut the door behind him. Without his coat. Bemused, she headed down the hall and opened the door, arms crossing over her chest. It was still dark out, although the sky was starting to lighten just a little toward the east.

The bright security lights she had installed lit up the grounds enough that she saw Elliot just fine as he came jogging his way back up to her. "What are you doing? It's got to be ten degrees outside," she snapped at him. "Are you . . ."

He crowded her back into the house, dipped his head, and smothered the rest of her words with his mouth. "Remind me to tell my sister thanks," he muttered as he kicked the door shut.

She didn't even have any way of making sense of that. Not until he leaned back and reached for the hem of her shirt. "Didn't we take this off already?" he asked, toying with the fabric.

"I thought we weren't . . . we couldn't . . ."

He pulled something out of his pocket.

Blood rushed to her cheeks as she realized what it was. Condoms. Staring at the strip of foil packets, she said, "You mean to tell me that your sister left rubbers in your car after you called her last night?"

"Yeah. Remind me to tell her thanks." He reached over and hooked his fingers in the front of her pants, tugged her against him. "Come here . . ."

"Why would your sister do that?"

"Probably because she knows I'd never think of it, and because she's always hopeful." He pressed his mouth to her shoulder. "She kept telling me I needed to get back with you. I guess she got all excited when I told her where I was." He lifted his head and studied her, eyes thoughtful. "Are you mad?"

She shrugged. "No . . . I'm not mad. I'm a little embarrassed, thinking that your sister knows, or is maybe thinking . . . hell. Can we stop discussing this? I'm not mad, isn't that enough? I'm not entirely comfortable with this sort of thing, you know."

"We can stop discussing this." He curved his hands over her waist and eased her body against his. "I think we should get right back to where we were . . . and we were right about here, I think. I'm pretty sure I was about to talk you out of your pants, if I remember right."

"I think that sounds just about right." Catching her lower lip between her teeth, Shay glanced around. "We . . . um. We're in the hall."

"Yeah." He frowned, and then caught her hand. "Come on."

She followed along behind him, but he didn't lead her to the bedroom. They stopped in the living room, where the fireplace still crackled along merrily. "I should put out the fire," she said, distracting herself.

She was about to have sex with Elliot—

"No. I like it." He pressed his lips to her neck.

"But . . ."

"Shhh . . ." He guided her to the couch. But not to the front. He leaned against the back, legs spread. He settled his hips against the couch as he guided her closer.

"Here?" She stared at him.

"Why not?" Trailing his fingers down the midline of her body, he said, "Let's get you out of those pants now."

But when he went to reach for the waistband, Shay caught his hands. He stilled.

She reached up and plucked at his sweater. "You're about two seconds away from having me naked and you're still completely dressed." With a glance down, she added, "You even went and put your damn boots on."

"I wasn't about to go out in the snow barefoot," he pointed out. But obligingly, he kicked his boots off. He went to reach for the hem of his sweater, but stopped and let his hands fall to the back of the couch. "I think if you want it off, you should do it."

There was a look in his eyes, Shay thought. She couldn't tell if it was a challenge or an offer . . . maybe it was both. Her heart was practically lodged in her throat and she had to take short, shallow breaths just to get enough air into her lungs. But that was okay.

Taking one small step, she put herself between his wide-spread thighs and fisted her hands in the bottom of his sweater. Staring into the rich, potent gold of his eyes, she dragged the sweater up.

When it caught under his arms, he helped her and in another few seconds, he was naked from the waist up.

Her breath caught. A silver chain glinted around his neck. Curious, she reached up and touched it, tracing its shape. It was a simple silver cross. Cocking a brow, she studied his face. "Am I about to make you commit a carnal sin or something, Elliot?"

"I think I'm pretty involved in anything carnal going on here," he said. He glanced down, then back up at her. "It was my mother's."

"Oh . . ." She knew about his mom. Knew both he and Lorna had loved her, that they still missed her. "I'm sorry."

He shrugged as he dropped his sweater over the back of the couch. "Now do I get to get you naked, Shay? I've only been trying to do it for . . . hell, two years, now?"

"Two years, huh?" She laughed, caught off guard by how amazingly . . . easy . . . it felt to be there with him. It hadn't been like this the one time she'd tried. But then that one time, she hadn't felt like this, either. As her laugh faded away, she smiled at him, resting her hands on the waistband of her pants. "If you've been waiting that long, does a few more minutes really matter all that much?"

"Yes." He tugged her against him.

Shay went willingly, but then she stiffened. "Oh . . ."

"What is it?"

She swallowed, closing her eyes as she let herself absorb the feel of him. Naked skin pressed against her own . . . that was . . . *wow.* She couldn't think of any way to describe it.

"Shay?"

His hand feathered across her brow and she made herself open her eyes, smile at him. "This is going to sound stupid, but I . . ." She looked down, staring at his bare chest pressed to hers. "Damn it, Elliot. All of this is new, okay?"

"That's not stupid." He kissed her, sucking her lower

lip into his mouth, as one hand came up to cup her breast. "It's not stupid. It's amazing . . . you're amazing. And I'll do my damnedest to make certain it's amazing for you."

This time, as he reached down for the pants, she had nothing to say. She suspected they'd already said enough. She let him strip them away and then, without another word from him, she stripped his away. He caught the denim from her before she could toss it on the floor, though, and she watched as he took one of the foil packets from the pocket.

Her breath caught as she stood there, distracted for just a brief moment, as he did that.

She was really going to do this—

Don't think, she warned herself. *Whatever you do, don't think.*

She stared at Elliot. She'd think about him. About this . . .

He dropped the condom on the back of the couch— she was so damn glad she'd bought the one with that wide, fat-pillowed sort of top—and shifted back toward her.

Wearing nothing but a snug-fitting pair of boxers, that silver chain, and that intense look on his face. All of it focused on her.

"Shay?"

She swallowed and then whispered, "Quit looking at me like you expect me to change my mind."

"Are you going to?"

"Hell, no." And before he could do or say anything, she hooked her fingers in the waistband of her panties and dragged them down. As she straightened up in front of him, she wondered if she should warn him . . .

Elliot groaned. And as he reached for her, all thoughts fled from her mind. She was done thinking, damn it. She could just feel, right? Couldn't she just *feel* . . .

As he pulled her against him, she braced herself once more for that shocking, heated sensation of his bare flesh against hers. Once again, it was completely breath-stealing. And she felt more of him. Almost all of him now. Just his boxers separated them and as she slid her hands inside the waistband, cupping her hands over his hips, she whispered, "Now you're the one who needs to get naked."

"In a minute," he rasped, his hands settling on her hips.

One hand slid around, cupping her between her thighs. Shay tensed.

"No," she said, shaking her head. "Now . . . please. Elliot . . ."

She pushed his boxers out of the way.

"Shay, what's wrong?"

"Nothing!" She closed her eyes, resting her head on his shoulder, struggling to calm the terror that was trying to edge inside. She wasn't afraid of him. She just couldn't explain anything else right now and if he touched her there—

"Can you just let me do what I want, Elliot?" she asked quietly. "Please?"

He was quiet.

Lifting her head, she stared at him, certain she'd screwed it up. She had . . . she knew it. But as their gazes locked, he dipped his head and pressed his lips to hers. "Have your way with me, baby. I'm yours . . . always."

"Then can you just . . ." *Do me* . . . That didn't sound right. She was too nervous to say *fuck me*. Desperate for this to happen before she lost the words, before she lost this delicious heat, she reached out and grabbed the condom he'd set on the couch and pushed it into his hand. "I don't want to wait. Not this time. Not for anything. Is that okay?"

"Anything you want is okay."

She closed her eyes and rested her head against his shoulder, breathing in the scent of wood smoke, after-shave, and Elliot, listening as the foil tore, feeling the warmth of his skin. Thinking about him, just him. Only him. As long as she did that . . .

"Look at me," he whispered, a moment later.

She felt his hands on her hips as she lifted her lashes and tipped her head back to study him. Dark eyes—liquid gold—stared into hers and she fell. Lost in him, so lost.

"You can't know how many times I dreamed about this," he muttered, pulling her closer.

She wrapped her arms around his neck. She wanted to tell him that she dreamed about it, too. Swallowing, she pressed her lips to his. "I've thought about this. A lot. I don't dream nice things too often, but maybe you can give me better things to dream about."

"Yeah. Let's see if we can do that."

She felt the length of him against her belly, slick and sheathed with the rubber. Then she felt him lifting her, turning so that her weight was braced on the couch. "You okay?" he asked softly, drawing her knees up, opening her.

"Yes . . ." She gasped as the head of his cock brushed against her. *Ohhhh* . . .

For a brief moment something ugly and dark danced in the back of her mind. *Cunt—stupid cunt, did you think I wouldn't find you* . . .

"Look at me, Shay," Elliot said, his voice gruff, steady.

Her head fell back. And once more, he was all she saw, all she felt, and every thought was of him.

"Just keep looking at me."

As she watched him, he slowly pushed inside.

Her eyes darkened almost to black . . .

But they stayed locked on his. That was all Elliot

needed to see. A slow flush crept up her neck, her face, staining her cheeks a light pink as he eased deeper, deeper into her body. Tight, so fucking tight. She gripped him like a fist. And all the while, she watched him, as if nothing else existed. Under his fingers, her skin felt soft as silk, and her slight, lean body felt both fragile and strong against his.

She caught her breath and he shuddered as she shifted, moving against him. It had her tightening around him and it was just too much—she was so fucking tight already. He groaned and released one hip, resting his hand on the couch next to her, gripping the fabric desperately. *Breathe . . . just breathe . . .* he told himself.

When she wiggled again, he slid deeper, and he had to bite back a curse as she tightened. Withdrawing, he sucked in a desperate breath. There were stars dancing in front of his eyes—he could practically count them.

"You okay?"

He smiled down at her. "Never better." It was both the biggest lie he'd ever told and the most honest he'd ever been. It was possible to be in both the most excruciating pain and to experience the sweetest pleasure, all at once. And right now, he was there. Trapped right there on the razor's edge of pain and pleasure, and Shay was asking him if he was okay.

Stroking a hand up her back, he twined his fingers in her hair and leaned in, pressing his lips to one eye, then the other. Each cheekbone. The scars along the side of her face. Then her mouth. And with each brush of his lips, he worked deeper into her body. Fighting against that delicious, and deadly, tight embrace. It drove him insane the way she kept wiggling against him, trying to adjust to him.

Easier, he thought, to do it this way.

Then, he was buried inside her, so deep inside, he thought he just might be able to feel her heart beat. So deep inside her, he could feel her in his soul. But then again, she'd been there for quite a long while already.

Lifting his head, he stared down at her and asked, "What about you . . . are you okay?"

The black fringe of her lashes swept down, shielding her eyes. And there was a Mona Lisa smile on her lips . . . one that set his blood to burning, just to see it. "Oh, never better," she murmured, her voice barely above a purr. "Never better."

Then she arched her neck back and rocked against him. The action lifted her breasts and he caught sight of the scars again—it was a hot, dangerous punch, and the grip he had on her hips tightened. Dipping his head, he buried his face against her neck as he started to pump within her. *Not here . . . not now . . .*

It was nothing like she'd imagined. And yet, it was everything. She really could experience that pleasure, and she really could experience that connection. And when he took her, he made all those silly things she'd read about in romance novels seem not so silly. But then again, Elliot had always been like that . . . he'd always made her heart race, had always made her breath catch . . . and when he looked at her, he made her feel incredibly beautiful, despite her scars, despite her flaws.

Right now, as he stroked inside her, she felt no fear. It was a miracle. His big hands stroked over her body and there was no sign that her scars bothered him. It was amazing. When he tilted her head back and kissed her yet again, Shay could have cried, it was so amazing. Then he cupped one breast in his hand and dipped his head, catching her nipple between his teeth to give it a gentle tug and she heard somebody shriek—it was her own voice. Hot, fiery pleasure bolted through her, from her breasts straight down to her core, and she arched against him. It drove him deeper inside her, changing the angle so that he hit a certain spot. Shay knew all about that spot, but it wasn't anything she'd ever tried to experience on her own. For a second, she froze. Every muscle in her body tensed and she felt herself clamping tight around him.

Elliot gave a ragged groan and she stared at him. Gold eyes locked on her own. "Shay . . . ?"

With a whimper, she moved—it was the slightest movement. She needed to feel that again . . . *oh*.

Just . . . *oh*.

She cried out. Gripping his hips with her knees, she started to move, slowly at first, then harder. Again—again. Each time, it had the head of his cock brushing just there and it was more than she could take, more pleasure than she knew how to handle. She fought to balance her body, but then his hands were there, gripping her butt and steadying her weight as she rode him. The climax hit her and it was every damn thing she'd never even thought to hope for.

Elliot rasped out her name, but she barely heard him over her own broken moan. The pleasure exploded through her, shattering her . . . completing her.

When she could think again, Shay realized they were lying on the couch. Or rather, Elliot was. She was lying on him. The fire had warmed the room, which was good, because she was a little bit chilly in the spots where his body wasn't touching her. Sweat was drying on her skin, and she could smell the scent of him on her.

His fingers combed through her hair and she lay there for a moment, just enjoying it.

Eyes closed, smiling, and just . . . enjoying.

"I think I might be able to move sometime in the next century," Elliot said softly. "Hope that's soon enough."

"Hmmmm." Shay stretched and smiled when she felt the length of him against her belly. He was already hard again. How about that . . . hard, already, and she liked it. She was actually kind of excited about that. "I don't think it *is* soon enough. I think I'd like to do that again. Is that okay?"

"I don't know. I need to think about it." He was quiet for a beat of two seconds. Then he said, "I've thought about it. It sounds good to me."

Shay giggled and lifted her head, staring down at him. "I'm questioning my sanity, you know. I don't know why I was so nervous about this. I shouldn't have been."

"You're too hard on yourself." He stared at her, a dark, brooding look on his face. The burnished auburn of his hair framed his face and his golden eyes looked even more intense in the flickering firelight. He lifted a hand and traced the top edge of one of her scars. "I knew something bad had happened to you, Shay." Through his lashes, he shot her a quick look and then lowered his gaze again. "I just knew. But I didn't know . . ."

She closed a hand around his wrist. "I'm glad you didn't know. You really think I *want* people knowing it was something that bad, Elliot? I have a hard enough time living with the knowledge on my own. I don't want others having that in their head."

"I'm not others." He left off tracing the scars to reach up and cup her cheek. "You know that, right? You're more to me than just . . . this. I'm serious about you and I have been from the beginning. Whatever is happening here, it's not casual for me. It never was."

She blushed, averting her eyes. "Yeah. I know that." Scowling, she shot him a sidelong look. "You know, in theory, it's supposed to be the guy who has trouble talking about his feelings . . . not the girl."

"Well, in theory, lots of things are true. We're not theories . . . we're people." He hooked a hand over the back of her head and tugged her closer.

Shay went willingly, cuddling against his chest and smiling as he kissed her. "It's not casual for me, either. It never was. If it was casual, this wouldn't have happened."

"I know." He had his other hand resting low on her spine, doing things that made it hard for her to concentrate on the conversation. "Since it's not casual, I guess you probably realize that it makes sense that I know certain things . . . right?"

Shay made a face at him. "Things, yes. The ugliest shit in my head . . . no. The nightmares? That's not so easy to share."

"I could share mine," he offered.

She cocked a brow. "What kind of nightmares and shames do you have?"

Elliot's face darkened. "There are things. Things I'd rather never talk about but they are there. We'll talk about them, if you want to. But my screw-ups are mine—messes I landed in. What happened to you— Shay, this was *done* to you. My fuck-ups happened because of bad choices for the most part, or accidents. But what happened to you . . ."

"Yeah." She wiggled around until she was wedged into the small area between his body and the back of the couch. Staring at the fireplace, she said, "I get that. I really do. But there's no denying I've got issues, Elliot. I'm going to have them all of my life, and anybody who wants to be a part of my life needs to be aware of it."

She slanted a look at him. "Obviously you're aware and you're just too stupid to care how much this fucks up my head."

"You're not fucked up." Poking her in the ribs, he settled around on the couch a little more and then propped his head on his hand. "You're looking comfortable there. Does that mean you're not jumping me again?"

"Did I jump you?" She grinned at him.

"Just about. I think I've got scratch marks on my shoulders. I loved every second."

Still grinning, Shay said, "I don't think scratch marks count as jumping. But maybe it's a starting point. I think I'll work my way up to jumping you. It could be fun."

"Well, you already had your way with me . . ."

Then the phone rang. Once more, the outside world shattered Shay's peace.

The events of the past few days had her scrambling off the couch, even though she doubted it was either of the people she wanted to reach.

For once, she was wrong.

Or almost. It wasn't her agent, and it wasn't her editor—but it *was* the assistant editor.

CHAPTER
TWELVE

Two minutes into the conversation, she wasn't entirely certain this was going to be much help.

"Hmmm . . . well, this is strange. But you're certain it's not your page. You have an assistant, after all. This isn't something she set up for you?"

Distantly aware of Elliot's gaze, Shay stopped in mid-step and lowered the phone, staring at it. *Did I fall into the twilight zone?*

Once she'd managed to snap her jaw shut, she lifted the phone back to her ear and managed to snap, "Yes. I'm pretty damn sure it's not my page. If it was *my* page, I wouldn't have sent about a dozen emails to you guys over this, now would I?"

"Okay . . . just bear with me. I want to help, Shay, really."

You want to help. Then tell me you can get the damn page down, she thought sourly.

"If you're certain your assistant didn't set it up, do you have any idea who might have done it?"

Shay had to bite her lip, because she couldn't *say* she was certain Darcy hadn't done it. The problem was Darcy hadn't done it with her authorization and if Darcy was doing it, she was *pretending* to be her, damn it.

Once more, Shay found herself thinking, *Darcy, is it you . . . ?*

"No, Julie. I don't know who is doing it. I just know I want it down."

"I understand. You know Maurice is still out for a few weeks with his wife and the new baby, but we'll get to work on this and see what we can find out," Julie said. "I'll look around, see if I can find out more information, and I'll speak with the legal department. If the page is a fraud, I'm certain Facebook will take action. I'll be in touch."

Then she was gone.

Shay was left there, holding the phone and listening to dead air.

Frowning, she lowered it, staring at the handset. "If." Narrowing her eyes, she tossed the phone onto the couch and started to pace. "*If* the page is a fraud."

"What do you mean . . . *if*?"

Turning around, Shay stared at Elliot and said softly, "That's how she said it. *If* that page is a fraud. I don't get it. Why would she phrase it that way? I'd know if it was my page, right? So if I'm telling her it's *not* . . ."

That tension continued to churn in her gut and she groaned, dropping to the window seat.

"I take it that didn't go exactly as planned." He settled down next to her.

"Elliot, my *life* hasn't gone exactly as planned in so many months . . . hell, longer." Then she made a face and glanced at him. "Well, to be honest, my life was never really planned anyway, but every once in a while, would it really be so bad not to have a huge wrench thrown into things when I'm finally coasting by? Is that too much to ask?"

"You managed to go awhile with me without a wrench," he said, nuzzling her neck.

"True." She pursed her lips, studying the flames of the

fire as they danced. "Then I just turned myself into a wrench, remember."

Huffing out a soft breath, she eased away from him and swiped her hands down her pants. She'd tugged them on in the middle of the phone call—she just couldn't have that conversation naked. Too bad it hadn't helped. She swallowed as she tried to figure out where to go from here, tried to pretend she wasn't as nervous as she felt. Nobody needed to know she was scared, after all. She'd lived with fear all of her life, and other than Virna . . . and Elliot, most people hadn't ever realized it. No reason for that to change now.

"You didn't turn yourself into a wrench," Elliot said from behind her.

"No. I just made it all but impossible for you to be with me." *If I kept you away, you couldn't hurt me. If you couldn't hurt me, I was safer.*

But she'd also been lonelier. A fact she could admit, now.

He moved to stand in front of her, cupping her face in his hands. "You let me close enough last night. Earlier."

Heat buzzed along her skin as he dipped his head and pressed his lips to hers. "Yeah. I guess I did."

"You don't plan on pulling back, do you?"

The raw vulnerability she heard in his voice hit her square in the gut. Easing her head back, she stared into his eyes. "No," she murmured. She touched her fingertips to his lips and shook her head. "I plan on not pulling back. And that's one plan I don't mind making."

"Good."

Sighing, she rested her head on his shoulder and just let herself relax. Take in his warmth, his strength . . . and *him*. He was there. He knew her secrets, knew her scars . . . most of them, anyway. Grimacing, she pushed that thought out of her head. She had enough to deal with, just trying to adjust to what had happened with them, what *was* happening . . . and the hell that was going on in her business life.

Speaking of which . . . she had to get back to that hell, and she couldn't do it with him here. She'd never be able to concentrate, never be able to think. "I need to get to work," she said softly. "I haven't written more than a few pages since the accident. And I have to try to get hold of my agent again. She's not returning my emails, and that's not like her."

She gave him a glancing kiss on the cheek and then made her way to her desk, acutely aware of his intense, watchful stare. "That sounds a lot like 'you're dismissed,'" he mused.

"It's not a dismissal." Shay settled her weight into the chair, grimacing a little as muscles she wasn't used to using twinged in protest. Then she spun around and made herself look at him. It would be a lot easier to stare at the monitor, but if she'd told him she wasn't going to run, she *wouldn't* run, not even in a situation like this—and avoiding his gaze while she talked was a form of hiding. "I'm not trying to run away or hide or anything," she said, reaching for a pen and turning it over and over in her hands. "But my head is still spinning. Things are insane up here."

Closing her eyes, she thought of the episode from last night . . . *Michelline* . . .

Even now, goose bumps broke out over her skin and she could almost feel the weight of something enormous pressing against that impenetrable wall of her memories. There were things waiting back there. Just waiting for her to look at them. And she had to look. Had to keep pressing against that wall until it crumbled.

Do you remember what happened . . . ?

"There's too much going on. It's not just us," she said, staring into his eyes. "Although that's big enough for me. And it's a good thing, but it's still weird. There's this mess going on with my career, and I've got to get it sorted out. My writing . . . Elliot, it's my lifeline. I have to find this person and deal with it."

"I understand."

Those words, so simply stated, had her throat knotting up. "Thank you."

He jerked a shoulder in a shrug. "Doesn't mean I like leaving." He scowled a little, bumping one of the boxes of books with his foot. "What about the woman from earlier . . . Darcy?"

"My assistant." Shay sighed and closed her eyes, resting her head on the back of the chair. "Damn it. She's involved in this somehow. I just need to figure out how."

"Somehow?" He stared at her. "She's the one who called you *Michelline*. She triggered . . . whatever happened last night. That memory thing. She's got to know something."

She triggered it . . .

Staring at him, Shay felt as though the earth had opened up and swallowed her whole.

Shit.

Oh. Fucking. Shit.

She hadn't made that connection—

Why . . . ? Immediately her brain popped up with a dozen reasons why—the shock of the nightmare, stress, lack of sleep . . . sex with Elliot. Any of the above, all of the above. But the connection was there, and damn it, she had to look at it.

Son of a bitch. She'd already accepted the fact that Darcy was the one jacking around with her life. But *how* did Darcy know about *her*?

"Shay?"

The overly bright smile she gave him was enough to make his heart hurt.

"Yeah?"

"Are you okay?"

"I'm fine," she said, and he knew, as sure as he knew his own name, that she was lying through her teeth. "Is it okay if I call you later? Maybe I can come into town, we can go out to eat or something . . . ?"

"Sure." He waited a moment.

All she did was nod. "Okay. Great."

A moment later, she spun around in her seat and he watched as she started to peck away at the keys of her computer furiously, shoulders hunched in a way that made him understand why her neck was always so damn tight.

Blowing out a soft breath, he closed the distance between them. She stiffened. But he'd be damned if he let her put them back where they'd been yesterday. Gliding a hand down her shoulder, he pressed a kiss to the nape of her neck. "If you don't call me, I'll probably call you. See you soon?"

She surprised him by turning her head around to meet his. "Hmmm, definitely."

"Good." Slanting his mouth over hers, he stole a quick kiss. "Think of me, Shay."

"How can I not?"

Before he could try and push for more, he made himself leave. She needed some room. Needed to settle, to think. He could understand that, mostly. But damned if he had to like it.

Besides, once he was out of here, he was going to start trying to see what he could find out about this so-called *Shane*. Not Shay, but the other one.

He knew more than a few of his friends had been caught off guard by her accusations and he remembered some of the names from her "friend" list. Lorna, smart woman that she was, had made screencaps of the fake Shane's account.

He was going to start asking questions. After all, she

was screwing with *his* life, too. Shay had been more than clear about that. He might as well start working on getting some of those answers.

The sound of Elliot leaving had to be one of the loneliest sounds she'd ever heard. But she had to get him out of there; she had to think, and she didn't think she was going to be in a good place when she was done. If he was there, she was going to let herself weaken, maybe let herself lean on him.

Maybe even let herself not do what she knew she had to do. Now wasn't the time to be weak.

She triggered it.

That was what Elliot said—Darcy had triggered whatever episode Shay had had last night. That memory blip. Shay didn't particularly *want* to remember those years; all the dragons, all the nightmares she dealt with, stemmed from those years. But maybe if she faced them, dealt with them, she could banish them forever and move on.

After all, how much worse could those years *be* compared to what had been done to her fifteen years ago?

Did you really think I wouldn't find you . . . little cunt . . .

"Not *now*," she muttered, fisting a hand and pressing it to her forehead.

But what had Darcy said?

Shay couldn't remember much more than a few minutes into the conversation, and then the name. Everything else was a hazy fog of fear and adrenaline.

Can you tell us what happened, Michelline?

"No. That's not right." Shaking her head, she rose from the chair and made her way to the window. Past and present tried to come together on her, but that wasn't it. That was Virna's voice.

Memories from the night she'd been rescued from hell.

Leaning against the solid wood casement of the window, she let it support her body as she stared outside, watching Elliot deal with the snow that had fallen, watching as he knocked it off the car, then as he went and did the same to her truck. The sight of it brought a smile to her face. Nobody ever did that for her. It was . . . nice. Yeah. It was nice, she thought, having somebody there to take care of her. Nice having somebody trying to take care of her . . .

"That's it," she whispered, stunned.

Elliot was circling around his car now, and she straightened, staring at him but hardly seeing him as that voice echoed in her mind.

Taking care of her . . .

She did such a wonderful fucking job taking care of you . . . didn't she . . . Michelline . . . ?

Darcy's voice had been angry. Hurtful. Hateful. And certain—

Swaying with the knowledge that flooded her head, she lifted her hand and braced it on the window, her gaze seeking out Elliot's face. Just one more look. One look, and she could think her way through this.

He slanted his gaze in her direction and mouthed, *Bye.*

Swallowing, she nodded.

As he drove away, she turned back to the computer.

Before she went and lost her mind, before she went and did *anything* else, she needed to know—who *was* Michelline?

There was only one person who might know some of those answers. At least, one person who was alive. But the question was . . . would Angie tell her?

Pacing the floor, holding the phone, Shay called Angie.

When she wasn't there, she left a message.

Then, because she couldn't take the chance that she'd chicken out, she sent her sister an email.

Angie . . .

I know this isn't easy, but I have some questions about my life before I came to live with you all. Mom never told me much. Did she ever talk to you about it? Do you know what my name was?

Leaning back, Shay stared at the screen and went to hit *send*. Then she stopped herself. Before she could change her mind, she added:

Was my name Michelline? I'm not talking about the name change after Mom. From before. When I was little.

Shay didn't mention their mother's death. That wasn't needed. Angie would know. Holding her breath, she hit *send*. Then she logged into her online diary, desperate to do something, *anything* that would get that name out of her mind. Anything that would *clear* her mind, and maybe silence the screams that were trying to creep in. The screams, and those whispers that usually only crept in during the dark night hours.

Can you tell us what happened, Michelline?

While the voices and memories and nightmares raged in her head, she started to write.

I've had a couple of different names . . . more than most people, I know. But I think this was my *real* name—the one I was given when I was born. V changed it. I was too little to understand, and it didn't occur to me to care. I was loved, cared for, and she had made sure I had plenty to eat . . . what did it matter if she wanted to call me a different name?

But there shouldn't be anybody who really knows that name.

Anybody who remembers it, really.

I don't. Or I didn't. Because I'd blocked it out.

Only a few people would know it.
Somebody used it earlier.
Called me by that name.
How would she know it?
How would anybody know . . . unless they knew me then?

Brooding, Shay skimmed the post and then published it to her diary. It didn't help things solidify in her mind any. It didn't seem possible, or even likely, that Darcy *knew* her from back then.

How could she?

But if she didn't, how would she know that name?

She couldn't think of any answers, though, and until Angie got back to her, it was just speculation anyway. Maybe that hadn't even *been* her name. Sighing, she skimmed through her email. It was all but exploding now that she didn't have Darcy accessing it anymore to clear out the business issues and the spam. Nothing from Anna, and nothing from Julie.

But hallelujah! There *was* an email from Facebook. Shay could have wept. There was one from Twitter, too. And *yes*—both pages were down.

"Thank God," she muttered. "Finally."

One thing off her list. Now . . . for another.

If Anna wasn't emailing, then it was time to call the office.

CHAPTER
THIRTEEN

"LOOK AT YOU . . ."

Elliot came to a stop, standing in the doorway, not caring about the 12-degree weather at his back. Lifting his hand, he pointed at his sister. "Don't say a damn thing," he warned. That cat-ate-the-canary grin on her face boded bad things, and he wasn't having this conversation in public. Preferably *ever*.

"Hey, is that any way to speak to somebody who went out of her way to bring you a present?" Lorna asked, smiling angelically. Leaning forward, she braced an elbow on the counter and waggled her eyebrows at him. "So . . . did you need it?"

"I'm a grown man, damn it. I can take care of myself, you know."

"So you did need it." Lorna's grin widened. "If you didn't, you would have just laughed at me."

Elliot rolled his eyes and came inside, letting the door shut behind him. After he hung up his parka, he glanced around the store. The store was empty. Normally, he hated that, but just then, he was just fine with it, because he was not in the mood to see anybody, except Shay. "You okay if I go take a shower, grab a bite?"

If he could eke out a few more minutes, he might even send out a few emails, check with those friends of his.

All he wanted to do was see if this Darcy chick or Shane or whoever in the fuck she was had contact with anybody besides him. It wouldn't take long.

Of course, judging by the look in his sister's eyes, she wasn't going to give him time to *breathe*, much less shower and send out emails.

"She such a party animal you couldn't eat all night?" Lorna grinned at him, a sly look in her eyes.

Under any other circumstances, it would have just made him shake his head.

But these weren't normal circumstances. And all of a sudden, it dropped down on him. The weight he'd been trying to ignore, the rage he'd been fighting to hold back.

All of it hit him and it was now crushing him.

Closing his eyes, he said, "Lorna . . . don't. Okay?"

"Hey . . . is everything okay?" Lorna cocked her head, studying him.

She must have seen something in his eyes, heard it in his voice. "Oh, shit, Elliot, don't tell me you two fought already."

"No." He gave her a tired smile. "No, it's not that. I think . . ."

Memories of the scars flashed through his mind, and abruptly, the fury he'd been holding in check exploded. "*Fuck*." He slammed his fist down on the counter, but it didn't do a damn thing to expel the rage he had trapped inside him.

"Whoa . . ." Lorna moved around the counter and rushed to the front door. She locked it and flipped the *Be Back Soon* sign over, then came to him. With the bravery only siblings can possess, she grabbed his arm and started to pull on him.

"Leave me alone now, Lorna—you want to leave me alone." *Leave me alone so I can fall apart. Explode. Something—*

"No, I want to kick your ass the way I did when we were kids, but you had to go and grow a foot and a half taller and join the military," she snapped. "But I can kick you in the balls and I remember most of the dirty tricks Paul taught me, so I can still hurt you."

"Lorna . . ."

But he was too tired to fight her. Fighting his fury was draining. It didn't help that every time he closed his eyes, he saw those scars. Those awful scars. How could somebody do that—

Stop it, he told himself. Not now. He had to get a grip on this fury because if he didn't, he was going to find himself on a flight to Phoenix, where he'd be hunting that son of a bitch down and killing him.

Slow.

And then he'd end up with his ass in jail and he wouldn't be able to be with Shay.

Sometimes, subtlety wasn't his strong point.

So because Shay mattered, he had to get this fury under wraps. Had to.

He let Lorna take him to the office and he threw himself down on the couch, staring up at the ceiling with eyes that burned while the acid of his rage ate a hole inside him.

"What's wrong, El?" Lorna asked softly.

"I can't talk about it." He shook his head. Those were Shay's secrets, and he'd be damned if he broke that confidence.

"How much of this has to do with Shay being Shane Neil?" Lorna asked quietly.

Elliot shot her a look.

She arched a brow. "Hey, what am I, stupid? You beat it out of here like a bat out of hell, and then a couple of hours later, call me from her place. She up and buys all of the signed books, she takes the ARC, the bizarre message pops up . . . and you *believed* it. You wouldn't have bought it from just anybody, you know. It's the only thing that made sense."

"Shit." He covered his face with his hands. "Don't go mentioning it to people, Lorna. And I mean *to anybody*—not even your boyfriend. She keeps it quiet for a reason."

"I kind of figured that out already. Otherwise, she would have told you ages ago." She leaned against the desk, watching him. "You're not mad at her about this, are you? I mean, she had to have her reasons."

"I'm not mad at Shay," he said quietly. His heart was fucking breaking for her, but he wasn't mad.

She blew out a breath and shoved a hand through her red hair. "Damn it, is everything okay with you two? I mean, I keep hoping it will work with you. I see how—"

"We're fine. I broke it off because she kept pulling back and I couldn't keep falling harder and harder for a woman who held me at arm's length." Closing his eyes, he said, "She's not doing that anymore."

"So what's the problem?"

Slowly, he sat up, opening his eyes to stare at her. Easier, he thought, to look at her, look at anything. When he closed his eyes, he kept seeing those scars, what had been done to Shay and how she must have suffered; and he remembered how they'd let that bastard out. *Why?* He'd served his time?

Fuck.

Reaching for one of the worn pillows on the couch, he shook his head. "You know that saying . . . be careful what you wish for? I got what I wished for. She was always so closed off, wouldn't open up to me, wouldn't trust me. Things changed. I want her, I always have. I just don't know if I'm strong enough to handle everything I'll have to handle now."

"What do you mean?"

He shook his head. "Those are her secrets, sis. Goes a

lot deeper than her Batman writing persona thing, too."
Twisting the pillow in his hands, he wished he could
just tear it apart—tear *anything* apart. It might help
lessen the rage. Maybe.

Feeling the weight of his sister's gaze, he looked up.

"So it's her burden . . . one she chose to share with
you," Lorna said slowly. "I think that means you're already strong enough. She's cautious for a reason, El.
You and I both figured that out awhile ago. Don't sell
yourself short; don't go doubting yourself already."

She came over and bent down, pecked his cheek. "It
will be okay."

Then she left.

Elliot was alone with nothing but his rage and the
memories of scars he couldn't heal.

Her gut was in knots.

The day had come with good news and bad news.
Twitter and Facebook were down. An hour after they'd
gone down, she'd heard from Goodreads. *That* page
was down, too.

Finally. Progress . . . on one front.

She'd left message after message at her agent's office,
and now it was almost four o'clock New York time. If
she didn't hear something soon, it would be tomorrow
at the earliest before she heard *anything*.

Then the phone rang, and *yes*. It was the agency.

But not Anna . . . it was Trish, Anna's assistant.

"I'm sorry, Ms. Morgan, but she's not available to
return your calls at this time."

"What do you mean, she's not available to return my
calls?" Shay asked, her voice shaking. She hated the
sound of that. One of the few people she'd been counting on, and Anna wouldn't *talk* to her? *Fuck*, what was
she supposed to do now? And damn it, why wouldn't
Anna talk to her?

That ugly monster of paranoia grew another ten or twenty feet, at least.

"She's just not available to nonclients right now. Ms. Kent is extremely busy. I'll take your information and if she has time—"

For a moment, the words just didn't connect in her brain—she'd *heard* them and she knew what Trish had said. The words just *didn't make sense*. But once they made sense, panic wrapped its tight, slimy fist around Shay's gut and the words exploded from her in a hot, uncontrolled rush.

"What do you mean, *non*client? Trish, she's my damn agent!" Shay squeezed her eyes closed.

"No. She's not." There was a brief pause, and then the assistant said softly, "You ended the relationship between you and Ms. Kent nearly four months ago."

Ended the relationship.

All the strength drained out of her legs and she sagged against the nearest upright surface. It happened to be the bar. Convenient, that.

She reached for the nearest bottle of liquor. It happened to be rum. Even more convenient. Rum might just help her get through this.

She splashed some into a glass and hoped her legs would be steady enough to carry her into the kitchen so she could get some Diet Coke. She needed a fucking drink *now*.

"Ended the relationship . . ." she echoed. "No, I sure as hell did not."

"Ms. Morgan, you did."

As pain started to pulse once more in the back of her skull, Shay shoved off the bar and started for the kitchen. "Exactly *who* says I ended the relationship?"

"Your email to Ms. Kent, if I recall correctly. There was an attachment, a PDF with your signature on it, stating that while you'd enjoyed the arrangement you had, it was time that you branched in a different direction. There's a copy of both the letter and the email in your file. Would you like me to forward it to you?"

"Yes." She just barely managed to keep from growling the word. Anger gave her the strength she needed to get into the kitchen, though. Diet Coke in hand, she splashed some into the glass and then tossed back half of the drink. "I also want to know *what* email address it came from, when it was dated, and why Anna didn't call me to discuss this, because I damn well didn't *send* it and if she'd called me, I could have told her that."

"I believe she did call. You never returned her calls."

Shay took another gulp. Ever since Elliot had left, a malicious, nasty headache had been brewing in the back of her head; now it struggled to break free of its chain. She knew if it got the better of her, it would be taking gleeful, happy bites out of her brain matter and she'd be lucky if she didn't end up puking her guts out.

A migraine—just wonderful. On top of everything else.

"I never received any calls," she said quietly. "Not one."

"I don't see how, Ms. Morgan. I called you three times myself."

Setting the glass down, she pressed her fist to her brow. Then she took a deep breath. She needed to get Anna on the phone. Somehow. Anna knew her. Knew she wasn't a ditz, knew she wasn't crazy—or too crazy, anyway. But she wasn't going to get Anna on the phone if she was mean to the assistant on the phone now.

"Can I ask you a favor, Trish? What number did you call?"

She heard a faint sigh across the line. "Ms. Morgan—"

"Shay. And please. Humor me. Something seriously fu—ah, really weird is going on. Just help me out a minute more. Did you call me at this number? Or a different one?"

"Hmm. No. Actually, I was surprised that you'd called from this number . . . we received an email last summer that you'd changed your home number." She recited a number that wasn't familiar to Shay.

She jotted it down and she'd damn well be calling it, but it wasn't *her* number. "That's not my number, Trish. I don't know *who* that number belongs to, but it isn't me."

This time, there was just silence on the phone. After ten seconds of it, Shay said, "When you couldn't get hold of me on that line, did anybody call my cell? Anna had the number."

"We were given a new cell phone number as well. I believe it was the same area code as the other number, but I'd have to check my records to be sure."

A humorless laugh escaped Shay. "A new cell. How come I'm *not* surprised . . ." She stared at the number she'd written down. "Can you get me that number?"

"Ah, perhaps I should speak to Ms. Kent . . ."

"Yeah. You do that, and when you do, tell her I'd like to speak with *my agent*. At *this* number. No matter what you get via email, don't change the number you have on file for me unless I call you from *this* number and ask you to change it." She gave her the right number and then asked, "Any idea when I can expect to hear from her?"

"Well, it could be a couple of weeks." Trish's voice had more warmth to it, maybe even a hint of an apology. "She's in Europe for one of the big conferences she attends every year."

"Great."

"She calls a couple of times a week. I just spoke with her yesterday so I'm not expecting to hear from her for a few days, but I do have a number to contact her for emergencies. I'll contact her, let her know there was some sort of misunderstanding."

"This isn't a misunderstanding, Trish. That email you have is a fake and the agency accepted it, without even talking to me." She shouldn't have said that—things were bad enough without putting anybody on the defensive. But damn it, *she* was on the defensive now. "Please, if you can get Anna to call me, I'd appreciate it."

She forced herself to smile, although she doubted it would show in her voice. "She's the only agent I've ever worked with. I can't imagine working with anyone else."

"I'll pass it on." Trish hesitated for a moment and then added, "I know she was really upset when she got the letter. If you didn't send it . . . well, do you know who did?"

"Possibly, although I can't be absolutely certain. I can say that it's probably part of the problem I need to discuss with Anna, though. I also need to see that letter."

"I'll do what I can. I have that cell phone number." Trish gave her the number and Shay jotted it down as well.

"I'll have Anna get in touch with you as quickly as I can," Trish promised.

"Thank you." Shay wrapped up the conversation, and although Trish didn't outright say it, she had a feeling she'd be getting a copy of that email shortly. Good. Bits and pieces of information—it was more than she'd had earlier in the day. Staring at the phone number she held, she took a deep breath.

Then she dialed the number—a home phone, she thought. Anchorage area, she thought.

Her breath gusted out of her when she received the disconnect message.

"Son of a *bitch*!" She slammed the phone on the counter, fury tightening her muscles until she was shaking. Adrenaline crashed through her body, and with it came much-needed strength.

Her gut was a tight, hard knot and for a few moments, she was so pissed off she couldn't even see.

"Breathe," she muttered. "Just breathe."

She knew how to think when she was upset. She'd done it before and she'd been in worse shape then, much worse. She could be all but bleeding and still make herself do what she had to do.

"One more drink," she murmured. With her eyes closed, she took another, smaller sip, let it roll over her tongue and down her throat, and for a moment, the heat of it was enough to warm her belly. Thirty seconds later, she was under control as she reached for the phone and when she dialed the second number, her fingers were steady. They even stayed steady when the voice mail started to play.

It was full of static and unclear—*very* unclear. But she did manage to hear, *This is Shay. Leave a message . . . beep-beep!*

Shay . . .

The freaky thing was, as unclear as the message was, the voice sounded . . . well, kind of like . . . *her.* Including the way she always ended *her* messages . . . *beep-beep.*

Swallowing, she lowered the phone and stared at it. The seconds kept ticking by, reminding her she hadn't disconnected the line. Abruptly, she did, and then she dropped the phone as if it were a snake.

A poisonous one.

"What is this shit?"

Emails that came from her.

Phone calls that sounded like her.

But they *weren't* her.

None of it was *her.*

Yet whoever was doing it managed to do a damn good job at pretending to *be* her.

Elliot read the email. Deleted it.

He read the next one. Deleted it.

It was an endless, ongoing annoyance and something he'd been at for more than a few hours. Many people expressed sympathy. A few talked out of the side of their mouth, although he wasn't exactly sure what the correct phrase would be considering it was all done via email.

But so far, nobody except him and Lorna seemed to have had any direct contact with the Shane imposter—

"Wait," he muttered.

The email in front of him.

Somebody in Westland, Michigan.

Hey, Elliot . . .

Man, I'm sorry to see all the problems you've been having. Yeah, I met her, briefly. And I've gotta say, I wasn't impressed. Sucks, because I always liked the Neil books. Most of my customers are more into romance, but I turned quite a few of them on to the Neil books and it bites that this bitch turned out to be . . . well, a bitch.

She came into my place last summer. Had some bookmarks and wanted to sign stock. And that was cool. But one of my readers was here and made a comment about how she hadn't liked the ending of one of her books and the woman practically jumped down her throat.

Elliot, it was scary. I'm talking borderline 9-1-1 scary. My husband was in the back and I think if he hadn't come out when he had, I might have had to call the cops. The woman was furious.

I was about to go postal and blog about it, but the customer is a friend and she was so embarrassed, and to be honest . . . she was kind of scared. So I agreed not to post anything. But I no longer order any of her books. If somebody requests one, I direct them to another source or I order it used. I won't give that crazy bitch a red cent.

Something is wrong with her, man. I mean, *really* wrong. If I were you, I'd call the cops or something.

M.

Narrowing his eyes, Elliot kept that email, and then continued on. Delete, delete, delete.

Another one in Michigan. Two people in Michigan and that was it. But somebody besides him had met her and at least *one* person had the same impression he had—the woman was off her rocker.

The big thing now was figuring out just where to go from here.

Screaming—

Bright flashes of light—

Blood—

Over and over. She saw it all and she ran from it. Ran and hid. Someplace dark and quiet, where the things that hid in the dark couldn't find her. But still, they came. Giggling. They came giggling.

A hand touched her cheek—it was hot, that hand, so hot. Hot and wet, and it made her hurt. "Aw, what's the matter, princess? It will be good, you'll see. You'll be the princess and I'll take care of you, just the way I should."

In her sleep, Shay flung out a hand and gripped one of the pillows, clutching it to her chest. It was the one Elliot had used, and she clung to it as tears crept out from under closed lashes.

The lights were too bright. Michelline wanted to hide from them, hide from all of them, but she couldn't get away. They stood by the door and every time she tried to get up, somebody would stop her.

People with sad, worried eyes stared at her, but she

didn't trust them. Not at all. And they asked so many questions . . .

"Do you remember where your mother is?"

My mother . . . she remembered her mother. Her mother had been called Jeannie, or Jeanette. And her girls had called her Mama.

Softly, she whispered, "Mama." Tears stung her eyes as she stared at the lady with tired, nice eyes sitting at the table across from her. "Mama left us. That's what he said. The baby took her away."

Around her, people shared that funny look they sometimes used around kids.

"The baby took her away?" the lady asked.

Michelline nodded, and she thought of her mother. She'd been funny, and nice, and sweet. "I miss my mama."

Mama had long, shiny hair that twisted and curled. She smelled like roses and vanilla and cut grass.

The closet used to smell like Mama. Not so much anymore, but it was safer there. That's why they stayed there. Why they hid. But it wasn't safe anymore and she hadn't hidden them well enough . . .

And somebody had been giggling . . . giggling, and playing with something that dripped with dark, dark red . . .

Abruptly, Michelline started to scream.

It took a very, very long time for her to stop—and the woman who held her was crying along with her by the time Michelline's screams faded to sobs.

Shay came awake, her breath trapped in her lungs like a sob, the dream frozen right *there*, a perfectly formed image, at the front of her mind.

It hadn't been just Virna that time.

Not just Virna.

She remembered others.

She remembered herself. Remembered the name they'd called her.

"My name," she whispered. Michelline *had* been her name. She could remember the way Virna had said it that day, as they sat in that quiet, too bright room, with a plate of doughnuts between them . . . and then something else.

Shay could remember a sudden, dark flood of terror, grief, pain . . . and confusion. The screams. Absently, she reached up to rub her throat in memory of the way it had ached from the screams. But she didn't remember what had caused them. It was as though the child she'd been had just blocked all of that out.

She pushed, but even just trying to remember made her head hurt and the harder she pushed, the worse the pain got.

Swiping the back of her hand over her mouth, she swung her legs over the edge of the bed and stared off into nothing. The room was night dark. Her head was muzzy; the migraine had finally grabbed her by the throat and she'd been forced to take some medicine. The nightmares always left her feeling weird, and the dregs of the migraine were still there, too.

The migraine and the nightmare.

Honestly, she'd rather deal with the migraine.

* * *

MyDiary.net/slayingmydragons

It was different this time. I remembered more. There was giggling. I've remembered bits and pieces of that before, but it was more vivid.

She was laughing, laughing and happy and singing. The cops, asking about my mother.

And I remembered her name.

My mother's name was Jeanette. And I think she loved me. She smelled

like flowers and grass and my stepfather said the baby took her away
from us.

But my mother loved me.

I remember that . . . my mother loved me.

"She didn't love you," Darcy muttered, staring at the
diary entry. "Nobody fucking loved you. Ever. Except
me. I'm the only one who loves you."

But Shay didn't seem to *get* that.

Shay didn't realize that Darcy was the one who cared,
the one who would take care of her, always.

The one who would never, ever go away or disappear,
no matter how ugly Shay's secrets were, no matter how
bad her scars.

Everybody else ran away, or left, or died. Sooner or
later.

But Darcy would *always* be there.

"She didn't love you," Darcy whispered, touching the
screen. "But I do."

Her mother had loved her.

It was a bittersweet thing to carry in her heart that day,
but somehow, it managed to steady her. In the back of
her mind, she had odd flashes of memory. Almost memories, more than anything else. The scent of vanilla . . .
something richer, sweeter. Cookies . . . ? A laugh, husky
and soft. *Come on, princess, that's enough . . .*

Off in the dark, quiet house, the phone rang and the
memory shattered, falling apart like gossamer threads.

"Damn it." But even as she grumbled, she felt her
heart kick up a little bit. Elliot . . . he'd said he'd call.

A smile was already forming as she went to answer. It
stopped ringing before she made it to the phone, but a
quick look at the caller ID was enough to dash that rising hope in her heart.

Not Elliot. Darcy. Again.

And she'd called several times. Twice while she'd been sleeping, and then once while she had been writing in her diary; Shay hadn't even noticed.

The low, angry hiss of Darcy's voice came back to her, echoing through Shay's memory . . . *Michelline* . . .

"How do you know about me, Darcy?" she asked, staring at the phone. She wasn't going to pick up. She didn't care just then *how* many times the woman called. "Just who are you?"

It was, she realized, a question for which she really, really needed to have an answer.

Too bad no easy answer existed.

The data search she'd run on Darcy was several years old. She'd stayed off the general search engines, going instead to a public records base—she didn't want to spend time combing through a thousand *Did you go to school with Darcy Montgomery* links—but the info she'd come up with was sketchy at best. The latest address wasn't even listed. It looked like a bust, but Shay *knew* that address was legit, damn it. She'd been sending books there for two years, and she knew the books were sent out to contest winners and received. She also sent bookmarks and promotional shit, and knew *that* stuff was received, too.

Booksellers emailed her to thank her, to update mailing addresses, to request a higher quantity—all sorts of shit.

Contest winners emailed her to thank her.

That stuff wasn't just sitting in a house somewhere.

So if that stuff was being sent out, just who in the hell was taking shipment if it wasn't Darcy?

"This just doesn't make sense."

But lately, that seemed to be the sum of Shay's entire life.

Nothing made sense.

Absolutely nothing.

CHAPTER
FOURTEEN

"YOU'RE SERIOUS."

Staring at the computer, reading through the data she'd found, Shay sighed. "As a heart attack."

On the other end of the line, Elliot was quiet. Finally, he said, "That's disturbing on so many levels, I don't know where to begin, Shay."

"Tell me about it. The address where I send books . . . it doesn't belong to her. It's like she doesn't even exist."

"So what are you going to do about it?"

"I don't know," she said. But she was lying. She had a few ideas, but she wasn't ready to speak them aloud. Not yet. It would make them too real, for one thing. And she had to handle this *now* before it got worse. If she told Elliot, he'd probably want to come with her, but he had a business to run and it wasn't fair that either he or Lorna had to pay for the mess in her life.

"I heard a new blog popped up."

Shay closed her eyes. That hadn't been the highlight of her day. After the migraine, the revelations, the memories . . . she'd been sitting at her computer when she saw an email from somebody she knew only vaguely. Apparently a new blog had been set up under *her* name, but not on her site and not hosted at wordpress.com. Which,

Shay had already discovered, was going to make it harder to get down. It was now at www.shaneneilblog.com.

"Yes, I've learned." Absently, she hit *refresh* on her screen, checking her email. "I've sent a notice to the ISP, but who knows when they'll do something about it."

"Are you still thinking it's this assistant of yours?"

One of the emails all but grabbed her around the throat—the subject line was like a red flag waving in front of her.

It was from Darcy.

That book where the author loses his identity?

For a few seconds, Shay sat there, staring at the screen, at that new email, hardly able to breathe.

"Shay?"

Swallowing, Shay whispered, "Yeah?" Her fingers were shaking as she clicked on the email.

"Do you still think it's her?"

As she started to read, she mumbled, "I don't know what to think anymore."

Was it just her imagination that this message seemed vaguely threatening?

Shay,
Did you forget, you were going to send me that book . . . the one where the author loses his identity for being an idiot? I really want to read that. I can't wait to see how it ends.
Darcy
PS: Where are my new passwords?

"Elliot . . . I have to go."

Earth's End was a small town. There, everybody knew everybody else's business.

That was why she didn't do much in the way of business there; she didn't bank there, she didn't use an accountant or lawyer there. All of her business was done out of Anchorage.

She had to drive a lot longer, but it was worth it.

The drive seemed especially long today and her skin was crawling. All she wanted to do was go back home and maybe dig a moat. It would be hard as hell, considering she'd have to dig through snow and frozen ground, but if she had a moat all around the house, would anybody be able to get in without her help?

A moat and a drawbridge . . . to keep her brand-new dragon out . . .

Hysteria bubbled up in her throat and she gripped the steering wheel desperately. *I can't wait to see how it ends.*

"Yeah," Shay muttered, a chill running down her spine despite the fact that she had on her parka, boots, a hat, gloves . . . despite the fact that her truck was cranking out the heat, despite the fact that it was actually nice and toasty in the interior. She was cold, but it had nothing to do with the temperature, and everything to do with the implied threat.

I can't wait to see how it ends.

"I bet you can't."

But if Darcy thought she was going to bully Shay into silence, bully Shay into *anything*, she was in for one very rude awakening.

Shay wasn't letting anybody take her life over. Maybe it was empty as hell—or had been, until Elliot came along. Maybe she was lonely a lot of the time, and maybe she was afraid of her own shadow. But it was her life, damn it, and she'd protect it.

So she had to take precautions. Maybe she was being paranoid, but she wasn't going to take any chances, especially since the moat option wasn't exactly viable.

If that made her paranoid, so be it.

Shay could live happily being paranoid. Well, maybe not happily, but it wasn't any skin off her nose.

Maybe Darcy shouldn't have sent that email, because now Shay was being precautious in the extreme. She kept remembering what had happened in that book she'd read—all the hero's documents had been burned and he'd almost been killed. Nobody knew who he was, really.

Everything had been on paper for him.

Most things were online, or in email, for Shay.

But the paper trail Shay had wasn't about to get burned up; she figured a nice, safe place for *her* legal documents would be a safety deposit box. Just in case. Being as paranoid as she was, she also thought she'd leave a set of copies with her lawyer in town.

She already had a safety deposit box that she kept a few things in, so at least she wouldn't have the hassle of obtaining the damn thing. Moreover, nobody knew she *had* the box. She'd gotten it years ago, and had never mentioned it to anyone. Only she had the key. She was also going to stash some cash and other valuables in there. She'd heard all the hype about not storing that kind of stuff in a safety deposit box, but Shay figured she had enough issues to worry about without jumping onto the government conspiracy and bank theft bandwagons.

She just needed to make sure she'd have resources, if she needed them. That was all. In case her impersonator decided she wanted to do *more* than just take over Shay's life online.

Even as she thought this, she told herself, *You're getting carried away.*

Except she wasn't so sure. Somebody was stealing her life. Kicking her agent to the curb. Trying to take on a persona for her online when she didn't *want* one.

And sending her creepy little email messages.

Calling her names that nobody should know.

Giving her addresses that weren't real.

If that wasn't enough to make somebody paranoid, what was?

By the time she made it to Anchorage, she had herself good and worked up. Not the ideal way to meet with her lawyer, Noelle.

Looking like a paranoid lunatic wasn't going to endear her to the woman.

Tap-tap-tap. Tap-tap-tap.

Tap-tap-tap. Tap-tap-tap.

The white light of the screen glowed, turning the woman's face into an even paler oval.

Highlighting her smile.

So far, Shay hadn't answered her calls or emails.

But that was fine. None of that really mattered. She could still do what needed to be done. Although she did miss talking with her.

This would all pass, eventually, and things would go back to how they were. With a little bit of work, of course. She wasn't so blind that she couldn't see that things were a little off-kilter.

She would have to fix things, but first, she had to make Shay understand why she had to do this. Why she had to do things this way, and why, really, it was just better if Shay would leave things alone and let her handle this end.

She'd been doing it for years and everything had gone just fine.

It would be best, though, if she didn't have to wait too long to get a start on cleaning up the mess. No telling how long it would take to get back in control if she had to take the direct route, so she'd go for the indirect one and see if that would get her anywhere.

Plus, to be honest, all of the emails she was getting

now were a pain in the ass. It was a hassle dealing with Shay's daily emails, but the hate mail made Shay's regular email look like a dream.

At least she'd been smart. She'd set up the blog on its own site, away from WordPress. She'd backed it up so all she had to do was import the posts and everything looked as it had before the site was shut down.

She had all the comments moderated, and those ugly or negative ones never cleared.

She'd even designed the new site just like the real website. Once she had access to Shane's website, she would merge them. But that wasn't anything she could think about until she had access to the site. Too fucking bad Angie was the one Shay trusted to design it—she'd tried to talk Shay into giving her a chance to do that, but she'd brushed her off. *Angie's always done it and she does a good job. Why fix what isn't broke?*

But once she had access to the site, she could lock *Angie* out, too. She'd damn well do it; should have *already* done it.

Which was what she was working on now. It would be hard, because she couldn't even access the email accounts anymore. Except one. It was an old one, one Shay had used years ago when she was still on AOL. She'd found the password in one of the old emails she'd printed out, stored in one of her many file boxes.

She'd get back in. Take the site and then move it away from that bitch Angie. Once it was out of Angie's control, it would be harder for Shay to do anything about it. She could work on convincing Shay that she needed to just relax and let her handle this. She would even take over Angie's job. There wasn't anything Angie did that she couldn't handle anyway.

It would all work out.

In the end, she'd get this all done, all taken care of. Once things settled down, it would all be okay.

She knew what she was doing . . . she'd been doing it a long, long time, after all.

Angie Lassiter knew weird.

She was an artist. She worked with writers. She *knew* weird. And she *liked* weird, for the most part. But this . . .

Scowling, she read the email and then read it a second time. It was enough to make the hair on the back of her neck stand on end. It sounded like Shay. If Shay had been kind of cracking under the pressure. And yeah, Shay had enough to be stressed about.

And the email address was definitely one she recognized. It had been one of Shay's first, but Angie hadn't seen her use that one in years.

Oh, shit, Angie, I just can't handle it. I think I'm going to lose my mind. I've been locked out of my site and I don't know what to do about it. I'm freaked out and I'm scared and this is just so insane.

You're the web genius—isn't there something you can do about this? You know how to get me back in, right? Please, you've got to say you know how to fix this because I'm going to really, really lose it if you don't . . . lol . . . like I haven't already lost it, but man, I'm going to lose it *bad* and I mean postal bad if I don't get my website back.

That crazy person is trying to ruin me or something. Can't you do something . . .

And the ramblings just went on. And on. Like insane bullshit. No. Not *like* insane bullshit. It *was* insane bullshit.

No matter how much it sounded like Shay, the thing ranked so high on Angie's bullshit meter, it was almost off the charts.

Not to mention that the idiot writing this shit just had no clue what she was doing—she thought *this* would do it? That some freak trying to take Shay's life over would be the thing to break her?

After what Shay had lived through?

No. She'd lived through the likes of hell people couldn't imagine and it hadn't broken her. This crazy bitch, whoever she was, didn't have any idea just what kind of steel Shay had in her . . .

"The steel," Angie muttered. Sometimes, Angie let herself forget about the strength Shay had. Scowling, she leaned back and pulled up another email. She'd been ignoring it, unable to bring herself to answer it. Even after all this time, she wanted to protect Shay, shelter her from the bad shit. But there wasn't any way to protect Shay when the bad seemed to hunt her down, when the bad came in the form of memories creeping out of her clouded mind.

Was my name Michelline? I'm not talking about the name change after Mom. From before. When I was little.

"Michelline . . ." Angie closed her eyes. "Steel, Ang. She's got steel inside her."

Then she clicked back to the other email and printed it out. She'd keep a copy and she'd forward it to Shay. That was about as much as she was going to do with it. But she did need to answer Shay. She'd been holding back, trying to figure out how to answer that question, but there was no right way.

Yes . . . you were Michelline. That was the truth, but it wasn't a truth she wanted to give to her adopted sister. It wasn't a truth her mom had ever shared. Angie knew some of the details about Shay's earlier years, but that was information she'd ferreted out on her own.

She'd been eleven when Shay came to live with them. Old enough to remember, and old enough to understand that bad things had happened to the pretty little girl who hid from everybody except their mother.

Virna told them to call her Michelle.

But after a week had passed, the little girl had started

to talk to Angie, and she had once whispered, "Michelle isn't my name . . . it's Michelline."

"Michelline . . ." Angie rubbed her hands over her eyes and then groaned, leaning back in the seat. "Shit."

Okay. She needed to handle one problem at a time. The crazy first, because that was easy. Or easier. Leaning over the desk, she studied the email again. It was from Shay's imposter, Angie knew it. Shay needed answers . . . and Angie wouldn't mind a few herself. And she was curious. Just how far would this person go?

Common sense told Angie that she needed to be careful.

And she would be careful—she'd learned caution the hard way. The attack on Shay, her mother's murder. Yeah, she was careful.

She didn't leave the house all that often, and she didn't open her door to strangers. Plus, she had an ace in the hole. Something not too many people knew: Angie lived with a big, mean cop and they had a big, mean dog. Plus, she was pretty mean herself, even if she wasn't precisely big. This chick, whoever she was, was a stupid coward, hiding behind computers and lies.

Hunching over the keyboard, she emailed back.

Considering all the trouble you're having, I'll feel better if I call. I'm calling your house.

She smiled thinly as she hit *send* and then grabbed the phone.

She'd barely managed to dial Shay's number before the response appeared.

Oh, call my cell—please! I'm having some trouble with the number at home and . . . well, look. This is weird, but I think . . . I think somebody might be—Shit. You'll think I'm crazy, or crazier, anyway! But can you

call my cell? It's a new one. I bought it a few weeks ago and you don't
have the number yet.

"I don't, huh?" Angie muttered as Shay's voice mail
kicked in.

"Hey, sweetie. It's me. I just got a message from one
of your old email addresses . . . the AOL one? Do you
even use that one anymore? Anyway, just wanted to ask
you about it—you there?"

When nobody answered, Angie wasn't really surprised.

After she hung up, just for fun, she dialed the other
phone number.

It was almost freaky, though, when a voice came on.
If she hadn't been prepared for something weird, she
almost might have believed it was Shay. Almost.

"So how do we get back in?"

Angie studied the notes she'd made. There wasn't
much. The Shay impersonator was claiming that somebody had hacked into her site. Of course, the bitch
claimed she didn't know what that note on her news
page was about—but they needed to get it down because she was dealing with all sorts of crazy over it.

And again, it did sound like Shay.

Sounded—but it wasn't. There wasn't much else that
Angie could get, though. When she tried to get an idea
about what was going on, the only response she got
was, "I just don't know . . ."

When Angie asked what the deal with Elliot was—
had he tried to hurt her? What was the deal with the
note about the rape and shit?—all she got was *I just
don't know* . . .

Nothing to go on. But hey, Angie had gotten a phone
number.

And she'd pass it on to that big, mean cop of hers who
had just come into her office. He bent down to kiss her

cheek and she smiled at him before focusing back on the
phone call. *Sorry, Shay . . .* She'd wanted to get more
information than this, but there just wasn't anything to
find.

"So, Angie, how do I get back into my site?" the
woman on the other end of the phone asked, her voice
taking on a needling, *annoying* whine.

Sighing, Angie dropped her pen. "Well, you see, that's
the problem, sweetie. I don't know how to help you. It's
not *your* site."

As the line went dead, she just sat there. Darcy had had
her fingers poised over the keyboard, ready to type in
the password.

Her heart had started to pound when Angie spoke
again, though. Her voice had lost its understanding,
we're girlfriends tone and in its place was a ball-busting
bitch. Half of the words didn't even make sense. But one
thing had been clear . . .

"It's not your site."

And then, dead air.

She'd hung up.

Angie had hung up.

Without giving her the information she needed.

No way to get into the site now. No way to move the
site to a different hosting service. No way to change
that message.

"That *bitch*. That *fucking* bitch!"

Fury ripped through her.

She shoved back from the desk so hard, the chair
overturned. In a rage, she grabbed it and threw it as
hard as she could. It didn't go far. "Fucking cunt."
Reaching out, she grabbed whatever was closest—
a heavy glass paperweight in the shape of a chess piece.
She threw it and it went pretty damn far, much farther

than the chair, hitting the wall on the opposite side of the office and tearing into the drywall.

She grabbed something else—a pair of scissors. They didn't do as much damage as the paperweight, so she picked them up and attacked the drapes.

This wasn't going to be the end, damn it. She'd put too much work into this. Into *everything*. She'd spent too much *time* on this—almost half of her life waiting for just *this* and she wasn't losing.

Not now.

"This. Isn't. Done." The drapes were in ragged shreds on the floor by the time she was finished with them. Bit by bit, the rage was lifting. Bit by bit, it eased. It wasn't gone, though. Not yet.

She put the scissors between her teeth and grabbed a framed poster from the wall, slamming it down until the glass shattered. Heedless of the sharp edges, she reached inside and grabbed the poster. It tore as she jerked it out, but that wasn't enough. She cut, and she cut, and she cut, until nothing but tatters was left.

There was one large, ragged piece left in the frame. Her breathing came in gasps as she stood up and stared at it. She pushed her hair aside, looking at remains of the oversized cover Shay had sent her. It had been signed. A gift.

Now it served to remind her . . .

She hadn't wasted these years, and she hadn't wasted her time. She wasn't giving up now. She wasn't.

She'd keep trying to get control of the website. But there were other avenues she could explore. Plenty of them.

She shoved her hair back from her face, unaware of the blood dripping from her fingers as she turned away.

"I need to make a plan," she muttered. She'd figured out a long time ago that she worked better with a plan, especially with something as big as this—and this was *big*.

CHAPTER
FIFTEEN

Okay. That was done. Shay had turned over the papers to her lawyer. The originals were locked in the safety deposit box.

Now she was going to find out some answers on her own. She was going to find out who in the *hell* was taking receipt of her books in Michigan.

But that meant . . . *leaving.* She hadn't left Alaska since she'd moved here. She didn't *want* to leave Alaska. She felt safe here.

Panic swelled inside her and she squeezed her eyes closed. Maybe there was another option. A better one. There had to be—

The phone in her pocket buzzed and she reached for it, feeling the ache in her chest ease as she saw Elliot's face on the display. She answered on the second ring. "Hey."

Another option . . . no, there isn't. Come on, Shay. Don't be such a coward.

Somehow, just listening to him grounded her.

"Hey back . . ." His voice was subdued. Quiet. "I tried calling your place."

"I'm in Anchorage." She chanced a quick look down the street and then zipped up her parka, tugged her cap and gloves out of her bag. She had to do this. She had to, because she had to know. "I . . . Elliot, I think I'm going to do something drastic."

"Oh?" There was a world of tension in his voice.

"I'm going to Michigan."

A beat passed and then he laughed. "You call that drastic? What would New York be . . . earth-moving?"

She swallowed. "I haven't left Alaska since I moved here," she whispered softly. "I just need to go for a day or two, but I'm terrified."

He was quiet. Then he said, "When are you going? Give me a day or two and I'll go with you."

"I can't." She checked the time on her watch. "I'm leaving today. In a few hours. I don't know when—just as soon as I can find a flight into Detroit." She didn't know when the next flight to Detroit was, but she'd be on it, damn it. She had to be, because if she thought about it, she'd freak *out*.

"Shay, damn it."

Wincing, she said, "If I don't go now, I'm going to chicken out and I have to go—I need answers. I'll call you once I land." Then she hung up and took off, moving out of the mall toward the parking garage. *Don't think, Shay . . . just don't think.*

Elliot stared at the phone and then hurled it down on the counter. "Shit." Glaring at it, he tried to decide if it was worth the trouble to call her back.

"What's wrong?"

"Shay's going to Michigan."

Lorna gaped at him. "For good?"

"No." Then, as his heart clenched on him, he muttered, "Hell, I hope not."

He hadn't asked *that* question. Rubbing the heel of his hand over the knot in his chest, he said, "She has some stuff she needs to do."

"And this is bad . . . ?"

He grimaced. "I don't think she wants to go alone. But she can't wait."

Lorna came deeper into the office and plucked the phone from his desk. As she pushed it into his hand, she advised, "Then I suggest you haul ass. Go pack some shit. I'll see what I can do about flights."

"I can't just drop everything and go to Michigan," Elliot muttered, even as he stood up, staring at his sister.

"You're not." She gave him a smile that reminded him of their mom. "You're dropping everything to go to the woman you need. Right?"

He stared at her. Then, without wasting another second, he tore out of the office and headed to the back of the store. The stairwell that led to their shared apartment was there.

He could pack *fast*. He just hoped his sister could get him a ticket that fast.

As Shay stood on the curb outside the airport, she swallowed.

"Miss?"

She glanced back over her shoulder and saw a guy standing a few feet away—it was one of the porters, she thought. He had on a uniform and a kind smile graced his face. "Am I in your way?" she asked wanly.

"No. You're fine." He smiled again and came another step closer.

Immediately, she tensed up.

He saw it and halted, lifting his hands, still smiling. "Are you okay? You look kind of nervous. Upset."

She forced herself to smile. "Yeah. I'm fine."

"Don't like to fly, huh?"

"Kind of." She gave him a weak smile and went back to staring at the airport.

Here in Alaska, she'd found anonymity. And slowly,

she'd come to find safety. Maybe she hadn't exactly
found the home she'd known with Virna, but it was still
her home. Usually, she felt safe. There were exceptions,
of course. Like when *he* had been released—

Her heart jumped into her throat, just thinking of it.
But he'd never come looking for her. He was still living
in Phoenix—she had monthly reports on him, courtesy
of a contact there, and if he left for even a day, she'd
know.

It was another way for her to feel safe. Just like the
security system. Just like the name change. Just like
the move.

All of it.

And now she was leaving the only security she'd
found in all that time.

Shit, maybe she should have waited for Elliot.

Swallowing, she made herself take one step.

Then another.

"It's not going to get any easier with those baby steps,
sweetheart."

"No." She glanced back at the porter and grimaced.
"I guess it's not. I'm just having a hard time moving
much faster than this."

An understanding smile creased his face. "Just go on
and get it over with, that's what I'd do. It won't help
drawing it out." That wide smile changed his whole
face, lit it up and made his dark eyes sparkle. "You go
on now. You'll be fine."

Man, I hope so.

Taking a deep breath, she turned back around and
squared her shoulders. She'd damn well better be *more*
than fine. She'd gotten away. She'd gotten here.

She'd spent all these years in hiding, yeah, but she was
doing a pretty good job of living.

She hardly ever woke up screaming anymore. She
dealt with the nightmares—so what if they choked her?

And hell, she was even in a relationship—that was something, right? She'd had sex. Normal, healthy sex. She wasn't the useless, cowering victim he'd tried to make her. Not anymore.

Taking one big step, then another and another, she headed inside.

She could damn well do this.

She'd had enough things stolen from her. Half of her childhood, all of her innocence, her family.

The pain, the memories, all of it haunted her. But she'd fought past that, past the horror, past the screams, past the nightmares, the grief, the pain.

She'd made a life, damn it. Now somebody was trying to take it away.

And she'd be damned if she let that happen.

"Okay, there's no direct flight to Michigan. Help me out here. There are two with connections, both of them within a couple hours of each other. The cheaper one is US Airways, connects in Phoenix and leaves sooner—"

"Not that one," he cut in. Images of the articles he'd read slammed into his mind. *Phoenix*—she'd avoid that place if at all possible, his gut said.

"You sure? It's more than a hundred bucks cheaper and it's the one leaving sooner. Thought she was in a hurry."

"I don't think it's that one. What's the other one?"

"Delta. A few hours later. Connects in Minneapolis–St. Paul."

"That's the one. Book me that one."

"Are you *positive*? If I book this one and she's on the other one, then you're out the money."

"No. I'll just catch up with her there." But he knew he wasn't wrong.

Cutting into the next lane, he eased his way around a

semitruck. It was a nice day and he'd actually made it out at a good time to avoid traffic—now if it would just stay that way. "When does it head out?"

"You've got four hours. How far away are you?"

"Still thirty minutes." He checked the clock. "As long as I don't hit traffic, I should be good." He blew out a breath and asked, "What do I say?"

"Just tell her the truth. You knew she didn't want to do this alone." He heard a voice over the line and then Lorna said, "I need to go. Customers just decided to attack the store. You be careful—don't crash trying to get there."

"I won't. Thanks, Lorna."

Tossing the phone down on the seat, he focused on the road. No, he didn't want to crash on the way. He needed to have his wits about him to convince her that he really needed to be with her on this trip. Lorna could handle the store for a few days on her own.

But Shay needed him.

That was what he'd say . . .

"Shit." He dragged a hand down his face. "Is that the right thing to say?"

I knew you didn't want to go . . . and I didn't want you to have to go alone if I could be with you . . .

This relationship crap was way too complicated. And they'd just gotten started.

He made it to the airport in record time. Now all he had to do was find Shay.

Lorna had already taken care of the ticket, but he wanted to make sure Shay was actually *on* this flight before he checked in. That way he could change it if needed.

With his duffel bag at his feet, he sent her a text, scanning the crowd every few seconds, hoping he'd see her.

Have you booked your flight already?

Thirty seconds passed before she answered.

Yes. I leave in just over two hours. I'll call you when I land.

Just over two hours. That had to be the same flight.
But just in case . . .

What's the airline?

She texted back and added:

You're not mad at me, are you?

No. I know you need to do this.

Then he tucked the phone away and went to check in.
It took a while to get through security, but forty-five
minutes later he was heading down the walkway, phone
in hand. Once he saw her bent head, he sent her another
text.

Remember how I said I wasn't mad? Because I knew you had to do this?

He watched her from the side of the corridor and as a
faint smile curled her lips, it punched him straight in the
gut. She texted him back.
He glanced down to read the message.

Yes. Thanks for understanding.

Repay the favor . . . don't be mad. I had to do this, too. Look up.

As she lifted her head, he shoved off the wall and
started toward her. He saw the puzzled expression on

her face as she looked around, then the look in her eyes as she saw him—at first, delight, followed by dismay. Then she slumped back into the seat, her eyes closed. By then, he'd reached her. Dumping his duffel bag on the floor by her feet, he crouched down and rested his hands on her knees. "So. Are you mad?"

Shay scowled at him. "You make it kind of hard—being so understanding and all. I'd look like an ass if I got angry at you. Although where in the hell were you when you texted me?"

"Getting ready to check in." He shrugged, rubbing his thumb back and forth across her knee. "I wanted to make sure I had the right flight—if it wasn't, I'd change it."

"That's cheating."

"We're not really playing a game." He studied her face another moment and decided she wasn't mad. Moving to the seat next to her, he took her hand. "You don't want to leave. I could hear it in your voice. I don't want you leaving here if you're not comfortable doing it. And I don't really want to go a few days without seeing you." He paused, and then softly, slowly, added, "Besides, all of this shit is crazy, and it's getting crazier. I'd feel better if I could sort of watch your back."

Shay glanced at him, that scowl still twisting her lips. "Don't be so logical. I'm still trying to sulk here."

"Why?" Stroking a hand through her hair, he cupped the back of her neck, digging his fingers into the tight muscles.

"Because I had myself all psyched up to do something that terrifies me and I was ready to do it, all by myself. Now I'm not. It feels like I'm being a coward."

"Well, you didn't ask for my help. If it makes it any easier, consider me an intruder or something."

She made a face. "Yeah, like that's going to happen." With a groan, she shifted in the seat, leaning against him as well as she could with the armrest between them. "I'm kind of glad you're here, though. If I had to be honest, I have to say I'm really glad you're here."

CHAPTER
SIXTEEN

In some ways, the north of Michigan looked a hell of a lot like Alaska.

And it was cold. Like Alaska.

As they came out of the terminal to find their rental car, Elliot sucked in a deep breath of air. Then he glanced at her. "Man, it feels like home."

Shay shivered in her jacket and stared at the rows of cars. "She should have lived in Florida. That would have been a nice change."

"Nah. That would be too easy. *Too* nice," he told her, ambling toward the cars. "So did you find a nice, sexy little convertible for the balmy weather?"

She was pretty certain she had icicles dripping from her nose. "Since I wasn't expecting this to be an *us* when I landed, sexy wasn't on the brain. It's an SUV."

"Oh, even better. We can get some blankets and snuggle up in the back somewhere. I hear Michigan's got some prime waterfront." He gave her a playful leer and despite herself, she laughed.

"Are you trying to talk me into going somewhere to make out with you?"

"Yes."

Shay grinned at him. "That could be fun." Actually, she was rather certain it would be. It might be the only fun they managed to get in, too, because she wasn't expecting her confrontation with Darcy to go well.

"There it is," Elliot said, pointing toward a rather bland-looking SUV. At least it was clean and in a few minutes, it would be warm. That was good enough.

"This is one boring-ass drive," Elliot muttered. "I thought we'd at least see some lakes."

Shay glanced at him. "Sorry."

He smiled. "Hey, *you* didn't tell her where to live, did you?" He jerked the wheel to the right, barely avoiding a pothole in the road. "Shit, this road *sucks*."

"Yes." Absently, she shivered. The cold really wasn't bothering her—she was used to it. But as she and Elliot drove over that miserable, rutted excuse of a road, Shay realized she was shaking. Not from the cold, but from the fear. She wanted, so much, to knock on the door of the upcoming house and see Darcy with her own eyes, ask her if she was behind any of this.

Face to face, Darcy wouldn't be able to lie, would she? She'd never been very good at it before. Shay had always known when her friend was being less than honest—it had shown on her face.

"This is killing me, you know," she said quietly. Sighing, she rested her head on the back of the seat and fisted her hands in her lap. "It's killing me."

He reached over and laid a hand over hers, his thumb stroking her white knuckles.

"If I get there, and I see her, is she going to be able to actually lie to me? To my face?"

Swinging her head around to look at him, she asked again, "Is she?"

He sighed. "Shay, I don't know. I've never met her . . . but some people can do it. Is she one of them?" He glanced at her for the briefest second before diverting his attention back to the road. "Some people can. Some can't. But is that why you're going out to see her? Or is it because you need to look at her? Do you really need to ask her if she's doing this . . . or do you already know?"

In the pit of her stomach, she felt very cold.

Closing her eyes, she drew her knees to her chest. She didn't want to answer that. Not at all. "I want to be wrong."

Blowing out a breath, she added softly, "I want to look at her and somehow know that I'm wrong."

"But that's not going to happen. And you know it. So why are you here?"

"Because I want to know why. Because I just have to see her." No matter how much it hurt. At least she'd feel some sort of closure. Plus, she was going to get it through Darcy's head that this shit would stop. Here and now. Because if Darcy didn't stop, Shay was going to go postal on her.

"You got any idea what you're going to say to her?" he asked.

"No. I don't have the slightest clue." With a nervous laugh, she added, "I gotta admit, I'm playing this thing completely by ear."

"I'm going to ask you something and I want you to answer, straight up, no thinking it through. Okay?" He slid her a glance.

Shay nodded.

"How do you think she'll play it . . . assuming you're right, and she is behind this?"

"She's going to lie." Then she groaned and covered her face with her hands. "Shit . . . *shit*. This is a friend of mine. And I'm sitting here talking about something that could tear my life apart if she got away with it. How can that woman be a *friend*? And I'll tell you this . . . if you'd asked me two years ago? Three? I'd tell you that there's no way we'd be having this conversation. But lately . . . lately, she's just different. She's the *same*, but she's not. And the Darcy I know now would lie in a heartbeat."

"What makes you think that?"

She looked down, staring at the hand he had on her thigh. Resting her hand on his, she twined their fingers and closed her eyes. "She . . . manipulates. She wasn't always like that, but lately . . ."

With the knot in her throat trying to squeeze out the ability to speak, Shay paused to take a deep breath. As she did, Elliot turned over his hand and tightened his fingers around hers. "She manipulates me . . . or tries to. It wasn't like that before, but over the past few years, she started doing it. She was so *obvious* about it, I could see it. I even called her on it a few times, told her to chill out. Now, thinking back, I think there were other things . . . subtler things that I didn't see, and part of me wonders if she didn't use the obvious shit to hide the subtle shit. Now here's the really crazy part . . . it doesn't make *sense*. Because that's not the Darcy I remember. She couldn't have manipulated me for anything. It just wasn't in her."

"Except that's just what you said she's doing." He stroked his thumb over the back of her hand.

Amazing how such a light touch could be so soothing, so comforting.

"I know." Closing her eyes, she gripped his hand in hers, squeezing it. "I feel like I've been played, and I never even knew it. You can't imagine how sick this makes me feel."

"You might be surprised." Elliot's voice went gruff, tight.

Opening her eyes, she looked at him, but he wasn't looking at her. He was staring out the windshield with a dark, distant expression on his face. "I might be able to understand better than you think."

"How?"

He shook his head. "We'll go into that later." Nodding, he said, "I think we're here."

They came to a stop in front of a small house—small and run down but well cared for, it seemed—and got out. Shay could see what looked like flower beds, although it was hard to tell under the snow. That was weird. Darcy said she hated gardening shit; it was something they had in common—Darcy wouldn't do it and Shay rarely tried, because of her allergies.

As the cold lashed them, she pulled up her hood and shoved her hands into her pockets.

"What do we do if she's not here?" Shay asked. The driveway had a little red Corolla, but Darcy had said she drove an old, beat-up truck she'd had since high school.

"Then we come back," Elliot said. He came around the car to stand beside her and hooked an arm around her neck. "Quit stalling."

She couldn't seem to move her feet, damn it. Wheezing out a choked breath, she forced herself to take one small step. Then another. Remembering what the porter had said back at the airport about baby-stepping it, she took bigger steps, and each one got easier.

By the time they hit the beat-up little porch, she'd found her resolve, and when she reached to knock on the door, she knew she'd done the right thing.

"You ready for this?" Elliot asked.

"Yeah." She nodded. "I've got to know—even though in my gut I *do*, I have to ask her. I have to look at her face . . . I have to see what she has to say. And . . ."

He slid his hand inside the hood of her parka and touched the back of her neck. "You need to know how she knows your name. If she's connected."

"Yeah." She smiled at him and murmured, "I'm glad you decided to show up at the airport, you know."

If Darcy wasn't here, then Shay would just come back. They'd get a hotel, and come back. It might be . . . interesting, she decided. She'd never stayed at a hotel with a guy—hell, she *rarely* stayed at one, period. Room service, sleeping in. Assuming she could sleep.

Why don't you stop trying to distract yourself and just get this over with?

Lifting her hand, she braced herself and knocked.

The door opened.

Shay froze as a pair of dark eyes, set in a wizened old face, met hers. "Yes?" The woman's voice was soft, heavy with a Spanish accent.

"Ah, I'm looking for Darcy Montgomery."

The woman frowned, puzzled, shaking her head. "There is no one by that name here . . ."

The pit of Shay's stomach crashed, even though she'd been expecting this. All too aware of Elliot's presence at her side, she kept the smile on her face as she said, "I think there's some confusion going on with deliveries I've had coming here. I send packages here, regularly. My friend Darcy gets the packages, but if she doesn't live here . . . did she move?"

The woman's warm, honey-brown skin paled and something flickered in the dark depths of her eyes. "Ah, yes. The packages, yes. I receive packages, but I only hold them. They get picked up. There is no Darcy Montgomery. I'm sorry." She tried to smile, but the smile wobbled and fell flat.

Shay continued to stare at her, watching as the woman tried to pretend that she wasn't suddenly terrified. *I receive packages . . .*

Something hard and cold settled in the pit of Shay's stomach. "You receive them . . . I take it this is some sort of arrangement? Did you arrange this after she moved?"

"No." The woman shook her head. "I've lived here

for many years, with my husband. We lived here a very long time. He's gone and now the house is mine. I am sorry. There is no Darcy Montgomery here. There never has been."

She went to close the door but Shay reached up, touched her arm. "Wait."

"Yes?"

"The packages. What . . . what's the deal with the packages?"

A guarded look entered the woman's eyes. "Perhaps that should be discussed with your friend."

Then she withdrew into the house and shut the door.

Shay turned her head and looked at Elliot, then closed her eyes.

Coming here hadn't shed any light at all, it seemed.

Except for one thing—she now had more proof that something really, really screwed up was going on with Darcy. She *knew* Darcy. They'd been in school together, had spent a lot of time together. The woman was *real*. But according to the public records search she'd done on Darcy, there wasn't anything current—there hadn't been for quite some time, and this address was a fraud.

Swearing, she shoved a hand through her hair and spun away, staring out at the rental car. If she didn't know better, she'd wonder if Darcy existed. But Darcy was real. Damn it, she was *real*.

"Maybe I'm just crazy," Shay muttered. "Aw, hell. This was a waste of time."

"No. It wasn't." Elliot stood there and continued to stare at the door. "She's scared. Didn't you see it?"

"Somebody was there?"

Darcy gripped the phone, staring at the computer screen, hardly able to believe what she was hearing.

"Yes. A young woman. Her face was scarred."

"Describe her."

As Selena ticked off the details, Darcy felt both nervous and full of pride. Shay had gone to Michigan looking for her? How had she managed that? She hardly ever left the damn house!

"Do you know this woman?" Selena asked softly.

"Yeah. Don't worry about it. I'll handle her."

There was a pause, and then Selena Campbell said softly, "What are you doing to this girl? Haven't you caused enough grief?"

"Shut up," she said, but it was more offhanded than anything else. Selena didn't mean anything, couldn't do anything . . . *wouldn't* do anything. Because Darcy knew Selena's most secret fears. Darcy made it a habit to learn those things. They came in handy. "What was she doing there?"

"She was looking for you—or who you say you are." Selena laughed bitterly. "Looking for the woman she sends packages to. And she didn't look terribly surprised when I told her you didn't live there, that you never had. Neither she nor her man."

Darcy tensed. "Her man?"

Elliot . . .

"Yes. She had a man with her."

"Son of a bitch," Darcy growled. Slamming the phone down, she surged out of the chair and started to pace. "What in the *hell* are you doing, you crazy little bitch?"

She paced across the floor, then back. Spying her phone, she grabbed it again—she could hear Selena's voice. Ah, that familiar old voice. ". . . *please, don't do anything . . .*"

"Shut the fuck up," Darcy muttered, ending the call. Then she dialed another number. Usually, dialing it made her smile. Made her feel . . . *something* close to happiness.

But not now. Now it was rage. Gut-wrenching rage. But as the phone started to ring, she cleared her voice.

Made herself smile. All of that would show in her voice and she didn't want Shay suspecting anything more than she already did.

When the phone rolled over to voice mail, she almost lost it a second time. Breathing shallowly, she grappled it all under control and waited for the beep. "Hey, it's me, girl! Why don't you call me back . . ." She injected a bit of sadness into her voice and heaved out a sigh. "You know, I miss talking to you. I'm sorry we fought. Can you please call me? I . . . hell, Shay. I'm sorry. Just call me."

You stupid bitch.

Tossing the phone down, she grabbed one of the throwaway cells and dialed another number. As a female voice came on the line, she asked, "Can I speak to Elliot?"

"Sorry, he's out of town for a few days . . . can I take a message?"

"No." Disconnecting the call, Darcy lowered the phone. And stared at absolutely nothing.

"Why was she afraid, I wonder?"

Elliot shrugged. "I don't know, but she was. Something had her nervous, though, and she doesn't know you, so it stands to reason it's something to do with the packages, or the person who picks them up."

"Darcy," Shay whispered. "But why would she be afraid of Darcy?"

Elliot was silent.

Shay sighed, staring at her phone. They were in one of those little bar-and-grill restaurants. It was early and the place was mostly dead. As she hit the button on her iPhone, her gut went tight with dread. Darcy had tried to call. Twice.

"She keeps trying to call." Flipping the phone around,

she showed him the screen. "Just a few minutes ago. She tried to call, just now and about twenty minutes ago."

"You going to call her back?"

She dropped her head down on the dull wood of the bar. "I don't know."

"Well, you might want to figure out the answer to that." He rubbed his hand up and down her spine. "You need to track her down and face her over this, or maybe turn it over to the cops. Do something."

For a few minutes, she just let herself relax under the soothing motion of his hand. He could make millions, if he could just find a way to bottle what he did with his hands.

Then, because she couldn't block it out of her mind, she focused on his words. Rolling her head to the side, she watched him from the corner of her eye. "Calling the cops won't do a damn bit of good right now, Elliot, and you know it. She hasn't *done* anything we can prove and she hasn't done anything she can be arrested for. Hell, this probably isn't even legally harassment."

"So you just plan on ignoring it?" He tugged on the ends of her hair, shaking his head. "That's not the answer either."

"No. I'm not going to ignore it. I just . . ." Sighing, she closed her eyes. "I need to think. I was only thinking about seeing her, confronting her. Beyond that? I don't know."

"You need to figure that out before you talk to her. Don't let her keep jerking you around."

Next to her, the phone vibrated, signaling a text. Shay groaned and pushed a button, going to the screen that showed Darcy's info. The bartender passed by, and she flagged him down and showed him the phone. "Is that a local area code?"

He glanced at it and nodded. "Yeah." Then he

squinted. "Darcy . . . Montgomery. That's a familiar name."

"She lives around here," Shay said, smiling absently. "Or I thought she did. Thanks."

He gave her a tired smile. "I've probably met her somewhere, then. Small towns. We know everybody." As he wandered off, she resumed her contemplative study of the phone number, but no matter how long she stared at it, it didn't yield any secrets.

"I've been calling her at a Michigan number, sending packages to that house for years. But she doesn't live there." Her gut clenched tight. "And she knows my real name."

Nausea punched at her hard and fast. Lifting her head, she swallowed the bile churning its way up her throat. "I feel like I might be sick," she muttered. "Really, horribly, terribly sick."

"Just breathe."

Breathe—she felt a hysterical giggle bubbling up in her throat. She didn't want to breathe. She thought it might be better to hold her breath until she passed out and just slid into sweet oblivion for a while. Then she wouldn't have to think about answers or anything . . .

Answers—

Cocking her head, she studied the phone. Answers. She needed answers and she'd asked somebody for them.

Then she'd ignored her fucking email for the past day.

"Angie," she muttered. As the fog in her brain cleared, the swelling tide of nausea went with it and she reached for her phone.

She hit the email, scrolling through the hundreds of messages that had piled up. The second she saw Angie's name, her heart leaped into her throat. Lifting her gaze, she found herself staring at Elliot.

"Virna was one of the social workers who took me

in," she said, her voice barely above a whisper. "That's not exactly kosher—she had to call in all sorts of favors and shit to get me. She was a widow—her husband had died a few years earlier—but I couldn't cope with anybody else and in the end, the family court system wanted me with somebody who could relate to me, who *could* connect with me. Virna was the only one who ever could. I think I might have gone crazy without her. I mean *really* crazy—like bad. I was in rough shape when they found me. I don't know much about it—she never would tell me. Nobody really knows what I saw or anything. Anyway, she had kids. Most of them were grown, out of the house. But Angie was there. She was a few years older than me and it took us awhile to hit it off."

Staring at Angie's name, at *nothing* but Angie's name, Shay whispered, "She's the only person from my family that I keep in touch with. I broke all ties—changed my name after the trial and everything. But Angie knows about me."

"You don't think—"

"No." Shay jerked her head, staring at him. "No," she said again. "There's no way." And there was no doubt in her mind, in her gut, in her soul. "But if anybody knows anything about my past, it's Angie."

Taking a deep breath, she tapped on the screen and waited for the email to load.

Hey Sweetie

Man, this is hard to talk about. You were so little then, and so scared. I don't remember all of it, either. So I can't tell you much. I hope you understand. But when you first came to live with us, when Mom told us to call you Michelle, for the first few weeks, you didn't answer very well. And one day, out of the blue, you started talking to me a little. And you told me your name wasn't Michelle. It was Michelline.

But Mom never, *ever* wanted us to call you that. As a matter of fact, I once got in a lot of trouble for doing it. I didn't see the big deal—you were so little and nothing was the same for you. What did it matter if you were called your old name? She grounded me for a month and took away everything but books.

It wasn't until I was older that I figured it out.

I don't want to pry, but I hope you're okay. You forgot so much of everything before you came to us. If you ever need to talk, I'm here, Shay.

Tears burned her eyes but she blinked them away. Filing the email, she put the phone down and covered her face with her hands.

Can you tell us what happened, Michelline?

No . . .

She sat there and shuddered. *Do you remember . . .*

No. She didn't. But a part of her was trying to, and she really dreaded the day those memories finally crept into the open.

Selena Campbell stood at the back window, staring outside.

Darkness had fallen.

She hated the night with a passion. These hours were when she missed Lance the most. He had been the most wonderful man. He had made her laugh, had made her smile. And he had told her something was wrong with the girl who had come to live with them.

But Selena had always wanted to look for the good in people. After all, the dark-haired child had been so young. So sweet and kind when they first brought her home. How could there be anything wrong with her?

Lance had been right.

It had just taken her several years . . . and several losses . . . to see that.

Selena pressed her hand to her belly, grief gripping her brutally.

Mrs. Campbell, we found traces of something unusual in your blood.

Her heart raced and she blinked away the tears. It was foolish, really, to cry over it now.

It caused your body to go into early labor. That's why you lost the baby.

A few days later, Lance had found the little bag in their foster daughter's room. The girl had been a nice, neat little monster and she'd had it labeled. He'd researched it and discovered that the herbs inside weren't drugs. But they could induce a miscarriage. And when they'd confronted her, she'd just smiled.

"Child, what are you out there doing now?" she whispered.

She should have warned the woman who'd come to her door. But she hadn't.

And now, if that woman was harmed, she'd have yet another death on her hands. Staring at the spot where Lance's workshop had once stood, she let a tear fall.

They'd left Arizona to get away from all of that grief.

But the grief . . . and the monster who'd caused it . . . had followed them.

CHAPTER
SEVENTEEN

"Do you want to go downstairs and get some-thing to eat?" Elliot asked after they'd stowed their bags—her duffel bag, his, and her briefcase—and carried up her laptop.

Shay wandered around the hotel room, pausing only long enough to kick off her shoes. By the window, she glanced back at him and smiled. "Do they have room service?" Curling her toes into the plush carpet, she decided it was . . . nice.

It wasn't home, but it was a nice room.

And it was kind of fun being in such a small space with Elliot. They'd headed on to Detroit, getting the hell out of that small, tired town. Nothing had been there for them anyway, and the only hotel hadn't been much more than a single strip of rooms. They hadn't even slowed to check it out.

"I'm sure they have room service," he said, padding across the floor to her. "If you're too tired to go down-stairs, room service sounds good."

She shrugged. "It's not that I'm tired. Although I am. But I've never stayed in a hotel room and done the room service bit. It might be fun."

"Sure. Paying a fifteen or eighteen percent surcharge for the same food you can get downstairs sounds like a blast," he drawled, rolling his eyes. But he'd smiled and reached up, stroking her chin as he said it. "I'll dig up the menu."

As he did, she turned back to the window and stared outside. Detroit was all lights, she decided. There were a lot more lights than Anchorage, at least. And it was a bigger city. But not as pretty. She wouldn't be able to see the northern lights from here . . . too much light from the city.

But then again, no place was like Alaska. No place was like home.

"Here you go."

She turned around and saw the menu he held out. Taking it, she headed to the bed and stretched out on her belly, studying it. "Man, do they price things up or what?" she muttered.

"Yep." He stroked a hand up her thigh. "May I?"

She shot him a look over her shoulder. "May you what?"

"I was going to give you a back rub."

"Oh." She shrugged. "Okay." But when he straddled her thighs, her breath lodged in her chest. Panic swelled inside her—

"You okay?"

Elliot's voice called her home. And she managed to blow out the air threatening to explode inside her chest. "I'm fine," she squeezed out. Gripping the menu desperately, she stared at it even though the words didn't make any sense.

"You sure?"

"Right as rain." *No, I'm not.* But she wasn't going to admit to that. *Make it until I fake it* . . . Because damned if she was going to freak out because the guy she loved . . .

Shit. The menu fell from numb fingers. She might

have wilted if he hadn't slid his hands under the hem of her shirt. "You with me?" he murmured.

"Yes . . ."

The guy I love . . .

Oh, shit.

Strong, gentle hands worked their way up her back. "Why don't you lie flat?" he suggested. "I can get to you better that way."

Unable to argue, she stretched out, her mind still reeling. *The guy I love . . .*

I love him.

His thumbs ran along her spine, working it in a way that stretched those muscles. "You're too tense," he said softly.

No shit.

"Know what you want for dinner?"

"Ah . . . I'm still trying to decide," she hedged.

"Okay. We got time."

Closing her eyes, she folded her arms under her and buried her face, hiding it from him, and the world, while she tried to come to grips with what she'd just admitted to herself. She loved him.

Damn it all to hell.

Brooding, Elliot opened the door for room service as he admitted to himself that he'd pushed too hard. It hadn't been completely intentional. But he'd sensed her nervousness and instead of backing off, he'd pushed.

Which would explain why she'd been staring at him with dazed, glassy eyes for the past hour. Which would explain why she looked completely and utterly shocked.

After the guy finished setting up the food, Elliot tipped him and shut the door behind him, bracing himself to turn around and apologize. But when he turned around, Shay was on her feet.

And she was halfway across the floor.

"Shay, I'm sorry if I . . ."

"Shhh." She reached up and touched her fingers to his mouth, lightly. Then she replaced her fingers with her lips. "I was kind of wondering . . . can the food wait a little while?"

Elliot groaned as he opened his lips for her.

Staggering back against the door, he pulled her against him. It took everything he had not to clutch her tight, not to tear her clothes away. Instead, he kept his hands loose at her waist. He kept the kiss light . . . or tried to. She bit his lower lip, nuzzled at his mouth, and when he tried to ease up, she followed him, hungry. Almost as hungry as he, it seemed.

She pulled away for a minute, stripping her shirt off, her bra, and then she reached for his clothes. This time, she didn't make any attempt to hide the scars and he didn't try to pretend they weren't there. He cupped her breasts in his hands and dipped his head, skimming his lips along the ridges, then lower to catch a nipple in his mouth.

Shay cried out.

Bracing an arm around her waist, he lifted her. *Where* . . . he thought, his thoughts muzzy and hazed.

As though she'd been reading his mind, Shay whispered, "Bed, Elliot. Take me to bed."

He stiffened. Fuck, he'd already pushed her tonight just by putting some of his weight on her. She thought he hadn't seen, but . . .

Her hands fisted in his hair and she tugged his head back, peering down into his eyes. "Bed," she said again. Then her lashes flickered. "I . . . I need to show you something first. And I need to do it now before I lose my nerve."

The pit of his stomach dropped out.

On wooden legs, he carried her to the bed and lowered her. When she reached for the waistband of her jeans, he felt as if somebody had wrapped barbed wire around his gut, his heart, and his throat.

Her hands were shaking, shaking so hard she kept fumbling with the zipper. And there were tears.

Shit. Elliot eased her hands away and unzipped her jeans. It was the hardest thing he'd ever done. And part of him wanted to leave. Part of him wanted to run away and hide. He didn't want to see whatever it was that had her crying when she'd been so sweetly kissing him just a moment earlier.

Instead, he pressed a kiss to the soft curve of her belly, the dip of her navel. With his hands on her hips, he stroked down, taking both the denim and the silky scrap of her panties with it. Her thighs were strong, slender, and pale—he could still remember how she'd gripped his hips and rode him, the strength in that seemingly delicate body.

Once he had her jeans down to her ankles, she stepped out of them and then settled back on the bed. Her breath was coming in harsh, ragged pants and she didn't speak, just caught his hand and tugged him down next to her on the mattress. Elliot went, still braced on that razor's edge, wondering. Waiting.

She took one of his wrists and guided it to her breast, to the scars.

Her eyes stared at him, begging for him to understand. To see something. Elliot didn't know what.

Then she guided his hand lower.

What—

At first, he didn't know what it was he felt under his fingers.

Then, as realization dawned, he closed his eyes. Yeah, that part of him that wanted to run was really jeering at him now. Running would have been so much easier.

Easing up, he moved to his knees and settled between

her thighs. She had her face averted and there were tears streaming endlessly now. But she didn't fight him.

That fucking monster had cut her here as well.

Through the neat little curls between her thighs, Elliot could see hair-thin scars, even more delicate than the ones on her face. Five of them, it looked like. Unable to breathe, he bent over her and pressed his face to her neck, breathing in her scent and just trying to take it in.

He wanted to ask why.

But he knew she had no answer.

He wanted to rage.

But he knew it would serve no purpose.

He wanted to undo every fucking hurt that had been done to her. That, damn it, he'd at least try to do.

"If anybody else ever tries to hurt you, Shay, I'm going to kill them," he whispered against her skin.

Her arms curled around his shoulders.

Then she stroked her foot up his calf and murmured, "I want you to touch me. I'm so tired of the strongest memories I have being *those* memories. Give me better ones, Elliot." She turned her face to his and pressed her lips to his cheek. "Can you give me better ones?"

Fuck. He felt gutted. Destroyed. As though somebody had hollowed him out and left nothing but the dregs of him. But he couldn't say no to her. He moved to roll to his back, but Shay tightened her arms. "Here," she whispered. "Like this."

"Shay . . ."

Before he could say anything else, she raised her head and pressed her lips to his. "Like this," she said again. Then she twined her legs around his waist and arched up.

It was awkward, unpracticed . . . and as he felt the brush of her naked flesh against his cock, he almost exploded.

"Okay . . ." He groaned. "Like this . . . just give me a minute before you kill me."

Shifting his weight to the side, he reached down and covered her sex with his hand, watching as her eyes went wide. Fear skittered across her face but it didn't consume her. Didn't take over. Still staring at her, he pushed a finger inside her. Hot . . . she was hot.

And as he started to stroke, she grew wet and slick, rocking up to meet him. Her gaze sought out his, her eyes glassy, almost black. A broken gasp escaped her and it was the most erotic sound he'd ever heard. Almost enough to wash away the fury that tried to creep back in as he brushed against one of the scars as he added a second finger, screwing them in, then out of her sweet, sweet heat.

"Elliot!" She drove her heels down in the mattress and lifted her hips high while her hands gripped the comforter beneath her and twisted it in desperation.

There were tears glinting in her eyes as she climaxed. Elliot kissed them away as he settled between her thighs, watching for any sign of fear, any sign of nerves.

And he would have been fooling himself if he hadn't expected to see anything.

Almost as soon she felt his weight, her body tensed. When he went to pull away, Shay curled her hands around his biceps, her nails digging in. "Stay," she muttered, her voice hoarse and broken, her breath coming in ragged gasps.

Her midnight eyes stared into his as she said it again, "Stay . . ."

Elliot reached up and cupped her cheek in his hand. Pressing his brow to hers, he closed his eyes. "Shay."

Keeping his weight braced on his other arm, he muttered against her lips, "You do it."

She tensed. "Me?"

"You want me here . . . you take me here."

He lifted his lashes and stared at her, watched as her cheeks flushed. But she surprised him by reaching down. Then, as her fingers closed around his naked cock, he groaned. "Damn it, I need to get a rubber."

"Do you?" Her fingers tightened, stroking him with a hesitant little caress, from about the midpoint up to his tip.

Elliot could have whimpered, right then and there. "Fuck, Shay . . ."

"You feel soft. How can you feel so soft?" Then she grinned at him. "But not?"

"Telling a guy he feels soft when you got his cock in your hand isn't exactly nice," he muttered. But he didn't care what in the hell she *said* as long as she kept touching him. Her grip tightened and she gave him a longer stroke. He rocked against it and shuddered. "Shit, I need to grab a rubber before I do something embarrassing."

"Do you really need it?"

He stilled and made himself look at her face.

"You do know what happens when people have sex, right?"

Shay stuck out her tongue.

Dipping his head, he caught it in his mouth, sucked on it. She laughed breathlessly when he lifted his head. "Yes, you moron. But . . . well. There are no issues on my side, and . . . um. Well, I just got off my period a few days ago—the day before you and I . . . actually. So. Anyway."

"Anybody ever tell you that you're really cute when you stammer?" He nuzzled her neck and rocked against her hand again. She'd stopped touching him, and that had been the last damn thing he'd wanted. "Shay . . . are you sure you want to do this? And you need to be sure, because the more we do things like this, the more I'm going to think we're getting serious and it's going to kill me if things end up ending on us again."

"Yes." She rubbed her thumb around his head and he hissed, his eyes all but crossing from the sensation.

He held her gaze. "Then like I said . . . you want me here, you take me here."

And that's what she did. Gazes locked, she shifted and squirmed beneath him while he held himself, muscles tensed, over her. When he felt the first brush of her naked, slick heat, he groaned. Her hand fell away and he surged inside, watching her . . . waiting.

Shay smiled.

Seeking out her hand, he twined their fingers and rode her.

He could feel her heart slamming against his chest. He could see the dazed pleasure in her eyes. And he wanted to see it again, and again, every day and always.

"Shay . . ."

Then she completely shattered him. Lifting her hand, she touched his cheek and whispered, "Elliot . . . I love you."

Groaning, he dropped his head, covering her mouth with his. He rolled onto his back, taking her with him and clutching her tight, so tight. Rocking up, he took her fast, desperately. *I love you, Shay*, he thought.

But he didn't dare take his mouth from hers to say the words . . . not yet.

He was afraid if he so much as spoke, he'd wake up and realize all of this was just one very, very strange dream.

As she climaxed around him, he pulled her down, burying his face in the curve of her neck, and threw away his shaking grip on control . . . and just gave in.

To her.

To the need. And the love.

* * *

Shay smiled against his skin as he stroked a hand up her back.

"Did you mean that?" he whispered, his mouth moving against her shoulder.

"Yeah." Rising, she braced her elbows on his chest and stared at him. The dark, tumbled red-brown of his hair was damp with sweat, framing his lean face, and his eyes glinted as he watched her. She touched his lower lip with her finger. "I figured it out while you were giving me a back rub and trying not to freak me out. And for the record . . . I was freaked out over what I'd figured out. Not the back rub."

Elliot grimaced. "And here I thought I was good at covering things."

"You are." She smiled. "I'm just good at reading you."

"Are you?" In a flash, he moved, rolling over so that she was under him. "What am I thinking?"

Grinning, she shrugged. "I dunno. I said I could *read* you. That doesn't mean I can see inside your thick skull."

"Good. That means I get to do the same thing to you that you did to me." He lowered his lips to her ear. "Shay . . . I love you."

Lorna was in there.

Darcy curled her lip as she studied the woman bent over the counter. What an ugly-ass name.

It sounded like it belonged to some backwoods, backward country hick. The woman with the russet-red hair might not be completely backwoods or backward, but Darcy figured she wasn't as smart as she thought.

Customers had been coming and going all day. Darcy had been in and out several times.

Lorna hadn't once noticed her, even though she'd rung her up twice. Hell, she'd sat in the back of the store, using up the free Wi-Fi while she sent Shay some very interesting pictures.

Shay thought Darcy didn't know about the little things that kept her awake at nights. But Darcy noticed *everything* . . . she watched everything. All it took was the mention of an article she read about a child being locked in a closet—*oh, the poor thing*—and Shay wouldn't sleep for days. Then there had been one post where a couple of guys had kidnapped a girl from their school and kept her tied up for several days, playing with her, raping her . . . *that* had really set Shay off.

And she'd written one of her most twisted books afterward, too.

"Really, you should thank me," Darcy murmured, thinking about how many of Shay's fucked-up nightmares had led to fucked-up books. And how many times Darcy had fed those nightmares. It was a partnership—one Shay didn't even know existed.

Absently, she wondered if Shay was keeping up with her email . . . because that *last* one had been a trip. She hadn't sent it under her name. That would be stupid at this point. Shay was starting to remember more and more—she had said as much in her diary. Couldn't let her piece together too much, not until Darcy was back in control.

Shay lay sprawled next to him, half dozing. Every now and then, because he just couldn't stop himself, he reached over and stroked a hand down her arm, brushed her hair back from her face.

Once, she'd opened her eyes a little and smiled at him. But then she wiggled closer and buried her face against his neck and sighed her way back into sleep. It made his heart ache, watching her sleep. If anybody had ever told him it would be such an amazing thing to watch a woman sleep, he would have laughed.

But it was.

Amazing, and erotic, and beautiful.

He couldn't sleep. Part of it was because he couldn't stop thinking about what she'd said. She loved him. It was a gift he'd hoped for. Longed for. Now he had to hope he didn't fuck it up.

But those softly spoken words weren't the only thing keeping him awake tonight. The rest of it was something he could only attribute to feeling *twitchy*. He was damn twitchy, adrenaline cranking on high, and although Shay had yet to fully see it, he knew there was something really, really fucked up going on with her friend.

With her laptop open on his lap, he logged into his email, hoping there would be something from Mike. Something that would *hopefully* explain some of that fucked-up shit.

When he saw the new email, he practically pounced on it. *About damn time,* he thought sourly. It shouldn't take a cop a whole fucking *day* to run a background check, should it—what the *fuck*?

His eyes narrowed as he read the report.

Then he read it again.

When he came to Mike's question down at the bottom, his gut was as heavy as lead, twisted into hot, slippery knots.

Buddy, I don't know what the deal is, but it would appear you have me running a background check on a woman who has been missing for over two years. When you get back in town, you owe me a beer and an explanation.

What the hell was this?

Sliding Shay a look, he blew out a breath.

Okay. Well, it appeared he'd found an answer for the fucked-up weirdness they were dealing with.

Now he just had to tell her.

* * *

Shay read the email.

Hands shaking, she scrolled back to the top and then read it again.

Finally, she minimized the window and then got to her feet and walked away from the bed to stare outside.

It was dark out, although the streets were far from quiet. Apparently midnight in Detroit didn't mean much. The streets were still busy with cars and she stared at them, focusing on the blur of light and motion for a moment while she turned things over in her head.

"Why did you have Mike run a background check?" she asked quietly.

"Because I wanted answers."

Turning, she stared at him. The dim light cast by her laptop played with the planes and hollows of his face, neck, and shoulders and his expression was grim at best.

"Answers about . . . ?"

"Everything." He rose from the bed, the sheet falling away from him. He came to her, wearing nothing but a close-fitting pair of boxer briefs. The muscles in his arms bunched and relaxed as he opened and closed his hands. "Shay, none of this makes sense and *all* of it is seriously fucked."

"You think I don't *realize* that?"

"I think you do. But have you considered just how fucked up this woman is? She's obsessed with you, Shay. That's dangerous."

"She's not—" Then she groaned and turned away. Her belly hurt just thinking about this, but she had to admit it.

If it had been anybody *but* Darcy, she would have been a hell of a lot more cautious about this, and she probably would have been a hell of a lot more scared. And she was already plenty scared.

"Missing," she murmured. "For two years. But it doesn't make sense. I talk to her, Elliot. All the time."

Shaking her head, she moved to the bed and reached for the laptop.

Maybe it was another Darcy Montgomery. She'd just do that deeper search now. She'd meant to do it, anyway. Why not now? It wasn't as if she was going to sleep anyway.

Half desperate to prove Elliot wrong, to prove Mike wrong, she did a Google search and found the typical *Find Darcy Montgomery* . . . blah, blah, blah. There were numerous hits on Facebook and she went there.

After several minutes of searching, she found the right one.

Or at least she thought she had. But the only person she was going to prove wrong, it seemed, was herself. Reading it sent a shiver down her spine.

The picture was right.

Completely right.

And Darcy Montgomery was indeed missing.

Darcy . . .

Two years. Squeezing her eyes closed, she tried to think back. Thought about the emails she'd been going through. The weirdest changes had been in the past year or so, yeah, but the smaller things, those had started about two years ago, give or take.

As fear gripped her heart in a tight, desperate fist, she focused back on the monitor and clicked on the link for a Facebook page. Here, she realized, she'd found Darcy. The Darcy she knew . . . the Darcy she remembered. A Darcy others had known . . . and missed.

I'm thinking about you today, sis. Part of me still thinks you're out there and you'll come back to us. Darcy's brother . . . Shay remembered him. Darcy had talked about him endlessly.

Don't forget, there's a reward posted. A cousin, according to the profile.

Effing spammers—don't see why they have to hit the page of a dead woman. A friend.

"A dead woman," Shay whispered. "Oh, my God."

Her belly clenched.

That wasn't right, damn it. That wasn't fucking *right*.

But there was something in the pit of her gut that said it *was* right. So many things hadn't made sense. Until now. *This* made sense. It wasn't right, and it hurt. It was like acid and glass and nails in her gut . . . but it made sense.

"I didn't want you to be right," she whispered, looking up to find Elliot standing with his back to her, staring out the window.

Slowly, he turned around and met her gaze.

She closed her eyes and pushed the laptop away, drawing her knees up and resting her forehead on them. "I really didn't want you to be right."

Hearing a sound, she turned her head and watched as he came over and crouched by the bed, studying the laptop. "I guess that's Darcy," he murmured.

"Yes. And some of her friends, family." She closed her eyes. "I saw one of her brother's posts. I know him— never met him, but she sent me pictures. It's really her. There are articles from newspapers and everything. She really is missing."

He wrapped one hand around her ankle, his thumb stroking lightly. "I'm sorry, Shay."

She didn't say anything. What was there to say?

After a few moments, he closed the laptop and moved it over to the bedside table. Then he settled on the bed and pulled her against him. She snuggled against his chest and wished she could just stay there. Forever sounded like a good time frame, really.

"What now?" she whispered.

"I don't know." He stroked his hand down her thigh and pressed his lips to her temple. "But we need to start looking at things deeper. You realize that, right?"

Shay squeezed her eyes closed. "I don't even know where to start. I don't know what to look at, what to think . . . I just . . ." She trailed off and wished, yet again, she could just stay where she was. Forever. Not thinking about anything but her and Elliot.

"I've got an idea where to start, Shay, but you might not like it."

Opening her eyes, she tipped her head back and met his gaze. "With the exception of *you*, I haven't liked anything that's happened in my life over the past few weeks. Hell, the past few *months*. But I'll deal. What's the idea?"

"You need to think about who all knows who you are." He reached up, cupping her cheek in his hand.

"Who I am now?" She stared at him, her heart racing, fear turning her hands cold, her heart to ice. "Or who I *was*?"

"What do you mean you're not coming home yet?" Lorna asked.

"There's just some other things we need to check out," Elliot said, sighing. He turned away from the computer, staring at Shay. She stood at the window, her gaze locked on something he couldn't see.

She had come out here to speak with a woman who had been missing for two years.

Fuck, everything was *insane*.

She glanced over her shoulder at him. He smiled at her, but the smile she gave him in return was so broken, so sad and strained. She turned away and went back to staring out into the night.

"Can you do me a favor, Lorna?" he asked quietly, turning back to the computer.

"Yeah, sure."

"Remember . . . you already agreed," he said. "Go stay with Mike for a few days."

"*What?*"

Covering his eyes with one hand, he braced himself for the argument he knew was coming. "Please just do it. I've got my hands full worrying about the mess going on now. I'll feel better if I'm not worrying about other shit," he said flatly.

"Why should I go stay with him?"

"Because you're sleeping with him anyway and he's been trying to talk you into moving in with him and you're acting like nobody knows and everybody does, and for God's sake, because I asked you to . . . *please*," he snapped. He glared at the computer, not seeing anything, too aware of the burning in his gut, too aware of the fear that had been in Shay's eyes ever since she'd seen that fucking *eerie* Facebook page about her friend.

Missing . . . for two years.

Yet she was still getting calls from her.

"What's going on, Elliot?"

"I can't explain now. But if you go stay with Mike, I'll explain as soon as I can. I swear."

Lorna was quiet for a second. Then she sighed. "Fine."

He hung up the phone and then turned back to Shay, wishing he knew what to do, what to say.

It was edging up on two o'clock now, but he doubted she had any more interest in trying to sleep than he did.

Shay stood at the window and he was pretty sure she wished she were anywhere but here. Maybe even with anybody but him—

"I'm glad you're here," Shay said softly, her voice cutting through the turmoil of his thoughts.

He stared at the back of her head, scowling. "Are you?"

"Yes." She turned to look at him, a faint smile on her face. "Why do you sound so surprised by that?"

Elliot jerked a shoulder. "Doesn't seem like I'm making things any easier."

"This isn't meant to be easy." She slid her fingers through the dark, choppy strands of her hair before linking them in front of her neck. Lifting her gaze to the ceiling, she sighed. "My best friend has been missing for two years, Elliot. And I didn't know. I've talked to somebody who sounds *just* like her. How is that possible? How did I not know?"

He studied her. "Is that rhetorical, or are you asking me for ideas?"

"I don't know." Lowering her hands, she met his gaze and said again, "I just don't know. Hell, I don't want to *think* about this for a while. I don't want to think, I don't want to dream. I'm tired but I know if I lie down, I'm going to have all of this in my head, and then what?"

Closing the distance between them, he rested his hands on her waist.

"Well, if you're open to the idea, I've got a suggestion or two on something that might help both of us sleep," he murmured.

A smile tugged at her lips, a little nervous. A little shy. But heat bloomed in her eyes. It was a deadly combination, Elliot thought. And yeah, this right here . . . this was what they needed to do. Forget about the craziness they were caught up in and get caught up in each other for a little while.

"Why don't you tell me about these suggestions of

yours?" she murmured, laying her hands against his chest and stroking them down.

"I've got a better idea." He caught her around the waist and boosted her up. "Why don't I show you?"

She pressed her mouth to his and murmured, "That sounds like a fantastic idea."

CHAPTER
EIGHTEEN

SHE'D ALMOST VISITED LORNA THE NIGHT BEFORE.

Almost.

But Darcy had stood outside and heard the phone ring, then listened to the conversation . . . courtesy of some of the toys she liked to play with.

Elliot.

She'd been talking to Elliot, and then she'd started to pack. While she was packing, she called her boyfriend.

Darcy knew about the boyfriend. He was a cop in that Podunk little town. *Shit*. Not what she needed just then. But she knew when to retreat. Smart women knew when to do that, after all.

Lorna could wait.

Since she knew Shay was most *definitely* not around and wouldn't be coming back for a little while, Darcy was going to take care of other matters—like finding those fucking passwords.

Getting past Shay's security system wasn't the problem—she had the code. "She didn't think to change *that* one," Darcy muttered. She still couldn't believe Shay had gone and locked her out of everything. After all the stuff they'd shared, after all the work she'd done for Shay. "How can she not trust me?"

No, getting past the security system wasn't the issue;

it wasn't even using the bump key. After all, Darcy had used that before, too. Using it in the dark complicated things a little, but she managed.

No, the *problem* was when she got inside and couldn't find the damn passwords.

Shay made notes *everywhere*.

And as expected, Darcy found plenty of notes.

She found notes on stories.

Notes on all the sites she'd changed the passwords on.

But not the passwords.

"Where the hell are they?" Darcy whispered. They had to be somewhere. Had to be.

Fury burned inside her. "Think." She needed to think. Sitting down at the computer, she turned it on, keeping an eye on the driveway. Although Shay wasn't in town, she couldn't risk being seen. She'd parked her truck around the back and the snow was coming down steadily. In no time, nobody would be able to see the tracks left by her truck. As long as she was in and out, everything would be fine.

But she needed to get back in the damn site.

This was a new experience.

Shay woke up sprawled over more than half of the bed, twisted in the blankets, her legs tangled with Elliot's and her head resting on his chest. He had his hand curved over the back of her neck and hers was low on his belly.

Very low.

She flexed her fingers and then bit her lip as she felt the head of his cock.

Heat burned inside her. *Damn.* All these years with her libido lying dormant and she was ready to go for a third round with him in less than twenty-four hours. She needed to get a grip.

Closing her eyes, she told herself to get out of bed. She

needed to shower. Get her game face on and all of that, because today was going to be sheer hell. They had to go to Ann Arbor and find Darcy's family. Talk to her mom and see if she could find any answers.

No time for fun and games, right?

That was what she told herself.

Except she wasn't listening.

Biting her lip, she slid her hand lower and closed her fingers around the warm, rigid flesh of his cock.

"You're awake," Elliot mumbled, his voice husky with sleep.

"No. I'm sleep-groping."

He slid his hand down and closed it around hers, guiding her hand into a slow, steady rhythm. "Well, if that's the case, let me help you out there . . ."

She laughed softly. "Worried I'll wake up and stop?"

"Yes." He arched his hips, moving into her palm. "Fuck, that feels good."

Abruptly he let go of her hand and shifted, sitting up and urging her onto her back. He watched her, with that careful, intent stare that seemed to see straight through to her soul.

She eased back, smiling at him. "I thought you were enjoying the sleep-groping," she teased.

"I think I want to do some groping of my own." He settled between her thighs, lowering his head to nuzzle her through the shirt she'd tugged back on before falling asleep. "These tank tops you like ought to be illegal, I swear. Why do you even bother?"

"Huh?"

Instead of answering, he closed his mouth around one nipple, tugging on it with his teeth. He teased and toyed until he had her gasping, and then he shifted to the other one and repeated the treatment. "I can see right through them," he muttered. "And it just makes me want to do things like this."

With a shaky laugh, Shay said, "Well, if wearing a tank top is going to incite that kind of behavior, I'm going to buy even more of them."

"As long as you only wear them for me." He moved lower, shoving the blankets out of his way.

But when he went to press his mouth to her sex, Shay tangled her hands in his hair. "Elliot—"

He pressed his lips to her hip bone, gently. "Shh . . ."

He eased back to her belly, rubbing his lips along her skin. She jumped as he stroked one hand up her knee, catching her behind her thigh and spreading her open. Blood rushed to her face and she squirmed.

She reached for him, but all he did was meet her hand and twine their fingers. "You're so fucking pretty, Shay," he muttered against the skin of her hip. "So damn pretty. Fuck, just let me . . ."

She flinched as he went lower. Bucked as she felt his breath stir the curls between her thighs. "Hush, baby," he whispered.

"Elliot—"

The strangled cry bounced off the walls and she bit her lip to keep from making another noise, painfully aware of how late it was, of the fact that other people were sleeping on either side of the walls.

Then she forgot all about them—all about *everything* as he stroked her with his tongue.

Blood rushed to her face. *Too much, too much—*

She tangled her hands in his hair and went to jerk him away, but then he groaned against her, sliding one hand under her butt to arch her closer as he muttered, "Let me, Shay, I've dreamed of this . . ."

The naked, raw need in his voice gutted her. And she closed her eyes. Tried to forget just *what* he was doing and just let herself feel . . .

That was all it took.

Shocked, desperate pleasure slammed into her as he

swirled his tongue around her and then pushed it inside. She clutched him closer and drove her heels against the bed, arching to meet him as something hot and wickedly sweet unfurled inside her.

Closer—closer—

But right before she went screaming into it, he stopped.

"With you, damn it," he growled, crawling up the length of her body and settling between her thighs.

Gasping for air, she stared at him as he hooked his arms under her shoulders and caught her head between his hands.

"Wrap your legs around me," he rasped.

Shaken, Shay did just that and then cried out as she felt the head of his cock nudging at her gate. His gaze sought hers out, glittering and hot, all-consuming. Slowly, he pushed inside one slow inch at a time as she stretched around him and arched against him. She sucked in a desperate breath just before his mouth took hers.

"Hold on to me," he said against her lips.

She reached for him, clutching at him with a desperate grip.

As he drove himself home, she choked out his name, barely able to find the breath for even that.

He pulled out and surged back inside. Slowly at first, and then faster, and she arched to meet him. She clawed at his shoulders, straining to get closer. It wasn't enough, not nearly.

She could get lost inside him and it would never be enough.

One burning, hungry kiss after another stole her breath away. Overwhelmed, she was lost in him . . . lost *to* him, but it was wonderful. It was everything.

That burning, sweet oblivion raced closer but stayed tauntingly out of reach. Tearing her mouth away from Elliot's, she cried out in frustration.

He raked her neck with his teeth and pulled away.

Shay swore, but then he eased her over. Startled, a little nervous, she shot him a wary look over her shoulder. "Trust me," he whispered, nudging her onto her hands and knees.

Because it was him, because she could, she held still and then had to bite her lip to keep from screaming as he drove inside her again. Deeper, harder, fuller. One hand came around and she stiffened as he teased the hardened peak of her clitoris.

"That's it," he muttered, twisting his hips and surging deep. "Damn it, you're so fucking soft . . . do that again—"

She whimpered and clenched her inner muscles again, shuddering as he rewarded her with another teasing stroke against her clit.

"That's it . . . aw, *fuck* . . ."

He tightened his grip on her hip, leaned into her, and moved harder. Faster—

With a gasp, Shay went flying. Spinning out of herself.

It might have been terrifying. But she felt his arms come around her.

And even as she shattered into a thousand pieces, he was there to hold her together.

"You should have worn that skirt."

"What skirt?" she asked absently as she stared at the emails that had amassed in her inbox. She had a headache, just thinking about dealing with them.

"That long denim one you like so much," he said, glancing in the rearview mirror before cutting over into the other lane.

Frowning, she looked over at him. "Why should I have worn it?"

"Because if you had . . ." He laid a hand on her thigh, then slid it up until he was cupping her in his hand.

She gasped, sagging back in the seat. Her lids drifted down low and she muttered, "Oh . . ."

"Would have made the drive a lot more interesting," he teased.

Swallowing, she let her chin drop down to her chest as he rubbed the heel of his hand against her. Yes . . . yes, it would definitely have done that. "Well, it's definitely a better option than going through email."

He teased her for another few seconds and then pulled away. "Yeah. Too bad you didn't wear the skirt."

Shooting him a dark look, she shifted in the seat. A hollow ache throbbed down low in her belly and she ended up crossing her legs just to ease it a little. "That was mean," she muttered.

"Then why are you smiling?"

Absently, she touched her lips before looking back at her phone. "I'm plotting my revenge."

"I can't wait." He glanced at the phone. "What has you glaring at the phone so hard?"

"Email," she muttered glumly. "Lots of it."

They lapsed into silence, him playing navigator while she dealt with all those messages.

I hope you'll understand, but I'm unable to do a book signing . . . I don't travel . . .

I hope you'll understand but there's been some confusion—the Facebook page wasn't mine . . .

After about ten of those, she hit a spate of reader emails and breathed a little easier. It was much easier to respond to those. Up until she hit one that wasn't an email.

It was a picture.

Just looking at it—

Elliot just happened to glance over at her in that second. If he hadn't, he wouldn't have seen the way she suddenly clamped her hand over her mouth or the odd, greenish-white tinge to her skin.

He cut across two lanes of traffic and she barely got out of the car in time. He heard the wail of sirens approaching, but ignored them as he ran around the car. Shay was on her hands and knees. As he knelt beside her, she tried to wave him off. He ignored her, stroking her hair back from her face.

"Don't," she whispered feebly in between bouts of retching.

"Shut up," he ordered, continuing to stroke her hair.

"Everything okay here, folks?"

He glanced up as the police officer approached; Shay moaned and doubled over, another bout of nausea grabbing her.

The officer stood a good ten feet away and watched as she once more started to puke.

Elliot cocked a brow. "Well, I guess it depends on where you're standing, Officer."

"You going to tell me what set that off?" Elliot asked after Shay finished swishing some water around in her mouth.

She spit it out and then shut the car door. The cop was still behind them.

"Later," she said quietly. The image . . . *fuck, what was that?*

"Shay . . ."

"No. Not while we still have a fucking cop behind us. Come on, we need to go."

And she needed to see it again. She still wasn't completely sure what she'd seen—some part of her brain *knew*, but the rest of her just didn't.

"Look, just drive," she said quietly. She glanced at the rearview mirror one more time and then over at Elliot. "I have to get moving. Or I'm going to lose my mind."

He stared at her, that gaze searing deep into her soul. "That won't put me off for long," he warned her.

"I don't need forever," she promised him.

No, she didn't need forever. But she needed a few minutes. Elliot was wonderful enough to give her those few minutes and more. As the minutes stretched out into an hour, he still hadn't pushed, and she was eternally grateful.

It gave her time to settle, time to think, time to focus.

As they cut through the early morning traffic, Shay focused on the cars around them, on the sun beating down from the sky overhead, on anything but Elliot.

"Have you ever been to Ann Arbor before?" Elliot asked.

She glanced at him out of the corner of her eye, a faint smile on her lips. "Elliot . . . I've never been *anywhere* before. Arizona. Alaska. That's it."

"Hey, it's an 'A' place." He squeezed her thigh. "I thought maybe you'd decided to try it out. You've got a thing for 'A' places."

She snorted and fiddled with the red and white paper bag on the seat next to her. He'd bought it earlier and she'd eaten half of the sausage biscuit before digging into her email. Now, there was no way she could possibly eat, not with the way her belly was pitching and rolling. Not considering that every time she closed her eyes, she saw that image—

"Why don't you nap?" he asked. "We've still got some driving to do."

Shay snorted. "There's no way I can sleep," she muttered, sighing. The smell coming from the bag was making the nausea worse, too. Crumpling it up, she tossed it in the back and slumped low in her seat. No. She couldn't sleep, but she could keep messing with the nightmare of email and she could maybe try to work her way through the nightmare that was her life—

Or she could answer her phone. Which had started ringing again. *Damn it.*

Dread gripped her and she looked down. "If that's Darcy . . ."

Elliot picked up the phone, glancing at the display. Then he pushed it into her hand. "It says Anna Kent."

"Anna . . ." Clutching the phone in a hand that had suddenly gone sweaty and damp, she closed her eyes. Nerves swamped her, desperate and raw, dancing in her already uneasy belly.

Trepidation was a nasty, ugly beast. It wasn't a beast she normally had to deal with when talking to her agent, at least not in recent years. But it was there now, clawing at her and turning her brain to a stone.

The phone continued to ring. Praying her voice wouldn't shake, she finally answered, sounding cautious and reserved. "Hello?"

"Shay. Hello." There was some reserve in Anna's voice as well.

That actually made Shay feel a little bit better. Closing her eyes, she blocked out everything. Elliot, Darcy, the lingering nausea, the awful email. Nothing existed right now except the woman on the other end of the phone.

"So did Trish explain to you what was going on?"

"Yes." There was a brief pause. Then Anna sighed. "I have to be honest, Shay, I'm confused, I'm worried, I'm angry . . . can we just take it from the top? This just seems so . . . well, bizarre."

Bizarre. Yeah. That about covered it. Shay had spent the past fifteen years of her life living in paranoia, certain something would happen, go wrong. She'd been right, damn it.

She just hadn't expected *this* sort of thing to go wrong.

"From the top," she whispered. "I can do that."

"And you think it's Darcy," Anna said about ten minutes later, after Shay had explained everything that had happened.

"Does anything else make sense?" Shay hadn't even tried to explain the convoluted problems surrounding Darcy. Darcy's disappearance, her imposter . . . how the imposter seemed to know so much about her. She'd told Anna just enough . . . and still, it was too much.

"Well, *none* of this makes sense . . . but she's the only person who'd have the kind of access needed to do what was being done with your email. Not to mention the times when she tried to cause problems with us." Anna muttered, "I need a drink."

Shay scowled. "I want one, too. But I'm on the road and it's too damn early for a drink."

"You should have one, too. Considering this mess, it's definitely *not* too early for a drink. Okay, first things first . . . so you didn't send the letter to my office. Is that correct?"

"Damn straight."

"Okay." Anna blew out a breath. "I have to admit, I'm so glad to hear that, even as I'm . . . well. Never mind. And I'm so sorry this happened. I should have tried harder, something . . ."

"We can talk about all of that later," Shay said quietly, still staring at the trunk of the car in front of her. They'd covered it with bumper stickers. Everything from election campaign slogans to MADD stickers to

SAVE A HORSE—RIDE A COWBOY. "I need to know what to do, Anna. I've done what I can about the crazy pages and most of them are down, but there's still a blog, and she started another Facebook page . . ."

"Does this mean I'm still your agent?"

Shay closed her eyes. "Would you rather not be?"

"Of course, I still want to be your agent. But . . ."

"Anna, you're the only agent I've ever worked with. The only one I want to work with. Unless you'd rather not come back into the middle of this mess, I don't plan on going elsewhere."

"Well, then." Even over the phone line, Shay could hear the woman's smile. "Considering some of the mess happened because of a lapse on our part, my office is definitely going to help get this straightened out. I'll get with the people here and see what they suggest. I'll also contact your publisher, see if there's anything they can do."

A knot settled in Shay's chest. "Thanks." Closing her eyes, she told herself she didn't need to ask. There was no reason, right?

But she had to . . . "Anna?"

"Yes?"

"You believe me, right?"

"Why wouldn't I?" Anna's voice was firm. "Look, this is some crazy shit, I'll give you that, but we'll get it straightened out. I want you to be careful, though. This lady—if she's that obsessed with you, there's no telling what she might do."

Shay grimaced. "Hasn't she done enough? She tried to take over my life. She accused the guy I'm involved with of trying to rape her." *And a friend of mine is missing* . . . She didn't say that, though. Not yet. First she needed to see just what was going on with Darcy. The *real* Darcy. Then . . . then she'd figure out what to do next.

"No. She pretended to be you. And although it's bizarre, she may have thought she was helping you . . . and when you didn't get it, she was pissed, wasn't she? Now her house of cards is really toppling down. We don't know how she's going to react, do we? She could try to do a lot of damage."

Those words made Shay shiver.

Because she already suspected that this woman had done quite a bit of damage.

Part of her wanted to ask . . . *Just how much more can she do?*

As the echo of a child's scream danced through her mind, as the memory of horrendous pain rippled through her body, she knew the answer to that unvoiced question.

Worse. Much, much worse.

"This is the place."

Elliot's hand rested on the back of her neck.

"You're sure?"

Shay nodded. "I had her mom's info buried in my laptop from ages ago. Darcy used to move around a lot, and her mom was how I could reconnect if I lost her phone number or something."

She blew out a breath and muttered, "This is going to suck, Elliot. I mean . . . if I go up there and say, *I need to talk to you about your daughter* . . . What's that going to do to her? If she really is missing?"

"If she really is missing, and somebody is pretending to be her, you realize the imposter, whoever it is, may know something, right?" He brushed a kiss against her brow. "And you can't just ignore that fact. You can't tell me you haven't thought of it."

"I've thought of it," she said, anger and resolve settling inside her. That was why she was here. If nothing else, she had to do this . . . for Darcy. For the friend she remembered.

She swallowed and made herself take a deep breath. She needed to do this. No matter how much it sucked, no matter how much it hurt, the woman in there needed to know that somebody might well be masquerading as her daughter, and Shay needed to know what had happened to her friend.

If there were any answers, *anywhere*, they needed to find them.

There was no mistaking the woman at the door for anybody other than Darcy's mom, Shay thought.

Even the eyes were the same.

Though older, sadder, faded.

They were the same gentle brown. From the lines that fanned out at the sides, she looked like she laughed a lot. And the smile on her face was one that made Shay think of Darcy.

"Mrs. Montgomery?"

"Yes . . . can I help you?"

Shay swallowed. "I . . . I'm here about Darcy."

The older woman lifted a hand. "Oh, dear Lord. Please tell me you know where she is."

"No. I'm sorry." She licked her lips. "I'm a friend of hers . . . we were in school together in Anchorage." Shooting a look at Elliot, she glanced back at Ella Montgomery. "Ma'am, this is terribly complicated. Would it be okay if we came in?"

Ella nodded. "Darcy was terribly proud of what she did with you, you know. She . . ." The woman paused and looked away. "Don't be mad at her. I know you didn't want her discussing her job with others, but I'm her mother."

"It's okay." Shay smiled awkwardly. She twisted her

hands in her lap, uncertain where to go from there. Ella looked like she was ready to cry at any given moment and Shay knew that if the woman did start to cry, she wasn't going to be far behind.

"Can you tell me what happened with Darcy?" Elliot asked quietly, drawing Ella's attention toward him.

Shay could have hugged him. Taking the chance to suck in a breath and settle, she swallowed and looked up to see Ella's face take on a far-off look. "Lord, if only we knew. One day, she was just . . . gone. Just like that. She'd been living with me again for a while. You were sending the books here, do you remember?"

Nodding, Shay murmured, "Yes. For a year or so."

"About two and a half years ago," Ella whispered. "Six months before she disappeared."

Two years . . . It was two years ago when Darcy gave me a new address. That fake one. That was when she started acting different. Shay's gut turned to ice.

"Was there anything going on?" she asked softly. "New friends? Anybody she mentioned?"

As Ella lowered her head, Shay wished she'd just kept her mouth shut. Awkwardly, she searched for the words, but before she could find the right ones, Ella lifted her head and gave a sad sigh. "You have no idea how many times we've wondered that very thing," she said, her voice hitching a little before steadying. "I've gone over things with the police so often I could quote those last few weeks in my sleep. I can't recall any new friends, but while we were close, Darcy didn't share every detail of her life with me. There were some things that she just . . . wouldn't. You know?"

"Boyfriends?" Elliot asked.

"Darcy didn't date much." Ella absently smoothed her hair back and leaned forward, picking up a framed picture from the coffee table and studying it. It was

Darcy—Shay recognized that bright, open smile so easily. "There was a guy she'd been seeing off and on a few months before she moved, but it was more of a friendly sort of thing, I think."

"Maybe we could talk with him?"

Ella closed her eyes. "No. I'm afraid you couldn't. He was in the Marines—died overseas a few months after Darcy disappeared." She opened her eyes and looked back at Shay, that sadness still there. "But Ty didn't have anything to do with her disappearance, sweetheart. I know he didn't. He wasn't even in the country when she disappeared. They'd go out when he was back home, but that was it."

Gently, she touched her fingers to the pale, golden wood of the frame and then set it back on the table with that same gentle, loving care. "If there was anything I thought might help, Shay, I'd tell you. I would have told the police. But there's nothing. Dear God, after two years . . ." She tipped her head back, staring up at the ceiling. "My daughter just disappears one night and nobody sees anything. It's like she vanishes into thin air, taken by a ghost or something."

Taken by a ghost . . . A shiver raced down Shay's spine and an icy sweat broke out over her body. Deep inside her heart, she knew; just as she suspected Ella knew. Darcy was dead. What had happened remained unknown. But Darcy was dead.

Which only left more unanswered questions.

Who in the hell was calling her? Pretending to be her? Pretending to be Darcy . . . ?

And she did such a wonderful fucking job taking care of you . . . didn't she . . . Michelline . . . ?

Michelline.

"Shay?"

Swallowing, she jerked her attention back to Ella.

"I'm sorry. I'm just . . . my head is a mess. I don't know what to think. Darcy . . ."

The grief reached up and grabbed her, choking her.

Elliot wrapped an arm around her and she was tempted, so very tempted, to just press her face against him, let him get her out of there. He would. She knew he would. All she had to do was let him know. But it wasn't right. She'd spent too much time hiding, and this woman had lost her daughter.

Calling on the strength that had gotten her through all the hellish nights, the nightmares, even the trial when she'd had to sit across from her stepfather and say what he'd done to her, she eased away from Elliot and made herself breathe. Level out. And then she stared at Ella Montgomery.

"Your daughter was one of the best friends I had— one of the only friends. I don't make them easily. She all but chased after me in college and dragged me out of my hole, wouldn't give in. She was my first real friend. You have no idea how much I miss her."

Through her tears, Ella smiled. "That . . . well, that sounds like Darcy. Thank you."

Shay nodded.

"Well, was that helpful or not?" Elliot asked as they left.

Shay paused outside the car, staring at him over the roof.

"Two years ago . . . that was when Darcy started to change on me. Little things. Always little things. Then, gradually things got bigger and bigger, but when you're used to things being how they are . . . I guess I just never noticed." She licked her lips and then said softly, "It was helpful. It hurt like hell, but it was helpful."

He continued to watch her, his eyes blank. "You talk to her on the phone. Right?"

"Yes." He didn't have to say anything—she already knew what he was thinking. Looking away, she stared at the house, at the woman who stood at the window near the door, watching them with that sad, heart-breaking look in her eyes. "Come on. I want you to listen to something, but not here. You can listen to that, and I'll show you the email that freaked me out."

"It's a hand," he murmured.

"Yes."

She'd pulled it up on her laptop.

Ugly, brutal. Skin that had been soft and pale was now pallid and chalky, splotched with blood. A close-up of just that small hand. Nothing else.

Tucked in their room at the hotel, Shay sat on the couch, clutching a glass of rum and Diet Coke that held more rum than soda. She sipped at it in numb horror and stared at the monitor.

It was gruesome and horrifying—and oddly, revealing it was the easier of the two tasks. She had to show him this and she had to let him listen to the voice on the message. Let him hear that woman who sounded so much like Darcy.

Listen to the woman that Shay suspected had killed Darcy.

Shit, yes, this was easier. Right now, she was pretending that hand wasn't real and for all she knew, it wasn't.

"Damn it, this just keeps getting more fucked up," Elliot muttered. Shoving up off the couch, he prowled the room. "Who would send that? Is this related to . . . hell, why would it be related?"

Shay swallowed and looked down at her lap. She didn't know if there was an answer to that. If there *was* one, it was trapped back in the black depths of her memories, in that ugly pit that she didn't want to look at too closely.

Shut that fucking baby up . . .

Shay flinched as that voice echoed through her memory. So much louder. So much clearer. And then, that giggling. That mad little giggle, followed by a singsong voice.

Somebody finally shut that baby up . . . know who did?

"Stop it," she muttered, covering her eyes with her hands, swaying slightly.

Warm, strong fingers closed around her wrists, eased them down. Shay found herself staring at Elliot's face. "Are you okay?"

"No." Desperate, she flung herself at him and buried her face against his chest. "No, I'm not. Damn it, Elliot—those voices, the memories. They're getting louder, clearer, all the time."

Blood . . . bright red . . . dripping . . .

Do you remember what happened, Michelline?

Turning her head, she stared at the laptop, at that ghastly, gory image. "Shit." Easing away from him, she sat back on the couch and stared at it another minute. Whether it was real or not, just seeing it made the voices in her head scream louder and louder.

Unable to take it another second, she archived the file. She'd show it to somebody in the Earth's End police department. Filing it away didn't do anything to silence those screams in her mind, though.

Shifting her gaze away from the laptop, she focused on Elliot. He wore another one of those old Bob Marley T-shirts; he seemed to have a hundred of them. The dark auburn of his hair was falling into his eyes, and he looked ridiculously alert. Ridiculously calm. There was a bottle of beer sitting next to his elbow and he looked so . . . normal. So calm.

She'd never felt normal. But she'd found that calm before . . . she didn't think she'd ever have it again, though.

He certainly didn't look like he'd just stared at a small, severed hand or like he was involved with a woman who dreamt of screams, and blood, and mad little giggles.

He looked so calm . . . so normal.

So not for her.

"Tell me something about you," she blurted out.

He'd been in the middle of lifting the bottle to his lips and now he paused, eyeing her curiously. "Shay, you know all sorts of things about me."

"I know that. I just . . ." Groaning, she shoved her hands through her hair. "I've been stripping myself bare and everything I know about you . . . it's all wonderful. It's so normal, and even in the middle of this chaos that's my life, you're so calm. You have a great sister, even if she does crazy shit like bring you rubbers in the middle of the night—which is freaky. You had great parents. You own a bookstore, you were in the army . . ."

"That wasn't so great," he said sourly, lowering his gaze to stare at the bottle of beer. He leaned forward, elbows braced on his knees, dangling his beer there and staring at it. "You sure you want to hear this, baby?"

"If I didn't want to hear it, I wouldn't have asked."

He nodded and took another drink from his bottle of beer.

"You know that shit the woman pretending to be you posted? About how I supposedly raped her?" He lifted his head and stared at her, his eyes burning.

Shay curled her lip. "Don't get me started." Even now, it sickened her and fury beat through her, hard and fast and wicked.

"She isn't the only woman who tried to say that—somebody else did. When I was in the service." He continued to watch her, his gaze steady, eyes unwavering, mouth grim.

Shay's heart stopped. The air in her lungs froze even

as everything inside her tried to whisper . . . *lies . . . just lies. This is Elliot.*

And she knew that. She *did*, but the memories were beating at her, sucking her under. She shoved them back and focused on him, just him.

Drawing in a desperate breath, she looked back at Elliot and stared at him. "You would never hurt a woman."

"Don't bet on it," he muttered, lowering his gaze to his beer again. "If I ever find the woman doing this to you, I just might hurt her. A lot. But no, I haven't ever hurt a woman that way. I wouldn't."

Shay nodded. "So what happened?"

A bitter smile twisted his lips. "She was trying to fuck with her boyfriend's head. From what I was able to piece together in the aftermath of it all, I think he was getting ready to dump her. He was in line for a promotion and a transfer, and she was always pushing for a ring. He was on the fast track, too. Heading for big things. She knew it. She was an army brat—knew where he was heading, what he had coming toward him. She wanted to go along for the ride but when he told her he wasn't going to play, she got mad. Went out slumming."

His words were so flatly spoken, so coolly stated . . . and she could see the emptiness in his eyes. Hear the echo of pain, the lingering whisper of sadness.

"What happened?"

"I didn't know her," he said quietly. "Hadn't ever seen her before, although I did know her boyfriend. We were friends. I guess it says something that I hadn't ever met the woman—I'd met one of his girlfriends before. She came on to me at a bar and it was one of those stupid things. I was still young enough to think with my dick and we went back to her place. I spent the night."

He paused, lifted his bottle, and half-emptied it in three long gulps. "I left and didn't think about her again until a few days later when the MPs showed up. They told me a civilian had filed charges against me for rape." He shrugged and fell silent.

Shay remained quiet, waiting.

The silence didn't last. Surging up off the floor, he slammed the bottle down and started to pace. "The MPs took me in, questioned me. I got an attorney and I didn't talk to anybody but him—only smart way to play it."

All of that calm was gone, Shay thought. He paced, wild, restless. One glimpse at his face revealed eyes that burned, swirling with emotion. "My career was hanging in the balance; I'd planned on making a life out of it. I didn't have high aspirations, but my dad—the guy who fathered Lorna and me—he'd died in the army—Desert Storm—and I was following in his footsteps, or trying to. Wanted to serve. That was all. Now I've got this woman who I'd never met before, didn't even really know, and she's accusing me of rape—she's got this crazy story, telling them that she tried to fight me off, but she couldn't, and telling them how I made her lie down and told her if she fought me, I'd kill her."

"That's kind of contradictory," Shay said, forcing the words out through a throat gone tight. Her mouth was dry, she realized. Terribly, horribly dry. Tossing back half of her rum and Coke, she clambered to her feet and made her way over to the bar. Another drink and maybe she could get through this without freaking out.

It wasn't that she believed the woman's accusation. She didn't. At all. But it was hard to hear . . .

Go ahead and fight me, you stupid little cunt—

"Yeah. It's one of the things my lawyer grabbed and used. There were a lot of inconsistencies. First she said I used a rubber, then I didn't. Then she made her clean up before I left so there wouldn't be any evidence. People reported her coming up to me at the bar, but she tried to say I dragged her out of the parking lot . . ." He shook his head, staring down at nothing, his beer bottle now hanging, forgotten, from his hand.

"So if her entire story was shit, I guess it didn't go anywhere, did it?"

He gave her a look over his shoulder. "The military has a harsh line on these things. I was basically screwed from that point on. The charges were dropped—she had a history of false allegations and she recanted, then later tried to press charges against a different man. But the stain was still there. And I came up against a wall everywhere. Worse, the guy who used to be my friend . . ." He shrugged. "Well, I guess he wasn't. I tried to ride it out, hoped it would get better, but it didn't. Once I realized there were always going to be whispers, rumors and shit, I decided I was done. I finished up my time and got the hell out. Came home. End of the story."

Shay stared at him, bottle of rum in hand. "They shut you out, didn't they?"

He emptied his bottle and tossed it in a garbage can sitting a good ten feet away. It hit with a heavy thunk that made her jump even though she'd known it was coming. "Hey, I could have kept trying."

"Why bother? They had a crazy bitch spouting lies and they knew it and they still didn't care. They shut you out. Completely. And your friend. He'd rather listen to some idiot he was getting ready to dump anyway? That's insane."

"Yeah." He gave her a savage smile. "Fuck them."

Putting her glass aside, she crossed the floor to him. Her belly was a tight, ugly mess and her legs felt quivery and weak. What she wanted to do was hide in a corner until she felt a little more steady, a little more secure. But she wouldn't. She couldn't. So she didn't.

"You look afraid," Elliot said, his voice raspy.

Shay shook her head, knowing she was probably

going to mess this up. "I'm not . . . not exactly. I'm not afraid of you." With her heart tripping in her chest and blood roaring in her ears, she swiped her sweaty palms down the sides of her jeans and then reached up, resting them on his waist. "When I read what she'd written on Facebook, it took about four tries before I managed to get through it without a panic attack. But it had nothing to do with *you* or even what she said about you. It was just her words."

He continued to watch her, waiting, showing no sign of emotion, barely any sign he'd even heard her.

"Any time I even write a book that deals with assault, I have these mini-attacks. Not full-blown ones, but sweats, rapid heartbeat, nerves. It's nothing like dealing with it in real life, though, thinking that somebody else has dealt with it—I used to not even be able to watch the news because I knew it would be mentioned." She tried to smile and failed. "Once Darcy . . . my *real* friend . . . we'd gone to a sports bar and a news blip came up about this football player who'd raped his girl-friend . . . I passed out. Darcy lied and told everyone I'd had an anaphylactic reaction. She couldn't think of any-thing else to say. I woke up in an ambulance."

Nervous, she reached down and caught his hand. His fingers linked loosely with hers as she whispered, "It's not you. It's me."

"No." He sighed and lowered his head, pressing his brow to hers. "It's not you. It's the fucked-up world around us and what it let happen to you."

As he eased her body against his, she sighed and snug-gled closer. Some of that weird, nervous weakness drained away, replaced by a warm, loose feeling . . . al-most contentment. *Almost peace*, she thought.

"I guess you weren't expecting that kind of some-thing, were you?" Lips pressed against her temple, he slid another hand around her waist, then skimmed it up her back, settling her more firmly against him.

"I knew there was something." She grimaced and rested a hand on his shoulder. "I guess I should have been more prepared. Ah, maybe I should warn you. I think whoever is doing this has been poking around in your background. She said something . . ."

He tensed.

Lifting her head, she looked up at him.

"What?"

Shay swallowed. "She . . . whoever *she* is . . . said something about how you'd done this before after that shit went up on Facebook. I thought she was just trying to freak me out, and she was. But she was using your past to do it."

The gold in his eyes chilled to ice.

Reaching up, she touched his chin. "Elliot?"

"That bitch," he muttered. Anger vibrated inside him, crashing like waves on the sand.

But then he blew out a breath. "I should have figured as much. The shit she was saying . . . it was too similar."

She bit her lip, waiting.

The tension slowly eased out of him and then he shifted his attention to her.

"I'm sorry," she said quietly.

"Why? You didn't do it." He grimaced and said, "I was talking to my lawyer . . . he wouldn't be able to handle anything like libel, but I figured I could use some advice. I guess I could update him on how things are going, but it all seems kind of pointless right now. She doesn't give a damn about me—I was right about that. I'm just a casualty."

She opened her mouth to argue, but he cupped his hand over the back of her neck and eased her back against him. "It seems like this bitch is leaving lots of casualties around us," she murmured. "You. Darcy . . ."

Her gut twisted and she closed her eyes. *Darcy* . . . "Fuck, I've been so frustrated with Darcy lately. Even before this. Just irritated with her—I couldn't figure out what her deal was, why she'd changed, but she was my friend and I didn't want to rock the boat . . . why in the hell didn't I rock the boat, Elliot?"

He was silent as it all came pouring out.

"And then everything starts happening and I *still* don't see the problem. I think it's her, even though it doesn't seem like anything Darcy could have done. It didn't fit. It never fit. And that's because it *wasn't* her."

"No." He caught her hand in his, stroking his thumb across her skin. "It wasn't her. Your friend didn't set out to hurt you, Shay."

Grief grabbed her heart and twisted it, all but wrenched it from her chest, squeezing it in a merciless fist.

"You know, I'd rather it be Darcy. I'd rather deal with the fact that one of my best friends had decided to stab me in the back than this. Anything but this," she whispered.

"I know." He kissed her temple. "But I'm right here. I'm staying right here."

Blowing out a breath, she looked up at him and said, "I'm glad." Then she turned away and reached for her phone. "You mentioned her voice . . . it's something else that's bugged me. For a couple of reasons."

Sitting down, she opened up her contacts and found the number she'd saved.

Her hands were shaking, Elliot thought. And he'd seen the tears she'd fought back. She needed to let herself grieve. Mourn. But she was holding those feelings back. He didn't know if that was the best way to handle the situation, but he figured she was handling it the best way she knew how.

Still, looking at her made him ache. In so many ways. There were dark circles under her eyes, so dark her eyes looked bruised, and she'd never looked so fragile.

"Just listen to the voice," Shay said quietly, shooting him a look.

He nodded, hoping he'd be able to understand just what it was she so badly needed to share with him.

But he was clueless. The voice that came on the line was the message one got when a number was disconnected.

Shay scowled, staring at the phone. "That's *bullshit*," she snapped after about thirty seconds, snagging it and scrolling through the numbers. "That's the right . . ."

Then she lowered the phone, a distant look on her face. "That bitch. She disconnected the number. I called it just a few days ago—it's right there in the call log, but she's already disconnected it."

"Who?"

The smile on her face was a bitter mockery of a real one, he thought. "Isn't that the question, Elliot?" Rising from her seat, she paced the room slowly, almost absently, as if she didn't have a clue where she was stepping, nor a care. She shot him a look over her shoulder and her eyes snapped with fury. Her voice was short and clipped, all but vibrating with anger. "That's the number she gave my agent when she fucked up the works there, too. I called the number and it went to voice mail. The woman on the line? She sounded like me. *A lot* like me. It was freaky, Elliot."

Her eyes stared off into the distance but Elliot knew she wasn't seeing anything there. "And now the number is disconnected. We don't have any fucking *clue* who she is," Shay whispered.

He closed his eyes, clenching his jaw as the words burned inside him. The clues were there. Shay just couldn't see them, although he could understand why.

The horror of whatever she'd lived through, both as a child and as a teenager, was blinding her, and he didn't blame her for not being able to look beyond it. Now she had the trauma of losing one of her few friends. Sometimes being so close to something made it impossible to see the whole picture, he guessed. He wasn't that close and even *he* couldn't see it all.

But if she couldn't find a way to see past it to the thread that connected everything, this was going to continue to wreak havoc on her life.

"Shay . . . there is something that connects everything, you know," he said softly. "And it's pretty obvious. It's been right there, all along."

As she turned to face him, something glinted in her eyes. It might have been anger, might have been fear. But the look on her face was blank, almost carefully so. "Oh, really?"

"It's you."

Shay curled her lip. "I'm *aware* of that, damn it. It involves me and it's hard to connect *to* me without involving *me*."

Sighing, he rose and came around to face her. The choppy strands of her hair framed her face and he reached up, catching one lock in between his fingers, stroking the silken strands as he watched her. "She knew your friend . . . one nobody could really connect to you. She knew how to get to your agent, knew other things that really nobody but you should know. And she knew your name. Not the name you've got now and not just your pen name, although you kept that a secret, too. But she *knew* your *name*. Just how many people would know that, baby? How many *could* know that?"

"Hello?"

A long, sleepless night had passed. She'd lain curled in a ball with her back tucked against Elliot's front, but even his warmth hadn't done anything to ease the fear and aching lodged deep inside her.

"I need to speak with . . ." Shay paused, uncertain whom to ask for. A name flashed through her mind—she'd done a check on the address after she'd failed to find Darcy . . . or answers . . . there. Selena. Selena Campbell. "Ms. Campbell, please. I need to speak with Ms. Campbell."

"It's Mrs. Campbell. May I help you?" Her voice, cautious but polite, faintly accented with the sound of Mexico, was clear on the line.

And Shay had no idea what to say. None.

"Mrs. Campbell." Toying with the phone line, she stared out the window into the early morning sunlight. Elliot was out getting coffee and breakfast. She'd told him she needed a few minutes alone, so she could do her journaling and freak out in private. But here she was on the phone. With a woman she didn't know, and Shay didn't even know why she was calling her.

"You were at my house," Selena Campbell said quietly.

Shay closed her eyes. "Yes."

"I cannot help you."

"But . . ."

"There is nothing I can tell you. I truly wish I could, but sh . . . but I cannot. Please do not call again."

"Wait!"

But Shay feared it was too late.

Despondent, she stared at her phone. She'd been staring at it a full ten seconds when she realized the call hadn't been disconnected. Lifting it back to her ear, she said, "Mrs. Campbell."

There was a soft, sighing sob on the other end of the line.

"Mrs. Campbell, please. This woman . . . I need to know about her. Something. *Anything.* I think she's hurt a friend of mine. I don't know for sure, but . . ."

Closing her eyes, she pressed a hand to her brow and groaned. "Please. Just help me."

"We took her as a child." There was a pause. "Such a pretty child. Such a sweet smile. But such evil in her soul. We tried to do right by her, but she had a monster in her . . . and it got worse. All the time. Little by little. There was no help for her. Eventually, she crossed lines that must never be crossed. We left Arizona . . . but she found us."

Arizona . . .

Dumbstruck, Shay dropped the phone and stared at it as if it were a snake.

CHAPTER
NINETEEN

ANGIE DIDN'T EVEN LOOK AT THE NUMBER WHEN SHE answered. It had been ringing off and on all damn day and she had projects on deadline and she was in a bad, bad mood.

"What?" she growled into the phone.

"Did I have a sister?"

Shay's voice was harsh and edgy, full of something that Angie couldn't quite define. Scowling, Angie peered at the computer screen and changed the shading around the model's face. "A sister? Sweets, you got three of us."

"I mean from *before*," she snarled. "Somebody from before Virna found me. Was there a sister? Was there somebody else?"

The fury and the fear in Shay's voice finally penetrated and Angie straightened up, turning away from the cover she'd been working on. Rising from her desk, she stretched out the kinks in her back and stared out the window.

"Shay, I don't know anything about your life before Mom brought you home," she said quietly.

"Bull*shit*."

"I don't," Angie snapped, shoving a hand through her hair. Her fingers caught on a tangled curl and she swore. Grabbing a clip, she twisted her hair up and back, shoving a couple of sticks into it to keep it out of her face. "Shay, you were brutalized and you were traumatized. You screamed at night and you cried all the time, and you talked about a baby, and how you never had enough to feed it and the little kitty and how he hurt it. You cried about how you never wanted to be the princess and you were sorry. There was a lot of crazy, crazy shit, crazy shit I couldn't make sense of, and I don't know *what* was real and what *wasn't*. I just knew you'd been hurt, and that you were terrified, and that I wanted to kill anybody who tried to take you from us."

On the other end of the line, there was a silence.

Then a man's voice.

"Shit. I gotta go. Angie . . . I need more than that."

Closing her eyes, Angie shook her head. It didn't matter that Shay couldn't see her. "Sweetie, I don't have anything more for you. For the very longest time, I don't think you even knew what parts of your life were real, and what wasn't. Eventually, you just forgot. And it was better that way . . . why remember it if you don't have to?"

An ugly laugh came from her sister, one that sent chills down Angie's spine.

"That's just it, Ang. I *have* to. But there's *nothing* there."

* * *

MyDiary.net/slayingmydragons

I think there's another dragon in my life. Well, I knew there was a dragon, but all this time I thought it was like a pesky little dragonfly, something I could squash if I just tried hard enough.

This is a big-ass motherfucker and I think it's been there all along.
I just never knew.

Such a short little note.

It was bothersome, really. It didn't tell her *anything*. The whole point of the diary was to let her know what Shay was thinking, what had her worried, what had her scared.

This told her nothing. Sighing, she touched the screen on her phone and went back to studying her scrapbook.

It was stuffed full with pictures.

As the plane flew south, she made plans. She'd be in Phoenix by nightfall and she had plans to make.

The first task . . . find him. Find Shay's true dragon.

That wouldn't be too hard.

After all, Jethro Abernathy was a registered sexual offender and a convict. His crimes were many.

Even thinking about facing this dragon made her belly burn hot, filled her with anticipation and need. Everything went back to him.

Somebody shut that baby up . . .

Humming to herself, she continued to line up the pictures. All the pictures she could find of him. From those years so long ago to the more recent ones. She'd be able to find him anywhere, she imagined. She'd *know* him anywhere. But she wanted to study him. Know his face, know every wrinkle, every line.

And she wanted to look into his eyes as he died.

She thought maybe she'd even want to carve lines into him, to do to him what he'd done to Shay.

That was what she really hated him for. He'd had no reason to hurt Shay. And he'd made her break her promise to Mama. She'd promised. All those years ago.

Take care of Michelline for me, sweetie. And I'll see you soon . . .

Mama had broken her promise. But she never broke promises.

She'd go to Phoenix. She'd find him. And then, she'd kill him . . . kill Shay's true dragon.

The last thing Shay should have done was have a glass of wine on the flight.

Much less two. Except wine made it easier to think—or *not* think—about what she was doing. Flying to Phoenix. Back to hell. It had been fine, up until the wine hit her system. But now she was tired, so damn tired, and she couldn't fight the exhaustion dropping down on her.

Shay felt as though her eyelids had gained about five pounds each, sometime during the second glass of wine. Leaning her head against Elliot's shoulder, she stared out the tiny window at the fluffy white clouds and tried not to think.

Somewhere off behind her, a baby cried.

Squeezing her eyes closed, she whispered, "I don't want to hear that right before I fall asleep."

Elliot caught her hand in his. "You okay?"

"Yes."

But she knew she was lying.

The baby continued to cry. Soft, plaintive little sounds.

Vaguely, she heard a woman's low voice, then the baby stopped crying. Finally. Sleep rushed up closer.

She squeezed Elliot's hand tighter. "I don't want to dream."

His arm came around her.

She hoped he might chase the dreams away—

The baby cried. . . .

"Shut that fucking baby up! Shut it up or I fucking will—"

That giggling little voice. "Aww, it's okay now. You'll be the princess again . . ."

Trapped in the dream, Shay flinched. Turning her face toward Elliot, she bit back the moan.

"It's all your fault!" the dragon shouted. "Your fault . . . because you had to be the fucking princess."

The dragon roared . . . and a baby still cried.

Shay came awake to hear a baby crying—a real baby, whimpering and sobbing pitifully as his mother tried to console him.

"Are you okay?"

Elliot still held her hand.

She had no idea how long she'd been asleep, but the vague, hazy exhaustion caused by the wine had faded, so it had to have been at least an hour. Swallowing, she rubbed at her eyes and muttered, "Good enough."

The baby continued to cry, the pitiful sounds getting louder and louder. *Poor thing*, she thought.

"Damn it, that bitch needs to shut the fucking baby up. I'd smack the shit out of it if it were mine," the guy sitting next to her muttered as he shifted in his seat, jabbing his elbow into her arm.

With those fading screams from her dreams still dancing through her mind, she gave him a cool look. Without thinking, she said, "Yes, because slapping an upset baby is certainly the way to get him to stop crying."

He stared at her. "It's annoying as hell having to listen to that on a plane," he snapped.

"Maybe. But the baby can't help being miserable a few thousand feet up in the air." She smiled at him. "I find it annoying as hell to listen to *you* on a plane. *You* can help it, but I don't see you shutting up."

He curled his lip at her. "You're a mouthy—"

Elliot leaned in around her, reaching one arm over and laying it on her hand. "Sir?"

The guy glared at him.

Elliot just stared back.

As the dumbass went silent, Shay grabbed her iPhone and plugged in her earbuds. "Stupid asshole," she muttered. "Hit a baby—that's really a good way to make him feel a little less scared. Shit, did you eat lead chips for breakfast or what?"

Elliot laid his palm on her thigh and squeezed.

From the corner of her eye, she saw the passenger going red, sputtering as he tried to say something.

Either he figured it was a waste of time or he didn't like the way Elliot was eyeing him, because he settled back and folded his arms over his chest, glaring at the back of the seat in front of him.

Behind them, the baby settled down into soft, sad little snuffles.

But the baby's broken cries continued in her mind. Shay couldn't silence them there and no matter how loud she blasted her music, she couldn't block them out.

Do you remember what happened? Virna's voice, so soft and gentle.

Stupid bitch. You think you got away with it, don't you . . . Jethro, so angry and full of hate.

Even now, after all that time, she could feel the hard press of hands around her throat. Hear the rasp of his voice.

Her dragon.

Her stepfather.

For so many years, she'd kept his name tucked away and deliberately made herself *not* think of him, although she'd never forgotten. She didn't want to remember, but she couldn't forget him as easily as she'd forgotten the earlier years of her life.

Thanks to the security checks she kept up with, she kept track of him. She didn't stalk him, but she knew when he'd been released and where he lived, that he was still in Phoenix, working at a store. She knew just enough to make sure he was staying very, very far away from her.

In the depths of her mind, she could still hear him rasping in her ear as he dragged her out of the house.

Not yet, little cunt. You don't get off that easy. Not yet.

One hand closed into a fist.

You can't get away. You won't forget again, damn it. You stupid cunt—

Unconsciously, she reached up and rubbed her throat, remembering the brutal, hard press of his hands.

Elliot rubbed his hand up and down her thigh. Slowly. Soothingly. But the images continued to flash. Voices echoed in her ears. The echoes of laughter. A girl . . . it had been a girl's laugh she heard.

Swallowing, she bent down and grabbed her laptop, flipping it open, almost desperate to purge those images from her mind.

* * *

MyDiary.net/slayingmydragons

I left Arizona the day after my name change was final. My stepfather was put in jail for raping me, and for the attack that ended in my adopted mother's death.

It's been years . . . a lifetime ago since I left, but in some ways, it feels like yesterday. Once I left, I never returned.

I was sixteen when he took me, and it took almost two years to see him locked away.

I don't want to go back now.

But I've spent too many years not knowing what really happened to me as a child and somebody is using that against me.

Somebody knows things about me that they shouldn't know.

The name I'd forgotten.

My friendship with D.

There are probably other things, too.

But I need to go back and figure out who all knows about me.

And I need to understand more about that life . . . about who I used to be. Because there are so many things that don't make sense . . . so many loose threads. But like E says, there's one thing that connects all of them. Me.

Until I understand how I connect them . . .

CHAPTER
TWENTY

THE HEAT WAS A SHOCK AFTER THE FRIGID TEMPERA-
tures of Alaska and Michigan.

Shedding her coat, Shay stuffed it in the trunk of the
car, giving the task a lot more attention than it required.
The absolute last thing she wanted to do was look
around.

Phoenix, Arizona.

Sky Harbor wasn't a place that really stood out in her
memory and she knew the entire area was likely to have
changed, but she didn't want to look around and she
didn't want to be here.

The stark beauty of the desert was one that called to
many, but it wouldn't call to her. She was so desperate
to leave already; if she thought she could outrun the
screams in her mind, if she hadn't determined to find
some answers, she would have taken off for the terminal and been on the first outbound plane she could find.
Where it was going didn't matter. As long as it wasn't
here.

*You go ahead and run away now, you fucking
whore . . .*

Elliot skimmed his hand through her hair and then,
lightly, oh, so lightly, touched the back of her neck. She

leaned back into his touch and sighed, forcing herself to stare up at the sky. It was almost painfully blue.

"It's five o'clock. And it's not dark yet. Seems so weird."

"Give it an hour. It will be dark and you'll feel like you're home."

"Fat chance. It's hot." She grimaced and glanced down at her boots and sweater. "I practically need shorts."

Somebody bustled by in a hoodie and jacket, with the hood pulled up, and Shay laughed. "I guess cold is all relative. I'm burning up and that woman looks like she's freezing."

"They haven't spent their winters living in subzero temperatures." He tossed his parka in the back of the car before turning around, crossing his arms over his chest. She wanted to be there, right up against his chest where she could listen to his heart beating and forget about everything and everyone else in the world.

"You have any idea where we're going?"

Shay swallowed, her throat aching as if she'd just been forced to swallow an iron ball the size of a fist. Bruised . . . battered . . . broken. That's how she felt. Bruised, battered, and broken. "Yes," she said quietly. "I know where we need to go. For now at least."

Elliot waited patiently.

She really, really loved his patience. Usually.

Under the warm light of the sun, though, as she shivered and tried to accept what her brain was telling her, she wished that he wouldn't always be so patient. If he would push, if he would nudge, if he would do anything but let her think her way through this . . .

"I dream. And I remember things I've forgotten. Lately, I remember more . . ." She swallowed and lowered her head, staring down at the black toes of her boots. "But some things, I never forgot. Not the way I'd like to forget them."

"Shay?"

Unable to linger another second, she grabbed the door's handle, jerking it open. In a rush, she clambered into the driver's seat and gripped the steering wheel. "I want to find out more about my mother, Elliot."

Find out about her . . . and if there were others besides me . . . and the baby in that house.

The baby.

A child who Shay was more and more convinced was her brother.

A child that Shay was more and more convinced had died that last night . . . the night the police came and took her away.

But what had happened to him?

A blood-drenched scream.

"Somebody finally shut that baby up . . ."

A hand touching her cheek.

"Do you remember what happened that night?"

This time Shay had an answer.

I don't want to.

* * *

MyDiary.net/slayingmydragons

Until I understand how I connect them . . .

Frowning, she read the last line over and over. "Connect them? Connect *who*?"

Damn it, this wasn't what she'd expected to see. She was looking for a response to the emails she'd been sending—such as the hand. It wasn't a *real* hand. It was a doll's hand, but it still looked pretty damn lifelike and Shay should have been freaked *out*. But here she was talking about the search for answers and connections? Who in the hell did she think she *was*?

The *E* she mentioned, yeah, she *knew* who that was. Elliot . . . poking his nose where it didn't belong.

Rolling a pen back and forth between her fingers, she thought about the unfinished business she'd left behind in Alaska. If she'd *finished* it then, he'd be back there, dealing with the mess she'd wanted to leave. Lorna. The store. Her heart gave a wistful little sigh. She should have just done it, really. It wasn't as if anybody could have traced it to her. Not really.

Now they were heading to Arizona?

Doing God knows what . . . looking for God knows what. Looking for . . .

Swearing, she shoved up from her chair and started to pace. She *knew* what Shay was looking for—what she'd always looked for. She'd made numerous references to it in her diary, even in her books, although Shay couldn't see it as easily as *she* could.

The silly little bitch wanted answers. And she wasn't content to look for them alone this time. She had him with her. She'd actually left Alaska and come back home. Did she need them that bad . . .

"No," she muttered, reaching up and grabbing a lock of hair, absently smoothing it between her hands, over and over. Shay didn't *need* anything, or anybody, except her. Coming here was stupid. It was only going to cause more nightmares and more problems and more sadness.

Bringing *him* along was just more proof of how fucked up Shay's head was. Did she actually think she could handle a relationship *now*? When she hadn't been able to hack them before?

Didn't she remember how bad it got the last time?

"Of course, she remembers." But remembering wasn't enough. She had to keep trying and when she failed, somebody would have to pick up the pieces, all over again.

"Me . . . it will be up to me." She'd have to pick up the pieces, help Shay move on.

As she said it, she smiled, some peace coming to her mind. Once the world fell apart around her, Shay would realize she couldn't do this alone.

"She'll need me again. And I'll be able to take care of her."

That was all she'd ever really wanted, anyway.

Well, mostly.

CHAPTER
TWENTY-ONE

"I'M GLAD YOU'RE HERE," SHAY SAID QUIETLY.

"Wouldn't be anywhere else." He kissed her fingertips and then looked over at the building that sprawled out before them. The police station, like many of the buildings, was done in tones of rust and earth, sprawling out across the city block. People came and went in an unending flood. "So why are we here?"

"There was this one cop who worked my case." Shay slid her hand up until she could grip his, squeezing tight. "I remember him . . . he was so kind when he talked to me, and when he was working the case, he made me a promise."

She blew out a breath and then continued, "He told me it wouldn't be easy to testify and that he'd understand if I couldn't. But he also told me that if I'd stand up against my stepfather, he'd do his damnedest to make sure the man went to jail for a very long time. He kept that promise . . . and he came to Virna's funeral. I saw him there, the day before I ran away. I think he knew what I was going to do. I think he knew, but he didn't seem to mind."

"You were just a kid, Shay. You had every right to run—it's not like there were a lot of good things here to hold you back."

"No."

After Virna had died, once Jethro Abernathy was in jail, there hadn't been much of anything for her here.

But here she was anyway.

Back in Phoenix and ready to go find a man who'd seen her at her absolute lowest . . .

The interior of the police station seemed terribly cold after the heat outside. She shivered, arms wrapped around herself, hunching in for warmth as she walked down the hall toward the round desk located in the middle.

Elliot reached up and in that easy, casual way of his, laid a hand on her neck. The warmth of his skin was a shock—she was so damn cold. So cold. She could remember being in this place. Too many times. All the questions. Accusations. People made the victim into the criminal and even as battered as she'd been, as young as she'd been, it had been no different with her. And that was all *before* she faced the bastard who'd destroyed her childhood.

"May I help you?"

The question came from the cop sitting behind the desk and the look on his face was anything but friendly.

"Shay . . ." Elliot leaned down, pressing his lips to her ear. "Shay, breathe . . ."

Breathe. Yeah. Good idea, she thought as she eyed the cop just a few feet away.

He had a grim, unamused expression, and he looked as though he'd rather be doing just about anything other than talking to her. No sympathy, and for that, she was glad. Whether he'd realized she was on the verge of freaking out or not, she didn't care.

She was tired of sympathy and understanding.

She just wanted to get this done. Without bothering to smile, she said, "I need to speak to Captain Hilliard, please."

"Is he expecting you?" the cop asked.

"No. Just . . ." She paused, and then, without letting herself think, said, "Ask him if the name Jeanette Hall means anything to him."

The cop stared at her narrowly and gestured to the seats behind them.

"Sit down. He's in a meeting that can't be interrupted, but he should be done in a few minutes."

Shay sat.

And as she did, she noticed he'd picked up the phone. He wasn't very good at being subtle. She could feel him watching her.

Elliot, too. Although his study wasn't quite so intense, she could feel the curiosity in his eyes, the wondering questions. As he reached over and took her hand, she swung her head around to face him. His hair was tousled and getting long. He needed a haircut.

There was stubble on his cheeks and he looked tired as he rolled his head around to smile at her.

"I think Jeanette Hall was my mother," she said, her voice sounding terribly loud in the room.

Elliot's lids flickered but he made no other sign that he'd heard her, that he was really even listening. It made it that much easier to pretend she wasn't really talking to him . . . almost like she was writing in a journal. Except . . .

His arm came around her, pulling her snug against him. That sense of comfort, of not being alone, that silent strength—she'd never gotten that from writing in her online diary. Had never gotten that sense of peace from anybody . . . except him.

Leaning into him as much as she could, she stared toward the desk, watching. Waiting.

"I don't remember her . . . at least not up until recently. I don't think you can even call what I have memories, really." Sighing, she plucked at a loose thread from his shirt and asked, "You know that weird déjà vu feeling, like a song you think you've heard, or the smell of something that seems really familiar, but not quite?"

"Yes."

"It's like that. The memory of her is *almost* there . . . something I can *almost* remember. But it's just not there. Not yet. Not completely. And I don't think it ever will be. I was too little when she died."

"You're sure she's dead?"

Shay closed her eyes. "Pretty sure . . . she wouldn't have left me. Not if she loved me, not if she's the person I think I almost remember."

A gentle hand stroked up, then down her spine. "Sometimes people do crazy shit."

That lingering ache remained. Sadness. Another thing that she couldn't completely understand. "I hear a voice in my dreams . . . a girl. She says Mama left us. She says the baby took her away . . ." Side by side with that misery was that black, awful horror. She cringed— something made her want to hide.

"Something awful happened," she whispered.

Just then, a shiver ran down her spine and she realized she was being watched. Lifting her head, she found herself looking into a pair of familiar eyes— the color of faded denim, light blue, bracketed by lines. She suspected that many of the lines were caused by laughter . . . and equally as many were caused by stress.

"Detective . . ." She stopped, shook her head. "Captain Hilliard."

He stopped a few feet away, his gaze lingering on the scars on her face. When he met her eyes, she saw that there was no need to introduce herself; he already knew who she was.

"You know, if it was me, I'd have them removed," he said quietly, flicking his gaze to the scars.

Shay shrugged. "I've gotten used to them . . . and for a while, these were a reminder."

"Of what?"

"To make myself stronger. To remember I had to hide. To remember that I'd survived hell . . . everything," she murmured, absently reaching up to touch one of the narrow marks. She'd thought about having them removed. For years. But then, when life got hard, when she was lonely and scared, she'd look in the mirror and see those scars and she remembered.

After what had been done to her, there was very little she couldn't handle.

Whatever truths awaited her here, she could face them.

"I'm here because I need some answers."

Hilliard's shoulders rose under the old, faded suit jacket he wore. She suspected he wore it more because he was expected to than anything else. "You do know that some of those questions you have may be things I just can't answer."

"Will you tell me what you can?" she whispered.

"It will be hard," he warned her.

Shay touched the scars. "I've lived hard . . . I survived it." Then she looked back, holding out her hand to Elliot.

She'd lived. She'd survived.

Surviving it wasn't enough anymore. She had to get through this. And she had to do more than survive it, damn it. The last time she'd just *survived*, she'd ended up living trapped inside the prison of her memories, her fear, and her misery. She needed more than that this time around, and damn it, she was going to take it.

It was about what she'd expected. Squalid, ugly, and simple. The windows were dark and dirty and the nasty little hellhole didn't look like it had been cleaned in a decade.

They had lived in a place like this. After Mama died. Before Mama died, it hadn't been so bad.

Shay . . . no . . . *Michelline* . . . that was who she really was . . . Michelline wouldn't remember any of that, but she did.

Michelline had been their little princess and Leslie had been Mama's best girl. Everything had been fine. Then Mama met Jethro. She got pregnant. Even then, it wasn't bad, but Leslie hadn't liked it. Not at all. Because people weren't talking to her so much and Michelline was suddenly supposed to be a helper, too. That was Leslie's job.

And Jethro . . . she'd always hated him.

Something mewled and she looked down. When she saw the pitiful little black ball of fluff, her heart skipped. Sinking to her knees, Leslie scooped up the woebegone cat and cradled him to her chest. Her kitten had been white.

Right up until that night.

When Jethro had cut him open and the blood turned his pretty fur red.

A scratchy tongue licked her chin. "Are you hungry, boy?"

I told you to keep that damn thing away from me . . .

After he'd cut it open, he'd thrown it at her. She'd been covered in the poor kitten's blood.

Mama had died only a few days earlier.

The baby cried all the time. The one thing that made her feel a little bit better had been her kitty and he'd killed it, the cocksucker.

Another pitiful mewl and two tiny teeth sank into her hand, letting her know she'd been squeezing too tight. "Sorry about that, fella." Leslie sniffed and then stood up, glancing back at her car. She didn't really have anything with her to feed him, but she couldn't leave him here. Had to be a stray. So skinny and pitiful, no tags, and she suspected he was crawling with fleas, too.

It would be nice to have a pet again.

CHAPTER
TWENTY-TWO

"YOU'VE READ THE INFORMATION I SENT YOU ABOUT him."

Shay gripped Elliot's hand, focused on Hilliard's faded blue eyes, and pretended she was just researching. That was it. Researching. She didn't have to see *him*. No reason to, right? She did have a contact in Phoenix—it was Hilliard. She'd contacted him months after she'd fled and asked if he'd be willing to let her know if her stepfather ever showed any sign of leaving the city. He'd been happy to oblige. But she could only handle so much at one time and she wasn't here about him.

"I . . ." Shay squeezed her eyes closed. "Can we come back to him later?"

Hilliard smiled. "Of course." Hands folded in front of him, he studied her face, his gaze thoughtful. "Just what do you want to know?"

"Other things." It was a bare whisper and she had to clear her throat before she could go on. "My . . . my mother. Can you help me find out anything about my birth mother? I . . . she . . ."

Shay groaned and tugged her hand from Elliot's, leaning forward to brace her elbows on her knees. Elliot rested his hand on her back, stroking it up, then down. "I have nightmares, Captain Hilliard. Before I went to live with Virna when I was little, I have no memory of much of anything—just these flashes from my nightmares. Sometimes, there's blood. I hear a baby crying . . ."

The tension in the air was so damn thick, it could have choked her. Slowly, she lifted her head, finding herself staring at a man who hadn't had any trouble looking her in the eye a moment earlier. He'd faced her and told her the man who raped her was still living in this same city and he'd done it without blinking.

Why couldn't he look at her now?

"Captain Hilliard?" she whispered.

"You really are piecing things together, aren't you?" he asked, his voice hoarse. A muscle jerked in his jaw. "Are you sure you want to hear this?"

Shay shook her head. "No. I don't want to hear it at all. I want to run away and hide, and never think about this again. But my life is falling apart, and it all seems like it goes back to then. It's somehow connected to my mother, to those nightmares . . ."

"Michelle . . ." He frowned. "It's not Michelle, now. I have a hard time thinking of you as somebody other than Michelle Lassiter, you know. You were the little lion who faced a monster."

She blinked, caught off guard for a moment. *Little lion* . . . no. She'd never been a lion. She'd barely made it through that time with her sanity intact. "Michelle. No. That's not me anymore."

"I guess not." He came out from behind the desk to squat in front of her. He held out a hand and although touching people went against everything she had in her, she placed her hand in his.

"Shay . . . your mother had nothing to do with the nightmares in your life. From everything I could find out about her, she was a good mom. I don't know anything about your father—there wasn't anything listed

on your birth certificate—but everybody I spoke to said
she was a good mother and they all said she loved you."

She nodded jerkily. "I thought that seemed right.
I've been having vague bits and pieces come through.
Nothing concrete, but . . . well. I was pretty sure I remembered that much." She blew out a breath and then
focused on his face. "Tell me what happened to her."

"She died giving birth . . ." He blinked and then
looked down. "I imagine the baby you hear in your
nightmares is your baby brother."

My baby brother . . .

The little kitty was sleeping comfortably in a box in the
hotel room.

He had food, so much his tummy looked about ready
to pop. He'd sleep for a while, she knew, which gave
Leslie some time.

This wouldn't take long. She'd kept tabs on the dragon
from Shay's past. Leslie had conquered all of her dragons. She'd conquer Michelline's now.

Life hadn't been kind to him in prison.

She'd been amused when she read the reports about
him.

There had been a series of bad fights in the prison where
he'd been serving his time, and one of them had left him
paralyzed from the waist down. He was in a wheelchair
now. He wouldn't even be able to run away from her.

As she made her way to his squalid little hellhole, she
planned.

Cut the phone lines. He had a landline, but she wasn't
sure if he had a cell phone. She'd figure that out once she
got inside. He wouldn't have a security system. The pathetic idiot could barely get by on the check he got
working the night shift at Wal-Mart.

It was getting late now, and she'd wait for him to leave
before she broke in. Once he left, she'd go in. And wait.

Get the lay of the land, so to speak.

And then she'd slay Michelline's dragon.

"I have a brother."

Shay closed her eyes. She'd known. Somewhere inside, she'd known it for a long time. But *knowing* it deep inside and having it confirmed, hearing it, were very different things.

"Shay." Elliot's hand closed around her neck—that gesture, possessive as all get-out, should have bothered her. Especially as often as he did it. But it comforted her. Usually. Right now, she didn't feel at all comforted. It was the tone of his voice, she suspected.

That . . . and her own deeply rooted fears. Swallowing, she made herself look at the cop. No wonder Elliot had sounded so tense. It was in Hilliard's eyes. Grim, bleak sadness. "Yes, you did. He died twenty-nine years ago."

Twenty-nine years ago . . . when she was four. When she was taken away, out of hell. A sob built in her throat, but she swallowed it back. "Jethro killed him, didn't he? He was always screaming about the baby—always wanted somebody to shut him up . . ."

Even as she said it, though, she knew. Hurtling up out of the chair, she rushed for the garbage can. There was nothing in her belly, but that didn't keep her from retching.

Images, so obscene, so vivid and real, danced in her mind.

Bloody. Vicious. Awful.

Somebody finally shut that baby up . . . know who did?

And a girl's voice. Laughter. *You'll be the princess again, now . . .*

"Oh, God . . . oh, God, oh, God, oh, God."

There had been blood on her face when they led her

out of the house. It hadn't made sense to her young mind, then. But now, as those memories sharpened with painful clarity, she knew.

It had been a partial handprint . . . mostly the fingerprints. From when somebody had touched her cheek. Somebody with a small, childlike hand.

"Oh, God . . ."

Pathetic, Leslie decided as she studied him.

He looked pitiful and pathetic.

Granted, he was too gaunt for the wheelchair—that might have something to do with his miserable appearance. Plus, there was the long, stringy gray hair that fell to his shoulders, the balding pate. Why did men do that? Bald on top, yet they let the hair get all nasty-long and stringy like that?

She just didn't get it.

From her rental, she watched as he let himself out of the house, maneuvered the wheelchair down the small ramp, down the sidewalk, and began to wheel himself to the bus stop. No car . . . she knew that, because she'd made it her business to know about everybody connected to Shay. Jethro Abernathy was a connection. Michelline's dragon.

She was going to kill this fucking dragon and if she could figure out a way, she might just drag the dragon's corpse back for Michelline to see. *See, sweetie? He's gone . . . you don't have to be afraid anymore . . .*

Of course, if Michelline wasn't afraid anymore . . .

"No." Leslie shook her head. She'd still need her. A little girl needed her big sister. Always. Mama had even told her that, before she left. Left and went away . . . never to come back. Instead that squalling, nasty little Jeffrey had come back. And Jethro had dumped the thing on Leslie. She was expected to take care of it, change it, feed it, make it quit crying.

Well, she'd done all of that . . .

Leslie grinned, amused. She'd definitely done that.

Through the windshield, she continued to watch Jethro as he wheeled his chair about a block down. He swung it around and just sat there, hands hanging limp in his lap, staring out, straight ahead. The guy didn't look around at *all*. If he had, he might have at least seen Leslie's car.

Not that it would do any good, really, just seeing her car. He wouldn't even recognize her. Maybe, like Michelline, he'd forgotten all about her, too. He'd given Michelline scars for forgetting. If he'd forgotten Leslie, she'd have to do something about that before he died.

But scars didn't matter to corpses.

She'd have to find another way to hurt him.

A way to horrify him. Scar him . . .

It would scar him, he knew. The look in her eyes. The horror. The pain.

He'd never seen anybody look that pale, that fragile. That broken. Crouching in front of her, he pushed a Coke into her hands and wished it were some sort of magic cure, something that would take all of this away.

Not only could he *not* take it away, it was going to get worse. They hadn't even learned how the baby died. And Elliot knew it was bad. The cop looked sick. It would take a lot to put that kind of look in a cop's eyes.

Shay held the Coke and stared at it dumbly. "Shay . . . baby, take a drink, okay?"

She grimaced. "I don't drink regular Coke. It's too sweet."

"You need it," he said. "Trust me." Considering the shock to her system, she needed more than a Coke. Whiskey. Something. But he doubted Captain Hilliard kept Jack Daniel's on hand.

Her hands were shaking and some of the fizzy drink

splattered out. He steadied one hand as she took a sip. A few seconds later, she took another. He wanted her to drink more, but he wasn't surprised when she put it down on the cluttered table at her side. "I'll try to drink more in a few minutes," she said, forcing herself to smile.

He doubted she'd remember. Sighing, he caught her hands in his; they were shaking, as cold as ice. He rubbed them between his own for a minute, then lifted them to his lips, pressing a kiss to one wrist, then the other. "Shay, I wish you didn't have to be here," he said quietly.

She just stared at him.

"Whatever you're about to learn, it's going to hurt, baby, and I can't stop it."

"It already hurts," she whispered. "And it would be better knowing . . . than not knowing."

As she shifted her gaze to the captain, who continued to wait quietly, patiently, Elliot stayed where he was. He couldn't get any closer to her unless he pulled her into his lap, and he wasn't ruling that option out, either.

"Tell me," she said, her voice shaking slightly, but beneath it, there was a steely undertone.

She had to know. He just hoped he was enough to get her through this.

"Your brother was murdered. Twenty-nine years ago," Hilliard said, his voice flat and steady. His eyes were also flat, and if you didn't look too closely, they might look steady as well.

But Elliot had already seen the lingering horror.

What in the hell had happened . . . ?

"Let me guess . . . it was October ninth, wasn't it?" Shay whispered.

Elliot shifted so he could watch the cop but still be right there, crouched by Shay's feet.

Hilliard inclined his head. The only answer he gave. But it was enough.

"What—" Shay closed her eyes and took a deep, uneven breath.

Resting a hand on her knee, Elliot stared at the cop. "She's not going anywhere until this is done. You already know what she's gone through. If she can handle that, there's little you can do that's going to sway her. Just tell her."

So I can start to pick up the pieces.

Hilliard's lashes lowered, shielding his eyes. Then, finally, he said, "Your brother was found butchered, Shay. Somebody had cut him. Very badly, very deliberately."

"My stepfather?"

"No." The cop stared at Shay, his eyes intense. Focused. As if he were trying to tell her without actually saying the words.

He'd have to say them, though. If Shay wasn't going to take the easy way out with this and hide, nobody else could do it, either, Elliot thought.

After a long, tense moment, the man sighed and passed a hand over his timeworn face. Then he looked back at Shay and softly said, "You weren't the only child in the house that night, Shay. Two female children were removed from the household."

Two female children . . .

Shay stared at Hilliard. If she allowed herself to look at Elliot, for even a moment, she was going to beg him to take her out of there. Far away where she never had to think about this again. *Ever.* But she couldn't do that. That little brother of hers . . . she needed to know about him. Needed to know more. Needed to know who had hurt him. And why.

"I have a sister," Shay whispered, forcing the words out despite the fact that she just wanted that knowledge to stay hidden deep, deep inside her gut.

"Yes. Jeanette Hall was survived by two daughters . . . Michelline Hall and Leslie Hall, and her infant son . . . Jeffrey Abernathy, as well as her husband, Jethro Abernathy."

The sound of *that* name was like a slap, but at that point, she was practically numb. She could take only so much shock before she exhausted herself. She was at that point.

"Leslie. My sister's name is Leslie," she said quietly.

Hilliard looked down, once more staring at the page. "I don't have much information on her. Her case was sealed and I'd need a reason to open her file." He flicked a glance in Shay's direction. "I have your information because of our connection. The report of your brother's death, all of that, was public record. Sealed records aren't so easy to access."

"Why are her records sealed . . . did he hurt her, too?"

Hilliard sighed, reaching up to rub his hands over his face. He seemed to be aging before their eyes. "Shay, how much do you remember?" he asked quietly. "Anything?"

"Screams. Blood . . . I had blood on me and I remember screaming." She flinched and when she started to tremble, Elliot muttered under his breath—he didn't give a damn that the cop was in the room. Scooping her into his lap, he cradled her against him, one hand cupping her head, the other draped over her legs. Shay huddled against him, shaking like a leaf. "I saw myself in a mirror, and there was blood all over me. On my nightgown. On my clothes."

"Yes. But you weren't hurt. There was blood on Leslie, as well. She wasn't hurt. And your stepfather had no blood on him. There was a knife found in the closet where you liked to hide . . . you told Virna about that closet on previous visits. That's where the police looked for you when the call came in about the screams. You were found in there. Alone. With a knife."

Shay jerked. "No. I wouldn't—"

Hilliard continued. "Your sister was found in the backyard. She was singing and trying to dig a hole. There was a baby's body beside her. She was singing about—"

"The baby," she whispered while that insane little giggle echoed through her mind. That horrid little whisper. *My little princess can be the princess again . . . you're our little princess.* "She sang about shutting up the baby," Shay whispered. "Didn't she?"

Hilliard just stared at her.

But both Elliot and Shay saw the answer. It was right there . . . in his eyes.

Somebody finally shut that baby up . . . know who did? I did.

My little princess can be the princess again . . . you're our little princess, Michelline.

"My princess," Shay rasped.

Clearly, for the first time in nearly thirty years, she remembered.

A girl—dark-haired, maybe a little plump, with over-bright eyes and a smile that was . . . off. Just off. She'd smiled down at the girl Shay had been, Michelline. *"He's gone and you'll be the princess again, now. Doesn't that sound good? I'll take care of you, Michelline. Just like Mama told me to."*

She'd patted the little girl on the cheek. Then, whistling, she'd picked up the broken, bloody body of their brother—just a baby—and she'd left Michelline alone in the closet. A traumatized little girl staring after her sister . . . a child murderer.

"She killed him," Shay whispered. "I have a sister . . . and I had a brother . . . until she killed him."

CHAPTER
TWENTY-THREE

"WILL SHE BE OKAY?" HILLIARD STARED AT THE small, slim form of Shay Morgan, crouched on a grave that hadn't had a visitor besides him in probably seventeen years. He knew that Virna Lassiter had come out here, before she'd died. But since then? He was the only one left to come visit them now.

Elliot stood with his hands jammed in his pockets, legs spread over the uneven ground, his gaze locked on Shay's bowed head. Just then, he wanted to be at her side, more than anything.

But she'd asked for five minutes alone. He could give her five minutes, damn it. That was about it. Even though it killed him not to be there with her. *Shit*. He felt like a fucking useless waste of air. He hadn't been able to stop any of this from hurting her. And that psychotic bitch was still out there. All he'd wanted to do was take care of her and—

"*Fuck*," he snarled under his breath, spinning away and staring out toward the mountains. He shoved the heels of his hands against his eyes and tried to breathe, tried to think. He had to hold it together, because if his rage shattered him, what good was he going to be for her? He blew out a breath, focusing on the feel of the air moving in and out of his lungs. Then he glanced over at the cop. Hilliard was still watching Shay.

"I've never met a stronger woman in my life," Elliot said quietly, answering the cop the best he knew how. "But . . . okay? I just don't know. This is just . . ." He paused, blowing out a breath.

"Yeah, it's some fucked-up shit, isn't it?"

"You're a master of understatement."

"So I've been told." Hilliard pushed a hand through a head of grizzled, gray hair. "Just what is it that brought her back here, Mr. . . . ah, Winter, right?"

"Elliot," he said absently. "Call me Elliot." He debated— did he tell him? Should Shay do it? He suspected if he waited for Shay to do it, she'd say nothing unless she had to, but he wasn't so sure that was the right avenue. Hell, he *knew* that wasn't the right avenue.

Shay's sister was the one playing games with her. How Leslie Hall had managed to find Shay after she'd moved and changed her name, Elliot didn't know, but it proved one thing—the woman was smart. Smart, clever, and she didn't lack for patience or persistence. Not a good mix, the way he saw it. Was it possible she'd been watching Shay all of this time? That was a thought that was absolutely terrifying. It was also a thought that couldn't be dismissed, he realized.

Sighing, he slid the cop a look. "Shay's been having some problems. Somebody is trying to take over her life. Bits and pieces of it. She'd thought it was a college friend, but apparently that college friend has been missing for quite some time. It looks like the person just moved in, took over the friend's life."

"Wouldn't the friend's family have noticed? Wouldn't Shay have noticed?"

Elliot smiled grimly. "Whoever did this knows Shay too well. She doesn't let people get too close—most of her life is through her computer. She used the computer, the telephone, that's it. She probably goes weeks without seeing people and she hadn't seen Darcy since college." With a shrug, he glanced over at the detective. "The woman up and moves—claims she was relocating, gives a new cell phone and all. Shay has no reason to not believe her."

"Voice? Wouldn't the voice be off?"

"I think she can mimic voices. . . . it's a complicated mess, but she had a number set up like Shay's and apparently Shay called it. It sounded enough like Shay that she was freaked out to hear it, but when we called it again, the number was disconnected. And that's just one of many weird-ass things going on."

He rubbed the back of his neck, staring at the dusty toes of his boots. In terse terms, he outlined what had gone on so far, finishing up with what they thought might have happened to Darcy. "The friend is missing. For two years now. Nobody has seen her, heard from her. Everything about *her* seems to just be gone."

"Fuck," Hilliard muttered, rubbing his hand over his mouth. "I don't like the sound of this. I'd hoped she was just coming down here because she needed closure, but this . . . shit. This is a fucking shit bomb waiting to explode. Shay has no idea who she is dealing with now?"

At that moment, Shay swung her head around, staring at them over the field of stone that separated them. As she rose, Elliot studied her face, the grief there, the misery, the sadness. And the fury.

"She knows," he said quietly as Shay started toward them. His heart slammed hard against his ribs at the look in her eyes. He hated to see her hurting, but the expression on her face was the look of a woman ready to go to war.

"I know we think it's her sister, but—"

"I don't think, Captain Hilliard," Shay said as she approached them. Her eyes were grim, dark. Determined. "I don't *think*. I know. She's let too many things slip that don't make sense in any other capacity . . . like my name."

"Your name."

Brushing her hair back from her face, Shay stared at him. "My birth name. Michelline. Unless she *knew* me, how likely is it that she could have been able to get that?"

"And how do you know this?"

Shay turned away, crossing her arms over her chest. "Because I heard her say it," she murmured. She flicked a look at Elliot and he reached out and caught her hand, tugged her close. *You can do this.*

She came to him and he dipped his head, rested his brow against her crown. *You can do this*, he thought again. She leaned against him for a brief moment and they just stood there. He didn't know if she was taking in any comfort from him or not, but just that brief, simple connection helped ease the ragged, jagged mess in his heart and soul. *They* could get through this, damn it. Get through it. Get it behind them and then focus on what mattered—the rest of their lives.

After a moment, she eased away. He caught her hand in his and squeezed. It wasn't much, but he wanted her to know one simple thing. He was here with her. No matter what happened.

"A few days ago, she was on the phone with me, yammering about taking care of me, and I told her that wasn't her job—I'd had a mom who'd taken care of me. She muttered something and then mentioned my mother. She knew me. She knew my mother. It's her, Captain. I know it is."

"Okay . . . let's assume you're right. Let's assume she has tracked you down. Why is she screwing around with your life? Trying to take it over?"

Elliot curled his lip. "Sounds to me like she's a crazy bitch. I think that's a reasonable enough explanation."

"No." Shay pushed her hair back from her face, tucking it behind her ears. She stared off into the distance, the setting sun painting her pale skin a delicate gold . . . highlighting the fine scars along the edge of her face. Somehow, she managed to look both incredibly young and incredibly ancient, Elliot thought.

"It's not because she's crazy—or not *just* because she's crazy," Shay murmured. The desert wind kicked up, teasing the hair back into her face. She ignored it, staring at the mountains. It was peaceful here, she decided. Of all places, she'd found some small bit of peace . . . at the graves of her brother and mother.

She'd loved her mother, that much she knew—it was more a feeling than true memory. But it was there. Just as she knew she'd loved her brother. She wished she had some memory of him, a real one . . . not just those screams.

Not just the terror.

"I was the little princess," Shay said, closing her eyes. "I was the little princess, and she was our mother's best girl. Then Mama went away. I don't understand all of that, although . . ." She opened her eyes and stared at the quiet cop standing at Elliot's side. "You said she died in childbirth."

"Yes."

Tears stung her eyes, threatening to fall. She blinked them back. "You know, in the scheme of things, it hasn't been that long since she died. You don't think about women still dying from childbirth in this country. But it happens a lot more often than people realize." She pressed her lips together. *I had a mother, a brother. I loved them. And at least my mother loved me.* She tried to hold on to that, but the horror in her mind was still so huge. Just then, she couldn't think about any of that.

so she made herself focus on the puzzle—the mystery, the riddle. She'd always been good at puzzles. Figuring out the answer . . .

"Me," she whispered. "It was me. Or, at least, I'm part of it. She was supposed to take care of me—I was Mama's princess. I remember her telling me that, and then suddenly I wasn't the princess and she wasn't Mama's helper, because the baby was there."

"She blamed the baby," Hilliard said quietly.

"Yes."

Elliot, grim-eyed, just stared at her. "Doesn't that pretty much mean the same thing? That she's crazy?"

"There are all kinds of crazy, Elliot," Shay murmured. And deep inside, she felt even sicker than she'd felt earlier.

Jethro's words came back to her. She'd blocked out a lot of what he'd always ranted about, railed about. *He's gone, you little bitch . . . because you had to be the princess. He's gone . . .*

"Leslie blamed the baby, and then Jethro blamed me," Shay said.

None of it would make any sense to the logical, rational mind, but they definitely weren't dealing with rational or logical minds.

"He blamed *you*?" Elliot's voice was a dangerous, dark rasp.

Looking up, she stared at him.

Hilliard, wisely, turned away, casually strolling out of hearing distance as Elliot reached over and caught Shay's arm, drawing her closer. "Did you just say that fucker blamed *you*?"

"Yes." She started to touch the scars on her face but made herself stop. Maybe it was time to have them removed. All of them. "I told you how he ranted, how he yelled and everything. A lot of it just didn't make sense. He said shit about how he was gone—I never knew who the bastard was talking about, but he meant Jeffrey. He blamed me." Her voice hitched and she stopped, waiting until she knew she could breathe, could speak without crying. "He'd rant at me about how it was my fault and he'd yell at me because I forgot. That was why he hated me . . . he blamed me. All that time, he blamed *me*."

"How could he blame *you*?"

A watery laugh escaped her. "Elliot . . . I don't know. He was drunk most of the time, pissed off over being in jail . . ."

Closing her eyes, she thought back to all the times her stepfather had yelled. Were there other memories? Maybe, she thought; she almost remembered hearing other sounds . . . like a man crying. Turning around, she looked back at the stone. Her brother's stone had nothing on it, save his name, his date of birth, and his date of death. It was pitifully naked. It should say something more. She'd have it changed if she had anything to say about it.

But her mother's stone read: *Beloved Wife*. It said nothing about her children, but it mentioned that she was a wife.

"I think he loved my mother. I think he blamed the baby . . . maybe while he was in prison, he started feeling guilty over that and the guilt just . . . hell." She shook her head, stared off into the distance at the mountains. "I don't know. All of this is coming from a time that I can barely remember, and it's not like I wasn't fucked up to hell and back at the time."

"You're not fucked up—and you weren't then. *They* were fucked up," Elliot snarled. He pulled her against him, the motion abrupt and jerky, as though he just couldn't handle not having her close for another second. Burying his face against her neck, he muttered, "I want to kill them, Shay. Both of them. For what they did to you then, what she's doing to you now."

Caught in the circle of his arms, the warmth of the sun beating down on them, with his heart beating against her cheek, she closed her eyes and let herself lean against him. Here, right here, she felt safe. Felt wanted, needed . . . almost normal, even. If only she could just stay here . . .

But those two stones behind her reminded her how very unfinished this was. "She can't hurt me unless I let her, Elliot," Shay whispered, hiding her face against his shirt. It was a lie; she knew it even as she said it. But she wasn't going to let that woman win. She'd done enough damage and it was past time that it stopped.

"This game she's playing, now that I've figured it out, it's going to stop. I'll stop her. I'm not a scared child hiding in a closet anymore."

No . . . she was a scared, horrified adult who didn't know which way to go, but she wasn't going to let that stop her.

Moments passed as she stood there, pressed against his chest, listening to his heart beating . . . letting the place of death wrap her in its odd web of peace. "We'll get this done," she murmured. Somehow.

But after that?

"Where are you two going for the night?" Hilliard asked as he walked them back to their car.

"We're staying at the Hotel San Carlos downtown." Downtown—in the middle of a bunch of people, surrounded by them. It should have terrified her, but she desperately needed it right then. Needed the thought of lots of people, lights, and chaos. Maybe it would keep the shadows in her memory at bay for a little while longer.

Maybe, but she wasn't counting on it.

"And then . . . ?"

She just stared at him.

"What do you plan on doing next?" he asked gently. "You didn't just come here for these answers. What about Abernathy? Your sister?"

"Abernathy . . ." She clenched her jaw. She wasn't going to think about him, because every time she did, her skin broke out in a cold sweat. Those nightmares, those memories—they were her dragons, the nightmares that had haunted her all of her life. Even as a child, before he'd hurt her so badly, she'd been afraid of him and in her dreams, she'd remembered it.

She didn't need to see him.

She'd come for answers; she'd found them. She'd found out about her sister and now she needed to figure out the next step. What to do about her, how to find her . . . *face* her.

That was her focus. Clenching her jaw until it hurt, she gave herself a minute and continued to stare at the mountains. *Breathe—focus—think—*

She could do this. She had to. "I'm not here about Abernathy," she said, her voice a bare whisper. "He isn't my concern or my problem—" *He's just the dragon from my nightmares* . . . "I'm here because of Leslie."

"Okay." He inclined his head. "And what do you plan to do about her?"

"Hell." Shay spun away. If it weren't for Darcy, she'd rather just do *nothing* about her. She'd rather never know about her, forget about her . . . but that wasn't an option. "She's a stranger to me, and a monster—somebody I really wish I'd never remembered."

He's gone now . . . you'll be the princess again . . .

As the horror rolled through her, she covered her face with her hands, wishing she could carve the sound of that laughing voice, so gleeful and happy, from her mind. Then bleach herself clean—she felt so unbelievably dirty.

"I don't want this inside me, Captain," she said quietly. "I don't want to remember, I don't want to think about her . . . I don't want to *know* her. If I never thought about her again . . ."

Her voice hitched and she stopped to take a breath. But it wasn't that easy. Even if she never heard from Leslie again, even if the woman left her alone, Shay couldn't walk away.

Because of Darcy.

Feeling the weight of a familiar, intense stare, she looked up and found Elliot's gaze resting on her. And in those eyes, she saw the knowledge. He knew she wouldn't let this go . . . knew she couldn't.

She looked at Captain Hilliard, as the horror and grief continued to riot through her.

His face was gentle, still so gentle and understanding. "You can leave . . . she's not a part of your life, and she never should be, Shay. Just leave. Let us handle this . . . that's what the cops are here for."

"I can't." Closing her eyes, she whispered again, "I can't. She's . . ."

I think she killed my friend. She's screwing with my life. I can't leave until I find a way to make her stop—

How did she even begin to explain?

"Elliot tells me there was a friend . . . a missing one. Is that why you can't leave? Is that why you're here to begin with?"

Shay nodded. Sinking her nails into her palms, she tried to ground herself, but that small pain wasn't enough. Darcy . . . "Her name was Darcy. She's been missing for two years. And Leslie has been pretending to be her. I never even knew."

"Didn't you recognize a change in the voice or anything?"

Shay sighed. "Shit, do you think I haven't thought about that? No, I didn't notice any difference in her voice. I can't explain that, either. Maybe she's just really good at mimicking other voices." *Voices* . . . She stopped and remembered the call to the number Trish had given her, the voice that had sounded like her own. "There was this weird thing, though. She had set up a phone number, claimed it was mine. It's complicated and it would take a while to explain it all, but I called that number . . . and she *sounded* like me. I don't *know* how she managed to pull this off. But Darcy has been missing for two years. You would think I would have realized something was wrong . . . I've been paying . . ."

She stopped and looked at him. "I've been paying her. Damn it, I PayPal money every single month—her paycheck. Wouldn't the cops have checked on that, with her being reported missing?"

"Yes." Hilliard nodded. "Assuming they knew—they'd be watching bank accounts. But PayPal accounts aren't always linked to bank accounts. If the money was just going into the PayPal account, the cops may well not have known about it, especially if the family wasn't aware of it. Maybe there was an email address they didn't know about, so they didn't think to check that one."

"The business email." Shay rubbed the heel of her hand over her chest and whispered, "I had her set up a separate account that was only used for my business stuff—it couldn't be used for anything else. I paid her through that account."

Closing her eyes, Shay buried her face in her hands, grief hitting her in a hard, heavy wave. She almost collapsed under it. She'd wanted her privacy, her anonymity . . . and because of that very thing, it had made it that much easier for her sister to stalk and hurt her best friend.

"God, what have I done?"

"You didn't do anything," Elliot told her. He laid his hand over the back of her neck, but she couldn't find the comfort in it that she usually did, and she doubted she deserved any.

"Exactly!" she shouted, spinning away from him and pacing. Arms wrapped around her belly, she stared off into nothing while her heart threatened to split in two. "She did something to my best friend—one of my *only* friends, and did I *know*? Did I realize anything was wrong? No. I quietly bitched to myself about what a pain in the ass Darcy had become. I never realized anything was wrong. I never tried to find out what was going on. I just . . ." She pressed a hand to her mouth and whispered, "I didn't do anything."

Hearing the soft sound of footsteps, she tensed as Elliot approached and stood in front of her. "This isn't helping," he said softly. He cupped her face in his hands, stroked a thumb over her lower lip. "I know you're angry, and I know you're hurt. I don't blame you. I don't even know Darcy and I'm pissed off. But how can you *help* her now if you let guilt tear you apart?"

"So what do I do, damn it?" she asked, her voice catching in her throat. "Just shrug it off? Say *oh, well* and let it be?"

"No." Dipping his head, he brushed his lips across hers and murmured, "Even if part of me wishes you'd just walk away from this, that's not who you are. You'll do what you have to. We'll find a way to get through this. But don't let what *she* has done tear you apart, Shay. You can't do that."

Reaching up, she curled her fingers into his T-shirt and battled the urge to cry, to scream. Anything. The emotion building inside her had no outlet and she felt as though she might explode. "Elliot, this is killing me," she whispered.

"You'll be okay," he murmured, wrapping her in his arms. "And I'll be right here. I swear, I'll be right here, no matter what."

Shuddering, she rested her head against his chest and tried to think past the anger, the guilt. The horror. *My brother—*

Stop it, she told herself. Swallowing the knot in her throat, she eased back away from him, lifting her head to stare at the gravestones. Her mother and her brother, people she'd never known.

"Shay, no matter how you're feeling, none of this is on you," Hilliard said quietly. Then he heaved out a tired, ragged sigh. "You know, I should have known it wouldn't be a simple thing when I realized you were here. This isn't just because you needed to find your brother. It's not just because you're looking for closure . . . is it?"

"No."

He nodded and stroked his jaw. "The wisest thing you *could* do is go home. I've already got a weird twist in my gut, just listening to the weird shit you've had going on. You can go home and I can start making some calls, see what I can turn up."

She stared at him.

"And that's not going to happen, is it?"

"I didn't come all the way down here just to get sent back home, Captain," she said quietly.

He turned away, hands planted on his hips. "She could be dangerous. If this is a matter for the police, you'll have to step back, let the police handle it." Shooting her a look over his shoulder, he added, "My gut tells me that if Leslie Hall is involved, you have to be careful."

Shay grimaced. "I already figured that much out," she said. "She killed my little brother. I think she killed my friend. I'm dealing with a monster . . ."

A monster . . .
She had a monster in her.
Such evil in her soul . . .

That was what Selena Campbell had said about her. Shay hadn't realized who she was speaking about at the time. But now she knew it had been Leslie. She'd been speaking about Shay's sister.

We left Arizona, but she found us . . .

"There was a family. They may have been her foster parents," Shay said quietly, looking up to find both Elliot and Hilliard staring at her. "The Campbells— the woman's name is Selena. They would have lived in Arizona at some point and they took care of Leslie for a while. I think she might have done something to them, or maybe another child they took care of."

Hilliard pulled out a notebook and started jotting things down.

Elliot just studied her face. "Campbell . . . Michigan?" he asked quietly.

"Yeah. I . . . ah, I called her when you left for a little while. I just hoped she'd tell me something. It wasn't much, but . . ." Shay shrugged. "Elliot, her voice. She was so terrified. Just even talking to me."

"How old would she have been when she lived with them?" With a scowl, he looked at Hilliard.

"She was six years older than Shay, so it just depends on when they had her."

Six years older . . . She'd been four when they took her out of hell. So her sister had been ten when she killed their little brother. Bile rose in her throat; she swallowed it, fighting the urge to start retching all over again. *Deal with it now—fall apart later,* she reminded herself.

"A ten-year-old killer. What would they have done with her?" she murmured, also studying Hilliard.

"It depends," he said, sighing. He looked so damn tired. "Therapy, counseling—back then, they wouldn't have done too much with a kid that young. These days, they sometimes try, but it all depends on the trial. Those records are sealed, so the best I can assume is that they had her get help. Then she was fostered out."

"I'm going to assume the *help* wasn't much help," Shay said caustically, looking back at the grave of her brother. How could you *help* a child-killer? "I wonder what she did that had a grown woman so afraid of her."

Hilliard stared at her, his face grim. "You should just go back home, Shay. Keep away from this—from her. I'll start asking questions and doing what I can—if there's something going on, we'll find it. But it doesn't need to involve you. You found the answers you said you needed—go home. File a restraining order. Hell, if you need to, hire a bodyguard for a while." Shrewd eyes shifted Elliot's way and he added, "Although that may not be necessary considering the shadow you've got."

"Shit." Shay turned around, staring back at him. "A bodyguard—do you really think she's going to care about that? She killed a baby—her own brother. And I don't think she wants to *hurt* me. She wants to freak me out, and she seems to want to control my life, but she doesn't want to *hurt* me."

Elliot reached up and laid a hand on her shoulder. "Shay . . . we don't know that."

Yes, I do. But she didn't bother arguing. She couldn't just go home and hide under her bed and pretend this would all go away.

She felt as if she was about to come out of her skin. Her brain all but buzzed with all the stimuli dancing through it. Go *home*?

With a smile that she hoped looked more real than it felt, she said, "I don't know, Captain. I think I should sleep on it."

* * *

"You don't lie well." Elliot noticed that the cop waited until they drove off before he left the cemetery and he gave them a tail for a few miles before getting lost in the Mesa traffic.

"Hmm. You know, it's very pretty out here. I didn't think I'd be able to say that, but . . . well, I can. Not that I want to come back and visit or anything. But it's pretty."

Sourly, he muttered, "You're not very subtle with your subject changes, either."

"I wasn't trying to be subtle."

"You're not just going to give up and go home, are you?"

"Do you think I should?" she asked quietly, resting her head on the back of her seat and rolling it over to look at him. In the pale, wan circle of her face, her eyes looked darker than normal and that frail appearance was disturbing.

"She's not going to quit." That much was certain. Although things had been oddly quiet. Scowling, he shot Shay's lap a glance. "Where is your phone? I haven't heard it ring lately."

"I turned it off." With a weary sigh, she reached into her purse and pulled it out, rubbing her thumb over the surface, staring at the dark, blank face for a long moment before turning it on. "I was a little tired of all the phone calls and texts . . ."

A few seconds later, she started to swear. "Although I'll pay for it now. Guess how many emails I have?"

"How long have you had it off?"

"Since before we left Michigan."

"I dunno." He shrugged and made a guess. "Two hundred."

"You're off by about three hundred fifty-four." Sighing, she started to tap the screen. "And some of them are from her . . . as Darcy, of course." Her throat spasmed and she pressed her lips together. "Just looking at that makes me ill, you know."

"You shouldn't delete them." He reached over and caught her hand in his, lifting it to his lips. "The cops may need them now that we know something screwed up is going on. Just file them away or something so you don't need to see them, but keep everything you can."

She nodded but instead of doing anything about the emails, she put the phone facedown in her lap and twined her fingers with his. "It's insane that you're here with me through all of this, you know. You don't have to be."

"I'm right where I need to be." He flicked a glance at her.

A knot of emotion lodged in her throat, but for once, it wasn't the horrified kind. As something warm and soft settled in her chest, she smiled at him. "You're messed up, Elliot. But I'm glad you're here."

Sighing, she squeezed his hand, then tugged her hand free, picking her phone back up. "Don't delete the emails from insane sister. Check." She started skimming the messages and the silence stretched out. "She's asking what I'm up to. What's going on. Like there's no damn problem at all."

It made her gut hurt, just to sit there and scroll through the emails, tapping them to archive. She didn't put them in the folder labeled *Darcy*. She just couldn't. She used her personal folder. She'd need to move them later, but for now, this was enough, getting them out of her . . .

The bottom of her gut dropped out as the subject of the most recent email caught her attention.

I'm going to slay your dragon . . .

"What are you doing now?" she whispered.
Elliot said, "What?"

But she didn't even hear him. Her hand shook as she opened the message, and she ended up having to put the phone in her lap just to keep it steady enough to read it.

Not that there was much to read . . .

I'm off to slay your dragon, sweetie. We need to talk and I'm not going to let you keep ignoring me, either. But we'll deal with that after I take care of this. Once I do, you'll understand just how important you are to me and just what I'll do to take care of you.

"Shay."

His voice sounded as if it were coming to her through a tunnel. Blinking, she turned toward him. He was watching her, his face stark, eyes burning—locked on her face. And not the road. Dazed, she looked around and realized he'd pulled onto the shoulder. In a reed-thin voice, she said, "I need air."

Grabbing the handle, she all but ripped it off the door in her hurry to get out. Her legs felt awkward, stiff, as if somebody had gone and replaced her knees with rusted metal. Stumbling away from the car, she walked aimlessly until Elliot's hand closed around her arm, drawing her to a stop.

A monster of a saguaro towered over them and she found herself staring at it. Its surface was brown, cracked . . . it looked half dead. "It looks broken," she murmured. "What can break a cactus?"

"Fuck the cactus," Elliot growled.

Forcing a smile, she glanced over at him. "Even though it's half dead, it's still a cactus . . . if you fuck it, it's going to hurt."

"Shay, damn it, what's wrong?"

"She's making another move . . . we can't keep this up, Elliot. I think I need to call her," she said quietly. She debated about telling him what was in the message, although it was so hard, so fucking hard to think. Should she tell him?

No. In the end, she knew she couldn't. Because he'd talk her out of what she had to do and it would be so easy to let him. She had to do this, face both Leslie and the dragon from her nightmares. Elliot would try to shield her. She'd rather he just be there *with* her.

"There's something I need to do," she said quietly. "I want you there with me. Sooner or later, I have to face her. And when I do, I'd rather have you with me."

"You heard what Hilliard said—what *you* should do is stay the hell away."

"How can I do that, Elliot?" She thought about what her sister had just emailed her and shook her head. She'd gone after her nightmare this time. But she'd already targeted Darcy. Who was next? Turning to face him, she lifted her hands.

"What am I to do? Live in fear until she decides to do . . . whatever she's planning? Elliot, that's no *life*, and I'm finally realizing just how little I've let myself live. I know I kept myself closed off, but . . ." The words trailed off and she just stood there, staring at him and trying to figure out what she wanted to say, what she needed to say. "If I let her chase me back into the hole I've spent so much of my life in, she wins. I lose. I'm tired of living in fear, Elliot. Even if I've got a right to be scared, I don't need to let fear control my life."

"Showing common sense and staying away from a crazy bitch isn't the same as being chased into a hole," Elliot growled. The look in his eyes made her heart skip a beat. Caught between heat and fury and desperation, he was focused on her, as if he saw nothing else. Just her. Only her.

Lifting a hand, she touched his cheek. She felt the rough rasp of stubble against her palm. "Elliot, I don't even know what she *looks* like," Shay said. "What am I supposed to do, never answer the door, never go to the store, never drive down the highway because I don't know when she'll decide to try to find me?"

"I can tell you what she looks like." He skimmed a look over her from head to toe and then met her gaze. "Your height, black hair, her eyes are lighter blue, and you can tell something is off if you look in her eyes. She probably weighs a good thirty pounds more than you do, if I'm guessing right. I only saw her the one time in my store, but there ya go. There might be a resemblance, but between the crazy in her eyes, the weight, and the fact that I wasn't *looking* for a resemblance, it's hard to say."

She glared at him. "So now I stay away from women my height with black hair, who weigh thirty pounds more than I do and look crazy? Damn it, Elliot, this is insane. I'm *not* going to cower for the rest of my life. I'm *tired* of being afraid—it's like I'm trapped in that closet all over again."

For long, tense moments, the silence stretched out between them. His golden eyes were snapping in fury, and she felt as though she would shatter if another word were said.

"Fuck," he muttered.

She managed not to flinch, but as he turned away, she covered her face and sucked in a desperate gulp of air. This was so damn hard. So hard. Even thinking about facing her sister made her gut hurt. And what she meant . . .

Slay your dragon—

Her dragon.

CHAPTER
TWENTY-FOUR

"WHY ARE WE HERE?" ELLIOT STARED AT THE DIS-
mally small, dank house.

There was a ramp that looked as though it had been
put together with cardboard, Popsicle sticks, and maybe
some spit. The windows weren't much more than a foot
across and they were so grimy, he doubted the sun could
penetrate them.

"Dragons," Shay whispered. She lifted a hand to knock
on the door.

It echoed through the night, and long seconds passed
before she knocked again.

This time there was a response, but it came from next
door.

A woman, graying and gaunt, jerked up a window
and stuck her head out. "Abernathy ain't there—and if
you find the asshole, tell him his boss called. His ass is
fired if he misses another shift at work."

Shay winced as she felt the weight of Elliot's stare drill
into the back of her neck. Without bothering to wave at
the oh-so-helpful neighbor, she turned back toward the
car.

"Abernathy," he snarled, stalking along at her side.
"You came here to face him and don't even bother to
inform me."

"I did better." Swallowing the knot in her throat, she slanted him a look and spoke the basic truth. "I brought you along. Yeah, I did it without warning you, but if I had, you would have tried to talk me out of this and I couldn't let you. It would have been too easy to let you be strong for me."

"Shay—"

Shaking her head, she said, "I had to do this. I had to at least try. Nobody slays my dragons for me . . . oh, *fuck*."

"Shay, what in the hell is going on?"

She didn't answer him in words, and maybe he wasn't expecting her to.

But when Shay pushed her phone into his hands, the email message already pulled up, Elliot had to admit he was confused.

"I dream of dragons," she whispered, her voice raw and ravaged. She was staring at the house again, as if it were made of her very worst nightmare. "Not the kind of dragon you see these days—those noble, elegant creatures—but these nightmare things. The kind that long to eat you, to tear you apart . . . the kind that just want to hurt you."

Already, he'd focused on the line in the email . . . *slay your dragons* . . .

Now he looked up and stared at Shay.

"My dragon has always had a name; my dragon is Jethro Abernathy," she said, her voice raw. "And now my sister is out to kill my dragon."

Elliot's gut response was . . . *let her*.

Judging by the look in Shay's eyes, though, he suspected that wasn't what she had in mind.

"You think I should just let her," Shay said, echoing his thoughts with eerie precision.

"Why shouldn't I?"

The thick black fringe of her lashes swept down, shielding her eyes. "Maybe I should. After all, that's what I *want* . . ." Her voice hitched and she averted her gaze, staring off into the distance. "It's what I want, almost desperately. But I can't find strength by letting somebody else face my dragons, Elliot. I've spent the past fifteen years of my life in *hiding*. If I can't face those fears now, I'll never do it."

"This isn't about facing your fucking fears," he growled. He closed the distance between them and caught her arm. Staring into her tortured eyes, he had to face his own demons. Hatred, thick and vicious, clawed at him. "Damn it, he *deserves* to die. For what he did? For what he put you through? He ought to be dead."

"I don't disagree," she whispered. "But I can't find myself, I can't find my own strength, by letting my dragons kill themselves. *I* have to face them, Elliot. *I* have to do it. And if I let her do this? And then she slips away? What's next? She got pissed off at my agent once because she didn't like that I didn't get a book deal I wanted. Is my agent the next dragon? One of my editors? A reviewer? She's gone on rants about them, too. Not to mention my friend, who'd never harmed me. It has to stop, and it won't . . . not until I face her." Carefully, she brushed his hand aside and then, without looking at him, turned away.

Barely able to breathe for the helpless fury, he watched as she took one step toward the car, and another step toward facing those dragons. Then another. It was almost as if she had to force herself to take each and every single step. And each and every single step was almost painful to watch.

Fuck.

This was . . . shit, this was killing him. Just how was

he supposed to handle this? *How?* He couldn't. He just . . .

"Hey!"

He heard the belligerent voice, but Shay just kept moving.

"Hey . . . *Michelline*."

Her shoulders were rigid, but she kept walking as though the kid hadn't said a word. Elliot saw him now. Mouthy, arrogant, too skinny . . . hungry, in more ways than one. Hard around the edges. Elliot had seen the type in his years. As the kid moved to cut Shay off, Elliot intercepted, subtly, placing his body between the two.

The boy, just barely old enough to shave, sized him up and smirked, and then grinned at Shay. "Ain't you *Michelline*?"

"No." Shay's voice was cool, steady.

Elliot doubted the kid would have heard the fear laced just under the surface. He heard it, but just barely. A fear that wanted to destroy her. But a fear she faced. A fear she wouldn't let *own* her. *Damn* it.

The boy's smile widened. "You know, she told me you'd say that. Maybe you know the name *Shay* better."

"Maybe you should just keep your nose out of my business," Shay said mildly.

"Hey, she made it my business when she paid me fifty bucks to give you a message." The boy stroked a thumb down his jaw and then shot Elliot a dark look. "Do y' mind? I need to talk to my girl, Shay."

"She's not your girl," Elliot said quietly. Angling his body, he turned so that Shay could put her hand in his. *She's mine.*

She *was* his, damn it. Damn it all to hell and back. If she had to face that dragon, then he'd be there with her.

Gently, he squeezed her hand. When she squeezed

back, he closed his eyes for a brief second. When he opened them, the kid was still staring at Shay, a put-out expression on his too-young face. "Yeah, yeah, fine. I was told you might have company, but damned if I wanna mess with it . . ."

CHAPTER
TWENTY-FIVE

If it weren't for the brave speech she'd offered Elliot not that long ago, she might have begged him to get her away from here.

She hadn't recognized it right away. A lot of it had changed.

Even the building wasn't the same.

It was the liquor store that sat on the diagonal that made her remember.

It alone was the same . . . unaffected by the passage of time or anything else. It was a brutal one-two punch, stealing her breath and momentarily stunning her.

Stupid cunt . . .

You won't forget . . .

No. She hadn't forgotten this time.

She remembered this place, remembered how she'd been trapped, helpless, tied down and brutalized. How she'd screamed and begged as he cut her, as he beat her, as he raped her.

No. She hadn't forgotten. It had just taken her all of this time to get a grasp on why he had done it—even the weakest grasp.

"This was where he took me," Shay whispered, staring in dazed horror at the long, low building. It looked like a warehouse. She didn't remember much of the

building where she'd been held—it had been dark and
dank, and her screams had echoed around her. The one
thing she remembered was that liquor store . . . the logo
on the door.

She'd run stumbling across the street, clutching the
tatters of her flannel shirt, and when she'd burst through
that door, the looks on some of the men's faces had
made her wonder if she'd found safety or not.

A few of them . . . yeah. She wouldn't have been any
safer with them, she knew that.

Then one of the men had stepped forward. He'd
been the roughest-looking one of the bunch—a gruff-
looking, mean-ass bastard who'd taken one look at her
and immediately removed his leather jacket. As he'd
draped it over her shoulders, he'd bellowed for the clerk
at the cash register to call the fucking cops, *now.*

*"Do you hear me, you fucking moron? I told you to
call the fucking cops! 'Scuse me, sweetheart, sorry
about that . . ."*

*Through the rush of blood pounding in her ears, she
could barely hear him. But she recognized the kindness
in his eyes. A big, blunt-fingered hand awkwardly
patted her shoulder, hesitantly, just once, as though he
knew she wouldn't want to be touched. "You just stay
right by me, girl," he said quietly, glancing around. The
store didn't seem as crowded just then. "Ain't nobody
gonna touch you. Ain't nobody gonna hurt you here."*

*A hysterical laugh bubbled in her throat, but she
swallowed it down. Safe . . . she was finally safe.*

*Tears blinded her but she blinked them away. She went
to rub her eyes, but stopped when she saw her hands.
Red. Covered in red. Her blood—she was covered
in it—*

"I was covered in blood," she whispered.

A hand came up and squeezed her shoulder.

"Shay, we need to call Hilliard." Elliot's hand stroked

down to her back to rub in soothing circles low on her spine. "If that crazy . . ."

When his voice trailed off, she slanted a look up at him and offered, "Bitch?"

"Well, yeah."

Shay laughed, but there wasn't much humor in it. "You've always been honest to a fault, Elliot. Don't go sugarcoating things now. She's a crazy bitch. Call her what she is."

Those intense eyes of gold stared straight at her and then he nodded slowly. "Okay. If that crazy bitch is in there, it's the last place you need to be."

Swallowing, she shifted her attention back to the warehouse. Back to the place of so many nightmares and horrors . . . the home of her dragon. "She thinks she's saving me, thinks she's helping me."

"She tried to help you when you were a kid and she killed a baby," he growled, closing a hand around her elbow when she tried to take a step forward.

"Exactly." She continued to stare at the warehouse. Was it stupid? Yeah. It probably was. But she had to do this—had to see this *sister* of hers . . . this monster who had caused so much hell. "And she most likely killed a friend of mine; the first real friend I had since my stepfather attacked me. If it weren't for Darcy, I don't know what I would have turned into. Maybe I would have become as crazy as Leslie is. Maybe I would have killed myself. Maybe I would have just withered away and died. I don't know. I do know that she saved me . . . and I know, in my gut, that Leslie killed her. I have to face her."

"*Why?*"

"Because I want to know what happened to Darcy." She swallowed and shook her head. "My friend deserves that, her family deserves that. And I suspect I'm the only person she'll give those answers to."

"Would Darcy *want* you doing something that could get you hurt?" He glared at her, his eyes all but burning, his mouth a taut, hard line. "Something that *will* hurt you?"

"She doesn't *want* to hurt me, damn it!" Shay glared at him.

"There are different kinds of pain." He reached up and touched her cheek. "You're bleeding right now. I see it."

Shay closed her eyes, covering his hand with her own. "I have to do this . . . and before you throw Darcy into this again . . . she'd do it for me. I knew her. You never did. And if it weren't for her, I'm telling you right now, you may never have had the chance to know me. She saved me."

"You saved yourself, Shay. You're stronger than you think."

"If I saved myself, it's because she gave me the chance—she brought me out of myself long enough to find the strength to do it." Shaking her head, she looked back to the warehouse and took a deep, steadying breath. "And it killed her. She would never have been brought into this, never would have met my sister if it weren't for me. I owe it to her to find out what happened. Call Hilliard. I'm not a complete moron and I know she's dangerous. But I'm going in there, and unless you physically try to stop me, there's nothing you can do about it."

Without waiting another second, she took one small step toward the warehouse. Then another. And another . . .

It's not going to get any easier with those baby steps, sweetheart.

Shit, had it been only a few days since that nice old guy had said that to her back at the Anchorage airport?

Yeah. A few days. A lifetime ago. When she hadn't known she had a murderer for a sister.

Squaring her shoulders, she took another, longer, step. Then another. By the time she'd taken the fifth step, she was almost running.

Elliot fell into a jog to catch up with her, dialing the number from the card Hilliard had given him. *Just in case*, Hilliard had said.

Either the guy was psychic or he was just one of those people who believed in covering the bases.

When the man came on the line, Elliot didn't waste two seconds with pleasantries. He fired off the address and said, "Shay's sister may or may not be here and Shay isn't waiting. I tried to talk some sense into her, but she's not in the mood to listen."

"Then sit on her, for fuck's sake," Hilliard snapped.

"Just get here," he bit off, ending the call. He shot a look heavenward. "Please . . . don't let her get hurt."

He drew even with her as she pushed through the door. The place should have been locked up tight. The "for sale" sign on the exterior wall wasn't exactly new, and it was covered in graffiti. Elliot didn't know if the unsecured door was courtesy of Leslie or the area. Part of him hoped it was the area—if Leslie was good at breaking and entering . . .

Hell, she's a fucking killer. Why should she blink an eye at breaking and entering?

Shay stopped dead center in the hallway. "I'm right here," he whispered, his heart shattering. The fear pumping through her was enough to break him. *Fuck.* He wanted to kill the bitch responsible for doing this to her. "Damn it, Shay, let's just get out of here."

"I can't. . . . Darcy." She sucked in a desperate breath. "I have to know what happened to Darcy."

Shit.

Elliot guessed the woman must have been one hell of a friend to invoke that kind of dedicated loyalty. He closed his hand around Shay's. Her fingers twined with his, squeezing with the strength of the desperate. "Don't go anywhere," she whispered.

"Not for anything."

CHAPTER
TWENTY-SIX

"YOU *WOULD* BRING HIM ALONG," LESLIE MUTTERED, staring at the computer monitor. She'd had to rig the camera on the fly, but it did a damn good job. Michelline looked upset. "Poor kid. She probably just doesn't get it."

Turning around, she stared at the man she had tied to the floor. She smiled at him. "Once she sees you, she'll understand."

Over the gag, his eyes were dull. Almost dead.

That bothered her.

She wanted to see him *afraid*.

He'd scared her . . . once. Or at least, she thought he had. She thought she remembered being afraid. But then he'd done it too many times. He'd done things like killing her kitty . . . Chuckles. That's what they'd named the fluffy little white kitten Mama had bought for her. He'd killed Chuckles. He'd hurt Leslie just a few times too many, and somewhere along the way, she guessed she just stopped being afraid of him. Stopped being afraid. The only thing that had bothered her had been when he'd hit her, or when he'd yelled at her princess.

"She's on her way," Leslie said, stooping down by one of the cinder blocks she'd used to restrain his hands. It was a rather inelegant setup, but she didn't need elegance for this dismal sack of shit. She just needed him dead.

So Michelline could see it was okay to stop being afraid as well.

Once her dragon was dead, Michelline would understand how important she was to Leslie and they could go back to the way they had been before.

Everything would be as it should have been, all this time.

Jethro Abernathy just stared at her.

"You do know who I am, right?"

That blank, dead stare continued.

Sighing, she slapped the side of his face with the flat of her knife. "Come on, you stupid old fuck. Don't make me do something just to get a rise out of you," she warned.

And still, all he did was stare. And wait.

Hell, did you go crazy in jail or what? Leslie stroked the tip of the blade down the center of his naked, scrawny chest, watching for any sign of a reaction. His skin prickled and she watched as his pupils swelled . . . *ah, yes.* "There we go," she murmured. "That's a reaction."

She continued to move lower. "I hear you don't feel anything below your waist," she said. With a smile, she sliced.

As blood flowed, he twisted against the ropes that held him restrained and his strangled scream was like music.

"I guess it doesn't matter if you feel it or not. A man never wants to lose that bit."

That eerie, eerie sound was one that would stay with her, Shay knew.

She halted just outside the door and looked at Elliot. "You called Hilliard, right?"

He nodded and showed her his phone. It displayed a text.

ETA less than five minutes.

Shay pushed through the door. The first thing she saw was the wheelchair. The second thing was the blood . . . always the blood.

There was a man on the floor with a bloody, gaping hole in the center of his body—it didn't make sense at the time, and it wouldn't connect until later. He wasn't familiar to her at first, but then his head swung her way and she saw his eyes. As he stared at her, those pale, almost colorless eyes left her frozen.

Jethro—

She'd been prepared to see him. She thought. But the sight of those eyes, the dragon from her nightmares . . .

Stumbling, she fell against Elliot, and the solid, secure strength of him steadied her. Desperately, she reached over, needing something to hold. His hand was there, callused, warm, and strong.

"Your dragon isn't much of a dragon these days."

That voice was eerily familiar. Like her own . . . and like another's.

My pretty little princess . . . you'll be a good girl while I'm gone, right? That almost memory snapped into focus, and Shay had a flash of her mother, standing in the door, a hand resting on the swell of her belly. *I love you, baby doll.*

It was obscene, she thought, that she should have that final memory of her mother, brought on by the realization that she and her sister sounded so much like her.

Obscene. And wrong. She wanted to scream at the unfairness of it, but even as the tears tried to fight free, the anger burned inside her. She could rage at the unfairness all she wanted, but this bitch was the obscene one. The wrong one.

You saved yourself . . . you're stronger than you think.

By God, Shay thought, *it's about time I showed it.*

"I don't know," she said, and the steadiness of her voice surprised her. "I'm looking at a dragon right now that looks pretty fucking awful."

In all honesty, Leslie didn't *look* like much of a dragon. As Elliot had said, she was Shay's height, but she was rounder, curvier. There was a resemblance, she thought, in the shape of the face, although Shay's features were sharper, more defined. They both had black hair. The similarities were definitely there, although Shay didn't know if she would have blinked twice if she'd seen this woman on the street.

Well, actually, she probably would have gone out of her way to avoid her. There was something in Leslie's eyes . . .

Crazy bitch.

Just like Elliot had said. Her eyes were off. And that was another thing Shay could remember from those vague, surreal days of her murky childhood. "You know when I'd go and hide away in the closet?" she asked softly, ignoring the man who lay bleeding on the floor, ignoring Elliot.

"Yes." Leslie smiled. "You hid away from the dragon. But he can't hurt you now. You're starting to remember more, aren't you?"

Shay nodded. "What happened to Darcy?"

Leslie shrugged. "She was in the way." She reached for a cloth on the floor, carefully wiping away the blood that stained the knife she'd been holding at her side.

"I spent two years talking to you, thinking you were her. How did you manage that?"

"Oh, that part was easy . . ." Leslie cleared her throat and then she smiled. It was unsettling, the change that came over her face. But it was nothing compared to what happened when she *spoke*. "Hey, girl . . . it's me! Darcy, you know . . . that silly little bimbo who jumps at your every little word . . ."

Shay squeezed Elliot's hand, shaking as she listened to her friend's voice coming out of a stranger's mouth. It was surreal—so fucking surreal. "Impressive," she said, her voice faint.

"Nah, that's an easy trick. I learned how to do that in high school. I didn't have any big problems with her, you know. She was just . . . in the way." Leslie rose, still holding the knife and eyeing Elliot with a queer little smile. "People can't come between us, Michelline. You're my baby sister and it's my job to take care of you."

Something wrenched in her chest. If she even dared . . .

"Darcy was my friend," she said quietly.

"I know you think she was. But she just liked you because of what you did. What you let her do. She didn't love you like I do." Leslie brushed it off and glanced over at a computer. Shay followed her line of sight and felt her heart bump when she realized she was looking at the front door of the warehouse.

A camera. Leslie had rigged up a fucking camera.

The cops—they'd be here any second. She shot Elliot a look and saw that he'd seen it as well.

Taking a step forward, desperate to get her sister's attention away from that monitor, she said, "Can you tell me where she is?"

"Why?" Leslie just stared at her, a puzzled look on her face. Genuinely puzzled.

She didn't get it. If it didn't touch her, it didn't matter.

"Because she was my friend," Shay said again. Shaking her head, she added, "Even if you think I wasn't her friend, that she didn't care about me, I cared about her. And her family deserves to know where she is. She had sisters . . . sisters are important, right?"

Leslie frowned. "This doesn't matter to me."

The man on the floor had been oddly quiet, but when Leslie looked down, he groaned, shrinking away as though that might protect him. "*This* matters . . . don't you care that I'm taking care of the dragon?" Leslie knelt by him and dragged the blade up his chest. "He can't hurt you anymore, princess."

"It will matter more if you tell me what happened to Darcy." She shot a nervous look at the camera as Leslie toyed with Abernathy. Still blank—*shit*. Then a cop car appeared. Followed by another, then an unmarked one.

Elliot shifted his body, minutely. Shay didn't dare look at him. Leslie barely seemed to realize he was *there*. It was as though he didn't exist for her, as long as he didn't get in the way.

Like Darcy . . . like Abernathy. They had gotten in the way.

Abernathy made another one of those horrible whines low in his throat, and Shay stared in horror as Leslie pressed the tip of the blade into the hideous hole in his groin. Suddenly Shay realized why there was a gaping hole there, why there was so much blood. *Oh, shit . . .*

"I just need to know what happened to her, Leslie. She had sisters, too. And they must be worried. Tell me, and then we can talk about him all you want," she said, her voice reed-thin.

"Fine." Leslie's voice was truculent as she jerked the blade out of Abernathy's body.

She stood and focused her eyes on Shay's face. Shay had the sensation of being a fly pinned to a board. It wasn't pleasant. "You, being the wicked smart writer that you are, have probably researched all the ways to dispose of bodies. I got the idea from you . . . you really are brilliant, you know. I'm so proud of you, sweetheart." Leslie laughed and the sound was high, almost girlish.

It sent chills down Shay's spine. "Which idea was that?"

"Alkaline hydrolysis."

Shay's belly pitched and hurled. *I won't be sick—I won't.*

"She was already dead when I did it, don't worry. It's that so-called *greener alternative* to cremation. And it was so simple. Some lye. Lots of heat. Water. Pressure. And in a few hours, she was nothing."

I'm going to be sick, I'm going to be sick, I'm going to be sick—

Elliot's hand gripped the back of her neck and squeezed. Gently, but firmly. Shay sucked in a gulp of air. The metallic stink of blood didn't do much to settle her belly, but as she stared into the mad eyes of her sister, she realized the very last thing she could do was get sick. The very last thing she could.

"That isn't exactly an easy process," she heard herself saying. Another glance at the computer—*shit, the cop cars.* If Leslie looked over there now and saw them, what was she going to do? "You need lots of heat. High pressure . . ."

Leslie nodded. "Yes, yes . . . I know all about that. Don't you remember me emailing you about what a fantastic idea that was? Do you know what I went to school for? Veterinary medicine. They never did let me in, but that was what I wanted to do. I worked at a vet's office when I met Darcy. All I did was schedule appointments and shit, but I knew how to work the equipment. All self-taught. And he had the equipment I needed. I did a few test runs on strays, late at night—I'd go in to file, help them get caught up. I'm helpful that way."

"How considerate . . ."

As though Shay hadn't said a word, Leslie continued. "Plus, I wanted to make sure I knew how to clean everything up—better to have to explain having a dead animal than a dead *girlfriend*. And she didn't suffer any. She was diabetic, you know. Had crazy problems with her blood sugar and she didn't control it too well. We were out drinking one night . . . she was totally wasted. I mean, trashed. When we got back to her place, she passed out. I checked her blood sugar . . . it was low. She never woke up." Leslie smiled and her eyes gleamed with pure madness. "I gave her some insulin to make sure she wouldn't. She died a little while later. You see, I didn't really *kill* her. I just let her die. She should have taken better care of her disease and she would have been fine."

"Yes," Shay mumbled. The monitor was blank again. She couldn't see the cop cars. Where were they? "Why did you have to kill her?"

"Why?" Leslie stared at her. The look in her eyes was the sort of look an exasperated parent would give a particularly frustrating child. "Sweetheart . . . she was in the way. And she was *using* you. I'd been watching you ever since college and I could see it then, but I knew you wouldn't listen to me. You never talked to anybody but her. I needed to get closer to you and she was in the way. I realized that she was my chance to help you. To take care of you again."

Take care of me—

Shay slowly started to see red. It had been creeping in over the past few minutes, but now, as she stared at her sister, it was as if a veil of it had fallen between them—an insubstantial mist that overlay everything she looked at.

And still, like an inane, *insane* chatterbox, Leslie carried on. "She was doing all of these silly little chores and she felt so important for doing them, but none of it really *mattered*. She also had ways to talk to you and I knew you weren't ready to talk to me yet. So I just stepped in. She'd already moved away from her mother's—it took me nearly a *year* to talk her into doing that, stupid girl. She was scared to death to tell her mom about the two of us and she never did. Which is good, because no one ever came looking for me."

"Tell her mom about the two of you . . ."

Leslie grinned. "Yes. I figured out the best way to get to her. Darcy never did come out of the closet, but that was fine. I went into the closet with her . . . I could swing that way if it let me take care of you, Michelline."

It was another brutal punch, because Shay remembered emails from Darcy. She'd met somebody. Somebody really special. Somebody who made her feel really special. Hatred, pure, bright, and shining, rushed through her but she throttled it down, refused to let it show.

Leslie turned her attention back to Abernathy. "Now, can we talk about *him*?" she demanded, her voice falling into that needling whine that Shay found all too familiar.

This was the woman she'd been dealing with for two years. The woman she hadn't particularly cared for, who'd pretended to be her friend. Darcy had died, been murdered by a woman she'd thought cared about her.

Darcy . . .

"Yes," Shay said quietly. "Let's talk about my dragons."

"Dragons?" Leslie shook her head. "There's just the one, sweetheart."

"No." Out in the hallway, she heard something . . . it was faint, but she thought it might have been a footstep.

Leslie's head cocked and she shifted her attention to the door for the briefest second.

"I went into that closet all the time to hide from *two* dragons." Shay dropped her gaze to the pitiful bastard bleeding on the floor. "Him." Then she looked at her sister. "And you."

CHAPTER
TWENTY-SEVEN

THOSE FOOTSTEPS HAD BEEN QUIET, ALMOST SILENT, but still, Elliot had heard them. Shay had heard them.

And so had her sister.

Leslie Hall moved over to the computer and reached behind it, and he tensed—everything was about to get ugly. Fast.

The gun in her hand looked small, unassuming.

It wasn't.

He knew for a fact that a baby Glock could do a hell of a lot of damage. "Who is out in the hall, Michelline?" Leslie asked, her voice disturbingly void of emotion. And her eyes . . . they were as lifeless as a shark's eyes.

Locked on Shay's face.

That crazed bitch killed anything and everything that got in the way of her goal—taking *care* of her sister. Would she even try to kill Shay if *she* got in the way?

Shay smiled.

"I made a stop on my way here," she murmured. "A few of them, actually. I visited my brother's grave, my mother's . . . and I spoke with the cop who arrested the guy you're torturing."

Leslie's face spasmed. "The cop . . ." She blinked, shook her head. "The *guy*? Don't you know who he is?"

She pointed the gun at his head. "That's the fucker who cut you up! Don't you want him to pay?"

Shay looked at the wheelchair, then looked at the skinny, scrawny man. He couldn't even move, Elliot realized. Oh, he was trying. But there wasn't much he could do. Even as she'd cut him, the man hadn't been able to move his lower body, and it wasn't because she'd tied him down all that well.

"I don't think he needs to matter to me anymore," Shay said quietly. Her lip curled and derision all but dripped from her words. "He's helpless. He's old. He's weak. There's nothing to fear from him. He's no dragon, Leslie. I'm not afraid of him. I don't need you to protect me . . . not from him. Not from anything."

Leslie's hand wavered. "You need me. You've always needed me."

"Up until today, I didn't even know *you* existed."

"I've been taking *care* of you for two years!" Leslie shouted, her voice harsh and strident.

To Elliot, her voice sounded like it was coming through a long, endless tunnel.

It was one of those moments . . . he knew it even before it started to really unfold. One of those moments where everything could change in the blink of an eye.

Every time his life had ever gone to hell, it had happened in the blink of an eye.

I regret to inform you of the passing of your parents . . .

She's accusing you of rape, Sergeant Winter.

Yeah. Two brutal, ugly events . . . but they both paled in comparison to seeing Leslie lift the gun and point it at Shay's head. "You fucking *need* me," she snarled.

Not this time, Elliot thought. Life, fate—nothing else was going to steal from him again. Not this time. Moving in front of Shay, he caught Leslie's eye. "She needs you. You don't want to hurt her, right? That's not how you fix things, not how you show her how much she matters."

Her eyes darkened. "You shut up. Cocksucker! You shouldn't be here. You fucked everything up."

"I know. Look, maybe I should go," he offered. The cops were out there and he knew they were listening. All he needed to do was make sure she kept that gun pointed away from Shay. "I can go, and you two can talk."

"Yeah. You go, and tell the cops out there what's going on in here . . . so they can get in my way," Leslie muttered. "I don't think so."

She shifted the gun.

As he saw her finger tighten on the trigger, he lunged for Shay.

CHAPTER
TWENTY-EIGHT

SEEING THAT GUN POINTED IN HER DIRECTION WAS
nothing compared to realizing Elliot had just been
hit—nothing compared to realizing he'd taken a bullet
for her.

Trapped under his bigger body, feeling the hot, wet
wash of his blood, Shay shoved upward with all of her
strength.

She heard the door slam open.

Heard screaming.

Heard, distantly, the fire of another gun.

But none of it mattered.

Elliot was bleeding. Leslie had shot at her and he'd
jumped in front of her.

She managed to wiggle out from under him, despite
the fact that he was trying to grab her and hold her
close. Shoving him onto his back, she crouched over
him, staring down at his face. He was pale, lines of
strain fanning out from his mouth and eyes. "Get . . .
down," he muttered.

Shay glanced around. They were surrounded by cops.

And there was a body on the floor.

Dark hair fanned out around Leslie's head and there
was a neat hole in the middle of her forehead, blood
pooling out from the back of her head in an ever-

widening circle. "No need to," she said. "You jackass, what were you thinking?"

The bullet had caught him in the right side of his chest. The heart was on the left. That was good, right? Except he was so fucking pale and his breathing was really, really weird. A strange sucking sound came from the area of the wound, too. *Cover it*, she thought. *He's bleeding, cover it—that's the smart thing, right?* She wiggled out of the long-sleeved shirt she wore over a tank and pushed it against his chest.

He closed his eyes. "I dunno. You . . ." He grunted as she applied pressure. "You were baiting a psychopath. I had to do something to keep up. Shit, that *hurts*, Shay."

"Let me see him," a gruff male voice said from over her head.

"Go away," Shay snapped.

Then, as somebody knelt down in front of her, she looked up and found herself looking into a pair of familiar, faded blue eyes. "Shay, you trusted me once. Trust me now."

She eased her hands back as Hilliard bent over Elliot's body. Nerves bit into her. It was one thing to trust the cop to do his job—another to trust him with Elliot's life.

"Of course, it might have been nice if you'd trusted me and just *waited* before you tore off into here to face a woman you knew was unbalanced."

Unbalanced . . . Shay shot a look in her sister's direction. Did *unbalanced* even begin to touch it? Numb, she watched as Hilliard lifted the shirt she'd used to cover the wound on Elliot's side.

"I think it hit a lung—ambulance is on the way," the older man said quietly. "Just be still, okay?"

"I ain't up to moving much," he gasped out. But he did reach for Shay's hand, holding on tight. His eyes were glassy as he looked up at her. "Don't go any-where."

"Not for anything."

The waiting room was done in soothing colors of pale pinks, blues, and cream. Shay decided that if she had to stare at those walls for much longer, she was going to go stark, raving mad. Then an image of her sister's insane eyes flashed through her mind. No. She wouldn't go mad. She'd just rip her own hair out by the roots.

"You're looking a little rough there."

At the sound of Hilliard's quiet, patient voice, Shay just sighed. She didn't even bother to lift her head. He'd been in and out of the waiting room much of the night which probably wasn't too easy, since he had a crime scene to work. Jethro Abernathy had already undergone surgery, although Shay hadn't asked for details.

She didn't care. She just didn't care, one way or the other, about Jethro Abernathy.

No, the only man she cared about was still in ICU. The bullet he'd taken for her had caught him in the lung, just as Hilliard had suspected. On the way to the hospital, he'd taken a drastic turn for the worse. They'd managed to get him stabilized in the ER. He'd needed surgery and he had a chest tube in place. Now he was in intensive care but he was stable.

Of course, Hilliard was the one who'd told her all of that—the doctors wouldn't tell her *shit*. Couldn't tell her shit.

Bastards. Damn confidentiality laws. She wished she'd lied and said she was his wife. Then they would have talked to her.

Worse, they wouldn't let her in to see him. She wasn't family. Hilliard had managed to talk a nurse into letting her in, but that nurse had since gone and nobody else would allow it.

"Can you see if they'll let me in to see him?" she asked tiredly.

"They won't let you in?"

At *that* voice, Shay looked up. "Lorna." She shot up from her seat, but halfway across the floor, she froze.

Lorna didn't, though. Before Shay could so much as blink, the other woman had her caught up in a hug, one that nearly bruised her. "Damn it, Shay, what kind of mess did the two of you get into?" Lorna pulled back and stared at Shay's face. "Aw, honey, you look like shit. Why in the hell won't they let you in?"

"I'm not . . ." The sob caught her by surprise. Tears, deep and wrenching, choked her, and Lorna pulled her close.

"Shhhh . . ." Lorna hugged her, patted her back. "Now you need to hurry up and get that out, because Elliot will have my hide if he thinks I let you cry over him. Hurry up, because I need to see my brother and you're going with me."

"I can't," Shay whispered. "I'm not family."

"Like hell."

He remembered hurting. He remembered that a lot.

He remembered not being able to breathe.

And he remembered Shay.

He'd told her not to go anywhere and she said she wouldn't.

He couldn't tell where she was, but he knew she had to be there.

That was the one thing he held on to.

He was too fucking weak, and too fucking tired, but he held on to that. Shay had said she wouldn't go anywhere.

All around him, he'd hear voices and he kept waiting to hear hers.

He thought he'd just heard Lorna's.

She's gonna be so pissed . . .

"You're such an asshole," she said, her voice shaking and soft. "Do you hear me?" Then she squeezed his hand.

He squeezed back. Wished he could figure out how to talk. He wanted to ask for Shay. She had to be there.

"Say something to him."

Who . . .

"Hi, Elliot."

Shay—

Lorna's hand pulled away, but then there was another . . . Shay's. He gripped it almost desperately. *Don't go anywhere*, he thought. But for the life of him, he couldn't find the strength to speak, couldn't find the strength to open his eyes.

The darkness that had gripped him endlessly rose and he sank into it, helpless.

Shay . . .

CHAPTER
TWENTY-NINE

"WE SPOKE TO SELENA CAMPBELL."

Shay stared at Captain Hilliard over a cup of lousy hospital coffee and braced herself. She knew whatever he had to say wasn't going to be easy to hear.

"And . . . ?"

He sighed and dumped what looked to be two quarts of sugar into his coffee, stirring it absently. "She was pregnant when they took Leslie as a foster child. They didn't know. The lady was about five months along when they decided to tell the kid. When she was seven months along, she went into early labor. The baby didn't survive. Something screwed up showed in her blood work—she was crying as she told me, and I couldn't understand at first. But they found something in Leslie's room a few days later. Leslie told them that they already had a child and they didn't need another one. She killed that woman's baby—dumped shit in her tea and fed it to the lady. Killed the woman's baby while she was still carrying it."

Shay closed her eyes and covered her face. "Dear God."

"Yeah. They reported it, but nobody believed that the girl could do such a thing. Sounds like Mrs. Campbell's doctor thought *she* had done it intentionally. Suggested the woman get counseling . . ." He paused, took a sip of coffee, and made a face. "This crap is even worse than the shit they serve at the station." He took another sip. "Damn. So the husband puts in for a transfer out of state. Leslie goes back into the system, stays there for a while. She ends up with three other families and one of them . . . there was another baby, this one was a foster child who died of mysterious causes. The official cause was SIDS, but there were doubts. One social worker tried to blame the foster parent, but another had worked with somebody who had heard of . . ."

He trailed off and Shay gripped a juice bottle in her hands, clenching her jaw until she thought she could speak without screaming. "My brother? Me?"

"Yes. This lady realized there were some problems and pushed for more intensive residential treatment. Leslie was only fourteen and there was nothing conclusive. Likely nothing could ever be proved even now. She was kept in the facility until she was eighteen."

"Eighteen and no longer the state's problem," Shay said flatly, looking up at him. "Right? They just turned her loose on the world. She was a fucking lunatic and they just let her go."

"Yes." He met her gaze without flinching. "That's exactly what happened."

"*Fuck.*" Remembering the terror she'd glimpsed in Selena's eyes, the horror in her voice, she stared at Hilliard. "She said my sister followed them to Michigan. Did she do anything else?"

Hilliard sighed and reached into his suit jacket, pulling out a neatly folded sheet of paper. It was an obituary for Lance Campbell; he'd been sixty-one years old when he died nine years earlier. "I've got a call in to the local police department up there. I don't know if this is anything, but Mrs. Campbell says she tried to tell them her husband's death wasn't an accident. Nobody would listen."

Shay read the short, simply stated obituary with painfully dry eyes. "A fire in his workshop."

"Yes."

"*Why?*" But even as she said it, Shay knew. "I bet it was his idea that they leave Arizona. That they send Leslie back. She goes back into the system and she blames him. He was in her way, so she got him out."

Hilliard just sipped from his coffee.

Unable to sit there another second, she shoved back from the table and stormed out of the cafeteria, down the hallway. Three innocent lives lost . . . no. Five. The unborn child. The foster child Hilliard has just mentioned. Darcy and Lance Campbell. Darcy hadn't been a helpless child, but she hadn't hurt anyone, hadn't done a damn thing to Leslie. Her only crime was knowing Shay. Lance Campbell—he'd just wanted to get away from the monster who'd killed his unborn child. And Jeffrey, Shay's baby brother.

So much death . . . all because of her sister. And Darcy . . . that was on *Shay's* head. Elliot, all of his pain, his suffering, that was on her head as well.

Self-hatred and revulsion churned inside her.

Hearing his footsteps behind her, she turned around and stared at Hilliard.

"You can't blame yourself for any of this," he said gently.

Shay bit back the words burning in her throat like acid. Yes, she could. She did, and she'd deal with it on her own.

Giving him her back, she stalked down the hall.

"She stole enough."

Those words froze her in her tracks. Closing her eyes, she stood there, unable to move as he came closer. "She stole the life of your brother . . . possibly two other children. We heard enough to know she probably killed your friend. It's possible she killed her foster father years after they left Arizona. Five lives ended because of her. Will you let her steal your life as well?"

"She's dead now. She can't take it from me," Shay said. *Yay, me. I won that battle.*

"She wanted to take your life over, didn't she? If you let her win, if you let this defeat you, let her take what you've built . . . she's won. Whether she's alive or not, she's won. Are you going to let her have that?"

* * *

MyDiary.net/slayingmydragons

It's not a game of winning or losing.
I know that much.
She's dead.
I'm alive.
In the end, that's the thing that matters, isn't it?

The light sound of fingers on keys had become strangely familiar in the few short days they'd been together.

Elliot already knew what it meant.

Shay was in the room.

And she was on the computer.

The pain that had been his constant companion was a little less and he wasn't quite so leery about opening his eyes. It was a hit straight to the heart, a pleasant one, though, when he saw her sitting cross-legged in the chair, her shoulders and back hunched in a position that he knew was going to leave her in knots, her head bowed.

"You ever go to the chiropractic in town?" he rasped

Shay started. As she peered up at him over the top edge of her monitor, he cocked a brow.

"Huh?"

"The chiro who set up office last year. You ever go see

him? Because you ought to. Your spine must be in knots the way you sit."

Shay wrinkled her nose at him. "No, thanks."

"You're probably right. If a guy is going to put his hands all over you and twist you into weird positions, I'd just as soon it be me." He waited for her to smile.

But she just looked back at her computer screen. "Lorna's gone to call and check on the store. It's going to be a few more days before you can leave, so she's making sure Becca is up to holding down the fort."

He scowled. "Lorna should head on back. I don't need her here."

"You shouldn't be here alone."

"I'm not." He stared at her.

"Hmm." Shay rose from the chair, setting her computer aside. "I actually have to go to Michigan. They . . ." Her voice hitched. "I heard from Hilliard earlier. Mrs. Campbell had an address for Leslie. She knew where she was staying. Apparently, she was keeping quiet out of fear—she had family and she was scared."

"That didn't stop *you*," Elliot said, disgust rising inside him.

"Leslie killed Selena Campbell's husband."

Injury forgotten, he went to jerk upright—the sudden pain had him hissing out a breath. Pain streaked through him and lots of pretty lights danced in front of his eyes for a minute. Even as they passed, he was left dazed and breathless. Staring at Shay, he managed to gasp out, "*What?*"

"There's no factual evidence, but apparently Leslie confessed to Selena after the fact. Nobody believed her when she reported it, but Selena believed it. She was terrified, Elliot. Terrified of the monster that was my sister," Shay said, her mouth twisting as though it hurt to even say the words. "Now that Leslie is gone, she's talking, and we know where Leslie had been staying. They found an urn—it looks all nice and official. Even has an inscription on it."

Shay lifted a photo from the desk where her laptop was and showed it to him. It depicted a little urn; it was bronzed and simple. On the front, it read:

D. M.

"You think it's Darcy?"

"It makes sense. I need to go. I need to be there. If it's Darcy, I need to talk to her mom . . ." Her voice broke and she shook her head. "You've still got a few more days here in the hospital and this *can't* wait. You can't travel until they are sure your lung has healed. I have to go."

He stared at her. He didn't want her to go.

He knew . . . somehow, he knew she was trying to pull away again. Holding out a hand, he said, "Come here."

There was a knock at the door. "Go away."

"It's probably the nurse," Shay hedged.

"I said *come here*."

"Mr. Winter . . ."

"Come back later," he barked out, still staring at Shay. When she took one step in his direction, he felt a little bit better. Only a little. But when she put her hand in his, he breathed easier. "I love you."

Shay's smile wobbled. "I love you, too."

He found the card when he was packing to leave three days later. Shay had put it inside his tote bag, tucked in a book. There was no mistaking who it was from, and now he had the pleasure of kicking his own ass for not finding it sooner.

He read it three times before he was absolutely convinced his mind wasn't playing tricks on him.

Dear Elliot,

Hopefully you're feeling better by the time you read this . . . and hopefully, you understand.

I won't be coming back to Earth's End.

I don't know where I'm going, but I can't come back.

My sister managed to do the one thing she set out to do—she destroyed the life I'd tried to build and she almost killed you in the process.

My family would appear to be toxic, harming everything touched by it.

You need more in your life than that—you deserve more.

Take care of yourself and heal.

Thank you for helping me through this . . . I never could have done it without you.

Good-bye.

Shay

"Good-bye . . ."

"Elliot?"

Looking up, he saw Lorna standing in the doorway. He stormed over to her, shoving the card in her face. "Did you know a damn thing about this?"

She blinked and then looked at the note scrawled on the card. "Aw, hell. No. I didn't know anything about it. Look, after they do the discharge, we can—"

"Screw the discharge. We're leaving now."

He turned away and made his way over to the bed, ignoring the pain, ignoring the lingering weakness. None of it mattered. Shay was what mattered. All that mattered.

He grabbed his duffel bag and finished shoving his stuff into it. His coat was hanging in the closet. He suspected he'd need it. He had an idea where he'd be able to find her, at least for a short period of time.

"Damn it, Elliot, you—"

Turning his head, he stared at his sister. "I have to find her, Lorna. I have to."

Shay was finally able to write.

The deadline was going to have to be extended, but she wasn't going to worry about that.

She spent most of the flight buried in the book, all but losing herself in it, because it was easier to do that than to think.

The same could be said for the next few days; she spent many of those hours holed up in her hotel room, writing. Trying not to think about anything. Not Elliot, not her sister, not Darcy.

But it was getting harder to hide away.

* * *

MyDiary.net/slayingmydragons

L. wanted to steal my life from me and I didn't let her. My dragons are gone.

But it seems like I'm empty now.

Isn't that a karmic joke?

She wins, after all.

Walking away from Elliot had been the hardest thing she'd ever done, but the poison that seemed to follow her family couldn't be allowed to hurt anybody else. Lives had been shattered, and most of the damage hadn't even come from the dragon Shay had spent her life fearing.

"Another karmic joke," Shay whispered as she published the post.

Shutting down the laptop, she stood up and checked her reflection. She didn't have much in the way of clothing, so she'd made a quick trip to the mall, picking up a plain black sheath, black boots, and a long black leather coat. Darcy's memorial was today. There were still matters that had to be seen to, but her mother hadn't wanted to wait.

And there was little doubt the remains found in Leslie's little house of horrors were Darcy's. She'd recorded the whole damn thing—from Darcy's slide into unconsciousness, her death, to Leslie's dispassionate disposal of her remains at the veterinarian's office where she'd worked.

The remains wouldn't be released until further testing was done, but the family was having the memorial. Shay couldn't say she blamed them. They needed the closure.

Shay needed it, too.

She needed to grieve for her friend.

Hell, she simply needed to grieve.

Her heart ached, so desperately. *Elliot* . . .

"Stop it," she whispered. He wasn't there. She couldn't let him *be* there.

Turning away from the mirror, she grabbed her new coat and pulled it on. The memorial was soon. She needed to get on the road.

"You're sure she'll be there?"

"Yes." Elliot wished he hadn't answered the phone. He knew his sister was worried about him, but he couldn't focus on Shay while Lorna was fussing over him like a mother hen.

"How can you be sure?"

"Because it's the only thing I can be," he muttered, staring out over the crowd. Hilliard had been kind enough to give him the details of the memorial for Darcy Montgomery and even if he didn't find Shay here, he was going to pay his respects to the woman. If she was the friend Shay said she was, he owed her. But he knew Shay would be here. Just because Darcy *had* been that friend.

It was all that had gotten him through the past few days.

"When is your flight?"

Lorna groused on the other end of the line, muttering under her breath. "You're so good at changing the subject."

"Yeah. So when is it? We can't both be slackers."

"It's in two hours. And I don't think you can consider yourself a slacker . . . you know, being *shot* and all. Maybe *stupid* for getting yourself in that position to begin with, but not a slacker."

"Maybe I did it to avoid having to deal with the Danver family for a while," he said. Shoving a hand into his pocket, he jangled the change there. He didn't see her. Why wasn't she here yet?

"If you did, I'll do you bodily harm—for worrying me like that *and* for dumping them on me," Lorna swore.

An SUV pulled up. It was simple and black, a Ford Freestyle that looked like it had seen better days. For some reason, though, as it sat there with the doors closed, Elliot felt his heart kick up. He took a deep breath and immediately wished he hadn't, as pain lanced through his slowly healing chest. "I think she's here, sis," he murmured quietly.

"Then why are you talking to me?" Lorna demanded. The call disconnected a second later.

Shoving the phone into his pocket, he realized his hand was shaking. Pulling out a pair of sunglasses, he turned his back and bowed his head, ducking behind a crowd of people for a minute. He needed to get a grip. Needed to get ready to face her.

Needed to know what in the hell he should say,

needed to have the right words, and damn it, there *had* to be the right words. If he lost her . . .

"No." Closing his eyes, he pushed that thought out of his head. It wasn't going to happen. He wouldn't lose her. He was sure of that—he had to be. Just as he'd told Lorna, he was sure because it was the only thing he could be.

It was ice cold.

But they didn't let that stop them.

People gathered all around the house, on the porch, inside, around the back. There were portable heaters, a couple of fire pits, and people. Lots of them. She wasn't going to let that scare her or stop her. These people were here because Darcy had mattered. Everybody seemed to have a story about her, Shay thought.

She had one, too, but it was trapped inside.

She was my best friend . . . and I'm the reason she's dead . . .

Desolate, lost, she wandered through the crowd of people and felt even more lonely than normal.

From the corner of her eye, she glimpsed somebody that made her heart race, but when she craned her head to look again, he was gone. She pressed a hand to her chest and told herself to stop it. She saw him everywhere, it seemed. Because she wanted to, needed to.

"Hello, Shay."

CHAPTER
THIRTY

"MRS. MONTGOMERY." SHAY FLOUNDERED, REACH-
ing for the words. She shouldn't be here, she realized.
Oh, hell. She was going to make things so much worse.
She shouldn't be here—

"I'm so glad you came," the older woman whispered, tears sparkling in her eyes. She reached for Shay.

She found herself wrapped in an embrace. Tears clogged
her throat and she stood there, numb, barely able to
breathe, barely able to move. "I . . . God, I'm so sorry,"
she whispered. It was a plea for forgiveness, a plea for
things she couldn't even voice.

As Ella eased back, Shay found herself the focus of
eyes that reminded her too much of Darcy's. A gentle
hand touched her cheek. "You blame yourself," Ella
said quietly.

"If it wasn't for me, Darcy wouldn't have ever been in
danger," Shay whispered.

"You didn't bring this on her," Ella said, shaking her
head. "There's a part of me, yes, that wishes I could
blame somebody . . . hurt somebody. But that somebody isn't you. The blame rests with the woman who
killed my little girl. It's not you."

Tears burned, pricking her eyes. "You're more forgiv-
ing than I ever could be."

"Am I?" Ella absently touched the scars on Shay's face. "The captain from Phoenix—he tells me your mother died a long time ago. Do you blame her? Could you blame your mother? For giving birth to your sister?"

Appalled, Shay jerked back. "No!"

Ella nodded. "Then perhaps you can understand. You, me, my Darcy . . . all of us were hurt by this woman. We can add to each other's wounds by placing blame where it doesn't belong or we can help each other heal by talking about what a wonderful girl my Darcy was. How she made people laugh. How she made them smile. And if I know my girl, she wouldn't forgive me if I added to your pain—I can see enough of it in your eyes."

Staring into Ella's eyes, Shay whispered, "You can't forgive me so easily."

"Shay . . . you just don't understand; you've done nothing I need to forgive. Now come on. Come tell these people a story about my girl."

Twice more, she thought she saw him.

After she'd finished talking, awkwardly, stiltedly, about the shy, terrified girl she had been—still was—and the determined woman who had been Darcy Montgomery, Shay found herself standing inside the house on the second floor, staring out a picture window at the crowd that was gathered on the deck. Despite the gently falling snow, there were more people outside than inside, gathered around the roaring fire, the portable heating units, talking, laughing, and crying, all in equal measure.

But she couldn't see that familiar head of auburn hair, the one she kept thinking she saw, just out of the corner of her eye.

Abruptly, she tensed, acutely aware of a heated pres-

ence at her back. Sucking in a breath, she closed her
eyes. *Please* . . .

"Looking for somebody, Shay?"

Her knees buckled. Slamming her hands against the
wall in front of her, she rested her head against it, reminding herself of one simple fact—*breathing isn't op-
tional.* "Elliot."

"Turn around."

I can't, she thought, hysteria bubbling up in her throat
in a nervous giggle.

He decided to help her out, even before she managed
to say anything, gentle hands closing around her shoulders, urging her around to face him.

He was pale, she noticed that right away. Paler, thin-
ner, his cheekbones standing out in stark relief against
his skin. But his eyes glittered with that familiar, burning intensity.

She couldn't have looked more stunned if he'd hauled
off and popped her one, Elliot decided sourly. He didn't
know whether that was flattering or not. He wanted to
kiss her, wanted to shake her, and he was hard-pressed
to stay upright. He hurt like hell, his stomach was
queasy from the pain meds he'd popped without any
food, and if he didn't sit down soon, he was probably
going to fall down.

But none of it mattered.

He finally had her alone and damn it, they were going
to have this out.

"What are you doing here?"

Elliot stared at her, clenching his jaw to keep from
shouting. A week. It had taken him a fucking *week* to
track her down and she wanted to know what he was
doing here? "What do you mean, what am I doing here?
You are here. Where else am I supposed to be?"

Shay stared off past his shoulder. There were family
pictures on the wall. She could recognize Darcy in a lot

of them—they all looked so happy. So damn happy, and she'd ruined that.

Ella's voice drifted back to her. *Could you blame your mother? For giving birth to your sister?*

No . . . shit. Confusion, pain, grief—they all ripped through her mind. "Elliot, you don't need to be around me."

Logically, he shouldn't be. He shouldn't *want* to be. "You should go," she whispered quietly, edging around him. She had to get away from him, before she grabbed on to him—grabbed on, and never let go. "Go back to Earth's End, be with your sister . . . run your store. Forget about me."

Forget about me. Go find some sort of life.

And she'd . . . hell. Do what? The fear that had kept her trapped for so much of her life was gone. She could take her life back, whichever one she chose, and not worry about being found, about being hurt. But the life before her seemed pretty damn empty. There was already a ragged, gaping hole in her chest.

There was a faint, muffled sound—footsteps on carpet—and then Elliot's voice. Closer. So much closer. She closed her eyes to keep from looking at him, to keep from reaching for him.

"Why shouldn't I be here? Why am I supposed to leave, Shay? *You* are here, damn it."

Harsh, bitter laughter escaped her—it hurt. Her heart *hurt*, damn it. She wasn't as empty as she'd thought; she was full of misery and heartache, and only some of it was related to her sister, her brother, and her mother. But that poison shouldn't touch him any more than it already had. "Elliot, yes. Exactly. *I* am here . . . that's all the more reason you shouldn't *want* to be."

"Shay, you're going to have to help me out here. I'm not following." He brushed her hand with his.

Just that light touch was painful—a slap to her heart, a blow to her soul. She'd never have this . . .

Jerking away, she hunched in on herself and glared at him. "Don't you *get* it?"

"Apparently not." He caught her hand and tugged her along as he started to walk.

Shay jerked against his hold and he shot her a dark look. "I need to sit down, damn it, and I need to do it soon. So you either walk with me or I'll pick you up and then when I fall down, you can feel nice and guilty over *that*, too."

Glaring at him, she said, "Nobody is making you pick me up."

"Nobody is making you pull the martyr bit, either, but you're doing a fucking great job." He paused at a door and frowned as he peered inside, then moved on down the hall. Shay grimaced as he pulled her into what looked like a kid's bedroom, complete with toys all over the floor.

"I'm not being a martyr," she snapped at him as he continued to pull her along. He sat and the bed was so low, she ended up half-crouched over. Feeling stupid, she perched at the edge, but he grunted and reached over, pulling her closer.

"That's better." He stared at her, and the look in his eyes made her heart race.

It made her heart race in a way that immediately had her looking away. She needed to get up. Run away. He wasn't moving fast and if she ran . . .

"Since when did you turn into a coward, Shay?" He brushed her hair away from her face.

"I've always been a coward." She closed her eyes.

"No. You've had plenty of reasons to be afraid, but you've never been a coward. Until now. You're thinking about running *again*. When there's no reason to do it, you're thinking about running from me. From us."

"There shouldn't *be* an us." Groaning, she looked at him and said, "Don't you *get* it? I'm poison, Elliot." She was still horrified over what she'd learned, still reeling over the truths she had faced . . . over what she was learning. *What if there's more?*

As he laid a hand on her knee, Shay shook her head. "How can you sit so close to me? Damn it, why don't you see me as a monster?"

"A monster?" Elliot shook his head. "Why in the hell would I see *you* as a monster?"

"My sister murdered my baby brother!" The words felt like they'd been ripped out of her and the pain of it *hurt*. It was visceral in its intensity. "She *killed* him, damn it. And why? Because my mother died in child-birth and because he cried. My stepfather gutted a cat in front of us. And I've blocked all of that shit out of my head. Monstrous, awful, evil things. Since then, she's killed four other people—two of them were babies. She was a fucking monster."

"Yes." Elliot cupped her cheek, stroked a thumb over her lip. "She was. There's no doubt about that. But Shay . . . she's *not* you."

He eased closer, pulled her against him.

"I'm poison," she choked out.

"No." He stroked a hand up her back.

"Yes, I am . . ."

"You were a child trapped in a kind of hell I can't even imagine. And you survived. *Sane*. And wonderful, and amazing, and strong. There's nothing poisonous inside you. There's nothing wrong with you and you're sure as hell not a monster."

She shook her head against his chest. She wasn't sane. Every damn second, she felt like she was losing her mind, that everything was slipping away. She wasn't wonderful. If she'd been wonderful, she could have done something to stop Leslie, or at least find justice before now. Nor was she amazing. Or strong.

She was just broken. Completely broken, completely busted inside.

"You *survived*, Shay. You survived not just one monster, but two of them, tormenting you throughout much of your life, and you never let it break you." Elliot stared down at her, brushing the tears from her face. Her tears, the very heartbreak coming from her, would end him. He knew it. If he couldn't make her understand . . . no. It just wasn't an option. He'd get through to her, because there was no other acceptable outcome. Cupping her face in his hand, he eased her face upright.

She resisted, not wanting to look at him, but he was patient and he didn't quit until she finally looked up to meet his gaze.

The misery there had him ready to do anything, *anything*, to take that pain away. But he couldn't. Not if she wouldn't let him help. *God, please don't let her shut me out again . . .*

Except he wouldn't let it happen. He wasn't walking away this time. Cradling her face in one hand, he stroked his thumb over her lip. "You may not see it, but I do. You survived hell on earth . . . you survived things nobody should see, much less a child. And it didn't break you. Shay, you're not a monster, you're a damn miracle."

"No."

"Yes." Cupping her face in his hands, he lowered his mouth and pressed his lips to hers. He kissed her—quick, hard—and then lifted his head just enough to stare into her eyes.

"And you're *my* miracle, damn it. I'm not letting you go, I'm not letting you run away. Not over this. If you've decided you don't love me, if you decide later on down the road you want out, that's one thing. But thinking you've got poison inside you, thinking you're a monster and walking out over that? No. This is *us*, Shay, and we deserve a fucking chance. After everything she did to you, what she tried to do to *us*, we deserve a damn chance."

She was silent, staring at him.

"Can you tell me that you don't love me?" He threw it out there, a challenge. No matter what he'd said earlier, he knew she wasn't a coward and damn it, if it took a dare, fine. He'd dare her into this. He didn't have a problem with that.

"You know I love you."

"Then why in the *hell* are you letting her win? She probably hated the idea of you having anybody in your life and you want to let her win?"

"It's not a game." Shay reached up, touched his lips. "This is life, Elliot. It's not a game."

"No. It's a hell of a lot more important . . . it's *our* lives. And I want to spend mine with you. It's all I've wanted almost from the first time I met you. Now just answer this—do you want the same thing or not?"

Just answer . . . Shay stared up at him.

Shit, he made it sound so easy.

"Don't think so hard," he whispered against her lips. "Trust me . . . just answer the damn question and we'll worry about the hard shit later. Do you want the same thing or not?"

Trust me . . .

She found herself thinking about something Leslie had said, back when she'd pretended to be Darcy.

Do you really think you can trust him?

Shay knew she could. Shoving thoughts of Leslie out of her mind, she thought of Darcy, wondered what her friend would have said—and she already knew the answer. Darcy would have all but been kicking Shay's tail for hesitating.

But none of that mattered if Shay couldn't work up the courage.

If Shay couldn't let go.

Easing back, she stared at Elliot's face, reached up, and touched his mouth.

Trust me . . .

She did.

She could.

She would.

Leaning in, she pressed her brow to his. "I want the same thing, Elliot."

His arms came around her, and all the tension just drained out of his body. He sagged back onto the bed, taking Shay with him. "You're not running," he mumbled against her hair.

Closing her eyes, she shook her head.

"Say it, damn it," he growled, squeezing her tighter.

"Hey, easy . . ." She could feel the bulk of bandages under her hand.

"Say it." Lifting his head, he glared at her.

"I'm not running."

"Thank God." He blew out a sigh, closed his eyes. "Shit, I'm tired. You're exhausting me, Shay."

She winced, guilt twisting inside her. "I'm sorry."

A big hand cradled the back of her head, easing her back against his chest. "Don't be. I'm not. Just be here . . . I think I might fall asleep here in a second. Pain pills. Evil bastards."

She scowled, tried to lift her head to stare at him, but he kept holding her tight. "Pain pills?"

"Yeah. Be here . . . if I go to sleep. You'll be here when I wake, right?"

In the darkness of the room, she shifted around and whispered, "Yeah. I'll be here." And this time, she'd stay.

ACKNOWLEDGMENTS

I should probably make a note . . . pretty please to my editor, Kate, my agent, Irene, and my admin, Nicole . . . the events in this book in no way have any bearing on anything, other than a wild imagination. ☺

Thanks to Sassy for refreshers on Phoenix.

Thanks to all my readers.

Thanks to Olivia Gates for the refreshers regarding the pneumothorax.

Thanks, so much, for the family who put up with the fact that I had to hide in my room and write at night, even while we were on vacation . . . I love you all, you're my everything, and I thank God for you.